# Reunion on Neverend

**By John E. Stith**

*Scapescope*
*Memory Blank*
*Death Tolls*
*Deep Quarry*
*Redshift Rendezvous*
*Manhattan Transfer\**
*Reunion on Neverend\**

(\*available from Tor Books)

# REUNION ON NEVEREND

## JOHN E. STITH

SF
STITH

**TOR**®

A TOM DOHERTY ASSOCIATES BOOK
NEW YORK

REUNION ON NEVEREND

This book is printed on acid-free paper.

A Tor Book
Published by Tom Doherty Associates, Inc.
175 Fifth Avenue
New York, N.Y. 10010

Tor ® is a registered trademark of Tom Doherty Associates, Inc.

Design by Lynn Newmark

Library of Congress Cataloging-in-Publication Data

Stith, John E.
    Reunion on Neverend / John E. Stith.
        p.   cm.
    ISBN 0-312-85687-3
    I. Title.
PS3569.T548R4   1994                    94-7150
813'.54—dc20                             CIP

First edition: August 1994

Printed in the United States of America

0 9 8 7 6 5 4 3 2 1

For Kathy and Brian Dahlin, Sandy and Ron Johannson,
Earle and Bonnie Turvey,
Greg and Linda Dunn, Diane and George Wilhelmsen,
Michael Ricciardi, Chris Bannister, Eric Sagucio,
Michelle, Debbie, Mike, and Ryan Blaha,
Melanie and Larry Eads, Grace and Earl Chamness,
and the Alamogordo High School class of '65.

# PROLOGUE

◆ KENTIN FARLON TURNED swiftly toward the chamber behind him and cocked his head in hopes of hearing the sound if it came again.

Except for the quick echoes from his own scuffing feet, the interior of the museum was quiet. As it should be. He listened intently as he took several deep and controlled breaths, willing his heart to slow down. Nothing.

Nerves, he told himself, feeling embarrassed even though no one had seen him flinch. He was entirely too jumpy lately. Nothing was going to happen.

Kentin Farlon resumed breathing normally and turned back to lock the museum's entrance, the door he had just let himself through. He needed to be open for the public in an hour and still had his morning routine to finish. He switched the overhead light-strips from "dim" to "full." The chamber he was in and the two adjoining caves filled with light. Kentin felt better. He'd been born in the underground city of Neverend and had lived there all his life, but he still felt reassured by the bright light.

He moved to the right-hand cavern network and began

his morning rounds, inspecting the displays in each of eighteen caves. Dark basalt walls and ceilings reflected a dull gleam through the clear protective coating. He heard no more suspicious sounds.

Kentin moved from the level floor in the early tool display room, up three steps, and onto the irregular, nearly level floor of a smaller cave containing artifacts from a site on Ooberhallew. No holograms here—here were actual artifacts, lifted carefully from their shroud of compacted soil on the distant planet, gently cleaned, catalogued, recorded, and then sent on display. Sent on display the way history *should* be displayed—with tangible, physical, real objects. No visitor to the museum could look at these mortars and pestles and decorated shells even older than early human life and not feel humbled. Sitting on cushioned supports inside transparent display cases, they seemed to say, "Be careful. Whoever made us thought their culture would last forever, and it didn't. Yours may not, either."

Kentin removed noseprints deposited on the display case by young visitors, visitors about the same age Tessa had been when she had made her own noseprints on the displays. At first she had been terrified when she realized what she had done, and she had almost panicked as she searched for a cleaning cloth to remove the evidence. Kentin had comforted her and told her she didn't have to worry, without ever mentioning her first father. He had felt such anger at the man he had never met, the man who had filled the child's heart with fear, that he was afraid his anger might show in his eyes.

Letting Tessa learn for herself that Kentin was not like her first father was a slow process that made gardening seem like a frantically paced activity, but when she finally understood that no harm would come to her from Kentin, she looked happy enough for any ten children. Kentin had felt a satisfaction then that had never been matched by anything else in his life. It wasn't until that day that

Tessa had begun speaking more than a few words a week. Sometimes she even had the strength to talk about her mother, who had obviously been driven away far too long before Tessa had been taken from her abusive father.

Kentin normally remembered Tessa's happiness the most clearly, but right now what seemed most fresh in his mind was her early fear, perhaps because he felt fear now himself. He made frequent backward glances, wishing he knew exactly what he was afraid of, and wondering if Tessa had ever felt the same.

He circled through the remaining caves, making sure they were ready for another assortment of people to file through, looking into windows to the past. Kentin had reached the next-to-the-last cave on his journey, almost back to where he had begun his inspection, when he noticed something wrong.

He hadn't owned and run the museum as long as he had without developing a cataloguing disposition, an almost instinctive awareness when things were out of their proper places. The display case near the far cave wall had been shifted. Someone had moved it too close to the wall. Visitors ran the risk of knocking their heads on the irregular cave ceiling with the case that close to the wall.

Kentin walked slowly toward the display case. Its contents were intact, all in their proper places.

So why had someone moved the case?

Crouching slightly to avoid hitting his head, he moved to one side of the case, meaning to get a grip on the back so he could pull it into its proper place. As he leaned toward the wall, he caught a glimpse of something even more wrong than a disturbed display case.

For just an instant, he saw four electric blue eyes, a central pair looking generally in his direction, and a wider-set pair on the sides of the small furry head. Kentin jerked his hand back. "What the—"

One pair of eyes blinked, followed quickly by the other

pair blinking, and then all four vanished. Kentin heard a scurrying, scrambling noise like a pet clawing on a smooth floor, and whatever had been hiding behind the case was on its way, vanishing into the network of caverns. He swung around and saw nothing but a fast-moving ball of green and brown fur. What was going on?

Astonishment held Kentin motionless for a brief moment, then he followed. The clicking against the hard cave floor grew more frantic before he caught another glimpse of the creature inexplicably trying to reverse its direction again. It was now racing back at him.

An instant later, Kentin saw what had spooked the creature into turning around. *Another* intruder was in the locked museum, this one human, wearing a blue jacket. But now things really made no sense. The man was stepping through the solid rock wall as if it didn't even exist. The man held a weapon, and he turned menacingly to face Kentin.

Despite his confusion, Kentin recognized the man's face, the face of the man responsible for the worry Kentin had been feeling for weeks.

Kentin fled, bumping into a display case and pushing through the narrow opening into the cave where he had surprised the creature. If he could reach the entrance and get through the door, he might have a chance. His breath grew ragged, and a pain stung his ribs.

But he would never reach freedom. He wasn't fast enough to outrun the intruder's weapon. Even before he reached the entrance to the next cavern, the fire from the weapon caught him high in the back, as if he were a bug being pinned to a specimen box. Fire boiled out of his spine.

Kentin lurched forward, and another kick of pain slammed into the small of his back. He fell. One knee bounced against the rock, and he slid on the floor. Despite the incredible pain, he tried to pull himself back up to face his attacker, but a final shot caught him in the back of the head. The flaring pain obliterated all hope of escape and stilled the last indications of life.

# 1

## HOMECOMING

"SHE PROBABLY WON'T be there, you know."

Lan continued reading the news sheet for a moment before he glanced up, his concentration broken. His gaze took in the empty seat next to him, then rose to the stocky man standing at the aisle.

Lan scanned the man's expectant face and said, "Parke? Parke Brenlek?"

"Have I changed all that much?"

Lan smiled at the not-quite-familiar face. Parke's hair had lightened slightly and he had grown a mustache clipped so short the hairs could have been just an ill-advised tattoo above his upper lip. He had put on maybe twenty kilos. Parke's ruddy cheeks were more rounded than they used to be. Despite the changes, he looked fit and strong rather than overweight. The faint pinch in the skin between his eyebrows gave an impression of cunning and maneuvering that was uncomfortably close to the image Lan still had of his friend.

Still smiling, Lan said, "No, not really. I'm just surprised that you're still alive. I thought by now some jealous husband would have vaporized you." He moved to extend his hand and began to rise, but the seat belt bounced him back into the cushion.

"Same old Lan Dillion," Parke said, grinning broadly. "You haven't changed a bit."

Lan unsnapped the seat belt. He turned off the news sheet and returned it to the pouch beside the seat, then stood up and shook hands. His hand felt small in the grip of Parke's large fingers, and his ring cut into his fingers. "I can't believe ten years have gone by so fast. You have to be on your way back for the reunion, too."

"Sure. I can't believe it either. You really haven't changed at all." Parke glanced at the display screen at the front of the cabin. "We've got plenty of time before changeover. How about a drink in the lounge?"

Lan nodded. Together they followed the aisle to the back of the circular chamber. Ignoring the shuttle's shiny zero-gee risers, they took the stairs leading upward, Parke in the lead. The spongy treads muffled the sound of their footsteps.

"I looked through every level," Parke said as they passed the passenger cabin above Lan's. "I didn't see anyone else familiar. It must be just you and me."

"Maybe the rest of them found out you were coming back for the tenth reunion and decided to wait for the twentieth. If I'd known, I certainly would have reconsidered."

"Take a long walk with a short bottle of air," Parke said good-naturedly.

They edged along the curved wall to make room for a cheerful trio of fast-talking, blue-scaled Merentos heading downstairs, then reached the landing on the lounge level. Thick viewports broke the expanse of walls curving around the dimly lit lounge, and directly opposite the doorway was a large screen similar to the one downstairs. The upper-right corner counted the time remaining before changeover and read,

TRANS SYSTEM SHUTTLE 2245
SEAT BELTS: MAY BE UNFASTENED
NEXT STOP: NEVEREND

Occupying the center of the screen was the image of a dark, slightly off-round planet that from this distance appeared to be banded with fine black circles. Through the edge of one filtered port showed the dim arc of the nearby sun. Most of the other ports were totally clear, admitting light from a star field so dense that it seemed to be an uneven expanse of white, veiled with a scattering of black specks. Surrounding the black specks were individual stars far enough from their neighbors that they showed blue and yellow and red and orange.

They found an unoccupied table on the sun side. Lan settled into a chair and swiveled to face his friend. "It's really good to see you. So, what have you been doing with yourself these last ten years? At one date a night, that would put you in the three thousands, but a schedule like that would take a lot of stamina." He used the tabletop controls to order a drink and Parke made a quick choice, too.

Parke looked up from the tabletop. "I've pursued lots of things besides women. School at Technigrad. I manage a materials production lab on Algontin. Did a little growing up." Parke's gaze flickered over Lan's shoulder. Lan turned to see what or who had attracted Parke's attention.

Lan grinned. "She's very pretty. How much growing up did you say you did? Maybe all you did was age."

Parke returned the grin, unabashed. "A little growing up doesn't mean I'm a little dead. But I'm more of a looker than a toucher nowadays."

"This is probably a stupid question, considering your old habits. Did you ever get married?"

Parke shook his head. "I don't think I'm ready to settle down. What about you?"

"No. Never seemed—" Lan paused as the waiter arrived to deliver their orders. "Let me." Lan retrieved a couple of coins, checked the displayed balance on each, and placed them on the waiter's tray.

As the waiter departed, Parke winked and said, "You know, you never did answer my first question."

"Which was?"

"Well, not a question, actually. I said she probably won't be there."

"Who's that?"

"Who's that? That's a stupid question. We haven't been gone *that* long."

"You mean Tessa?"

"Of course I mean Tessa. Come on, Lan. This is me. Parke. You're not fooling anyone."

Lan let his gaze slide past Parke and rest on the veiled image of the sun, its mottled sunspots giving the impression of some ultra-large-scale disease. Because the ferry slowly rotated, the sun had slowly moved since they sat down.

Tessa. Tessa Farlon. Even now Lan had trouble admitting his feelings to Parke.

If Tessa truly wasn't coming to the reunion, then Lan had wasted the trip. It was fun to see Parke again, and he could think of a few other people he'd like to see, but Tessa was the reason he'd taken time away from his job.

As the time of the reunion had grown nearer and nearer, Lan told himself he wouldn't go, that it made no sense to torture himself. Lan hated the closed-in feeling of the caves on Neverend, and Tessa wouldn't leave. Lan was just as stubborn as he had been, and surely Tessa was, too. But then again, maybe her feelings about staying on

Neverend had tempered. Lan doubted that, but at the last minute he realized that he had to find out. Too, he might find that being back on Neverend wouldn't make him feel as trapped as before. Maybe he would be able to forget or ignore the need for sunlight, for open air overhead, for the sense of freedom he had when he was far from Neverend.

But maybe all these questions were for nothing. Tessa could have married years ago. Who would blame her? Or she could have found a way to let go, to let her father have his own life and to start one of her own.

Lan looked back at Parke. "That was a long time ago. We were kids."

"We're not all *that* old right now."

"Why do you say she might not be there?"

"I hear from Toko Yinda occasionally. My folks left Neverend about a year after yours did, and I like to know what's going on. Toko says she hasn't seen Tessa lately. She thinks Tessa might have left Neverend."

"That would be too bad," Lan said finally. "I would like to see her again."

"*Now* we're getting some honesty here. I wouldn't mind seeing her again either. And maybe doing a little more than just seeing. From what I hear, she's gotten even prettier since school."

Lan grimaced and took a sip from his drink bulb. "Is that what you remember? Her looks were more a liability than anything else. I would have preferred her plainer, to keep guys like you away."

Surprise magnified the small folds in the skin between Parke's eyebrows. "What are you talking about? There's nothing wrong with beauty."

"Nothing more than there's anything wrong with loud noises or flashy clothes. They just distract people from what's really important."

"All right, mister wise old man. What *is* important?"

Lan was silent for a moment. "Do you remember the time when some caverns caved in, a couple of levels up, and south from Marrotto Junction? Maybe four or five people were killed."

Parke nodded.

"A young girl, I think her name was Meccer, was orphaned. Falling rock damaged one of her legs pretty badly. Even after they found a family to adopt her, Tessa spent time with her, helping her relearn to walk, and keeping her spirits up by reading to her and just being a friend."

Parke took a gulp from his drink. "I never knew that."

"I'm not surprised. Tessa never bragged about the things she did. She just went out and did them." Lan drummed his fingers on the table. "She used to go down to the museum after school and help her father with whatever exhibit he was setting up, more to be with him than because he needed the help."

"I'd figured she was always meeting you or one of the girls after school. Whenever I asked her if she wanted to go hiking or go for a meal or do anything together, she just told me she was too busy."

"I don't know if that was the only reason. I think Tessa was wary of people she thought were interested in her just because of her looks."

"Yeah, but I didn't just want to look," Parke said, leering broadly.

"You're disgusting." Lan grinned. "And incorrigible. You know, I still remember the time you and Valma got caught in the lagoon in Optner Grotto. You had told her if you stayed close enough together, you wouldn't trigger the alarm system. I bet she didn't speak to you for half the next term."

"It was worth it."

Lan shook his head in reproof.

"Please secure your seat belts and your belongings,"

said a voice from overhead. "Changeover is in two minutes. We are now halfway from the gateway to the Neverend dock." The voice droned on, asking people to be
careful with their drinks.

"Did you bring anything for changeover?" Lan asked.

"No. But I'm sure someone did."

Lan looked around the lounge. At least two people,
one child and one adult, both making fists, seemed to be
holding small objects. Changeover, the brief period of no
gravity, had long ago acquired traditions. Maybe people
figured if the law of gravity was temporarily suspended, so
were some other rules.

Shortly the voice said, "Changeover is beginning.
Please remain where you are until the maneuver is complete." As soon as the voice died, Lan felt his stomach
lighten as gravity began to disappear. He clasped his
hands to keep them from floating. Before twenty seconds
passed, he was weightless, held in place by only his seat
belt.

The child Lan had noticed, a boy with flaming red hair
and freckles, pushed his hand into the air and flung his
fingers open, releasing an insectoid. From Lan's left, another insectoid joined the first.

The little powered toys rose toward the ceiling. One
bounced off the ceiling and began to fly in a slow arc.

From behind Lan's head came the faint whine of another insectoid. The black-and-yellow gadget whistled past
his neck, then it, too, soared toward the center of the
lounge, moving in large circles, occasionally darting one
way then another, seeming to be genuinely alive. Several
people laughed when the device started generating a
noise that was a mixture of nasal buzzing and a moronic
happy humming. This one was obviously more advanced
than the average insectoid.

As the toy buzzed around the lounge, a smooth pressure pushed Lan briefly against the seat back, and the ferry began its 180-degree turn to aim the propulsion system toward Neverend. Directly ahead of Lan, the star field panned slowly from the bottom to the top of the window. In the window to his right, the star field pivoted. The insectoid careened off a passenger's head, prompting chuckles from the people around the victim.

A minute later Lan felt pulled away from his seat back, then weightlessness lingered several seconds before the ship began to decelerate and he felt himself pushed down into the seat cushion. The almost unnoticeable vibration Lan had felt before changeover resumed as the thrusters began to slow the shuttle enough for it to match orbit at Neverend.

The black-and-yellow insectoid had been freely cruising in the low gravity, but now it had to struggle against the increasing force, and finally it crashed into the floor a few meters away. The instant after it hit, it generated a programmed sound Lan hadn't heard before, an undignified *splat* followed by a sudden loud buzz that trailed off, as though a large, smart bumblebee had said "awwwwwww" and then died. Lan joined in the laughter at the pitiful wail.

Over the laughter came the droning voice telling people they could release their drinks and unfasten their seat belts. Two adults and the redheaded boy retrieved their insectoids.

At the table next to Lan's, a man, still amused at the insectoid's performance, either squeezed his drink bulb too hard or drank at just the wrong moment. He managed to get some of the fluid up his nose and proceeded to spray the woman sitting across from him.

Parke started laughing loud enough that the man glared at him. The woman wiped her sleeve with a napkin.

"I'm sorry," Parke managed, his voice high and tight.

"It's just that we made it all the way through changeover without an accident and—and—" He started laughing again.

The man and woman studiously ignored Parke as they left the lounge.

Lan looked at his laughing friend and said, "That's what I like about you. You take everything so seriously. You know, I was wrong to say I thought you might have been killed by a jealous spouse. I put way too narrow a definition on the possible murderer."

Parke laughed even louder, and several people looked their way. Lan turned to one of the nearby men and said, "You'll have to excuse him. He's always been a big fan of nasal spray."

The man gave Lan a puzzled look, and Parke's laughter grew even noisier.

"Stop." Tears glistened at the corners of Parke's eyes and his cheeks bulged. He always had been an easy victim for this kind of torture.

Lan waited a second until he caught Parke's eye again and smiled at him. "You know, I remember the time you tried to convince Shirl that the earlier you try sex, the more you'll enjoy it when you're older. And then she asked her mother if that was true. And then her mother had a talk with your mother."

"Please—stop." Parke's face was turning red.

Lan waited a few seconds until Parke had to drag in a deep breath. In the relative quiet, Lan said, "Mr. Tendals. You remember how you altered the picture database for the annual—"

Parke started laughing again, gesturing for Lan to stop. Parke's eyes squinted shut.

"—and inserted eye-stalks coming out of his forehead? Is nothing sacred to you?"

Parke managed to put his hands over his ears, but he

was shaking so hard that his hands didn't stay in place, so Lan was sure Parke could still hear.

"And that time he was answering questions after a session. He said something like 100,000 of our brain cells die every day, and wouldn't that be a problem if they weren't being replenished?"

Parke shook his head, as if denying the memory would stop Lan, and started shaking harder as Lan continued. "And you said it sure would be a problem unless you wanted a teaching job."

By now, almost everyone around the two men was staring at Parke, several of them grinning at Parke's discomfort. Parke's face had turned a painful shade of red, and he began to cough.

Lan let his friend calm down until he stopped laughing. Parke hesitantly looked in Lan's direction.

Lan simply gave him a sudden broad grin, and Parke was laughing again.

When Parke's laughter subsided, he looked back at Lan.

Lan put on a serious expression for a second or two as Parke took some deep relaxing breaths. Abruptly, Lan said, "You remember the time—" and Parke was once again out of control, quaking for a time before he finally regained control.

"You're going to kill me someday," Parke wheezed at last. "I wish you wouldn't *do* that."

"One does whatever one does best. I'm glad to see you haven't changed, either."

Parke finally began to breathe more normally. "What do you do, anyway? Besides tormenting people. We never got to that."

Lan carefully squeezed his drink bulb and took a sip. "Nothing special. I work for an import-export consortium. My job is to help balance the two wherever they send me. If I'm on a world that imports more than it exports, I help them find markets for more of their materials or products. Or help them match something they could be providing to a market need somewhere else. Dull work, but the travel makes up for it." Lan's story was a complete fabrication, but Parke seemed to accept it.

"So, have you been back to Neverend since we graduated?"

"No. If they've had any need for the kind of work I do, someone else must have handled it. And my parents migrated to Merohive not long after that. It will be fun to see the old place. See people I haven't seen for a long time."

"I warned you she might not be there."

"Right, you did. There are other people I want to see. The Newtons—they lived near us—Carrie, Eddar, several others."

"And Tessa," Parke added.

"And Tessa. If she's there. And her father."

"Somehow I—I thought you might have known." Parke was suddenly sober.

"Known what?"

"He's dead. He was murdered in the museum. A few months ago. Toko told me about it."

Lan was silent for a long moment, staring at the mottled sun. Tessa's father had been one of the kindest men Lan knew. Harsh words from him were rarer than pearls in the desert. He was a master of self-deprecating humor that could defuse almost any situation, and he was someone who avoided confrontation to begin with. What a blow to Tessa.

"I'm sorry," he said finally. "She was really close to him. And I liked him quite a lot. What happened?"

"I don't know."

"You mean Toko never said?"

"I don't think anyone knows. Except maybe the killer. Tessa's father didn't have any enemies. They found him in

the museum, but there wasn't any indication of theft."
Parke's eyes widened. "You were always interested in mysteries. Maybe *we* could find out what happened."

"I think you landed on your head too many times falling out of bed."

"No really. We could make a great team. You're intelligent and I'm strong."

Lan nodded. "Right. I can see it now. I figure out which questions to ask, and you punch whoever we're questioning until we hear an answer we like. We could call ourselves the brains and brawn brothers."

"Bad idea, huh?"

"Let's put it this way. I think you had a better idea when you organized the scavenger hunt that almost got us kicked out of school."

"We had fun, didn't we?"

"Yeah, but it was just asking for trouble to have an escalator tread on the list."

"Lan," Parke said, suddenly serious. "For your sake, I hope Tessa *is* going to be there."

"Thanks. But even if she is, she's almost certain to be married to somebody. It's stupid, but I don't know if I'll want to stay around if I find that out."

# 2

## TOUCHDOWN

◆ "THE PLANET HASN'T changed a bit," Parke Brenlek said. He peered out the cable car observation port at the surface of Neverend far below.

Lan said, "I bet nothing's changed down below either."

The two men had made the transfer from the ferry to Neverend's orbital dock, perched atop an invisible column extending from the planet's surface. There, they were ushered through zero-gee corridors to the beanstalk cable car ready to descend to the ground.

Lan glanced at the barometer gauge on the screen near the center of the cable car. According to it they were almost halfway down. The faint tug of gravity was finally beginning to make him feel that he was looking down on Neverend from a high observation point, rather than floating near it in space.

Below him lay a chain of safety reflectors stretching all the way down to the dark surface of Neverend. Faint narrow bands around the planet's actual surface were just beginning to show. Between the bands were the wider, dark and dull surfaces of enormous strips of solar panels, each individual section sucking up the sunlight so efficiently that little was reflected into the wispy atmosphere. The thousands of latitude lines made Neverend resemble a decorative paperweight.

"I almost decided not to come back," Parke said.

"Oh, come on."

"No, I'm serious. I wish I had done more since I left. I wish I was clearly on my way to being a company president or an explorer or something."

"You've done all right. You've still got your sense of humor, and most of your looks. What are you really worried about? That some of the folks we knew won't respect you? Or some of the girls you never slept with still won't? What?"

"I don't know. I suppose it's the girls."

"The girls. They're women now."

"Yeah, I know. But I still see them as girls. I still see the holos in the annual. I see myself grown up—no comments—and I still see them the way they were. Maybe I'll be more comfortable when we get there and I see faces as old as mine."

"They aren't going to judge you the same way they judged you back then, you know. They've done some growing up, too."

"I'm not convinced yet. Nothing ever seems to change on Neverend."

Lan looked back down at the surface. "I know what you mean."

Not far below them was a rising cable car. At its current distance, it seemed to be heading directly for the car carrying them to the surface. Both men fell silent as they watched the approaching vehicle. Moments later it flashed past them so closely that for an instant it blocked half the sky. Someone nearby gasped.

To Lan something didn't feel right. A second later he

realized that if they had just passed a tube car in the night, he would have heard the Dopplered roar of air. The silence here didn't fit the normal experience.

Parke said, "What do you want to bet that Lissa Tirn still has that high-pitched giggly voice?"

"I don't take no-win bets."

"Talk about things never changing. Good old stable, conservative Lan. You probably still don't go out on dates unless you've already heard the woman is interested in you."

Coming from someone else, Parke's words might have irritated Lan, but Lan felt no resentment. "I'll bet I don't hear 'no' as often as you do."

"Yeah, and I'll bet you don't hear 'yes' as often either. *That's* what I can do while I'm here. Work on you. You need to learn to take a few risks, live a little more."

"I take all the risks I need. I'm sitting here with you, aren't I?"

"Maybe opposites attract in friendships, too. Maybe that's why we're friends. You've probably always wanted to be bolder, more daring."

"And you've probably always wanted to be more careful, more painstaking, more discriminating."

They scrutinized each other for a moment, then both men laughed.

Lan looked down at the slowly approaching surface, now seeing small square equipment shacks edging the solar panel strips. He looked back at Parke and said, "It really is good to see you again."

Parke nodded and looked embarrassed.

"You're incredible, you know that? You probably pursue a woman you've known for less than a minute without giving it a second thought, and you get embarrassed when an old friend tells you he's glad to see you again."

"Yeah, well, you're not *that* old."

Lan smiled and let the subject drop.

As the planet's surface grew wide enough to become the horizon, Lan finally began to get the feeling he was home again, no longer a voyager. The horizon kept flattening until the rows of solar panels extending into the distance made the view suggest a crystallized field, with row after row of cultivated metallic plants. Both men watched as the cable car sped toward the ground. While the car began to slow, one of two circular hatches on the ground slid slowly open.

The car crawled as it entered the chamber. The edge of the hatch cover rose past Lan's head, cutting off the view of outside. Columns of soft blue lights in the docking bay rose slowly and then finally came to a gradual stop. Overhead, the hatch slid slowly closed, cutting off the view of the stars, protecting the subterranean world from the rest of the universe. Lan's stomach felt queasy for just a moment in the changing gravity, or from being sealed inside, then recovered.

"Welcome to Neverend," the generic monotone announced. "At the chime, the local time will be 11:42. All passengers please proceed in the direction of the moving arrows."

Lan and Parke merged with the other passengers following the lighted arrows in the ceiling. The exit door met an accordion-pleated pressure seal, and a spiral corridor led gradually down to the baggage level where the circular baggage compartment was ringed by a wide hallway. Lan found his bag under the panel reading "D," released it with his ticket, and slung it over his shoulder. Above the lighted alphabet was a display reading "1,228 passenger-parsecs without any lost baggage. If you are headed for Alpha Centauri, so are your belongings."

Parke joined him, swinging his bag to show Lan he was ready.

"Lucky your bag got here all right," Lan said, pointing to the display. "With a record like that, if you reported anything lost, they might kill you to keep the word from getting out."

"Or send you wherever your bag went."

Together they followed the green arrows to Customs. Parke's bag passed inspection, and then Lan's was on the conveyer. Lan swallowed as the bag passed through the scanner. The inspector gave Lan an indifferent glance as he handed over the bag. Good.

A moving walkway carried them into another tunnel, moving toward the waiting area.

"Looks just the same," Parke said.

Lan nodded. "Yeah, we haven't been gone quite long enough for civilizations to rise and crumble."

A dull and transparent protective layer coated the high rock ceiling and irregular walls. A sun-spectrum light-strip ran directly overhead, filling the passageway with diffuse yellow-white light. The walkway turned and twisted, rose and fell, as it moved through what was far more like a large tunnel than a corridor. From space, Neverend had looked inhospitable with next to no atmosphere, but, below the surface, ancient volcanic bubbling had turned much of Neverend's outer layer into a porous maze of pockets, caverns, tunnels, and grottoes.

Lan didn't know whether the tunnel they traveled through, with its black pitted walls and ragged twists and turns, was artificial or natural. Either way, it always gave him a touch of claustrophobia.

A soft breeze met them. Despite all the filtering and purifying stages in the recycling plants, the air still smelled faintly musty and dusty. They passed a low-slung litterbot on a programmed search for waste to suck up.

Parke said, "It's nice to be in low gravity for a while. But I'm not looking forward to the first few days when I get back."

The nature of the echoes ahead changed as the walkway began to curve downward and to the right. Added to the prompt echoes of occasional loud words and the clamor and clatter of many people moving, was a multitude of delayed echoes, some much softer than the prompt echoes, some almost as loud. Turning a final bend in the passageway brought them to where the tunnel mouth met the side of Majilly Cavern, a brightly lit, enormous chamber crowded with people, edged by shops tucked into small caves around the perimeter. The antiglare, poured floor was perfectly level and transparent, allowing a view of the natural contours below, and giving the illusion that the entire populace walked on water.

Holograms of large aquatic creatures moved beneath the surface, including a large fast-moving shark cutting its silent path through the pseudowater, leaving no wake, oblivious to the strollers overhead. Or oversnout.

Lan said, "You know, I can still remember the first time my folks brought me here. I was sitting, playing with a toy, and I caught sight of something moving down there, one of the holograms. Except I didn't know that's what it was. I jumped up and I was peering back down through the surface when I heard my folks and their friends. They were all watching me. Probably they'd been watching me ever since we arrived."

"So did they tease you?"

"No. They just wanted to see how I'd react. I don't remember them being condescending. I told my mother I was afraid of falling through the floor. I must have been really flustered, because I don't remember thinking that the adults were much heavier than I was, and so I shouldn't have been worried. Sometime later, I came back with them, and I brought a light so I could get a better view. And then I was mystified when it didn't help at all."

"That reminds me of one thing I never did that I wanted to do," Parke said. "If I'd had the equipment and some good images, I would have added a few more holograms."

"Don't tell me. Let me guess. You would have put some holograms of dead fish, all bloated and floating belly-up just below the surface."

"I don't have any secrets left at all, do I?"

The walkway carried them farther into Majilly Cavern. To the left were groups of people saying good-bye. To the right, where the ramped walkway followed the curving wall gradually to the floor, were people looking expectantly upward at the new arrivals.

Feeling annoyed at himself, Lan couldn't help scanning the crowd to see if Tessa Farlon was among them. A waving arm caught his attention and he heard a woman's voice call, "Parke. Lan. Over here."

Parke saw her, too. He pointed toward the waving woman, then waved back. "Toko's here to meet us."

Toko made motions indicating that she would wait for them.

The walkway moved them slowly down toward the main floor. Lan kept looking for other familiar faces.

They reached the fanout section of the walkway and had to keep adjusting their positions to stay together as the walkway mechanism spread into a 180-degree semicircle with spokes moving out from the center and growing as they traveled. Lan felt his feet trying to move in diverging directions and repositioned himself.

Near the edge of the walkway, the surface gradually slowed down. Lan and Parke threaded through the crowd and reached Toko Yinda. She gave Parke a big hug. She turned to Lan, and Lan could see that she was a little unsure whether to hug or shake hands. He spread his arms. Toko smiled brightly and hugged him, too.

"You two are really looking good," she said finally. "You guys look—I don't know—lived in."

Parke turned to Lan. "You know what that means?"

Toko shook her head in mock exasperation, then grinned lopsidedly. Even when she quit grinning, a faint crease in her cheek remained as evidence of frequent smiles. She wore her brown hair straight and long; it fell back over her shoulders and almost reached her waist. Her wide-set dark eyes made her seem relaxed, unlike the energetic, almost furtive girl she'd been in school. Her outfit, a zipped-up, one-piece garment with long sleeves, made of a thin tan material, fit her snugly.

"You look good, too," Parke said appreciatively.

"Come on. Let's get out of here," Toko said. She pointed to the largest exit.

Lan fell in behind Toko and Parke as they walked toward the exit. Near a group of adults, a young girl sat on the floor, her head just off the surface, her hands cupped to the sides of her face as she peered into the shallow pseudowater. The image of an octopus slithered close to the bottom surface. Not far from it was a portwesseb, rolling itself along with its clawed appendages. Near the top surface a small school of glitterfish weaved to and fro in unison. Probably no aquarium owner had ever owned an assortment of creatures that got along so well together and didn't even soil the water.

Toko looked back at Lan. "I don't know if Tessa's still here."

Lan's gaze snapped away from the crowd near one of the cave shops. For an instant he looked at Parke, who had also looked back, and Parke just shrugged his shoulders.

"What is it with you two?" Lan asked lightly. "I'm just here for the reunion."

Toko walked backward for a few steps as she watched Lan. "Yeah, but—" She looked quickly at Parke who had just nudged her in the ribs.

Toko held up her hands and smiled helplessly. "All right. All right."

Lan hesitated. "Have they found out who killed her father yet?"

Toko sighed. "Not as far as I know. It all seems so senseless."

"I'd like to find whoever did it and settle the score." He was still angry at the idea of someone harming such a kind man. Toko was right; it was absolutely senseless.

"Easy there," Parke said. "If you want to go settling scores, make sure I'm with you."

Lan nodded silently and tried to force the image of Tessa's dad out of his mind.

Toko turned back to face the direction they were moving. She tipped her head toward Parke, and Lan busied himself looking everywhere.

"What happened to Thonsdol's?" Lan asked a moment later, looking at an unfamiliar sign over a nearby cave.

"They retired," Toko told him. "And they apparently didn't want to sell the name, so the port set up a lottery. Obviously Wilkerrok won."

"It's amazing how some things haven't changed one bit, and others are totally different. I thought for sure that shop over there—the exotic food shop—would have gone out of business long ago. They don't have any more customers right now than the last time I was here. Parke probably goes out with more women than they have customers."

Parke said, "And they don't have to pay."

"You really haven't changed," Toko said and shook her head. "This place has probably changed more than you, if you can believe that."

"How?" Parke said.

"Expansion south of Arapiton Cavern. There's a whole new area for homes and some new shops. The main thoroughfare going up from Mepitas is temporarily closed because they're strengthening that section. There's a brand new extension from Trinity. I'll give you the guided tour when you're ready, but are you in sync yet?"

Lan said, "No, but I could probably get by if I can get a short nap in a few hours. And Parke's tough."

"I'm all right for now. I'll let you know if I get too tired."

"I bet you will," Toko replied.

Their walk carried them past shops selling a variety of fragrant foods. Occasionally Lan would smell something that brought deeper memories. The McPhetter shop sold small, chewy wafers that could last a half-hour when a small boy was judicious. The aromas made Lan hungry, but didn't seem to affect Toko or Parke, so he said nothing.

Neverend still had its small-town atmosphere, which was hardly surprising since the effect was deliberate. By Neverend's very nature, growth was more limited than on planetary surfaces where more room was available. Neverend had been founded by a group who wanted to create a perpetual close-knit community. They succeeded—only too well.

A central services area was the focus of a number of arteries leading out to smaller communities, like small towns all within commuting distance of a moderate-sized city, so the residents could have the benefits of local communities and the occasional trip to a larger metro area that was still a manageable size.

Due to the nature of the limited-growth design, most people held jobs that didn't rely on population expansion—simple shops that did a steady business, stores that anticipated a regular turnover of perishables or non-durable goods, schools that educated the sons and daughters of the previous generation. The occasional small spurt of growth was inevitable, but Lan felt he could take a time-lapse sequence of views of Neverend and an outsider wouldn't be able to tell the progression showed centuries instead of decades.

Nearing the west exit, where Majilly Cavern narrowed,

they passed shops selling tourist clothing, map datapacks, snack foods, subscriptions to the local newscasts, hiking boots, lamps, emergency rations, first-aid kits, locators, toiletries. A few young boys and girls lounged near the shops, keeping their eyes open for newcomers in need of a guide.

Lan followed Parke and Toko through the funnel leading out the west exit, and they stepped onto the moving walkway. Through an irregular portal wide enough for ten people standing abreast—five going in and five going out—they found the uppermost cavern in Main Slope: Cavern 1.

The exit walkway transformed into an escalator with short, almost unnoticeable steps. Lan adjusted his footing so he didn't straddle the steps, and within a few seconds the steps grew taller until the path of the escalator angled down at almost a thirty-degree grade following the angle of Main Slope.

Toko was saying something to Parke, but Lan didn't listen. He lost himself in his surroundings, paying only enough attention to the two people ahead of him to make sure he didn't get separated.

The top cavern in Main Slope slanted down toward the point where it met a still lower cavern, which in turn connected to the next in a rough series of caves and caverns that cut a generally straight swath, sloping downward through the heart of the unseen city, a string of extraordinarily large irregular beads stretched in a haphazard line.

The cavern ceiling had been turned into a dimpled mirror, reflecting a distorted view of the shops lining the walls as the escalator dropped them deeper and deeper. They passed near a six-arrowed hologram showing the four compass points and up and down. In the box surrounded by outward pointing arrows were coordinates that Lan found he could remember:

20.14 North
87.33 West
 0.20 Down
Main Slope

Lan could see two more distant grid holograms in line before the cavern wall blocked the view. They passed a platform level leading to a storefront cut into the cavern wall. The unfamiliar display above the door read "Benkton and Crossheld Investments, 20.141 N, 87.330 W, 0.213 D. Main Slope 1."

People on the up escalator to their left passed them indifferently, and Lan saw no familiar faces among the array of smiles, frowns, and preoccupied expressions.

The escalator turned to the right once, then again, and the step height increased for a short steep section, as the path through Main Slope angled through the junction between Cavern 1 and Cavern 2. From that vantage point, Lan could see one of his favorite views. The next five caverns were aligned closely enough that parts of each were visible. A string of grid holograms cut a straight line sloping down into the distance, in one of the longest possible views inside Neverend. The view had always given Lan the feeling that the maze of caverns never ended, that the visible parts were merely the outermost irregular cavities cut in a galaxy-wide honeycomb. Even though most large caverns retained much of their original open space to minimize the closed-in feeling, this was one of the few places where Neverend didn't feel so claustrophobic and static to him.

The escalator continued making occasional course adjustments as it carried the trio. Near the center of Cavern 2, Toko led them into a lateral tunnel and stopped in front of one of the down chutes. "Let's drop to Rockville."

She and Parke managed to squeeze onto one of the

slowly falling platforms. The transparent cylinder rotated ninety degrees so the doorway sealed. As their heads dropped out of sight, Lan stepped onto the next platform and turned to watch the tunnel behind him as his cylinder door shut. The platform continued to fall slowly until his eyes were about level with the floor. Chutes were among Lan's least favorite aspects of Neverend. Even by himself in a chute, he felt the claustrophobia as an almost physical pressure from every direction.

When the cylinder began to accelerate, it dropped almost fast enough to make Lan float. The smooth shaft walls made gauging the speed impossible, but the strong acceleration lasted almost half a minute and then reversed, so Lan felt his weight almost double and his knees flexed against the pressure. When the chute wall opened to reveal the next stop, Lan swung open the curved door and hopped out to join Toko and Parke.

Lan said, "One of my biggest worries used to be that I'd get stuck in one of those things between levels."

"I don't know." Parke leered at Toko. "It might be fun."

Toko punched him lightly on the arm. "Let's go."

Lan reoriented himself. On this level, the chutes were totally exposed, three ups and three downs. The six transparent tubes, with a dark, hand-width runner inside the back of each, joined circular cutouts in floor and ceiling. A nearby grid hologram said they were 1.2 kilometers beneath the surface and were on Rockville Boulevard, cave six.

This stretch of the boulevard was fairly level compared to Main Slope, but smaller and more uneven. Lan looked both directions and at the nearest businesses, and was instantly sure he was on the axis near the corkscrew. Not more than three or four caverns to the north, Rockville Boulevard began to follow a spiral path through a jumbled network of caves.

Here he saw fewer changes. Lan recognized most of the shops they passed. MacMetver's home-making shop still carried everything from poured-floor compounds to drills, grinders, shapers, wall-thickness sensors, lighting compounds, blower tubes, wall-sealing resins and pigments. He wondered if they still had the sign that read, "If you don't see what you need, are you sure you really need it?"

Adjacent to MacMetver's was the same old antiquities dealer displaying ancient eyeglasses, pill-boxes, jewelry, and calculators in the case at the front of the narrow store. Lan could see all the way to the back of the fissure that formed the dealer's shop space.

Next to the antiquities dealer was the entertainment store that Lan's parents had loved to visit. Their leisure time had been full of novels and vids from a variety of worlds and periods.

His parents had come to Neverend partly because they saw it as a good place to raise a son, but mostly for work. They were a team, specializing in trouble-shooting for small businesses. Sometimes they'd go to work as employees and then provide feedback and recommendations to management. Eventually they saturated the business market on Neverend. As soon as Lan graduated, they moved on to New Phoenix.

As the three continued walking along Rockville, Lan began to feel for a moment that he had never left. Memories of the old days came more frequently and more vividly. With the nostalgia came the recollection of the camaraderie he had felt back then. But moments later he realized he felt uncomfortable.

More than that, Lan felt angry with himself. Lying had become all too easy since he had left Neverend, and he found himself hating the fact that he had lied to Parke.

# 3

## SHOPLIFTING

LAN, PARKE, AND Toko had just entered one of the larger caverns on Rockville Boulevard when the sound of yelling came from behind.

"Stop them!" someone shouted in the distance. Echoes bounced from the rock walls and ceiling. "Thieves!"

This section of the boulevard wasn't nearly so busy as Main Slope. Instead of escalators and walkways, smooth paths cut through the long, narrow cavern. Correspondingly fewer people were out doing business, so the two running boys were readily visible as they headed toward the trio. The larger teenager wore a red shirt that flapped as his arms pumped. His companion, a blond boy with a slight build, ran right behind. As they came nearer, the larger boy shoved aside a pair of shoppers. Packages went flying.

"I'll get the one in red!" Parke said. "You get the other."

Lan glanced wide-eyed at Parke and swallowed. "I'll try. Er, Toko, you want to back away?"

The two boys raced closer, over a small rise in the path, and around a slight curve, weaving around the few people in their way. A customer came out of a food shop at just the wrong moment and was knocked spinning back into the shop.

The larger boy saw Parke blocking his path, and hunched down, throwing his shoulder forward. Lan moved just behind and to Parke's side. An instant after the first kid rammed into Parke, the other swerved to avoid the collision and headed straight for Lan. Lan shifted suddenly out of the boy's way. The boy's expression was just showing a touch of triumph when Lan took advantage of the boy's casual dismissal and stuck out his leg.

Perfect. The slight boy tried to leap higher, but tripped. He tumbled, lost whatever he was carrying, and went sprawling to the floor. As he did, Lan began to hop on one leg while clutching the leg the boy had collided with. He felt no pain, but the act would help maintain the image Parke and Toko had of him from the old days.

After Lan glanced toward Parke long enough to realize his friend had the situation under control, he hobbled after the other kid.

"I got it!" Toko cried in a satisfied voice. She retrieved the object the boy had been carrying, something encased in a gel wrapper.

The boy got back to his feet and had started to move toward Toko when Lan stepped between them. Lan knew he looked hardly more threatening than Toko, but the boy had to know time was running out. The boy's gaze flicked from his friend to Lan, and his small mouth twisted into a grimace. A faint scar above one eye whitened. Very quietly he said, "You'll be sorry." He turned and fled.

Lan watched the boy's retreating form for a second or two before he turned to Toko and smiled. "Great job." Then he limped back to where Parke had pinned the red-shirted boy's arm behind his back. The boy's features contorted as he struggled to get free, but then the muscles loosened as he apparently realized he wasn't going to break Parke's hold.

Lan looked past the boy's angry face to Parke. "Congratulations. Mine got away, but Toko got whatever he was carrying."

Parke was breathing heavily and had scraped skin on his cheek, but showed no other injuries. "No protest. This one can identify the other one anyway. And you did more than you would have ten years ago. You did good."

Lan grinned and ducked his head as if he were embarrassed. From the corner of his eye, he saw a wide smile on Toko's face directed his way. When he looked back toward Parke, he saw Parke's prisoner inspecting him balefully.

"We didn't have any argument with you," the boy said. Blood trickled from his nose. One of his eyebrows was blond and the other matched his black hair. Together they made his face look lopsided, as though Parke had hit him even harder than he evidently had. The boy tried to get a glimpse of Parke's expression, but couldn't.

"I know," Lan said. "We're just meddlers."

"Let me go and nothing will happen to you." The boy's angry face and raspy voice might have been more intimidating if not for the mismatched eyebrows.

Parke interjected, "You mean let you go and nothing will happen to *you.*"

Running footsteps that had been in the distance gradually grew louder. The runner was obviously tired, running slowly and flat-footed. Moments later, a middle-aged shopkeeper came into view. He trudged forward, and a smile transformed his round face when he saw the trio and their prisoner. "Terrific," he managed between deep breaths when he got closer. "You folks are great." From the way he swayed, Lan figured he wouldn't have been much more lightheaded if he'd just inflated a dirigible.

"His friend got away," Lan said. "My fault. At least Parke was ready."

The shopkeeper waved his hand while he drew a few deep breaths through his wide-open mouth. He leaned against the dark cavern wall and wheezed. "No matter," he said finally. "This one gets the penalty for both if he doesn't say who his friend is. Either way is fine by me."

The boy with mismatched eyebrows just glared.

"You called for the law?" Lan asked.

The shopkeeper nodded quickly and looked around. A small crowd had gathered around the group, but none of the bystanders wore the green uniform of peace officers. "Let me call them again and tell them where we are." He moved off toward a public call booth below a nearby grid marker.

Their captive spoke more quietly than before. "You're running out of time."

"You have that backward," Parke said.

The boy twisted suddenly to free himself, but Parke's grip was too strong. The boy said, "Let me go now, or you're going to be in for trouble."

Lan looked into Parke's eyes. "There sure are a lot of echoes in this place. Even more than I remember."

The boy said, "Joke about it. But I've got friends. Protective friends."

Parke applied more pressure, and the boy winced. Parke said, "You try anything with any one of us, there won't be enough holes here for you to hide in, or rocks for you to hide under."

The shopkeeper returned, his breathing more under control, but his face still florid. Toko volunteered the boys' spoils.

"So that's what they took," the man said. He looked down at Parke's captive, then back at the package. "A holo set." He turned the package in his hands until he was apparently satisfied that the casing around the projection receiver was intact.

Parke said, "He probably should have taken something that would be more useful in confinement. Like a marker for counting weeks on the cell wall."

The boy must have decided another threat would do no good, because he kept quiet as the law finally arrived, in the form of a man and woman team. From a distance they might have been mistaken for a father and daughter. The man was even taller than Parke, with wide shoulders and large hands. The top of the woman's head came up to the man's biceps. A name plate over one of the woman's pockets read *L. Akalton, NPO.* After a quick assessment of the situation, they locked a tamer on the boy's wrist and dispersed the few onlookers who had stopped nearby.

The belligerence in the boy's face faded into a dazed expression as the tamer began to function. When Parke let the boy go and the male officer took him by the arm, the boy was as docile as if they had shot him with a tranquilizer gun.

Officer Akalton glanced at the shopkeeper and the trio, said, "Good work," then activated her belt recorder. Her mouth was slightly pinched, and her firm chin added to the impression of duty-above-all that her rigid posture suggested. But the animation in her wide-set eyes made Lan feel she was enjoying herself. She said to the shopkeeper, "Let the record show that I am talking to—"

"Miles Westerk, Dock Seven Imports," the shopkeeper responded.

"And can you explain the events that led to this call?"

The shopkeeper explained that while the boy Parke had caught was providing a distraction, the boy's partner had tried to steal the holo set. When the shopkeeper noticed what was happening, both boys fled.

As the shopkeeper continued, Officer Akalton moved to open the prisoner's ID bracelet. She withdrew the boy's

ID pin and inserted it into her belt recorder, and the captive's picture and identification flashed onto its screen.

When the shopkeeper finished, the woman turned to the boy. She looked at the image on her screen. "Let the record show," she continued, "that the accused is—Rento Amello Queller." She reminded Rento that if he denied the charges and was later found guilty that the penalty would be increased, then asked him if he had anything to say in his defense.

Rento looked angrily at Lan and Parke. Thanks to the tamer, his actual expression was a little closer to being forgetful than vicious. He shook his head silently.

"Who was your partner?" she asked.

Rento remained silent. He could have been sitting in a doctor's waiting room, lost in thought or wondering what pamphlet to read next, for all the attention he paid Officer Akalton before she gave up.

She got names from Toko, Parke, and Lan, and asked for their versions of the story. "And the boy who got away," she said finally. "Can you describe him?"

Toko went first, followed by Parke. They mentioned his slight build and his blond hair and not much else.

"Can you add anything?" the officer asked Lan.

For a second Lan instinctively catalogued the fine scar above the boy's eye, the fact that he had threatened with his left hand, the emblem patch on his pants pocket, the tan-and-silver ID bracelet, then said, "I'm afraid not, Officer. Everything just went so fast."

# 4

## RECEPTION

A MAN WEARING a belt wider than Lan's hand stopped and peered at Lan's picture badge. Lan looked at the man's badge, saw an old school picture he recognized, then together their gazes rose to each other's faces. Lan remembered him as a stocky kid who knew all the one-syllable nicknames for muscles.

"Lan Dillion," the man said. "It's good to see you after all this time. You remember me? Makil Hendron. We were on the game team together." Makil hadn't changed a great deal except that whatever environment he'd been in had weathered his skin, eradicating the rather baby-faced look he'd had in school.

"Of course. How are you?" Lan shook hands. "I'll never forget the time you beat that egotistical redheaded girl from Alpinder. You had the winning marker and you led her on until she was convinced she had you. She was already bragging to her friends in the audience when you closed her out."

Makil's eyes widened. "That *was* fun. You know, we played them a few more times after that, and she actually changed—grew up a little. I wouldn't mind going to their reunion. I'd be curious to see how she came out." He looked around the cavern at the reception crowd.

Lan glanced around at the same time. Rippling reflections from the lagoon at one end of the cavern danced on the dark ceiling and high on the cave walls. The textured walls of the cavern could have been the interior of some enormous dark, oblong fruit with the meat eaten out by acid, leaving bubbly pockets covering the walls. A crowd of more than two hundred people around the edges of the water made Brownian motion a tangible action. Lan still saw no sign of Tessa Farlon, but he caught sight of Parke standing and talking with three women. "So, tell me, Makil. What do you do now?"

Makil pulled his gaze back to Lan and said, "I work on Metrohaven. How about you?"

Lan briefly considered the evasion. Obviously, saying where one worked didn't say what one did, but if Makil was doing something he wasn't proud enough about to mention, Lan wasn't going to prod. He could understand the feeling. "I work for an import-export consortium." Lan went on to tell the same story he had told Parke. He told it so often, it almost sounded true.

Makil said, "It seems that over half the people I've talked to tonight are living off-planet, but I'm still surprised at the number who stayed here."

"I guess not everyone felt that same need to get away. I know I did, but everyone's different. I think, too, some people always talk about leaving 'next year.' Maybe the low gravity traps people; if you live here all your life, and you wait until you're middle-aged, you might decide it's not worth the adjustment to somewhere else." Traps look a lot of forms, not all of them as obvious as gravity.

"It's good to be back for a short visit, though."

"Same here. But I'm still glad I left. I don't even have to look up to see the rock ceiling; I can just feel it. It's a constant pressure overhead, like the whole place is going to implode under its own weight someday. I like sky. I like horizons. I like atmospheric air cleaning, not pumps and pipes and filters."

Makil looked toward one end of the cavern, at the rock platform used for ceremonies. "I can still see us walking up the ramp to the left there, marching along and getting a diploma from old Mr. Marshelt, and then down the steps in front."

Lan looked where Makil was looking and said, "I guess I would have changed the ceremony so it resembled real life more."

"How's that?"

"After we got our diplomas we walked to the edge of the platform. Instead of having those comfortable stairs leading back down, they should have just led us to the edge and pushed us over."

Makil grinned and nodded.

Not far from them, Lan recognized one of the more vocal nonconformists from their class, a man who had been slender during school and now sported a small pot belly. A woman with her back to Lan said, "Why, Kert Bronnigal, I do believe you've put on a little weight. And are those a few gray hairs I see?"

Kert never lost his smile, and replied, "Well, hi, Barb. Good to see you, too. And my, aren't your breasts sagging?"

The conversation experienced a sudden lull. Barb's sudden silence would have been rare back in school. Lan had thought of her during a lesson on communication links that were loaded with error-correction bits and built-in redundancies. She used to talk so much that he had to listen only occasionally to be able to get the whole message.

A few minutes later, Lan excused himself and began to walk the perimeter of the lagoon, away from the crowd of people. Angry with himself, he strode along the narrowing walkway. He had told himself it wouldn't matter if Tessa wasn't here. For all he knew, she was on another world. And yet he kept waiting, expecting, hoping to see the crowd separate and for her to be there.

The clamor from the crowd gradually blended into a focused noise source behind him as he walked, but occasionally the walls and ceiling would play acoustic tricks and one voice or maybe two would be as clear as if the speakers were right behind Lan.

Lan was absorbed in the view and his thoughts when he heard approaching footsteps. He turned and found Carrie Helmstun, her dark eyes unreadable this far from the lights over the crowd.

She said, "You came a long way to stand out here and be alone." In school, she had been one of the few girls besides Tessa with whom Lan felt at ease. Carrie seemed a few centimeters taller now, and her brown hair was a little shorter, but otherwise she could have stepped right out of the past. She wore a simple, pale-blue, off-the-shoulder dress. On her wrist was a thin, glittery ID bracelet.

Lan moved to her and gave her a hug. "It's good to see you. I was going to come back to the crowd soon. I just needed a little breathing space."

"You amaze me. You really do. After all the years you lived here, to still feel closed in, even when you are in a room that is probably bigger than—I don't know—bigger than a hundred homes." Carrie's voice was sisterly rather than critical.

"Silly, isn't it? You don't look like you've changed either. You look terrific."

"Why, thank you, sir." She mock-curtsied.

"No, I'm serious. Don't do that. It makes it seem you don't believe it."

Carrie turned toward the water. "Sometimes I don't."

"Who was he?"

She sighed an I-have-no-secrets sigh. "Jarl Haxxon. We got divorced a few months ago. You know, I never felt old until recently."

"That's because you're *not* old. I'm sorry about Jarl. But life does go on. You'll find someone better. You deserve it."

"Easy talk, coming from a man who's standing out here because Tessa didn't show up. After ten years."

"Carrie, I don't believe you. Where did you get the idea—"

"Relax. I already talked to Parke. You're not fooling me either."

"Parke—" Lan hesitated. "Parke. You should spend some time with him. He'll perk you up."

"He probably would, if I thought I was the only one he was perking."

Lan looked sharply at Carrie and she grinned. She said, "Honestly, I like Parke. If he had grown up just a little more since school, he would probably be having to fight off the women. But you're not going to change the subject that easily."

"I didn't know we had a subject."

"I remember when you had your first argument with Tessa. You wanted to leave Neverend when school was finished. She wanted to stay."

"I don't know that we ever argued about anything else," Lan said.

"Parke told me what Toko said."

"And?"

"And Toko is wrong. Tessa is still here on Neverend."

Lan looked across the lagoon toward the crowd of classmates, then back at Carrie. "How sure are you?"

"Fairly sure. I saw her about ten days ago. She was at the museum. I think she's been running it ever since her father was killed."

"If she *were* on Neverend, don't you think she'd be here tonight?"

"I would have thought so. But the fact that she isn't here tonight doesn't prove she has left."

"I'm not disagreeing with that. I just don't understand."

"I don't either. I'm just telling you what I know."

Lan was silent for a moment, wanting to ask a question, but afraid of the answer. "Did Tessa ever settle down with anyone?"

"Yes. A guy you probably don't know since he got here after you left. Phil Damonka. They lasted maybe a year."

"You're teasing me by leaving the important information for the last, you know that?"

"Sure. You always were fun to tease."

"So, what else are you going to let slip if I ask the right questions?"

"If I had to guess, I'd guess Tessa hasn't been as happy as she used to be since you left. Maybe if you tried again you could talk her into leaving Neverend."

Lan stood still for a moment. As he looked into Carrie's dark eyes and tried to think of a reply, there came the sound of more footsteps. At first Lan thought they were another trick of the acoustics, but then he saw the man approaching.

"Well, hello, friends," the man said, his voice slurring slightly. "Good to see you, Carrie. And you, Lan. Don't you two make a handsome couple?"

"Hello, Jarl," Carrie said, and Lan recognized Jarl Haxxon. Her tone was cooler now.

Jarl had grown no taller, but had become more barrel-chested, more stocky than he was in school. A shock of sandy hair was combed forward to minimize the gap left by his receding hairline. He carried a glass with a blue drink, mostly gone.

"Hi, Jarl," Lan said. "It's been a long—"

"What are you doing out here?" Jarl interrupted, his tone switching from sarcasm to belligerence.

Lan and Carrie exchanged glances, and Lan said, "Talking. Care to join us?"

"I already have. I don't need your permission." Now, instead of his voice slurring, he had overcompensated, and each word came out carefully controlled, like a series of one-word sentences.

"Lan didn't mean you needed permission. He was just being friendly."

"Like he was when you two came out here, all alone, away from everyone else?"

"We're just talking," Lan said calmly.

"She's mine," Jarl said.

"What are you talking about?"

"She's mine. Carrie's mine."

"People don't own people. People own objects."

"Always Mr. Smart Person."

"If I'd been smart, I would have left when I saw you coming."

"Run away, huh? Just like always."

Carrie said, "You're drunk and you're not making sense. Avoiding a fight isn't running away. It's smart."

"See. Mr. Smart Person." Jarl grinned, as though there were some humor in his statement, or he had invented some cosmic truth.

"How about if the three of us go back to the party," Lan suggested.

"I've got a better idea. How about if you go back to the party by yourself."

"That sounds like a good idea, too. I guess I've had enough fresh air for now." Lan started past Jarl and said to Carrie, "You going to be all right?"

Jarl was instantly livid. "Of course she's going to be all right! We were married for five years."

"No harm meant. I was just—"

Jarl lunged and shoved. Lan was directly between Jarl and the edge of the lagoon. Less than a second later, Lan was weightless, arcing slowly into the dark water.

The water splashed high as Lan's body hit back first, arms spread. In the moderate gravity, Lan surfaced quickly. He shook water from his hair and wiped water from his eyes. Fortunately, the water temperature was comfortable, and his clothes were light enough that they didn't seem to be dragging him down. Treading water, Lan turned slightly and looked up at Jarl. Carrie stood near him, open-mouthed.

As the water drained from Lan's ears, he realized the dull rumble of conversation back in the crowded portion of the room had changed character, probably because people were now wondering what was going on over here.

Lan swam slowly toward a convenient handhold a few meters to the right of where Jarl stood silently. As Lan neared his destination, Jarl moved toward the same location.

"You going to help me up?" Lan said calmly.

"What do you think?"

Carrie must have recovered from her shock at the events, because she said to Jarl, "Just get away from there so he can get up without your interference. Haven't you done enough already?"

Jarl didn't move, so Lan reached for a handhold to pull himself out. An instant later, he pulled his hand back fast to avoid Jarl's foot as it pounded against the rock where Lan's hand had been.

Lan slowly swam to another way up from the water, and Jarl tracked his progress and barred his way again. Lan looked up and said, "Don't you have anything better to do? Like vandalism or adult delinquency? Uninformed voting?"

Jarl was silent.

Lan swam back to the first place he had tried to get up, and Jarl again moved to block his way.

Treading water, Lan slowly moved farther out into the lagoon. "Carrie, I think I've discovered the pattern. This may be making some big assumptions, but follow me here. I think Jarl is planning to keep me from getting out of the water here."

Carrie grimaced.

"Anyway," Lan continued, "as long as I'm here, I think I'll just go for a swim. I hope we can get a chance to talk more later."

"Lan, don't try to swim all the way across. I can reason with him."

"No, you can't," Jarl said with satisfaction. He hiccupped and put his hands on his hips.

"I'll be fine," Lan said. He started backstroking away from the shore, keeping his eyes on Jarl.

Lan was far enough away that he couldn't see Carrie's expression, but, judging from what she did next, she must have been angrier than he had seen her before. She moved behind Jarl, who was busy guarding Lan, and landed an unladylike kick on Jarl's rear, sending him windmilling into the water, glass and all.

Lan was still laughing when Jarl's head surfaced about midway between him and the edge of the water. "Good show, Carrie."

"Thanks," she called. "It was the least I could do."

Lan stayed where he was, treading water, thinking that as soon as Jarl picked where he wanted to get out of the water, Lan could swim for another spot and climb out without interference.

Instead, Jarl began swimming toward Lan. "This is your fault, Mr. Smart Person."

Not seeing any easy alternative, Lan turned and began swimming for the far shore. After a half-minute, he glanced back and saw Jarl following at about the same interval. Lan gave Carrie a final wave, and turned back to swimming, settling into a rhythm as comfortable as it could be, considering the drag generated by his wet shirt and pants. Occasional backward glances told him Jarl was keeping up, so he couldn't just turn toward a closer exit point without Jarl gaining on him. Occasional glances ahead showed far more faces than would randomly be turned in his direction in a crowd of people engaged in casual conversations. Obviously, he and Jarl had attracted some attention. Great.

Lan kept swimming, thankful that the low gravity allowed him to keep his clothes on in the water and still not sink. The evening was already turning out to be embarrassing enough without adding to it by having to emerge half-naked.

The lagoon seemed much wider than it had when he was on foot. For a short time, the shore seemed farther away every time Lan glanced ahead, but finally he was close enough that every glance told him he was obviously almost there. Jarl had fallen a little farther behind, so Lan quit pushing himself so hard.

As he neared the shore, Lan saw that Carrie had run around the lagoon and was waiting with the crowd. Parke was nearby. He had found a napkin and was holding it high, displaying large letters saying *9.5.*

When Lan was sure he was close enough for Parke to hear, he said, "Come on in. The water's fine."

Nervous laughter came from the nearly silent crowd.

Parke reached a hand down as Lan reached the edge.

In a moment Lan stood on the smooth floor, the water dripping from his soggy shirt and pants building a pool around his feet. He used his hand to comb hair off his forehead, and he looked around at the bemused crowd. He said, "It's a nice night for a swim, but they sure have stocked this place with some ugly fish."

As the crowd laughed again nervously, Carrie said, "I'm awfully sorry about all of this. Are you all right?"

"I'm fine. Really. And it wasn't your fault. But I think I've packed in enough experiences for today."

Parke said, "I can slow Jarl down until he's sober."

Lan looked back. Jarl was within a few body lengths from shore. "That would be great. Can you make sure he doesn't try to take his frustration out on Carrie?"

"Easy. Maybe Carrie and I could just vanish." He turned his grin toward Carrie, and she had recovered enough that she smiled back.

The crowd parted for Lan as though *they* were the water. Lan's shoes squished and squeaked as he walked, dripping and calm, through the gathering. This certainly wasn't one of the scenes he had imagined when he thought about coming to the reunion.

On his way out, Lan noticed Makil Hendron again and said, "The pool's great, but they should harpoon that lifeguard."

# 5

## RUNNING

◆ LAN'S CLOTHES HAD dried enough to be mostly cold and damp instead of actually dripping wet by the time he took the spiral escalator up from Windhove Cavern to the intersection of Krugon Street and Incline Boulevard. He had already experienced several puzzled stares and suppressed grins.

As the escalator carried him upward, it wound DNA-fashion around the down escalator spiral, constantly keeping him in view of the descending traffic. From somewhere above came raucous laughter and loud voices. The sounds grew louder, so they obviously came from the down helix. Moments later, a group of six teenage boys came into view. Four of them leaned carelessly on the escalator handrail. The other two gave their best impression of sprawling while standing upright. The first one to notice Lan's wrinkled, almost shiny clothes did a double take and then nudged a couple of his companions. Several of the boys had started to laugh when Lan's gaze locked for a split second on the eyes of a blond boy with a fine scar above one eyebrow.

Lan looked away as casually as possible, knowing that particular boy would have a tan-and-silver ID bracelet and might still be wearing pants with an emblem on the pocket. His refusal to show recognition did no good, though. An instant later the boy was yelling at his friends and pointing. "That's one of them!"

Lan felt immediately grateful for the double-helix escalator, but it was no guarantee of safety. The group of boys started to backtrack on their escalator, bumping into people who were on their way down, trying to keep Lan in sight. For several heartbeats, Lan didn't respond to the group of boys, wondering if that might shake their confidence that they had the right man. They kept on scrambling upward, making excited, angry noises.

Lan bolted. Only one person was ahead of him on the escalator, so he had an almost unimpeded path, and the advantage of steps moving the same direction he was. He took the steps upward two at a time, no longer making any pretense that he wasn't the one the boys were after.

As he raced upward, he tried to recall as much as he could about the cavern the escalator was rising into. If he ran outward from the point where his escalator stopped, that would give him another slight advantage. That way took him along Incline Boulevard. It would also take him in the general direction of Tessa's museum.

Lan whipped past a solitary man. The man, apparently alerted by Lan's pounding footfalls, held close to one handrail.

Lan reached the top of the escalator before the first of the gang reached the top of theirs. He ran to the right, up a sloping walkway, and down the other side into the adjoining cavern. The breeze made his rumpled clothes feel even cooler. For a moment, he thought he might have had enough of a margin to vanish from sight before they reached the top, but a cry behind him indicated that he hadn't been lucky.

The time being so late in the evening worked both for and against him. The number of people he had to avoid as he ran was small, but the likelihood of encountering help was also small. This part of Neverend held modest shops mostly dedicated to the service business, such as maintenance. The majority of the shops were closed and locked for the night, many of their barricaded entryways lit only by security lights near the rear of the store.

Three caverns met in an oblong antechamber that could have been part of a hundred-times-lifesize abstract model of a human heart. Lan sped into the passageway on the right and saw his goal ahead: a single pair of chutes, one up, one down. He reached the down chute with enough of a lead to jump into the next tube available and swing the cover closed in front of him. The floor was rising over his head before the first runner caught up, and by then there was nothing the boy could do but follow. Now the odds would change because six people wouldn't fit in one chute.

The chute fell quickly. At the next stop, Lan scrambled out, swung around a corner, and ran toward the nearby quicktrain station.

He was five seconds too late. As he neared the deserted platform, the quicktrain's doors slid closed and it accelerated swiftly into the dark tunnel. The overhead display said the next quicktrain was due in ten minutes. What a great night.

Lan considered his options for no longer than it took to verify with a backward glance that his followers hadn't seen him miss the quicktrain. First he moved to an emergency callbox on the wall and pressed his thumb firmly onto the plate. In response, the box lit. Peace officers would probably arrive after they were no longer needed, but there was always a chance that someone was close. He jumped down from the platform and landed next to the nearer monorail. He ducked below the level of the platform and ran in the same direction the train had gone until he found a shadow deep enough to hide him.

At least this time he had a little luck. He managed to settle into the shadow and turn around just before his first follower reached the edge of the platform. Lan could see the boy peering toward him, and had no doubt the boy could hear the same thing Lan could: the muted *whoosh* of a departing quicktrain in the distance slowly growing softer.

The boy swore and kicked his toe into the platform surface. Obviously he had drawn the desired conclusion.

Lan stayed perfectly still, trying to breathe quietly, looking back at the boy through squinted eyelids to minimize reflections from the moist surfaces of his eyes. As he rested there and the boy on the platform paced, the boy was joined by one of his friends. A conversation started. Lan couldn't hear every word, but the gist of the message was clear. At intervals determined by the down chute, the rest of the group formed, including the slight, blond-haired kid. The basic conversation was repeated more times than a politician's promises, so Lan heard the whole story.

The guy who had helped catch Rento had just managed to catch the quicktrain before it left. If they waited for the next one and tried to follow, they'd have no idea at which stop to get off, and even if they did, they wouldn't know which way he had gone. So, what was the point?

At first the blond kid didn't want to abandon the chase. "We can't just . . . now. He'll probably get away if . . . the next stop."

A taller boy, more Rento's size, said, "Maybe. Or maybe not."

At that point one of the sharp-eyed six noticed the lighted call box and told the others their time was running out.

Another said, "This is useless . . . down to Harper's."

Lan sat silently, wishing they would agree to abandon the chase before the next quicktrain came along. For the first time that night, he seemed to get his wish. The boys retreated from the platform, talking as they went. When the voices had been inaudible for more than a minute, Lan made his way carefully back toward the platform. At the edge, he cautiously peered onto the platform. No one was visible.

Wary of a trick, Lan waited where he was for several more minutes, until he saw the distant glow of warning lights on a quicktrain coming back from the direction the first one had gone. He carefully hoisted himself onto the platform and moved quietly to a nearby corner. He peered around the edge, in the direction the boys would have gone to reach Harper's, a night club half a kilometer down and south from the quicktrain station, and saw no one.

The quicktrain slowed to a stop at the platform, and Lan boarded. Benches occupied most of the perimeter of the single car and held only two other people: a man and a woman together. They gave Lan a nervous look, then ignored him. A brief inspection of his reflection in the glass told him he looked even worse than before. His clothes were still wrinkled, and they had been damp enough to pick up plenty of grime from his journey along the monorail track bed and his rest stop. He felt tarred, feathered, and run out of town.

The quicktrain hummed almost inaudibly as it traveled through the darkness. Wind rushed past the shell of the vehicle and gave Lan a comfortable feeling of putting distance between himself and his followers. He almost wouldn't have minded adding even more distance by dropping the group down a deep hole.

The couple showed no signs of getting off at the next stop, so Lan got off. He'd had enough attention already.

He'd already had enough adrenaline, too. He could have started back for his room at the Travelers' Territory, but he'd sleep better if he stayed up longer. Besides, he was close enough to Tessa's museum that he wanted to walk by the entrance. He paused at a call booth on the quicktrain platform and called the peace office.

When the call was answered, Lan said, "You'll find my thumbprint on an emergency call you got recently. I wanted to cancel the call but let you know it wasn't a prank. I was being chased by a group of young men, but I got away. I'm fine now."

The man on the other end told Lan he'd have to stop by the station the next day to verify what he was saying.

"Fine. I'll do that." Lan terminated the call.

Four tunnels fanned out from the quicktrain station. Lan took the second from the right, which led upward at a comfortable slope. Lan was sure the tunnel was not a coincidentally handy natural feature, but it, too, had been constructed to look as though it could have been. Its uneven walls stayed wide enough for four people abreast, the rough, lightpainted ceiling stayed safely high enough for people significantly taller than Lan, and the floor was regular enough for safety, but otherwise the tunnel could have been the result of a huge bubble forcing itself through slowly cooling lava.

The cavern at the end of the tunnel was much taller and narrower than most. It was barely wider than the tunnel, its ceiling almost invisibly high. Lightpaint swaths on the walls shed ample light. Some small businesses had doorways cut into the cavern wall at the street level; others had stairs cut into the wall, the narrow treads leading to doorways higher than Lan's head.

Beyond that cavern was one a little like it except for being laid horizontally. This one's ceiling might have occasionally been a problem for tall people, but the floor spread in an enormous circle with two other tunnels connecting at roughly equidistant points. A man walking toward the tunnel on the right entered it as Lan came into the disk-like cavern. A small group of rock benches provided resting places near the center of the cavern.

Lan settled heavily onto the bench facing Tessa's museum, which, as he had expected, was closed at this time of night. As his legs relaxed, he realized how good it felt to sit down. In the quicktrain, he had been too aware of the couple and the boys to care about much else. His clothes were even dry now.

Dry clothes and a place to sit unmolested. Amazing how one's priorities can change in an hour or two.

He and Tessa had used to sit out here sometimes, waiting for quitting time at the museum. He had always wished back then that the cavern would be as quiet as it was now, yet it never seemed to be. There were always other people around. Spread around the perimeter were other businesses, closed now that it was late, that during the day were almost always the source of at least a trickle of passers-by. Next to the museum was a toy shop selling educational toys and science aids like extremely low-power visible-light lasers.

Next to the science store was a holo theater. There Lan had been able to escape, to feel a world existed beyond the underground, many worlds in fact. Worlds where one could walk for days with nothing overhead but air and stars. Tessa had begun to dislike going to the theater with Lan; too often they would argue afterward. Lan would try to convince Tessa that she would like to travel if she would only *try*. And Tessa would try to convince Lan that if he had lived in Neverend for most of his life he could certainly live there a few more years. Lan hadn't know how to put the feeling into words then, but he feared being trapped.

Neverend held tightly to its citizens. Those who wanted to stay for a while seemed to grow wistful, but steadily more reluctant to leave. Those who managed to push themselves to escape velocity shot away, rarely to return.

Lan was thinking about how stubborn they both had been back in school, when a door on his left opened. The door led to one of the restaurants. The man who stepped out of the doorway carried a small package and seemed slightly startled to notice Lan sitting there, but closed the door behind himself, and walked undaunted over to the door of the museum. There he knocked.

Only a few seconds later, the door to the museum opened just enough to admit the package. The door closed, and the man went empty-handed back into the restaurant.

Lan was on his feet, moving toward the museum, thinking that no one else besides Tessa would be at the museum at this hour, and then he remembered his appearance. He hesitated, wondering if he should go back to Travelers' to wash and change. He took a couple of steps in that direction, thought about how he'd feel if he missed his chance to see Tessa, then headed directly for the museum door.

He knocked just the way the other man had: four evenly spaced firm raps.

# 6

## TOUR

THE MUSEUM DOOR didn't open promptly the way it had for the previous visitor. After a minute Lan knocked again, wondering if the person inside was Tessa and, if so, why she wasn't answering. Lan glanced around the low-ceilinged cavern as he waited.

Finally a muffled female voice came through the door. "Who is it?" Despite the distortion, Lan was sure the voice was Tessa's.

"Lan."

Silence. "Lan?"

"Lan Dillion."

More silence. "Lan? I—that's really you?"

"I know you never thought I could stand coming back, but it's really me."

A lock clicked and the door opened a few centimeters. Then it closed again and reopened, wider this time. Tessa Farlon peered around the door and said, "Come on in."

Lan hesitated. "If this is a bad time—"

"Hurry. Come on in." Tessa's voice was insistent.

Lan hurried. Tessa swung the heavy door closed behind her and locked it.

Tessa was barefoot and dressed casually, shirt tail hanging outside her pants, the top couple of hooks on her shirt unfastened. Her hair was a shade lighter than Lan remembered and her cheeks were maybe a little fuller. Her familiar dark eyes, almost level with Lan's, were filled with surprise and something more. "I didn't expect to see you here." She paused, then let her gaze take in Lan's appearance. "And I didn't expect to see you looking like this. Are you all right?" She wrinkled her nose and gave him a questioning grin.

Lan glanced down at his dirty and rumpled pants and gave her a wry smile. "I didn't expect to be greeted quite like this, either." He moved a step forward and reached a hand toward Tessa's arm.

Tessa came forward and put her arms around him.

"I guess it took a moment for everything to register," she whispered. "It's really good to see you. I thought maybe I'd never see you again."

"It's good to see you, too. I wish I hadn't been so stubborn."

She held him more tightly.

Finally Lan released his grip and said, "Tessa, what's the matter? Are you all right?"

She backed up. "What do you mean?"

"You look worried. Oh, I'm sure my showing up here has you a little off balance. But that isn't it. I know you too well. And there's this business of being super-cautious with the door, and a meal delivered from twenty meters away. And some of your acquaintances not knowing if you were still around."

"It's—it's not your problem."

"I never said it was," Lan said, then waited. "Sharing a problem doesn't make you dependent on the person you're sharing it with."

"Speaking of sharing problems, what happened to

you? You're going to tell me you choose to look this way?''

"I'll tell you mine if you tell me yours.''

Tessa was silent until a relieved smile finally dissolved her worried look. "All right. But come on in and sit down.''

Lan followed her from the museum entryway cave into the adjacent cave on the right where a folding partition formed a private niche across from an exhibit of early time-capsule contents from Earth.

"You hungry?'' Tessa asked, offering a small plate of broiled meat slices and vat-grown vegetables.

Lan realized that he was. Tessa pulled out a chair for him, found a pillow for herself, and sat cross-legged, leaning against the cave wall. The next cave in the large circle was dim, lit only by a small strip of lightpaint.

Lan looked at Tessa, and she responded with raised eyebrows and a gesture for him to start his story.

"It's fairly simple, actually,'' he said. "I took a swim and a hike. I think I enjoyed the swim more.''

"Try again. With more words.''

Lan backtracked to give her a brief description of the encounter with Rento Queller and his blond shoplifting friend. Tessa listened without interrupting as he told her about the conversation with Carrie being cut short by being pushed into the lagoon and then having Jarl join him in the water.

Lan took another bite of meat. "While I was going back to my room, I saw the blond kid again. He recognized me and he was with several of his friends. They looked like they wanted to talk and I wasn't in the mood, so I avoided them—by hiding near a quicktrain station until they decided tonight wasn't going to be the best time for conversation.''

"They chased you?''

"That would be fair to say.''

"What a terrible way to start your visit."

"Oh, I don't know. It turned out better than I had hoped for."

"Better?"

"I got to see you. Toko thought you might have left."

Tessa acknowledged the compliment with a brief steady look, then seemed to relax partially. "I've been here all the time. I just don't get out as much as normal lately."

"I'd say." Lan glanced meaningfully at the temporary living quarters behind the partition.

She took a deep breath but said nothing.

Lan put his plate down. "What's wrong? Are you all right?"

"I don't know. I—I don't know if you heard that Kentin was killed."

"I'm very sorry. He was a good man."

Tessa fidgeted. "Yes, he was. He almost made me forget my real father. I don't mean *real. Biological.*" She made the word sound filthy, as though she were describing a chemical disaster that had to be decontaminated.

Lan was sure he didn't know everything about her biological father. Tessa kept that part of herself as private as she could. The small white scar on her palm was a permanent reminder of the time the man had pushed her down some stairs, and the writing stylus she'd had in her hand had gone all the way through her hand. Her father had reportedly been contrite for a couple of weeks. Tessa told most people the scar was the result of her own clumsiness, but to Lan she had admitted the truth. Her mother was only a dim memory from the time before the woman had fled her abusive husband—leaving Tessa to face her father alone.

Lan considered Tessa's statement. In the old days, she had been even more uncomfortable talking about the fact that she'd had a father before Kentin. "Do you know why anyone would have killed him?"

"No. It still all seems so senseless. But it does appear to have something to do with the museum. He was killed here, and lately someone has been trying to buy the museum from me."

"And you don't want to sell."

"I don't know. But I do know I don't want to sell when I'm feeling manipulated."

Lan started slowly. "How sure are you—"

Tessa gave him a *stop* sign. "I know what you're going to say—that I'm *always* feeling manipulated. But that isn't true. I know you used to joke about it, and I know that's a sore spot with me, but this isn't my imagination."

As Tessa spoke, Lan was suddenly aware of how naturally their conversation was progressing. For an instant he felt he'd never been away. He had always felt more comfortable around Tessa than the other girls he'd known in school. Since he'd left Neverend, he hadn't ever found a woman who gave him that sense of comfortable familiarity. Suddenly he realized he'd missed Tessa even more than he had admitted to himself.

"All right," he said. "What's making you feel this way?"

"Well, for one thing, right after Kentin died a woman came around asking if I was interested in selling. I told her no, I wanted to have time to think things through. She told me the offer was good for only a day. Does that sound businesslike and professional to you?"

Lan shook his head.

"So I told her no and she got nasty with me. Not really threatening, but a lot more hostile than someone who was merely interested in a business that wasn't for sale. Since then she's made the offer three more times and virtually turned it into a standing offer. Not very consistent with someone who at first wanted me to decide in a day."

"But there's more to this than just dealing with a businessperson who's irritable and inconsistent, right?"

"Yes. A few days after her first offer, someone poured some hydrofluoric acid on one of the display cases. It ruined the case and some of the contents. Expensive contents. If it hadn't been for the insurance, I would have been in big trouble."

"Did you find out who—" Lan stopped as Tessa looked suddenly into the dark adjacent cave.

"Did you hear that?" she asked.

"Hear what?"

"I don't know for sure. No one else is in here, but it sounded like a muffled cough or someone clearing his throat or a shout somewhere else carrying through the rock—or just my imagination."

"You're sure no one could be in here without you knowing about it?"

"I really don't see how. At closing time I lock that set of bars across this doorway and circle through the rest of the museum shooing people out until I get back here. I don't let anyone get behind me."

Lan glanced at the bars. They certainly seemed secure enough. "How about if we do that now and take a quick tour? I haven't been here in a long time."

Tessa gave him a small worried frown, but she got up and swung the set of bars across the opening to the entry chamber. The lock engaged and the number buttons for the combination lit. Lan took one hand and shook the bars. They felt solid.

Tessa switched on the active lighting, and the cavern next to them lit brightly. "Ready for the tour?"

Arrays of early Tapthorn tools from the Remulary system filled the first display cases they came to. Sharp rings formed by firing husks of round fruits had found uses from jewelry to weapons.

Lan and Tessa walked through the first cave and into the connecting cave on the far side, encountering no one, and seeing no hiding places that could conceal a person. Lan said, "What else has happened besides the display case being vandalized? That wouldn't be enough to make you spend your nights here."

Tessa's soles padded softly on the poured floor. "A couple of things. For one thing, several small items have turned up missing."

Lan paused near a display case, then took the two steps up into the next cave.

"None of them was expensive, but the pattern made me think someone had managed to find out the combination to the main door. One time I was certain that when I locked up for the night I had left a writing stylus right on top of my desk. When I opened up the next day, it was gone. And then about a week later, it was back."

"That sounds like something the authorities would have a hard time getting excited about."

"I know. In fact I felt maybe it was deliberately low key. You know, enough for someone to be telling me, 'I know how to get in here,' and at the same time deliberately making it seem trivial enough to keep anyone else from taking me seriously." Tessa stopped in the middle of the cavern, looking somehow defiant and vulnerable all at once. "Do *you* believe me, Lan?" Her voice was firm, as if she wasn't asking for validation or a second opinion that she was sane, but rather wanting a calibration on Lan.

"You tell me that's what happened, so I believe it."

They moved into the next cave, which was also empty of other people. One side of the cave showed an irregular, vertical stress crack that had been filled with a lighter sealer.

Lan said, "You mentioned a couple of things. What else?"

"Threats. Threats that I can't really call threats. I was going home from here after I closed up one night. I was waiting at the quicktrain station and a small group formed. As a quicktrain was coming in, someone bumped me from behind, hard. The guy who bumped me also caught me and kept me from getting killed. He said someone had bumped into *his* back."

"But you didn't believe him."

"I might have. But a few days later almost the same thing happened again. And it was the same guy. That time he said to me, 'I sure hope bad things don't happen in threes.' "

They had walked through almost all the entire circle of caves so far, without seeing anyone else. "Were you able to find out who the guy is?"

"I didn't know what I could do even if I found out, so I didn't try. I figured it would be easier just to avoid him long enough for things to die down."

"Any indication that's working?"

"Not so far. I walked over to get dinner last night and the guy was sitting on one of the benches out there."

"Just enough to be intimidating, but not enough to be able to call a peace officer."

"Exactly."

They neared the opening to the entryway cave. If their tour had herded an intruder full circle, the intruder would now be trapped between them and the bars Tessa had locked.

Lan and Tessa moved into the entryway cavern. The front door was still locked, the bars were still in place, and no one else was in the cave.

"It's been a long day," Tessa said. "I must have been imagining things."

"I'd rather have that than think someone could get in here without you knowing about it."

Tessa entered the combination for the bar lock, and pushed it out of the way.

Lan said, "Well, I've certainly been a big help."

"You have, actually." Tessa looked at her bare feet and then back at Lan. "I feel better having someone to talk to about it all. And I'm glad it was you."

"I'm glad it was me, too."

"You know, talking with you is as easy as if you'd never left."

"I know." Lan almost told her then how much he'd missed her, but instead just said good night.

Lan knocked on Parke's door the next morning. The door was unusual for Neverend: a tall rectangle with hinges and a knob. The Travelers' Territory builders had started with a large cavern and subdivided it with real walls and corridors, so it was one of the few places on Neverend that could have been a typical building on any of over fifty worlds of the Commonwealth.

Not all visitors to Neverend liked the cave-like feel to most individual homes, so the Travelers' Territory hotel was one of the few places people could temporarily forget where they were. People joked about a hotel room on Neverend looking just like one on Tetra or High Vista, but that was not so much coincidence as market-driven customer service. Travelers' Territory was the only hotel near where Lan's parents used to live, but each primary neighborhood housed a hotel that looked a lot like it.

From the faces Lan had spotted on the way in, he guessed that about half the visiting reunion members were staying here, and presumably the rest were staying with friends.

"This better be important," Parke said groggily as he swung open the door.

"It is. It is. Morning is here."

Parke looked at Lan through one open eye.

"You might as well open both eyes. You'll wake up at the same speed anyway."

Parke opened his other eye and closed the first.

"Oh, good," Lan said. "Progress."

Parke backed into the room and sat down on the rumpled bed. "What's this all about?"

"You're awake?"

"I'm talking, aren't I?"

"With you that's no guarantee."

Parke simultaneously opened both eyes and said distinctly, "I am awake."

"All right. I believe you. I just dropped by to give you a warning."

"If you didn't want me spending time with Carrie, then you shouldn't have pushed us together last night."

"That's not what I'm talking about, but congratulations. Maybe she'll rub off on you."

"Now *there's* an interesting—"

"That's enough. I came here to warn you about something else. Rento Queller was released this morning."

Parke sat silently on the bed for a moment. Obviously, keeping both eyes open was a challenge. "So?"

"So, he may decide to take this out on you, or me for that matter, so I wanted you to know, so you could be careful."

"No little street punk is going to come after me."

"Maybe not by himself, but apparently he has several friends."

Parke seemed to make an instant transition from drowsy to alert. "How do you know all this?"

"I found out Rento was released because I stopped by a peace office this morning."

"Why did you go there? They already took our statement."

"Another matter. Just a small thing."

Parke seemed to consider that as he rose from the bed, moved to the bathroom, and splashed water on his face. Through the towel, he said, "You're leaving something out. What is it?"

"Nothing important. Look, I've got to run."

"Nope."

"I beg your pardon."

"Nope. You're not leaving until you tell me the rest."

Lan stared at him for a moment. "You know, you're tougher to deal with than you were back in school."

Parke smiled.

"All right. After I left the reception last night, I was minding my own business when the blond kid, Rento's pal, spotted me. He was with a few of his friends. They weren't a very good example of politeness or restraint. In fact, I had to run to get away from them."

"But you did get away?"

"Yes. No bruises or anything."

"Good. I wasn't looking forward to spending my day hunting for some punks to beat them up."

"Look, Parke. Even if they had done anything, you don't have to be my protector."

"What are friends for?"

"All right. I appreciate the thought." Lan moved toward the door.

"Isn't there any more?" Parke asked.

"More?"

"You know. Tessa."

Lan hesitated.

Parke said, "Come on. Carrie told you last night Tessa was still here. Are you going to tell me you didn't go look for her?"

"No," Lan said finally. "I found her—at the museum."

"That's working a little late, don't you think?"

"She wasn't working. She—oh well. She's got some problems with the museum." Lan looked away, looked back at Parke, then gave him the whole story.

"I've got an idea," Parke said when Lan had finished. "Let's find this guy who's been following her and I'll beat him up while you keep watch."

"Two problems. One, this guy may outclass you. Two, Tessa has—she has a real strong aversion to violence."

"Maybe we don't tell her. Any anyway, what's this aversion you're talking about? I didn't know about it."

"She doesn't talk about it with everyone. Even I don't totally understand. Kentin's not her natural father. I think her natural father abused her when she was small."

"Why do I have to leave for ten years to find out all these things? I would think that would make her prone to violence—ready to get out all that anger."

Lan thought about it. "I don't know. Maybe with some people it would. I don't know enough about it to say. But I do know that Tessa doesn't want any part of violence, whether it's on her behalf or not."

"She doesn't have to know."

"Let's see if we can come up with a plan that doesn't require it."

# 7

## CONFRONTATION

"SO, WHAT ARE we going to do if this guy shows up?" Parke asked. "Carrie should be here any time."

Lan was silent. He sat next to Parke on a bench near Tessa's museum.

Parke said, "I said—"

"All right." Lan held up a hand. "Here's a plan. Tell me if you see anything wrong with it. At quitting time, Tessa and I leave together and start walking. You and Carrie follow us. You look potentially intimidating, so having Carrie along makes it seem that much more likely that you're not with us. If someone confronts Tessa, I'll be close enough to know what's happening and call for you if need be. If she sees the man but he doesn't do anything, maybe you and I can try to discourage him. If he knows Tessa's got friends, maybe he'll stop whatever's going on."

"What if we don't see anyone?"

"Then we all have a great time at dinner. Good plan, huh? We can't lose."

"There's lots of room for error."

"Yeah, I know. The things we do for hormones and

pheromones. Which reminds me. I'm surprised I found you alone this morning.''

"Yeah. Me, too. Carrie and I had a great time last night, but somehow I didn't suggest anything more.''

"They say that's one of the danger signs.''

Parke grinned lopsidedly.

Lan checked his watch. "Not much time left for changes.''

Parke sat quietly for a minute, then finally said, "I can't think of anything better. Where are you going to dinner, in case we get too far behind?''

"Mercaldo's. Up on Boulder Pass. She's seen the guy there a couple of times.''

"We'll be right behind you. At a safe distance of course.''

Lan swung the round museum door closed. As it was almost touching the frame set into the cavern wall, he pushed a small wad of paper into the gap. The door completed the last few centimeters of its travel and wedged the wad into place.

Tessa pressed a few digits in an inset panel, and the lock inside made a soft *snick*. She looked back at Lan. She had changed from her casual at-home clothes and wore a transfiguration dress with turquoise birds in flight in front that gradually changed shape so they become fish in back. "It will be good to get out tonight. I'm glad you talked me into this.''

"Me, too. I just hope nothing goes wrong.''

On one of the benches in the center of the cavern, Parke and Carrie sat, apparently oblivious to Lan and Tessa. Lan ignored them.

"You really are looking better than ever," Lan said as they began to walk toward one of the tunnels leading north.

"I think that just means you're not very objective.''

"You still don't accept compliments all that well, do you?"

Tessa didn't respond until they had entered a downward-sloping tunnel. "I'll work on it." After another pause, she asked, "How long are you here for?"

"A couple more days. At least that was my plan. I don't like the idea of leaving, knowing about these threats. I wish we could find out soon what's going on and stop it."

They entered a larger, rounder cavern. Tessa said, "Have you ever thought about coming back here to live?"

"Only a few hundred times."

"But you still feel the pressure here? Still claustrophobic?"

"I think it's more than simple claustrophobia. My temperament is wrong for Neverend. I feel more comfortable when I have more room to stretch out. I like places big enough that the echoes go away."

They walked into the next cavern, seeing no sign of the man who had followed Tessa. Lan said, "Have you thought more about leaving Neverend?"

"Sure. Probably as many times as you thought about coming back. But it's still home."

In an alcove between two shops were a pair of chutes. Tessa took the next available tube up, and Lan followed. He would have liked sharing a tube, being that close to Tessa, but his claustrophobia peaked inside the tube, and even by himself he felt uncomfortably squeezed. He got a glimpse of Parke and Carrie before he rose out of sight. Tessa was waiting for him when the tube slowed to let him out.

The cavern floor sloped up almost twenty degrees, and Mercaldo's was at the top of the incline. Shortly Lan and Tessa found a table that offered a view of the cavern and the cavern next to it. The tables and chairs had all been carved from the rock, or, rather, the architect had started with a rough, hilly section of rock looking like a miniature hillside, and the builders had used cutters and abraders to scoop out space here and there so what remained were tables and seats and pathways that were all integral parts of the original mound. Tessa and Lan sat about two-thirds of the way up the hill. They ordered dinner from menus set into the tabletop. By the time they finished ordering, Parke and Carrie had been seated at a table to one side and lower than theirs.

Tessa said, "Does this place have enough space that it makes you feel comfortable?"

Lan glanced around. "It helps."

"What about on the tube coming up here? Did that bother you a lot more?"

"A little. But like I said, I don't know that my problem is literally claustrophobia. Maybe it's more that this place somehow makes me feel small. Part of that's the fact that everything seems to be pressing in, but part of it's that Neverend has a lot of inertia. It wants to stay the same as it always has been."

"You seem a lot like the way you were back in school. Maybe your need for change isn't as strong as you think it is."

Lan looked intently at Tessa for a long moment, thinking about how much he had changed in ways invisible to Tessa, and about how much he wanted her. "Maybe some things never change." He looked away, suddenly self-conscious, feeling helpless at wanting her so much, but unwilling or unable to make the sacrifice of coming back to Neverend to settle down.

"Things like what?" she asked.

"Tell me again what this man looks like."

"Deft transition, Lan. Maybe we should talk about something else, huh?"

Lan glanced back at Tessa, but she didn't seem to have taken offense. She looked at ease, calmer than the night before, and smiling. She said, "He's closer to Parke's build

than yours. Black hair, rounded shoulders, usually wears that blue jacket.''

"You had a great time in high school when you played Eleanor in *One Came South*. Have you done anything more about wanting to be a part-time actress?''

"No. I guess that's one more thing I just didn't make time for.''

"Well, here's your chance to act. Stay looking at me for now, but when you get a chance, look down near the path we took to get here. Just outside that shop that sells snacks. On the bench.'' It suddenly occurred to Lan that even though Tessa had been the one who wanted to act, he had been the one to develop that skill.

Tessa's eyes widened but she didn't look around. "He's here?''

"I don't know. I need you to tell me. Here, I'm going to point at a couple sitting below us. When I point, look for the man.''

"Right.''

A second or two later, Lan gestured casually at a nearby table. Tessa appeared to look where he was pointing. "It's him. I'm certain.''

"Then I'm really puzzled.''

Dinner arrived, so neither talked as the server set their meals on the table.

"Why are you puzzled?'' Tessa asked finally. "Didn't you believe me?''

"I don't think I've ever not believed you. What I meant was, now that you've broken your pattern of going from the museum to home every day at the same time, and the guy has still showed up, that must indicate some pretty strong interest. Otherwise, maybe he would have given up when he realized you weren't going to be panicked into doing what he wanted.''

"What *they* wanted. There was the woman who tried to buy the place, remember?''

"Have you seen her since then?"

Tessa shook her head.

"But she did tell you how to contact her if you decided you want to sell?"

"Yes, now that I think about it. I've got the information at home. Her name was something like Ellie Troughter."

Lan nodded, filing the information away. He let his gaze flick in the direction of the man below. "When we finish dinner, how about a walk?"

Lan and Tessa strolled into Cave of Breezes, moving slowly enough to make sure their follower didn't lose them.

Besides the normal openings to two caverns beyond were several grilled patches on the cavern floor where steady breezes blew upward through fissures too small for travel, yet large enough to present a hazard. From the roof high above hung an enormous mobile with pinwheels and paddlewheels and rotors and spirals, all steadily turning with the constant air flow. From a distance they suggested a bizarre machine doing some unfathomable task.

Lan glanced back and saw that Parke and Carrie had gained enough ground. "You ready to turn around and say hi?" he asked Tessa softly.

Tessa looked worried, but she nodded.

Lan turned casually. Tessa moved with him, and ahead of them their follower became engrossed in the display of electronic equipment in a store window. The store was closed, so he would not be able to enter. He was stuck in the narrow passageway between Lan and Parke.

Nonchalant, Lan strolled with Tessa, looking at store displays as they squeezed their follower more tightly. The man began to fidget slightly as they approached. Lan stopped at the store next to the electronics store. At about the same time, Parke and Carrie arrived at the store beyond.

Lan wasn't all that interested in work clothes, but he

and Tessa looked at the store display for a moment. Finally Lan reached a hand into his pocket as he turned toward their follower and said, "Nice night, huh?"

The man continued staring at the store display for a moment, but finally he looked all around to see if he was the one being spoken to.

Lan looked directly at him.

"You talking to me?" the man said.

"Yes. Nice night, huh?"

"Ah, sure." The man looked puzzled. He started to move away and Lan said, "Why are you bothering this woman?" He gestured to Tessa as he pulled his other hand from his pocket, holding a sticky little ball smaller than a pebble.

"What are you talking about? I'm minding my own business," the man said after taking another look around. The man was easily as muscular as Parke, with black hair that reflected almost no light. A heavy dark-blue coat rested on rounded shoulders and covered part of his thick neck.

Parke and Carrie were almost as close to the man as Lan and Tessa were, and Parke slowly moved forward.

Lan continued, "I'm talking about intimidation, and bumping people when they're at quicktrain stops."

The man's expression never changed, but suddenly he was in motion. Rather than try to get past Parke, he bolted in Lan's general direction, to one side rather than directly at Lan or Tessa. Lan put up a hand to block the man's path, but the effort didn't provide any interference. The man barreled past him, knocking against his shoulder and shoving him into the wall. By the time Lan stood steadily and knew his hand was empty, the man was in full motion and Parke had started after him.

Lan started to follow, and called to Parke, "Let him go!"

Parke ran another several steps before slowing to a halt.

"Are you all right?" Tessa asked.

"Sure," Lan said. "Fine."

Carrie looked concerned but kept silent. Parke walked back to the group. "Well, that was really productive."

"I agree," Lan said seriously.

The other three looked skeptical.

"I'm serious. One, Tessa can feel better because she's been validated. Oh, you know I believed you, but if you're like me, down deep you worried a little about it. Two, we all know exactly what this man looks like, we can identify him if there's further trouble. Three, *he* knows we all know what he looks like, and that should give him pause. Four, he knows Tessa's got friends so he can't just take advantage of one person on her own." Lan had additional items for the list, but he didn't verbalize them.

Tessa began to relax visibly. Parke said, "You're right as usual. Like I told you, your brains and my brawn."

Carrie said, "Parke told me about his conversation with you. When he suggested that you'd want to explore the big mystery behind what happened to Tessa's father. He said you denied it. Maybe we haven't changed as much as we thought, huh?"

Lan opened his mouth to protest, thought better of it, and said, "How about dessert? That guy isn't likely to come back around tonight."

"You're sure you two will be all right?" Parke asked.

"Positive," Lan said. Tessa nodded. The foursome stood outside Kimbollo's, in a cavern small enough that it held only three shops. Since the confrontation, there had been no sign of the man following Tessa.

Carrie stood at Parke's side. He took one step away, but Carrie didn't move. She said, "You're sure that guy won't be back?"

"I'm sure he went home to think," Lan said. "Until now he's had a single target. By now he's probably deciding whatever he was after isn't worth the extra trouble."

Parke nodded. "Let's talk in the morning then."

"Right. And thanks, Parke. And thank you, too, Carrie."

Carrie now seemed more relaxed than Parke. "I was happy to help." To Tessa she said, "I wish I'd known earlier what was happening. Maybe we could have put some pressure on this guy and stopped this already."

"Thanks," Tessa said. "Maybe I'm too independent sometimes. I appreciate your help."

Parke and Carrie said good night and took the stairs upward from the cavern. Lan and Tessa stood where they were and watched them depart. Finally Lan said, "You're better at saying thank you than you used to be. I haven't seen any negative changes at all."

"Thank you, thank you, thank you."

"You're funny when you're embarrassed, you know?"

Lan and Tessa walked across a small level patio under a low ceiling, and down the stairs. Tessa said, "I'm not embarrassed. I haven't felt this comfortable in a long time."

Lan looked straight ahead and said, "Now *I'm* embarrassed."

"You're not serious."

"No. I haven't felt this good for a long time either." As Lan realized the truth of what he had said, he felt a pain in his chest, a pang of loneliness and sadness that spanned too many years.

Tessa slipped her hand into Lan's and they walked down the stairs into the next cavern. By mutual and unvoiced agreement they avoided the direct route back to Tessa's and wandered from cavern to cavern with no particular destination in mind.

\* \* \*

"Don't look away from where you're looking," Lan said quietly and firmly.

Tessa flinched, but she kept looking at the waterfall at the end of Jiorton Cavern. Pinpoint lights aimed toward the largest plumbing exhibition on Neverend made the flowing, tumbling water sparkle and gave the rising mist the sheen of an avalanche of tiny gemstones. The echoing roar covered most other noises, but from behind Lan and Tessa came rowdy, drunk, and wired sounds of a couple of loud teenagers.

"What is it?" Tessa asked softly.

"Maybe nothing. But I caught a glimpse of one of the noisemakers back there, and he looks to me to be one of the crowd that chased me last night. I might be wrong, but, if we just stay here a few minutes and don't turn around, they should be on their way."

Lan and Tessa stood silently at the railing, their backs turned to the small park behind them. At first the voices seemed to diminish in volume, but then Lan heard, "Well, look who's here." He didn't turn around, but the voices began to grow in volume.

# 8

## BULLY

THE VOICES APPROACHED so closely that Lan had no alternative but to turn around. He moved forward a half-step. Tessa turned, too, and stood motionless.

Approaching them were the thin blond boy from the shoplifting incident, and a boy Lan recognized from the group he had seen on the escalator. The blond's companion looked sturdier than Rento, but not quite as burly. Lan saw no weapons. The blond kid whistled by putting his fingers in his mouth and produced two piercing sharp notes. A signal.

"So what do we have here?" the blond kid asked. "Mr. Meddler and his girlfriend."

Lan said, "In my book, stopping you two yesterday wasn't exactly meddling."

The blond kid's expression turned instantly from smug irritation to outraged anger. "It was none of your business."

Lan said gently, "I was prepared to apologize if you were doing something you had a right to be doing."

He turned to his friend, who wore a windbreaker with

wide horizontal stripes. "Oh, he might have apologized. That makes me feel a whole lot better. How about you? Doesn't that make you feel better?"

His burly friend, a kid with dark eyes partly covered by a shock of dirty brown hair, had his hands stuffed into his pockets. He said, "Oh, yeah. That makes me feel a whole lot better."

The blond kid turned back to Lan. "You know what would feel even better?"

Lan was silent.

"To hear you apologize. Why don't you go ahead and do that now?"

"Apologize for stopping you yesterday?"

"Yeah. That'd be good."

Lan looked toward Tessa for an instant. She stood perfectly still. Finally he said, "All right. I apologize for tripping you."

The blond kid and his friend exchanged glances. He said, "Somehow that doesn't make me feel as good as I thought it would. Too bad your big friend isn't around to help you out." As the kid talked, he edged to one side, and his friend moved the opposite direction.

"We're not looking for trouble," Lan said.

The teenagers continued to spread apart.

Lan moved another step in front of Tessa.

Tessa said, "I can scream really loud."

Lan didn't turn. "It certainly can't hurt now."

Her scream was loud enough to surprise Lan. The echoes were mostly covered up by the waterfall rumble, but the initial cry vibrated in Lan's ears.

Lan moved another step away from Tessa, and turned toward the burly kid. A quick sideways glance told him they were concentrating on him rather than one of them going for Tessa. Good.

The blond kid said, "Go ahead and scream. There's hardly anyone up this late."

As he spoke, the burly kid moved toward Lan. The kid feinted, then pulled back. Lan flinched and the kid smiled.

The kid with the windbreaker moved farther around so Lan was directly between him and the blond kid. Lan could move farther away from Tessa, move back next to her, or stay. He stayed.

Lan looked over his shoulder at the blond kid, then back to his friend. As soon as his gaze was off the blond, the blond shoved him toward his friend, who promptly took advantage and punched Lan hard along the jaw.

Lan quickly moved away. With a hand on his jaw, he said to the blond kid, "This probably evens us up, don't you think?"

"Not quite yet."

Lan backed slightly away, and both boys moved in closer. By now there was nearly enough room for Tessa to run. Lan backed another step and stopped.

Both boys were focused on him now. They spread out again, the blond behind and the burly kid in front. This time the friend feinted again and the blond shoved Lan from the back at the same time.

Lan half-turned and the burly kid grabbed him and twisted. A second later, Lan's arms were pinned and the blond stood in front of him, a wide smile on his face. He moved a step closer. There still wasn't enough room for Tessa to get by for certain. The blond kid moved another step closer. One more step. He punched Lan in the stomach. Lan sagged in the burly kid's arms, and in his most forceful voice said to Tessa, "Run. Now."

Instantly she started to move. But the blond was faster than he looked. He ran five long paces and caught her by the arm and twisted it behind her back. Tessa grimaced, obviously in pain.

Just as the blond finished dragging Tessa back, a new

voice came from nearby. "Well, well, well. What have we here?"

Not ten meters away were Rento, the blond kid's shoplifting companion, and two other teens.

As Tessa struggled to get free, the three newcomers drew closer. One of the newcomers, a kid with a gap between his two front teeth, swaggered forward as he reached into a pocket and drew out a small knife. The other kids flicked glances between Lan and the kid with the knife.

Lan spoke, his voice taking on a command tone that made one of the boys back up a step. "All right. You've had some fun with us. Roughing me up a little isn't something that would put you in a cell, but you're about to step over the line."

The kid with the knife stopped. "Just cleaning my fingernails." He grinned and proceeded to pick under one thumbnail with the knife, but then started to move forward, the knife still in his hand.

Rento and his blond companion, who held Tessa as she struggled, also seemed concerned about the shift. "He's right," Rento said. "We don't need that kind of trouble. Alab's got him nice and tight. Just work on him a little. That'll be enough."

The kid with the knife stared at Lan. "No, that's not enough. People have to learn that they don't get in our way." As he finished speaking, he shifted his gaze toward Tessa, and his grin widened.

Lan no longer had a choice. He let air out of his lungs and sagged forward in Alab's arms. As Alab shifted his weight to compensate, Lan lifted his foot and drove his heel hard into Alab's instep. Alab cried out in pain, and his grip relaxed. Lan drove one elbow into Alab's midriff and heard the cry turn to a yelp as the blow forced air from Alab's lungs. Free of the grip, Lan whipped his forearm upward and felt the back of his hand impact Alab's nose.

Surprise worked to Lan's advantage, just as it usually did. He was free of Alab even before shocked expressions had faded and turned to anger. Two strides brought him to Tessa and the blond kid. The kid obviously couldn't decide whether to let Tessa loose and have two potential opponents, or to hang onto her and have only one hand free. He hung on just a little too long, because Lan smashed a fist into his cheek. With the blond kid dazed, Lan pulled Tessa free and pushed her behind him so anyone coming for her would have to pass him.

As Alab fell to his knees in pain, one of Rento's other companions rushed forward, his anger stronger than his judgment. As he took a swing at Lan, Lan dodged it, bent at his knees, grabbed an arm, and pivoted, swinging the teenager in an arc that carried him to a hard landing on his back.

Rento and his remaining healthy companion wore expressions of shock and surprise as they moved toward Lan and spread apart. Lan didn't wait for the split to complete. He moved toward the kid with the knife. The kid waved the blade menacingly, but Lan spun, then whirled on one foot and kicked him in the stomach. The boy staggered backward and fell. Lan turned to face Rento, the only kid still untouched, and Rento stood absolutely still.

The blond kid didn't look so much hurt as he looked confused. The kid who'd had the knife reached toward it. Lan stepped on the knife, pulled it toward him with his foot, and picked it up. A flick of his wrist sent it spinning into the waterfall.

Rento moved forward warily. He motioned for the blond kid to circle Lan. The blond kid looked back at him in disbelief, shook his head, and sat down, holding his jaw.

Rento charged. He never had a chance. Lan waited patiently until Rento was close enough. Lan twisted at the right moment, reached for the necessary grip, and Rento flew through an arc that landed him heavily on the ground. Rento was starting to struggle back up when Lan knelt beside him, one knee pinning Rento's wrist, one hand against Rento's throat.

Rento tried to swing at Lan with his other arm, but Lan intercepted the blow, then quickly plunged a fist into Rento's stomach.

As Rento gasped for breath, Lan shifted position so he could face Rento, and spoke quietly. "I can keep this up for hours if you're that eager for the abuse. Now listen to me."

Rento must have believed him, or felt powerless without a gang to back him up, because he quit struggling.

Lan continued, his voice icy calm, nothing like his normal easygoing tone. "Good. Now I'm giving you a simple warning. If you bother me again, I won't hold myself back like I did tonight. Anyone who bothers anyone I know will never feel safe again for however little time they live. And don't even think about bothering the big guy I was with. He has a temper, and he thinks warnings are a waste of time. If he were here tonight instead of me, you wouldn't be alive to hear this conversation."

Rento's expression still contained anger, but his wide eyes told Lan that Rento was becoming a believer. That was good. Lan had no idea how well Parke could actually protect himself, but this was good insurance.

"Is all this clear to you?" Lan prompted.

Rento nodded, as much as he could.

"I hope it is, because I don't want to have to demonstrate how serious I am. I repeat. If you bother any of us again, you'll find your bothering days are over."

Rento nodded again without being asked.

Lan released his grip on Rento, rose to his feet, and backed up a step.

During the fight, Lan had paid little attention to Tessa, other than to make sure no one harmed her. Now he took in her dazed expression and thought about her aversion to violence. He reached her side, but she made no response. She stared ahead at the spot where the epicenter of the fight had been.

Lan reached gently for her arm. "I think we'd better go."

Tessa was trembling. She turned her head to look at him, but made no other response. She looked dazed, as if she'd received a strong blow to the head.

"Come on. Let's go."

For a long moment Tessa stood absolutely still, paralyzed. Lan wondered if she were reliving some earlier violent event in her life. He knew her opinions about violence, but he'd never seen her like this.

Finally, as if partly coming out of a trance, she moved with him and together they skirted the teenagers and walked away from the waterfall.

Tessa stayed beside Lan, turning from one path to another as he picked their route. The soft echoes of their footsteps somehow seemed to blot out the faint background noise of breathing, clothes rustling as they walked, and reverberations from sounds generated in adjacent caverns.

"Tessa, are you all right?" Lan finally asked, as they walked up a gentle series of steps into Hawthren Cavern.

She at least looked at him, but her eyes didn't focus on him. She seemed to be looking far into the distance.

Lan stopped walking and Tessa stopped beside him. "Are you all right?" he asked again.

Tessa shrugged, her expression glazed.

Lan moved his head directly into her line of sight. "Do I need to get you some medical attention? I don't understand what's wrong."

Tessa's lips moved soundlessly, then she spoke. "I—I'm the one who doesn't understand."

"What is it you don't understand? That I can defend myself now?"

Tessa seemed to come farther awake. She nodded. "You're not the man I knew. You're like my first father. When you beat up that kid, I could see my first father like it was yesterday."

Lan felt a strong chill. "Defending oneself from a threat isn't quite the same as striking a child who's crying because she's hungry."

Tessa went on without appearing to hear. A single tear slid from one eye. "He killed her, you know."

"Wait a minute. What are you talking about?"

"He killed her. He killed my baby sister."

Lan's chill spread along his back. "Dear God."

"He was always gentle whenever anyone else was around."

"How did it happen?"

"What?"

"Your sister. How did it happen?"

"I don't know. I mean I don't remember much about before. I mainly remember seeing her lying there. I kept expecting her to sit up, or stand up, or cry, or anything. And she didn't do anything. And then my father began to cry. I mean it was his fault for hitting her, and *he* began to cry."

"Tessa, I'm really sorry. I knew you'd had a terrible time with him, but you never told me this."

Tessa looked away, her expression still dazed.

"You want to find a place that's open late and talk for a while?"

Tessa backed up as though Lan had threatened her.

"Maybe that's *not* what you want, huh? Well, how about—"

A series of three *beeps* sounded from Tessa's wrist. At first she didn't seem to realize the source of the sound, but then she pushed her sleeve back to uncover a small module hanging from her bracelet. She looked at it blankly.

A puzzled expression slowly came across her face, and she looked up at Lan. "Someone's in the museum."

# 9

## FIRE DRILL

◆ "SOMEONE'S IN THE museum?" Lan repeated. "You've got an alarm set up there?"

Tessa nodded.

"Let's get back there and guard the place while we call the peace office."

Tessa took a deep breath and seemed to shake free from the spell she'd been under. "I guess we'd better."

They walked quickly through Hawthren Cavern, then took the narrow footbridge across Overhang. Minutes later they were in the low-ceilinged cavern in front of the museum. Lan hadn't known what else to say on the return trip, and Tessa had been lost in her own thoughts.

"You want to make the call?" Lan asked.

Tessa nodded and moved off toward a call box.

Lan tried the museum door. Satisfied that it wouldn't budge, he joined Tessa as she finished her call.

"They should be here in just a few minutes," she said.

"Does the alarm sound inside or just on your monitor?"

"Just the monitor. I wanted to be able to catch whoever it is, not scare them away."

"It only took us a few minutes to get here. Maybe you'll get your wish." Lan looked back at the door, which was still closed. "Who else has the combination?"

"No one."

For a moment they stood silently, both watching the closed door. Tessa looked toward Lan and he looked at her. Her gaze moved from his eyes to his cheek, and she looked suddenly away. Staring at the door, she said, "You haven't been honest with me, have you?"

"You mean that I can defend myself, but I don't brag about it?"

"No, you never brag about anything. That's one of the things I liked about you. I mean the act."

"The act?"

"Give me some credit. When those toughs first saw us, you were prepared to let them rough you up and then go on our way. It was only when they started to threaten me that you took off the mask. That means when you told me about Jarl throwing you in the pool, you knew full well that you could have beaten him up if you chose to. You didn't need to run from those kids last night. You're not the person I knew before."

"I'm still me, Tessa."

"But I'm not sure I like you now. You lied to me."

"Maybe I did. But I didn't do it to hurt you."

"Well, you did. What have you become?"

As Lan tried to figure out what to say, a uniformed peace officer appeared at the mouth of a tunnel across the cavern. Quickly Lan said, "Promise me one thing for now. Promise not to talk to anyone about tonight at the waterfall."

Tessa looked from Lan to the approaching officer and back. "Maybe." She turned to the officer and took two steps forward. "I sure am glad to see you."

The slightly overweight peace officer wore a name tag reading *Hintersal.* His utility belt held enough pockets and compartments to make him seem even more overweight. He looked bored. "You're the person who called about a break-in? Tessa Farlon?"

Tessa confirmed her identity and pointed out the museum door. She gave him a brief explanation about being out tonight and having her alarm go off.

"And so you got back here maybe five minutes after the alarm went off?"

"Yes. So I suppose that means whoever it was could have had time to leave, but it seemed safer to call."

"You did the right thing. That's what we're here for. Give me a few minutes to look around."

Tessa volunteered to unlock the door and she told him how to lock the set of bars inside to prevent an intruder from circling around to avoid detection.

Whatever the peace officer's belt contained in all those compartments was held securely, because he was no noisier than Lan and Tessa as the three of them walked toward the door. The door showed no obvious signs of forced entry.

Near the door, Hintersal retrieved a comm unit and spoke into it briefly, giving a description of his intended moves. When he was ready, Tessa tapped in the combination to the door and the lock clicked open.

Hintersal motioned Tessa and Lan to back up, then slowly swung the door open. Lan held his face blank as a tiny fragment of paper fluttered to the floor, apparently unnoticed by Tessa or Hintersal.

The peace officer cautiously entered the museum, then pulled the door slowly closed, leaving Lan and Tessa to wait outside. For a moment Lan watched Tessa, trying to guess her thoughts. She was aware of being observed, and avoided meeting Lan's gaze. She looked straight ahead at the closed door and blinked and swallowed more often than normal.

Eventually Lan looked back at the door. He felt sad

and for an instant thought he should never have come back. Beside him, Tessa seemed to relax. They waited in awkward silence for several minutes.

The door swung open. Hintersal invited them inside and said, "There's no one here. I don't see any signs of vandalism or theft, but I'd like you to take a quick look around before I go."

Lan could hear Tessa's sigh. She nodded to Hintersal. Together, she and Lan walked through the circle of caverns. Lan saw nothing changed since his last tour.

"Nothing," Tessa said to the waiting peace officer when they had covered the whole circle and unlocked the bars near the entrance. "I can't see anything out of place. I wonder if whoever it was somehow realized I had installed an alarm."

"What kind did you use?"

Tessa moved to the cave wall opposite the door, searched for a moment, and located a small, flat square. She pulled it loose from the wall and handed it to Hintersal. "It's a motion detector, from Big Ears. It's password-coded to the module on my wrist, so no one else should be able to know that it's been set off."

Hintersal briefly examined the back of the square. He shook his head. "These things are normally pretty reliable, but someone with sophisticated equipment might be able to detect the warning message being transmitted. If there was someone in here, he could have easily had time to get away before you came back."

Tessa nodded. There was nothing else for Hintersal to do, so he left.

Lan took a step toward the door. "I don't know how safe it is for you to be here. I'd be happy to pay for an overnight stay someplace else. How about it?"

"I'll be fine. I'll just prop something in front of the door. No one will be able to get in."

"Please? Humor me?"

"I'll be fine. There's only the one door to block."

"You're not going to be stubborn, are you?"

"No more stubborn than you."

Lan hesitated. "I'm worried about you. I don't think anyone came in through that door."

"That doesn't make any sense. It's the only alternative."

Lan told her about the tiny flap of paper.

"So all that means is that whoever was here noticed it when it fell out, and put it back in when he left, to make me think no one had been here."

"Maybe. But it was a really small piece."

"I'll be fine, Lan," she said. "I'm getting tired. I'll talk to you some other time."

The submerged anger in her words told Lan she hadn't forgotten their earlier discussion. He felt frustrated. "I'm nothing like your first father, you know."

"I know. I know."

"Look, Tessa. I'm the same Lan you knew before. So I can defend myself now. I'm not the meek, fumbling guy I was, but that wasn't why you loved me. And just because I'm capable of violence, that doesn't mean I use it indiscriminately. For God's sake, even though you're shook up, you should realize that I waited until the last possible moment."

"But you're still a violent man. You've changed a lot. I'm not sure I know you anymore."

Lan's frustration peaked. After a moment's deliberation, he took a small, thin disk from his pocket. The disk resembled a coin and even had the tiny display showing a balance of zero. He bent the disk in half, gave it a twist, and flattened it so it still looked like any other coin except for an almost invisible hairline slit. He handed it to Tessa. "Keep that somewhere where you won't lose it. If the guy we saw at dinner approaches within about fifty meters, that thing will beep twice."

Tessa took the proximity alarm and looked at it blankly for a second. "What *is* this?"

"It doesn't matter. Just do that one thing for me." Lan turned and opened the door.

"Lan—"

"I'm tired, too. I'll see you later." Lan stepped through the doorway. He pulled the door closed behind him and walked across the deserted cavern, feeling he'd lost everything he ever valued.

# 10

## CALL THE POLICE

THE NEAREST PEACE office occupied a cave cut into the side of a large chamber at the nexus of so many intersecting tunnels that little wall space existed. High on the wall opposite was a small medical facility. Lan entered the peace office, stood in front of the counter, and waited for someone to notice him.

Seconds later a uniformed man in his early twenties looked around from what he was doing and moved to the counter. "May I help you?"

"I'd like to talk to the officer in charge."

The man raised one eyebrow a millimeter, and said, "That would be Lieutenant Mahrig. Would you come with me?"

Lan nodded and moved to the end of the counter. The man swung a small gate out of the way. Lan stepped through, passing between scanner disks set into the opposite surfaces.

Lt. Mahrig's office was near the back of the cave. Half of her office was a depression in the back wall of the cave. The front half was fabricated and included a door, which stood open as Lan arrived. Lt. Mahrig was a woman perhaps ten years older than Lan, and she had dark hair pulled back away from her face. She was alert and calm, as if she had taken care of whatever emergencies had been waiting for her when she arrived this morning, and had been starting on the dull stuff.

Her desk top was a solid display of reference material. The surface was divided into more than fifty rectangular page images, some showing faces that might have been on the most wanted list, others showing checklists or summaries of key facts about how people die and how to keep them alive.

"What's this about?" she asked as soon as Lan had introduced himself and settled into a chair.

"I'd like to request some information, as a courtesy to a visiting person in the same line of work."

"What kind of information?"

"I took a picture of a man last night. I'd like to run it through your files and find out who he is."

"And just why would you like to do a thing like that?" Lt. Mahrig sat up a little straighter.

"As a precaution. He's threatened a friend of mine, and although he hasn't done anything he could be arrested for—that I can prove anyway—I'd like to find out if he has a record. I might be more concerned than I am now, if it turns out he's been convicted of murder."

Lt. Mahrig frowned slightly, as if having problems correlating Lan's small build with the stereotype of peace officers. "And this picture of yours is where?"

Lan took from his shirt pocket a photo he had printed an hour before. Lt. Mahrig had no need to know about the camera in his ring, so he didn't volunteer the picture's source.

If Lt. Mahrig hadn't taken Lan seriously at first, she did now. "I'd like to see some identification."

Lan withdrew a thin card from his shirt pocket, then

pressed his thumb into the card. As he handed the card to Lt. Mahrig, the card glowed orange.

The lieutenant put the photo on her desktop and held the card, clicking a corner of it against her fingertip. She looked from Lan to the card and back. Finally she leaned back in her chair and said, "That's very interesting, but just because you're affiliated with a peacekeeping office doesn't give you any jurisdiction here. You should know that."

"I do know that. I don't intend to try to arrest this guy or anything. I just want to know more about him. If there's any official work to do, obviously it's all yours."

"You haven't convinced me. There's nothing stopping me from taking this photo and deciding for myself if he has a record."

"But you don't know what he's been doing lately. Or who to ask."

"I could ask you to tell me."

"True. But no crime has been committed. I wouldn't be obligated to tell you anything."

"But you might do a thing like that if you thought it was the only way to help your friend."

"How about if we both tell each other?"

"I don't think so. How about if you just go ahead and tell me, and I'll decide for myself?"

Lan sighed.

She spread her hands. "Just go ahead and tell me."

Lan told her. He described the encounter with the man last night, and told the lieutenant about Tessa's previous brushes with him. When he finished, Lt. Mahrig turned to a small terminal near her desk and moved her fingers across the screen. Lan could see her screen brighten, but from his angle couldn't tell what it showed.

The lieutenant's jaws tightened and she tapped a few more keys. Light flickered from the screen. When she turned back to Lan, her expression was guarded. "How about if you have your friend come in and talk to us?"

"Because right now it's a waste of time. This guy's been very careful." Lan glanced toward her screen. "So, are you going to share some information with me?"

"No, I'm sorry. This goes a little beyond my idea of professional courtesy."

"I'm not asking for any information that wouldn't be freely available to me if I worked on Neverend."

"No. I just think this is a matter for us to handle."

Lan held her gaze long enough to convince himself she wouldn't change her mind without more persuasion. "You mind if I close the door for a moment?"

She shook her head casually, but her eyes grew wary, narrowing fractionally as Lan rose to push on the door.

When the door was closed, Lan pulled his card toward him until it lay near the edge of the lieutenant's desk, then he sat back down. Lan simultaneously put his little fingertips from both hands on opposite ends of the card. As he and the lieutenant watched, the card's fading orange tint dimmed still more, and a new image, in blue, poured over the card.

The new image showed block letters saying, "Commonwealth Covert Corps: Undercover Operations," and an emblem to Lt. Mahrig. Her expression changed from guarded to wide-eyed. She looked up at Lan with disbelief showing an instant before she masked it. "Why didn't you just say so at first?" she asked.

"I hoped it wouldn't be necessary."

"What the hell brings you here? Is there something we should know?"

"I'm just here on vacation." Lan told her the truth, aware that she probably wouldn't believe him.

She looked back at Lan's card. The blue image was starting to fade.

"What's the guy's name?" Lan asked quietly.

The blue image on the card faded completely, and the surface returned to its normal gray, almost as if the image had never been there. Lt. Mahrig picked the card back up and flicked the corner again with her finger. *Tick, tick, tick.* "Wilby Hackert."

Lan waited.

"He lives in Katteron Cranny." She looked back at her screen and supplied the address and the coordinates.

"Has he been in trouble?"

"Several times. But not directly for murder. He's been accused of embezzlement once, assault and battery several times. One of the witnesses in the embezzlement case disappeared. He just never turned up."

"But Wilby had an alibi?"

"Yeah." Lt. Mahrig looked back at the screen. "He was at a bar at the critical time. A friend of his vouched for him. Ellie Troughteral. She's had no trouble with us. And we found no evidence to the contrary."

"Ellie Troughteral sounds like the woman who made offers on the museum. That makes me wonder if she was a completely unbiased witness. What kind of jobs do they have?"

"Wilby is in construction. Home building, cave flooring, wall carving, damage repair, almost everything. He works for a small outfit called 'Home and Office.' " The lieutenant summoned more information to her screen. "Ellie works in hydroponics. Same job for five years. Good references. She lives in Katteron Cranny, too." She gave Lan the address.

"What can you tell me about a young man named Rento Queller?"

"How does he fit into this?"

"He doesn't. This is a slightly different concern."

Lt. Mahrig stared at Lan a moment before she put her fingers on the terminal. More shapes shifted across the screen. "He's a frequent short-term visitor here, usually for fairly minor offenses. We last saw him just a couple of days—" She looked suddenly at Lan. "I guess you know why he was here last time. Your name is in the report."

"Right. So that's typical of his escapades?"

"More or less. A few fights, mostly with males around his own age."

"What else? Where does he live?"

"He lives with his father, Walkark Queller, in Astrozoam Terrace. He's finished mandatory school. Bright, but hyperactive. He works part-time for Speedy Delivery. His father works for them, too."

"That explains why I've seen him a few times. They live fairly close to the museum. What's the exact address?"

She gave it to him.

"Thank you, Lieutenant. You've been a big help." Lan rose to leave.

"That's it? You're not going to tell me anything about your plans?"

"I don't have anything planned. Except a reunion dinner this evening."

"That isn't exactly what I meant."

"It's still all I've got planned. I don't know what's going on here." Lan hesitated. "Look, I know you're probably curious. But I really don't have a plan. I know I want to talk to Wilby Hackert and Ellie Troughteral, but I haven't decided when to do it or what my approach is going to be."

"That's the truth?"

"That's the truth. I'm just an impulsive kind of guy."

"I still don't understand," Parke said. "Where did you get this woman's name?"

Lan and Parke walked through Salahara Dome, an almost perfectly symmetrical, bubble-shaped cavern. A decorative, iridescent ball hung overhead in the center of the room, suspended by more than a thousand iridescent strands all anchored to random spots on the curved ceiling, as though the cavern had been designed with one purpose in mind: to accommodate the ornament.

Lan said, "From Tessa. She had the name slightly wrong, but it was in the directory close enough to spot." Lan neglected to talk about his other sources of information. He felt a little guilty withholding information from Parke and Tessa, but he'd just spent a number of years never telling anyone anything the person didn't need to know. His undercover training continually stressed how valueless agents like him would be if other people knew what they were.

"And what do I have to say?"

"That's the best part. You don't have to say anything. You're along for the intimidation value."

"That's it?"

"There's a possibility we'll run into trouble. I'd feel better if you were there."

They walked past a grid hologram, down a gentle incline, and through a narrow arch, into the next cavern. This one contained numerous small shops, most of them set into the walls, but a couple were free-standing in the center of the room, and the paths split to circle them. The men had walked partway around the perimeter when two teenagers walked out of a shop and headed in their direction. One of the boys was the blond from shoplifting and the night before; the other was one of his friends from last night.

When the blond kid saw Lan, his eyes widened. When he glanced at Parke, his expression turned to panic and he stopped right where he was. He grabbed his friend's arm and whispered something to him. His friend glanced at Lan and Parke and a second later, both teenagers spun around and ran.

"Did you see that?" Parke said, grinning with satisfaction.

"See what?" Lan said.

"One of the kids we saw shoplifting. He and his buddy spotted me and they went running. He looked like he'd just seen a squadron of peace officers."

"Good. The guy you caught must have passed on your message."

"Maybe. But I'm surprised anyway."

They saw no sign of the two teenagers as they moved into Katteron Cranny. There a long, twisty stairway led steeply downward through a fissure a couple of meters wide. Doors were cut into the walls at irregular intervals, some doors decorated with colorful designs, others completely bare. One they passed was nearly invisible because its rectangular surface was covered with a textured coating designed to match the surrounding rock walls.

"This is it," Lan announced moments later, as they stood on a narrow landing between tiers of steps. "Let me do the talking, all right?"

Parke glanced at Lan, then at the door, and grinned. "Sure, boss."

Lan pressed a switch set into the door. Moments later the door opened and a woman with brown hair and brown eyes stood there. She wore a limestone-gray uniform with a lapel display reading *Hydrogrow, E. Troughteral.* The cuff fasteners and the top couple of fasteners in the front of her tunic were undone, as though they had caught her just after she got home from work and was changing. Beyond her, a tunnel about two meters long widened onto a living area.

Ellie Troughteral squinted slightly and put several questions into one word: "Yes?"

"You don't know us," Lan said easily, "but a friend told us you were interested in acquiring a museum, and

suggested we talk to you about possible arrangements.''
Lan introduced himself and Parke.

Ellie's expression turned as pleasant as a first date's.
''Come right in. Where are my manners?''

She led them down the hall, then turned and said,
''Can I offer you anything?'' The men declined.

They reached her living area. The main room was a
rough oval, with two smaller tunnels leading off the back
wall, one going down to the left, one up to the right. The
floor was poured, an unblended mixture of blue and
green and silver and black that gave it the feel of turquoise. The rest of the room was understated elegance—
comfortable chairs with clean lines, a table with what
looked to be actual wood slats along the sides, cabinets set
into the walls, and gentle indirect lighting from a continuous ring around the ceiling.

Ellie looked about five years older than Lan and Parke.
She was a compact woman, about Lan's height, anorexic
or possessing either a racing metabolism or enough will
power to eat not much more than a subsistence diet. Her
wrists seemed no bigger around than a pair of Parke's fingers. When she sat, she hardly dented the cushions.

''You were saying,'' Ellie said as Lan and Parke took
seats.

Lan crossed his legs and leaned back into the chair. ''I
was saying that I understand you're interested in a museum. Are you interested in owning and operating, or
owning and letting someone else operate it?''

''Well, I guess I'd prefer to run it myself. Why? Does it
make a difference?''

''It may. I'm not sure. How soon would you like to
start?''

''As soon as possible.''

Lan was aware of Parke scratching his nose, something
he did when he was puzzled, but fortunately Parke didn't
say anything. Lan went on. ''I think the price is going to be

in the range of forty to fifty thousand. Does that eliminate your interest, or is it still worth discussing?" The figure was much higher than reasonable, and Lan watched her carefully.

"Oh, I think that could be arranged. I'd have to do some checking, but it's within reason."

This was interesting. She either had no idea what the museum was worth, or she didn't care. "The proprietor has a lot of sentiment tied up in the museum. She wants to feel sure the new owner would maintain the friendly atmosphere and keep the place functioning efficiently. How do you feel about that?"

Ellie didn't hesitate over that question either. "Oh, certainly I'd do that. She doesn't have a thing to worry about."

"Oh, and just out of curiosity, why do you want to run a museum?"

"I like old things. I always have."

"And would you want to pay for some indoctrination, training, that sort of thing?"

"I don't think so," Ellie said slowly. "I think I'll adapt just fine."

"That's good. So you must already be familiar with the methods of arranging exhibits to be sent, the deposits, the insurance, all that?"

"Well, I'm not an expert yet, but I think I'll be able to figure it all out. So tell me, how soon could the transaction take place?"

"I'm not sure, but I suppose it's mainly up to you. I need to give you a few more details to make sure you're interested. You see, this particular museum is the Art and Antiquities Museum on Harkener. You'll probably want to spend some time evaluating what your moving costs would be, and whether you really want to go ahead with this."

As Lan had spoken, the woman's expression changed to puzzlement, then to disbelief. "Wait—wait a minute. I thought we were talking about the museum right here on Neverend."

"Oh, I'm sorry," Lan said easily. "I apologize. I knew you were interested in a private museum, but I didn't know it needed to be that particular one."

# 11

## PARTY

ELLIE TROUGHTERAL DROPPED her mouth partly open. "This whole time you've been talking about some museum on Harkener? The one I'm interested in is right here."

Lan spread his hands. "I knew you were interested in that one, but I guess I got the message wrong. I thought you were interested in museums in general. I'm awfully sorry to have wasted some of your time." He rose to leave, and gestured for Parke to come with him.

"But what about this one?" Ellie asked. Both she and Parke got up.

"I'm afraid the owner isn't interested in selling right now. That's why I investigated some alternatives."

"But—" She stopped, looking as if she wanted to say more but was holding back.

Lan imagined Ellie was irritated at the false hope but not wanting to show her irritation in case Lan actually was in a position to handle the sale of Tessa's museum. He said, "Now that I know your requirements, I'll have to have another talk with Ms. Farlon, to see if she might change her mind any time soon."

Ellie was instantly understanding. "That would be fine. Obviously you know how to reach me."

Yes, Lan thought, and I know how to get to you.

"I still don't see any reason you needed me as a bodyguard, but forget it. What did all that prove?" Parke asked. He and Lan walked back through Salahara Dome.

"Several things. You haven't gotten any dumber since school. You tell me what we found out."

"I'll give it a try, but only if you'll come to the reunion dinner. It's only another hour away, and you've skipped almost everything else."

"I might as well," Lan said. "I don't have anything better to do."

Parke looked at him questioningly.

Lan said, "Long story. Go ahead and tell me what we found out."

"Well, Ellie didn't really seem all that knowledgeable about museums—and she didn't seem particularly interested in learning."

"That's good enough to make it worth the trip. In addition to that, she doesn't know what the place is worth. It's as if she woke up one morning and had this brilliant flash. I want to run a museum. And it has to be this one."

"So?"

"So maybe it isn't the museum itself that she's after. Maybe she wants that location for a new business that might be really profitable there. Maybe they're going to cut a new chute route through and the property will be worth much more. Maybe she's discovered that one of the artifacts on display is worth millions and wants to steal it. Maybe she's just crazy."

"Maybe she's buying it for someone else."

"Could be. But she seemed awfully emotional about it if some third party is the only one who cares."

"Unless she gets a big commission."

"It must be, to risk a sentence for murder."

They reached the station just as a quicktrain was pulling to a stop. Parke waited until they were settled into seats away from the other five people aboard. "You mean Tessa's dad?"

"Sure. He's dead and now people want to pressure Tessa into selling. Maybe he was being pressured and it didn't work. Now Tessa's being pressured and it still isn't working."

"So that means Tessa may be next?"

"I think she's fine for now. Ellie knows there are more people involved now—more people who know she wants what Tessa has."

"Maybe I shouldn't have talked you into going to dinner. Maybe you should be with her instead."

"No, dinner's fine. Tessa and I aren't really talking right now."

*"What?"*

"We had kind of an argument."

"You two sure are stubborn. What are you doing here with me? Get on over there and apologize."

"I tried that. Next suggestion?"

"What did you *say* to her to get her so angry?"

"Nothing I feel like talking about right now. It's private, all right?"

"How can you expect help from Doctor Parke if you won't tell me the symptoms?"

"I'm not looking for help. And I don't think the symptoms are fatal." Lan looked away and hoped he was right.

"Six ship changes to get here?" Lan repeated. "How far away is your home?"

Lellarah considered the question for a moment, then made a series of guttural noises that the voice box hanging around his neck translated into, "Many hundred light-years. My home now is Hanraketro Four, squatting on the edge of the Transfarr Domain. I had barely time to reach here upon leaving my home school reunion." The synthesized voice sounded as familiar to Lan as the other human voices he had heard during the dinner. As he had done in the past, Lellarah had the voice box set for literal translation rather than paraphrasing.

"I'm really glad you were able to make the trip," Lan said to the exchange student. "Besides the fact that it's good to see you, you probably win the prize for the most distance traveled."

The two stood at the edge of a large hall in which the rest of the class bounced around like a mob on tranquilizers, talking a few minutes here, a moment there. Lan tried to keep his mind on the conversation and off Tessa.

Lellarah's two large, dark eyes blinked in rapid succession, and Lan remembered one of his first impressions of his alien friend. How much more sense it made to blink Lellarah's way rather than the human way that leaves one blind for an instant.

Lellarah's body was closer to humanoid than many aliens were, but the shape of his head guaranteed there would be no mistaking him for human. Extending directly from his shoulders, with no intervening neck, his hairless head was more fish-shaped than round. His large eyes were set one on each side, so each had a view of almost 180 degrees, with enough overlap that Lellarah could see stereoscopically for perhaps the center quarter of his combined field of view. Like everyone else, Lellarah wore a name badge with a picture of him from school, but Lan could see no changes.

"I am glad you also came," said Lellarah through the voice box. "Not everyone here was as friendly as were you, or as willing to go slow enough to understand."

"I guess kids aren't always good examples. But I bet more of them would be better friends now than you might guess."

"I believe you are correct. I have already received good welcomes from people who I unexpected."

"It's fun to see people have grown up a little. I saw Pertain Havercomb tonight. The only things he used to talk about were getting loose and all-night parties. Now he's got a family and his job involves counseling kids. I think he still knows how to enjoy himself, but he doesn't focus every speck of energy on that one goal."

Lellarah tilted his body forward in his version of a nod. "That is true. We all change. But I expected to see you here with Tessa."

Parke interrupted from behind Lan's back. "It's probably just a game. If Tessa think he's aloof, then she'll want him that much more."

With Parke was Carrie, looking happy. As they exchanged greetings with Lellarah, his skin blued noticeably at the sudden attention.

Lan grinned. "Parke, on the other hand, will never grow up. This is like a time warp, seeing him just as immature and single-minded as he was in school. It's great having him here as a contrast while we're all trying to feel we've grown since we left."

"Maybe he *is* starting to grow up," Carrie said. "I've been around him off and on for more than a day, and he hasn't pulled one practical joke."

"Other than the sign on your back, that is," Parke said.

Carrie's eyes widened and she grimaced. She tried to look over her shoulder as she reached toward her shoulder blade to grab the sign if one was there.

Parke laughed gently. "I'm kidding."

Carrie punched him on the arm. "And I had such high hopes for you."

Parke hunched his shoulders as if to say, "I am what I am."

Lan looked over Carrie's shoulder and said, "I see Jarl

coming, and he looks unhappy. Maybe he didn't like the swim.''

Carrie took a backward glance. ''I don't think he did, but that's not your fault.''

The talk in their circle died, as the buzz of conversation seemed to grow louder all around them.

As Jarl reached the group, Lan said calmly, ''Hello again. Care to join us?''

''I don't need your permission, do I?'' At least Jarl Haxxon sounded sober tonight. ''And why are you still hanging around Carrie?''

''Friends do that kind of thing,'' Lan said.

''Why do *you* keep hanging around Carrie?'' Parke asked.

Jarl's features momentarily contorted and he blinked, obviously having trouble switching his focus from Lan to Parke. ''Why do I—that's *my* business.''

Lan stepped easily into the old divide-their-attention-and-confuse-them mode he and Parke had used. He said, ''Maybe you're in the wrong business.''

''Exactly what is that supposed to mean?'' Jarl asked. He flipped his attention back to Lan.

''It means if you don't stop harassing us, I'll have my trained mandorm here escort you outside,'' Lan said, gesturing at Parke.

Parke responded with a comic impression of a stupefied brute, blinking madly, his nose crinkled to the point that it looked more like a snout.

Jarl glanced at Parke, back at Lan, then at Carrie, and narrowed his eyes, apparently realizing that the fact that Carrie was closer to Parke than to Lan might be significant. He opened his mouth to say something, then closed it again. Finally he said to Carrie, ''Who are you—''

''Excuse me, will you please?'' Lan said suddenly. Not waiting for reactions, he moved behind and around Carrie and Parke, making his way through the throng of classmates, threading toward a face he had seen through a momentary gap between shifting people.

Jarl said, "Running away again?" but Lan paid no more attention to the comment than he would to a child who'd just deliberately dropped a toy on the ground for the fifteenth time.

He brushed past Teril Chow's welcome and extended hand with a quick "I'll be back" and stood in a small clearing in the forest of people, looking for Tessa. Or had his mind been playing tricks on him?

No. There she was, wearing dark pants and a lemon-colored blouse. Lan moved forward, cutting the distance between them, wondering why she was here and why she looked so nervous.

As Lan drew nearer, Tessa reached the bar. By the time Lan was close enough for her to notice him, she had already taken a large gulp from a goblet.

"What's wrong?" Lan asked as he reached her.

"What makes you think something's wrong?" Tessa asked back, glancing around the gathering, rather than meeting his gaze.

"We know each other too well for that kind of game, don't we? You look upset to me. I'm concerned about you."

"We don't know each other very well at all it seems." Tessa took another swig from the goblet. Her gaze drifted back to the entrance to the cavern.

"I'll try one more time. I care a *lot* about you, and I'd like to help with whatever's bothering you. If you don't want me around, just say so. I don't get any pleasure from doing things that annoy people."

Tessa said nothing. A tremor in her hand made her drink tremble. Lan almost convinced himself that he had read Tessa's actions wrong, and now *he* was the problem. He said, "Right. I understand. I didn't mean to bother you. I guess I'll see you later."

Lan turned away, feeling miserable. He started back toward the crowd of classmates, hesitated an instant, then turned toward the cavern mouth, suddenly feeling antisocial.

He was halfway to the exit when he heard rapid footsteps behind him. He turned.

Tessa halted suddenly, saying nothing. She looked more frightened than Lan had seen her before.

Lan softened his tone. "I don't understand. You want to talk or you don't want to talk?"

Tessa stood mute, just staring at him.

"What's wrong, Tessa? Please tell me what's going on."

"I—I don't know what to do. A voice inside me says don't let you go again. Another voice says anyone capable of deceit and violence has no part in my life. But I'm scared."

Lan moved closer. "What are you scared of?"

Tessa swallowed. "Somebody just tried to kill me."

# 12

## NONRESIDENT

◆ LAN SUDDENLY FELT cold in the warm room. "Someone tried to kill you? Where? How?"

Tessa took another large sip from her drink, then rubbed her temple. "Windhove Cavern. I stepped off the end of the escalator, and walked a few steps. A rock half the size of my head crashed into the floor not a meter away from me. I went back up to the top level and looked all around, but there were only a few people there and no one saw anything happen. A couple of peace officers took a long look around and asked me lots of questions before letting me go. I told them about the museum offers and the threats."

"Are you all right?"

"I'm here, aren't I?" Tessa's anger showed on her face, but Lan couldn't tell if the feeling was directed at him or the situation.

"I didn't mean physically. You want to sit down or anything?" Lan glanced back at the crowd of classmates, but no one was approaching them.

"No. I'm fine. It's just not every day that someone tries to kill me."

"And you're sure it was deliberate? I know it's really unlikely, but a piece of rock could have worked its way loose on its own."

Tessa took Lan's proximity alarm from a small bag hanging on her wrist. "As sure as I can be. I didn't see whoever did it, but this thing you gave me started beeping not five minutes before it all happened. What the hell is this, Lan?" Tessa's voice trembled.

Lan felt sick. "It's a proximity alarm. I stuck a beeper on your friend's blue jacket. But it doesn't matter. What really matters is that it's probably my fault that you were attacked."

"Your fault? How do you figure that? And how is it that you're so readily accepting all this? It took me almost all the way here to really believe it all happened."

"I went to talk to Ellie Troughteral today. I told her you still don't intend to sell the museum."

"You *what?*"

"I wanted to gauge her interest in your museum, as opposed to any old museum."

"What right did you—" Tessa's burst of anger faded fractionally, and her old familiar curiosity took its place. "What was she interested in—my museum or just any museum?"

"Yours. The most interesting part was that she doesn't seem to know much of anything about museums, and she apparently isn't interested in learning."

Tessa looked into the distance. "I wonder what it is she really wants." A moment later, she looked back at Lan and frowned. "So, what gives you the right to endanger my life?"

"Nothing."

" 'Nothing?' No excuses?"

"You want excuses? One, I really didn't think they'd react like this. Obviously I misjudged them or they just meant to scare you. Two, I didn't think you'd be out and around for them to try anything anyway. Three, I had planned to talk to the guy who's been following you tomorrow, and warn him that if anything happens to you he'll have a planetful of trouble on his hands."

Tessa just looked at him stonily.

"I'm sorry," Lan said. "I'm genuinely sorry about what happened on your way here, and if anything or anyone hurt you I'd probably turn into a raving lunatic. Just because I've changed a little, and just because I couldn't stay on Neverend doesn't mean you've ever left my thoughts. I've never stopped thinking about you."

Tessa hesitated. "I still don't have any real evidence to give the peace officers. Probably part of the reason I'm so angry is that your actions seem to have manipulated me into needing your help even more than before."

"I can understand how you'd feel that way. All I can say is that wasn't my motivation. I just wanted to help. I still want to help. And I think I *can* help."

"Help what?" Parke said from behind Lan's shoulder.

"Help discourage people from barging into conversations by killing the next person to do it." Lan turned and found both Parke and Carrie. "You're following me tonight?"

"Hey relax, Lan," Parke said.

Lan took a deep breath. "Sorry. Actually, I'm glad you're here. We need to give Tessa some protection tonight."

"Why protection?"

Lan looked at Tessa and got a nod indicating she was willing to share the information. "Someone just tried to kill her."

Parke and Carrie looked surprised, then Carrie said quietly, "You're not kidding, are you."

Lan and Tessa both shook their heads. Tessa explained what had happened.

Finally, Lan said to Tessa, "I don't know that it's a good

idea for you to stay here now. How about if the three of us escort you home, then Parke and I call on our friend from last night?''

Tessa said, ''If things got worse when you talked to Ellie, won't they get even worse now?''

''I don't think so. Now that the peace office has an open file and you've told them about the offers and the implied threats, whoever did this should realize that people will know who to blame if anything else happens. Plus, we can make up some story to get this guy to think he won't gain anything anyway. For instance, if you die your museum goes to a cousin off-planet. Maybe that will slow him down.''

Parke frowned. ''How valuable is the museum anyway? Are those artifacts worth a lot?''

Tessa shook her head. ''That's one reason this is so puzzling. The museum's really not worth much at all. I pay a periodic fee into a pool, and in return I'm on the list for a lot of traveling exhibits. It's actually more like an art gallery than a mainstream museum. Hardly any of the museum contents actually belong to me.''

''It could be this guy isn't clear on the concept,'' said Lan.

Parke turned to Lan. ''How do you know where to find him?'' Tessa's frown said the same question occurred to her.

''It's a long story. I'll tell you later.'' To Parke and Carrie, Lan said, ''Do you mind leaving early?''

Parke and Carrie glanced at each other and neither objected.

Lan glanced back at the gathering of classmates. ''Maybe we can spend more time at the next reunion.''

Parke caught his eye and added, ''Assuming we're still alive by then.''

\*   \*   \*

"See," Tessa said, "you can still see the fragments."

Less than two meters from the base of the escalator in Windhove Cavern, rock fragments and rock dust still lay in a heap on the scratched floor. Two larger fist-size fragments had shot in almost directly opposite directions.

Carrie kept watch on the railing far above to make sure no one tried the same trick while the foursome was vulnerable.

Lan said, "And when you looked up, you didn't see anyone at the railing?"

Tessa shook her head. "There were a couple of people on the escalator, but that was all."

Parke said, "The rock didn't land in the center of the path. You think this was maybe just meant to scare you rather than kill you?"

Tessa shrugged.

Lan said, "It's a possibility, but it's still not all that encouraging a thought. If whoever did this was willing to come this close to killing, I'm not sure the next step would be all that difficult." For the first time in several weeks, Lan felt afraid—afraid for Tessa.

Tessa looked at Lan. "That's very comforting."

"I'm not trying to be comforting. I'm trying to be realistic."

Tessa looked back down and kicked a pebble across the floor.

"You're sure Tessa and Carrie are going to be safe in the museum?" Parke asked. He and Lan had retraced the route they had taken earlier in the day and were nearing Katteron Cranny.

Lan glanced at him. "You mean do I think anyone is likely to blast down the door and force their way inside?"

"I guess they'll be all right, huh?"

"That's my guess."

They arrived at the number Lan provided and knocked on the door.

After a few seconds of silence, Parke said, "Maybe he's out causing more mayhem tonight. We don't know that Tessa's the only person he's trying to persuade."

"True. But let's try another place."

They walked up a series of winding steps and stopped in front of Ellie Troughteral's door. Lan knocked.

The silence lasted only ten seconds. The door opened, and Ellie appeared. Her features transformed from surprise to restrained optimism. "Hello. Did you bring more news about the museum?"

Parke looked at Lan, who replied. "No, I'm afraid not. We just wanted to leave a message for Wilby."

"Oh." Ellie's expression suddenly grew unreadable. "Wilby who? I don't understand."

"Wilby Hackert," Lan said. "We know you know him, and we already know he's also involved in this scheme to get the museum."

"Scheme? You're not making any sense."

"That's all right. You can pretend not to understand. Just tell Wilby the museum goes into a cousin's hands if anything happens to Tessa Farlon. You gain nothing by harming her. *And,* the peace office will know who's responsible if anything happens to her."

"I think you'd better leave." Without waiting for a response, she swung the door closed and it latched.

Parke stared at the closed door. "What do you say we leave?" he asked. "I'm not feeling welcome anymore."

"Me, neither."

"It's all so strange," Tessa said. "I still don't understand what they could stand to gain."

Lan and Parke and Carrie sat in the museum foyer with Tessa. Carrie said, "Isn't it time to ask for some protection from the peace office?"

Tessa shook her head. "I still don't have anything to prove to them that this last episode wasn't an accident or a prank."

Lan leaned back into his chair. He glanced at Tessa, saw her look away uncomfortably, and looked back at Parke. "Maybe—" he started.

"What?" Parke asked after a moment of silence.

"Did you hear something? From in there?" Lan pointed at the darkened adjoining cave.

"Hearing things now, Lan? You're getting too edgy with this business." Parke's voice held an edge that said he was more nervous than he cared to admit.

"I'm sure I heard something," Lan said, rising from his chair. He walked to the mouth of the cave and cocked his head. He heard nothing now. He turned toward the others. "I think we need to make a very careful search. Maybe you've got some rodent guest here, Tessa." He kept his voice calm, despite feeling nervous.

Minutes later, the lights were on in all the caves, and the four stood in pairs, Lan and Tessa ready to head one direction, Parke and Carrie ready to go in the other. Parke said, "Meet you on the way."

Lan and Tessa moved into the first cave. They both carried emergency handlights. As Lan peered behind a display cabinet filled with hand-beaten gold-foil jewelry from Talfor, Tessa said, "Do you really think this is necessary? Maybe you're overreacting to the whole situation."

"Maybe. Maybe not. But you heard something in here before, and your alarm went off, remember?"

Tessa made no response.

Lan said, "I hadn't looked at these closely before. Are there storage cabinets below these cases, or do they extend to the floor?"

Tessa reached one of the cases and pulled open a flat panel that had no handle. "There's a lip on the underside. There's space for power for internal lighting and any special requirements like flowing water. But no one can hide in there. It's too small.''

"Too small for us, but not too small for a rat or a marmoken." Lan swung his lamp over the interior shelf and the dusty tools lying inside. "Maybe even a small child could fit in here."

"Doesn't that seem a little unlikely to you?"

"Sure. But I'm positive I heard a noise." He closed the panel and looked behind the case. Nothing.

Tessa opened the panels on two more display cases, exposing nothing, then Lan went around behind each case, even the ones that afforded hiding places far too small for a person.

"Nothing in here," Tessa said.

"All right. Let's move on."

The next cave felt as silent as the first. Lan still felt edgy, but he began to wonder if he were overreacting. Maybe the sound had been a settling creak, the rock shifting a little under some pressure gradually built up as the caves and caverns overhead acquired inhabitants and their support functions.

Tessa and Lan opened more panels, and circled the display cases carefully.

Lan said, "Are you still angry with me?"

Tessa looked up suddenly from the shelf she had been checking. "We used to be honest with each other." Without pausing for a reply, she closed the panel and announced, "That's the last one here. Next?"

Her matter-of-fact tone was one Lan remembered from a couple of times he had hurt her in the past. Her hurt still showed, but Tessa must have felt she was successfully hiding it beneath a facade of mere irritation. Lan wanted to take her in his arms, to stop her from trying to pretend her emotions didn't exist.

They moved into the adjoining cave. Lan said, "It's not that I set out to trick you." He stooped next to a large display case filled with chunks of resin-encapsulated fragments of what looked a little like paper bearing hieroglyphics. He opened the door.

From inside the base of the cabinet came a cross between a squeal and a groan. The tone was decidedly not human, but it crossed language and culture barriers. Lan felt the mixture of terror and surprise in the first second. An instant later, a small furry creature bolted out of the enclosure and scurried into the cave beyond, going, Lan guessed, just as fast as it could travel. A green and brown blur with four blue eyes, it traveled a couple of meters on all four limbs. Then it rose slightly, running on its rear limbs and leaning forward.

Two seconds later, the small creature could have been a memory, but for the diminishing sound of clicking against the floor. Lan and Tessa looked at each other, their mouths hanging open.

Lan spoke first. "What the hell was that?"

"I have no idea. I've never seen anything like it before."

# 13

## NEW FRIENDS

◆ THE SOUNDS OF the creature's departure faded into silence even as Lan moved to follow it.

Tessa joined him. "I don't understand," she said. "How could a creature like that get *here?*"

They entered the next cave, not slowing down to search. Lan said, "I don't know. It's small enough that someone could have tried to take it through customs, but it's hard to believe no one would have spotted it."

"Do you suppose it's dangerous?"

"No idea. But most species have *some* means of protection."

"Maybe we'd better warn Carrie and Parke before we do anything else."

"Good idea."

They hurried through the next cavern and then the next, and stopped short as they encountered their friends.

"What's going on?" Parke asked.

Lan glanced back at the cave they had just left. "I don't suppose you saw a little guy about knee high race through here? Four bright blue eyes, green and brown fur. And toenails. Or claws."

Parke looked blank, but Carrie said, "We didn't see anything. But did it have a marsupial kind of pouch in front, or stripes down its back?"

"Stripes maybe," Lan said.

"Yeah," Tessa said. "It *did* have stripes—maybe three or four of them."

"It sounds like it could be a tekker. But what would one be doing on Neverend?"

"First things first," Lan said. "Are they dangerous?"

"Not unless you get them real mad. They're moderately intelligent—somewhere between chimps and debarters. Their personality is supposed to be something like a real smart cat—they're curious, too—but friendlier and less independent, and they use their paws more like hands. On their home planet, most of them know a little Standard mixed with a little signing. And their atmosphere's similar enough to ours that they wouldn't need life support."

"There's really one of them in here somewhere?" Parke said.

Lan said, "One of them, or something similar. We both saw it clearly."

"It couldn't have gotten out of a zoo here?"

Carrie shook her head. "If it's a tekker, not a chance. Nobody would have one in a zoo. They'd be in violation of a dozen covenants."

"What's puzzling," Lan said, "is how it vanished."

Tessa said, "Probably it saw Carrie and Parke ahead, and it hid behind one of the cases back there. By now it could be anywhere."

"I guess we'd better revise our search plan then. How about if you stay right here, Parke, while the three of us make a full circle. Don't try to capture it. Maybe if it sees we're not aggressive, it will stop running."

Parke agreed, and Lan, Tessa, and Carrie started their sweep. At each cave, Tessa blocked the path of retreat while Lan and Carrie opened panels and looked behind each display case. The first several caves revealed no small creatures.

Carrie said, "Maybe it's already gone all the way around and it's with Parke."

Lan said, "Could be, but I haven't heard anything from back in his direction."

They continued their search, passing through cave after cave, until they reached Parke.

"Any chance it got by you?" Lan asked, mystified.

"No. You people must have missed it."

"But we couldn't have," Tessa said. "We looked everywhere."

Lan said, "It sure seemed like it, but we must have missed something. We'd better try again."

Parke said, "You're *sure* you saw it?"

Stony glances shot his way.

"All right. I'll wait here again."

Lan and Tessa and Carrie began again, this time searching in the opposite direction. Opening panel after panel revealed nothing. They had covered about eighty percent of the circle when Tessa said softly, "Stay calm. And look down there, the shadow behind that display near the wall. The shadow doesn't look right to me. I bet our little friend is there."

"All right," Lan replied just as calmly. "I'll block the way back. Tessa, you want to block the way toward Parke? And Carrie, that leaves you to try to calm it. Maybe if you show yourself from a distance you won't spook it so badly."

Tessa moved into position as Lan did. Carrie moved quietly to a point near Lan, then edged sideways toward a point that would give her a view of the space behind the display case. She had to lean away from the cave wall to keep from hitting her head. Almost into position, she sat down, then scooted slowly along the floor for part of a meter. When she finally had a clear view, her eyes widened and she nodded.

Nothing happened for a moment except that Carrie grinned. She hesitated, then rapped her fingernails lightly on the floor. From behind the display case came a sudden squeal of what sounded like surprise, and something bumped against the cabinet.

"Surprised you, huh?" Carrie said softly, still smiling. Cautiously she gestured with her hands, pointing both index fingers together, palms toward the creature, and circling them.

An instant later she nodded, then made another gesture. She made a fist with only the thumb not tucked in and moved it forward and back under her chin, shaking her head at the same time. Then she put her palms together and moved her right hand quickly forward. Along with the gestures, she said, "No—run."

Carrie turned her head slowly toward Lan. "It *is* a tekker. And I think it's been frightened badly. Please stay where you are." She turned back and made hooks of her index fingers, looping them first right over left then left over right, this time saying, "Friend."

From behind the case came a noise that to Lan sounded almost the way a human baby would sound if it sighed in relief. A furry face showing two bright blue eyes appeared around the corner of the case. Lan smiled and stayed motionless. The tekker moved forward so its side eyes showed, too. The front pair of eyes blinked, then the side pair blinked.

Carrie said the "friend" word again and pointed at Lan. Lan nodded.

With its solid blue eyes, the tekker could almost have been some child's pet stuffed animal. It looked defenseless and cuddly. Now it sat on its haunches, revealing chunky hind legs, and slightly longer arms with tiny hands that looked like furry baby hands, with cat paw pads for fingertips. It moved an arm, revealing two elbows or at least two pivot points. Lan looked closer and saw that the tekker's legs seemed to have two knees each.

To seem less intimidating, Lan cautiously sat down. Tessa moved nearer and sat, too. Carrie said, "It might help if you tell it you are friends, too. And show it this gesture."

Lan and Tessa both said "friend" and copied Carrie's interlocking finger gesture. The tekker looked from one to the other, then it, too, made the "friend" gesture, raising its tiny furry arms. It looked back at Carrie, hesitated, then made a different gesture, with one hand moving toward and away from its mouth.

"Eat," Carrie said, and accompanied the word with both cupped hands suddenly dropping. "Now?"

The tekker nodded eagerly.

"We will find food." Carrie nodded, too.

The tekker nodded again. It seemed to like the direction the conversation was going.

"Come with us." Carrie beckoned with her index finger.

Another nod.

To Tessa and Lan, Carrie said, "I think we'll be all right if you don't try to get close to it right now. Despite being small, tekkers have a large personal space that they don't like strangers invading. I think the three of us should start out and ask it to follow."

"You're the expert," Lan said.

"I will get up," Carrie said to the tekker. She slowly rose. Tessa rose also, but Lan stayed where he was.

"Coming?" Tessa asked Lan.

"I'll wait here quietly while you two go with it to find food. When you're gone, I'll go tell Parke he can join us. He's probably hungry, too."

Carrie turned to the tekker. "Come." She and Tessa

walked toward the foyer cave, glancing over their shoulders to see if their undersized companion would follow.

The tekker looked at Lan with one side eye and one front eye. It wiggled and stretched as it got to its feet. It hesitated until Carrie said, "Come. Food," and then it scampered quickly after the two women.

"If tekkers are too bright to be put in zoos, how did one get here?" Parke asked. He and Lan were almost back to the foyer cave.

"You can ask it. Maybe it hitchhiked."

"Maybe Wilby and Ellie smuggled it to Neverend and that's why they want the museum—so they can get it back without anyone knowing what they did?"

"If that's so, how did it get here unseen?" Lan asked.

"I don't know. Maybe Tessa's father knew about it and was harboring it. Wait a second. You say Carrie talks to it with sign language? How does she know that?" Parke raised his eyebrows.

"She's got a way with languages. A kid she knew in school was deaf for a few months because the doctors were waiting for some other condition to change before they operated. While the kid was deaf, Carrie learned to sign. I guess that's when she got interested in other languages, too."

They reached the passage to the foyer cave. Tessa and Carrie sat near each other. On the far side of the cave, the tekker sat, looking worried, rapid breathing making its sides contract and expand.

Lan softly said, "Friend," and made the appropriate gesture. Parke followed his example. The tekker's breathing relaxed.

"What next?" Lan asked.

Tessa said, "In just a minute—"

A knock sounded.

Tessa went to the door and received several small bags. Turning back toward Lan, she said, "The restaurant had some things Carrie recommended."

Under the watchful eyes of the tekker, Carrie took the bags into the next room. There came the sound of running water, followed by brief sounds of tearing bags and tapping. Moments later, she carried in a plate of what looked like mushy, ground-up peanut shells. She set the plate on the floor, midway between Tessa and the tekker. Beside the plate, she set a spatula. Then she backed away. She put her right index finger to her temple, then pointed toward the tekker. "For you."

The tekker eyed everyone in the cave, no doubt gauging the distance from the plate to the nearest exit. Finally, it moved slowly toward the plate. In the almost silent room, it picked up the spatula and poked at the food on the plate. Maintaining watch on the humans, it scooped a dab of the mixture onto the spatula and moved it toward its mouth, which was nearly in the center of its face. The bright green tip of a tongue sprang out nearly as fast as a snake's.

The tekker sat there silently for almost half a minute, then suddenly put the spatula in its mouth and pulled it out clean. Its cheeks worked silently for a moment, then the tekker's eyes closed and it bowed briefly before the food. Eyes open, it began to eat in earnest, gulping down mouthful after mouthful. After several mouthfuls, the tekker suddenly looked up toward Carrie. It flattened both its hands and touched fingertips to its lips, then brought its hands forward until they were palm up.

Carrie responded with what seemed to be the same gesture and said, "You're welcome."

Lan kept his voice calm and low. "What's it been eating until now?"

Carrie said, "Hard to tell. Our metabolisms have enough in common that it could eat some of our food, although it wouldn't be nearly as nutritional as this. And their metabolism is almost a cross between an animal's and a plant's. Just being exposed to light can give it some energy."

Tessa rose slowly enough to avoid startling the tekker, then moved to the next room. Moments later she was back. "Apparently it also found my father's cache of snack food. I just left it where it was because there was no reason to move it." She looked down at the tekker and grinned. "This undersized person is fairly resourceful. The packages look the same as always, but the ones in the back are now empty."

As though it was aware it was the subject of discussion, the tekker stopped eating and glanced in Tessa's direction. Its blue eyes blinked in pairs. The lack of visible pupils made it difficult to know where it was actually looking.

Conversation stopped, so the tekker resumed eating. Finally, after eating almost half the food, it sat back and rubbed its tummy. It brought a tiny hand up flat under its chin.

Carrie asked, "Full?"

The tekker nodded and made the "thank you" gesture again.

The group sat in silence.

The tekker put its right-hand fingers together, touched them to its lips, then touched them to its right cheek.

"Home?" Carrie asked. "You want to go home?"

The tekker nodded energetically.

Lan said, "Can you ask it how it got here?"

Carrie looked at him. "You could ask it."

"Yes, but it seems the most comfortable with the signing language. I can figure out a nod means yes, but some of it isn't intuitively obvious to me. And besides, it seems comfortable talking to you."

"All right." Carrie turned to the tekker. She said,

"How did you get here?" and simultaneously made a series of gestures ending with her palms up, both hands
moving in a semicircle.

The tekker looked left then right, then pointed toward
one of the adjoining caves.

Tessa said, "It's taking your question too literally. I
think it means that a few minutes ago it was in there."

Carrie tried again. "Before that. How did you first get
here?"

The tekker cocked its head and pointed the same way
as before.

"This still isn't working," Carrie said.

Lan said, "Ask it to show us."

Carrie looked as puzzled as the tekker, but she complied.

The tekker rose from the floor and carried the plate of
food to Carrie. She accepted it and said, "Thank you."

The tekker walked toward the entryway to the adjoining cave. Almost there, it stopped, looked back at the humans, as if to say, "Aren't you coming?"

Lan and Tessa and Parke and Carrie all moved a couple of steps toward the tekker, and it started walking again.
The silent parade led through first one cave, then another, and then another. Finally, the tekker stopped in the
center of the fourth cave and waited for the humans to
reach the mouth of the cave. When they were assembled,
the tekker approached the cave wall until it stood about a
half-meter away. It stood up and pointed directly to the
blank wall.

Lan shook his head. To Carrie, he said, "It doesn't
seem to have understood your question clearly."

Carrie reiterated the question, going slowly with both
words and gestures.

The tekker began to look puzzled again and insistently
pointed back to the wall.

"I don't understand," Carrie said.

The tekker cocked its head again and turned toward the cave wall. It approached the wall, as though ready to scale it. Instead, it jumped straight up and spread its tiny arms against the wall. When the tekker fell back, it rocked on its feet for an instant and made a *tsk tsk* sound. It jumped again, once more seeming to be trying to touch two separate points on the rock wall. This time, at the top of the tekker's jump, there came a soft but distinct high-pitched beep.

The tekker looked back at the humans and nodded its head toward the wall. When no one responded, the tekker turned back toward the rock surface. Instead of jumping again, the tekker proceeded to walk straight through the wall.

# 14

## FIELD TRIP

 PARKE BLINKED AND took a deep breath. "What's going on here?"

Lan and Tessa and Carrie looked at one another, then back to the blank wall where the tekker had disappeared. There was no indication at all that the small creature had been there just a moment before.

Tessa said softly, "Maybe someone has cut a back way in here and covered it with a hologram."

Just as they started for the wall, the tekker reappeared. It squatted on the floor in front of the apparently solid wall and cocked its head.

Carrie spoke to the tekker, accompanying the words with gestures. "This is a surprise to us. What is on the other side?"

The tekker made a circling gesture with its hands.

Carrie looked at Tessa. "The world? What does that mean? That there's a tunnel from here back into one of the main caverns?"

Lan moved forward. "Maybe we'd better take a look."

Parke and Tessa moved to join him.

The tekker stepped back through the surface and disappeared.

Lan turned to Carrie. "Can you be ready to call the peace office if we're not back here in a minute?"

She nodded.

Lan and Parke and Tessa stood in a tight circle around the spot where the tekker had been. Lan stooped and moved one hand along the rock wall closer and closer to the point where the tekker had traveled through. Solid rock gave way to empty air. Lan moved his hand up and down, pushing only a fingertip through the imaginary surface. A nearly vertical straight edge divided what felt like rock and what only looked like rock.

On the far side of the opening, Tessa did the same thing. Together they traced the outline of a doorway slightly taller than Parke, a doorway wider at the base than at the top. Lan felt along the bottom edge of the outline and pushed his hand farther in. He couldn't see it but he could feel a smooth, level floor beyond.

"I'm going through," Lan announced. "The tekker seems to have survived fine."

Parke said, "I think we should draw lots. Or get a peace officer out here."

Tessa said, "I agree," just as Lan went ahead anyway and stepped through while keeping a grip on the side of the doorway.

Lan blinked as his eyes told him they were about to make contact with a rock cave wall. When they opened again, nothing visible suggested caves or Neverend. He was in a short corridor with perfectly flat surfaces that looked more like polished granite than natural lava. About three meters away, the tunnel ended abruptly with a blank trapezoidal wall. The tekker sat next to the blank wall, waiting patiently.

Lan started to back out, and collided with Parke who was on his way in. The two men untangled themselves and stood together for a moment, surveying the inside. "I'm going back out," Lan said. He turned and found the image of the cave wall had disappeared, or at least was transparent from the inside.

Lan took three steps forward so he was standing in the cave. Behind him the cave wall image was still in place. A moment later Parke followed, walking through the wall like a full-color ghost.

Tessa moved toward the wall. "What's in there?"

Parke said, "Take a look. It's a dead end."

Lan said, "If you and Carrie want to look, go ahead. But let's make sure at least one person is always out here, just in case that wall solidifies again."

Tessa and Carrie took their turns and finally all four humans stood in a circle in the cave, each looking puzzled.

Tessa pointed to a long thin discoloration on the cave ceiling. "That crack formed a few months ago. Dad had a team in to fill it in so it didn't get worse. Do you suppose they installed that dead-end tunnel, or whatever you want to call it?"

"No," Lan said. "But maybe that's when they found it. And that's probably at the root of why people would like to own the museum. This isn't any technology that I know about."

The tekker came back through the wall and sat down.

Parke said, "What makes you think they didn't do it?"

"I can accept the hologram as work they could have done. But that rock was solid before our friend here did whatever he did." Lan turned toward the wall and knelt in the place the tekker had jumped from. The tekker moved about a meter away and watched in silence.

Lan looked closely at the wall, trying to remember the two places the tekker had touched. Near each location, so faint as to be virtually nonexistent, were small black-and-white bull's-eyes. When Lan looked directly at them, they vanished. Only by using his peripheral vision could he make them out.

He reached a fingertip toward each bull's-eye. An instant after he simultaneously touched both, there came the high-pitched beep again and he felt force on his fingertips, pressing them away from the wall. When he reacted and tried to push with his hands, the rock was as firm as the side of a boulder. Lan rapped his knuckles against the wall in several places, meeting what felt like rock in each place.

Lan located the two bull's-eyes again and touched them simultaneously. The rock image remained after the new beep, and once again he could put a fist through it as easily as through smoke. Lan stood up and discovered yet another bull's-eye. He scanned more of the image. "Look," he said. "There are two more bull's-eyes up here." He again tried the technique of touching two of them simultaneously. "The top pair functions the same as the bottom pair."

Lan left the barrier turned off and stood back from the surface to see if he could spot any other features. He decided he couldn't about the same time the tekker went back inside.

Carrie said, "It sure seems an elaborate mechanism just for a dead end."

"You're right. It has to be more than that." Lan went back inside. The tekker was again waiting just in front of the panel at the back of the enclosure. Just like it had waited in front of the apparently solid cave wall.

Tessa was suddenly at Lan's side. "Is it going to do the same thing again? Go through *that* wall?"

"I don't know," Lan said, about the same time Parke entered. "Parke, can you trade with Carrie for a minute or two? We need someone outside just in case, and we need her here to talk to our friend."

"All right by me."

A moment later Carrie stood next to Lan and Tessa.

Lan said, "Can you ask if it can get through that wall, too?"

Carrie asked the question.

The tekker shook its head.

Lan asked, *"Did* it go through that wall once?"

Carrie relayed the question and the tekker nodded energetically.

Lan stepped forward, moving slowly to avoid startling the tekker. He stopped just in front of the rear wall. Etched into the surface were faint gray markings, some vertical groups suggestive of a written language. On the side wall were other symbols, surrounded with a series of long, straight lines.

"What do you make of it?" Tessa asked.

"I'm not sure," Lan said. "How about you, Carrie? You're the best language expert we've got."

"I'd have to have a computer to get started. Some of these characters have similarities with stuff on early Agnerbreet ruins. These figures here, the circles with dots inside, remind me of Yoltenk symbols for atoms."

"I'll get you one," Tessa said and left.

Where Carrie had pointed were four similar circles, four in a row next to a wide vertical bar. On the other side of the bar was a single circular symbol. Clustered in the center of each circle were various numbers of small gray dots.

Moments later, Tessa was back with a tiny screen-input unit.

"Thanks," Carrie said. "One thing's for sure. This certainly isn't the result of some workers cutting a hole in the side of the museum."

Lan glanced around the enclosed area. "Agreed. I think it's time we called the authorities in to take a look."

Tessa said, "I'll go call them now, if you want to stay here and see if you can figure anything out."

Lan and Carrie agreed. Lan said, "You might not want to explain what this is about until they get here. I couldn't blame them for thinking the call is a prank." After Tessa left, Lan and Carrie spent several minutes examining the inscriptions.

The tekker stood patiently near one wall, looking back and forth from the two humans and the symbol-covered surface. For just an instant it produced a humming sound.

Carrie knelt beside it. "Are you telling us something?"

The tekker made a series of gestures including two with palms forward, the first moving its two tiny hands together and apart, the second pivoting the hands as though they were double doors swinging open and closed.

"I think it's saying the door opens noisily or the door opens if you make a certain sound."

Lan started to speak. "I wonder—"

He got no farther because there came a frantic call from Tessa. "Lan, Carrie, come here, will you!"

Carrie slipped the computer into a pocket in her dress, and they turned from the panel and rushed back into the cave, nearly colliding with Jarl Haxxon, who stood silently in the center of the room, looking startled at her sudden appearance.

"What are *you* doing here?" Carrie asked.

"Good question," her ex-husband said.

Next to Jarl was Parke, no longer in his watch position. He stood near the portal between the cave and the one next door, his arms raised, the expression on his face filled with anger. Tessa wasn't far away, and she, too, looked angry. Holding a pistol to Tessa's neck was Wilby Hackert, wearing the same blue coat he had the night he followed Lan and Tessa. Tessa no longer carried the bag she'd had at the party. In case Wilby didn't have the situation in control, Ellie Troughteral stood ready, also armed with a pistol. And near her was Rento Queller, looking more nervous than when he had been caught shoplifting.

As Lan stood in the center of the cave, adjusting to the changes, the tekker poked its head through the cave wall image, saw Wilby, and gave a short squeal. The tekker's head vanished abruptly as it retreated into the hidden chamber.

"Don't anyone move," Wilby said. He didn't seem at all startled by seeing the tekker or its reaction, but his gaze flicked nervously between Lan and Parke.

"I'm sorry, Lan," Tessa said. "I called the peace office. When I heard a knock, Jarl and these three were here. Jarl came to see Carrie. These people must have got here just as—"

"Be quiet," Wilby said. "Everybody please move against the wall." He gestured at the wall opposite where the tekker had just shown its head.

Parke moved first. Lan and Carrie followed him, holding their arms up. Wilby edged forward, keeping his pistol against Tessa's neck. Wilby glanced at Ellie and said, "Turn it off, quick."

Ellie kept her back to the wall and her pistol trained on Parke as she edged toward the corridor. Only when she reached the opening did she take her eyes off the trio against the far wall. She went through the wall image and a moment later the image switched off, revealing the corridor, Ellie with her hand on the wall near the opening, and the tekker crouched fearfully back in a corner. She seemed more relaxed than Wilby did.

"All right," Wilby said. "Everyone inside."

Parke and Carrie led the way, then Jarl, then Lan. Lan tried to find an opportunity to act. With Wilby's pistol against Tessa's neck, the options were severely limited. Ellie got out of the way as the group moved to the back of the corridor and joined the tekker.

Wilby and Tessa came forward awkwardly, and finally Ellie joined them, still keeping her pistol trained on the group. Rento followed them in, looking almost as bewildered as Jarl did. Ellie touched a dark square Lan hadn't noticed earlier. Nothing seemed to change except that the square lightened, but Lan was sure the image was once again in place. Ellie then touched a circular outline above the square. When Ellie was finished, Wilby shoved Tessa forward and she stumbled into Lan's arms.

Wilby faced the group warily, ignoring Rento, and spoke to Ellie. "I told you when that stupid little animal got loose that we should have tracked it down and taken care of it. Now we've got a real mess."

"It's nothing we can't handle," Ellie said, also ignoring Rento. "Just stay calm." She glanced at Wilby and said with annoyance, "You're wearing your lucky jacket. How bad can things get?"

"Peace officers could be here any minute."

"So what? All they'll find is an empty museum, assuming they can get permission to enter. They'll never find us here." To demonstrate, she thudded a fist against what was now evidently a solid barrier but still invisible from inside.

"What do you people want with us?" Tessa said angrily.

"Nothing," Ellie said. "We just don't want you interfering."

"But what—"

"Be quiet!" Ellie said. She took an object the size of a large coin from her pocket. She pressed it and the device produced a four-tone chord. Lan was just thinking about the tekker's humming when the wall behind them began to slide open.

# 15

## REORIENTATION

As THE REAR panel slowly slid open, no one uttered a sound. The panel turned out to be heftier than Lan would have guessed, as thick as a spacecraft bulkhead. As the panel slid all the way into a slot in the wall, Lan became aware of a new smell in the air, like the stale odor of an animal pen.

Beyond the panel lay another cavity about the same size and shape as the one they were in, and at the end of that cavity was another panel. The interior panel bore large green lettering reminiscent of the characters on the first panel.

"Move ahead," Wilby said. He and Ellie Troughteral edged closer to the group of humans and the tekker. Rento followed.

The tekker moved first. Lan decided that it knew more about where they were than he did, and it didn't seem worried about the move, so he moved.

The walls held more green writing, too. On one wall, a blue rectangle enclosed several pictographs with words below each one.

"What the hell is this place?" Parke asked as the group backed toward the interior panel.

"You'll find out soon enough," Ellie said. She and Wilby and Rento passed the withdrawn panel, so everyone was now in the innermost cavity. Wilby's and Ellie's expressions were matter-of-fact, with some wariness keeping them from looking bored. Rento was clearly even more surprised than Lan's companions. Even whatever youthful pressures compelled him to appear blasé about everything in life couldn't keep the awe from his face. As Ellie and Rento moved together, Lan noticed the similarities in their noses, cheekbones, and eyes. So Rento was her son?

Wilby stared at the panel of pictographs as though he had forgotten which one did what he wanted. Finally he pressed one of a pair of trapezoidal images. The panel slid closed once again, sealing the group into what now felt to Lan distinctly like an airlock.

The trapezoidal image Wilby had pushed turned blue like its mate. Wilby pushed on the second image.

The inner panel began to open. Lan and Tessa and Carrie and Parke turned to see what lay beyond.

Carrie sucked in a sharp breath.

The view beyond looked nothing like Neverend either. On the other side of the panel was a large cubical room with a ceiling about three or four times Parke's height. At the far side of the room was a curved ramp about as wide as a normal stairway. The ramp led from the floor up the side of the wall. From there, it continued up the wall until, near the ceiling, the ramp bent back the other way and led into a room one floor above. On what looked to be the wall opposite the doorway were scuff marks and dust leading from the vertical section of the ramp sideways to a door on the adjacent wall.

Lan cocked his head. The only way anyone could conveniently go through the door was if the wall straight ahead was actually the floor.

"What the hell is this place?" Parke asked again, his voice hushed.

"Just move into the room," Wilby said.

The human prisoners and the tekker moved into the center of the bizarre room. Wilby and Ellie and Rento followed. As the door behind them slid shut, it exposed a handwritten legend saying "Neverend." Next to the legend were the digits "0, 0, 0."

"We're not going to hurt you," Wilby said. "We just need to keep you out of the way for a while. Go up that ramp." He gestured with the gun.

"To where?" Parke asked. "It goes up the side of the wall."

"Get on it and start walking."

Lan followed the instruction as Parke stood motionless. He reached the start of the ramp and began to walk carefully up it. As the ramp curved under his feet, his sense of up and down rotated synchronously, so that his feet were constantly on what felt like the floor. A few more steps brought him to the point where his body was parallel to what used to have been the floor. Wilby and Ellie and Rento and his friends all seemed to be standing on the wall. Lan felt his face and neck tingle with the rush of adrenaline. What an incredible place.

Lan waited where he was and said to his open-mouthed friends, "I think we'd better give up any notion that we're still on Neverend." He glanced at the door that now looked upright to him. On it was hand lettering saying, "desert planet." Near the words were the digits "0, 1, 0."

He beckoned the others to follow him. The tekker moved first. As the creature walked down the ramp to the new "floor," Lan kept expecting it to tumble, but it reached his side with no mishap. It seemed more at ease than before, having evidently decided that the latest events confirmed that its new friends weren't on the same side as Wilby and Ellie.

Tessa, Carrie, Parke, and Jarl followed. When they were all on the same surface, Wilby gestured with his pistol again. "Now go on over to the next room."

"Holy holograms," Parke said softly. "What *is* this place?"

The way to the next room was also by curving ramp, but the problem of changeable ups and downs made the path seem even more risky. Instead of curving from the current floor to what seemed to be a wall, the ramp cut downward into a room that now felt "below" their current location. Lan couldn't shake the feeling that he was about to do the equivalent of walking off a roof and trying to walk down the outside wall.

He took a couple of steps and felt much better when it was obvious that the same phenomenon was still hard at work. He took several more steps, feeling at each point he was vertical with respect to up and down, and when he stopped, he was standing on a new floor while his friends were following by walking up a wall to join him on the roof. This room had three doorways in it besides the ramps leading in several directions. One doorway was on the ceiling, another two on the walls. More handwritten legends said, "cinder," "pristine," "Lequwella IV ??" and "2, 2, 3." Lan noticed the tekker staring at the door to Lequwella IV and wondered if the creature's gaze was a little wistful, as though that was its door to home.

"Now that way," Wilby said.

Several more turnings and floor-wall-ceiling reversals later, the group stood before a door labeled, "thick plants." Wilby pressed a open circle next to the door, and the door slid open, revealing another airlock. Lan kept watch for an opportunity to resist as they were herded into the chamber, but Wilby and Ellie stayed separated and watchful.

Lan's ears popped several times as the airlock adjusted to a higher pressure. Beyond the airlock was another short corridor. Tessa gasped at the view through the end of the corridor. There could be no possible doubt about not being on Neverend any longer. Before them lay a sunlit expanse of rock and sand and unfamiliar plant life on a planet so large the horizon seemed a thousand kilometers away. Most of the vegetation clung low to the ground, with barrel-sized trunks and thick, stubby branches, all on the sunward side of the plants. The red-tinted atmosphere held no clouds. A fast-running stream ran nearby, its surface somehow unnaturally smooth.

"What *is* this place?" Rento asked.

Carrie gasped. "Incredible. This is some other planet."

"We'll explain later," Wilby said, without turning his head from the captors. "All right. We're going to leave you here for a while. There's plenty of water, and you should be able to survive on plant life until we've finished what we need to do."

"Wait a minute," Lan said. "If you intend to kill us all, what's to stop us from rushing you? You wouldn't be able to get all of us."

Ellie said hurriedly, "We're *not* going to harm you. We just need you out of the way for a while. This is the easiest way."

"Sending us out there is going to kill us."

"Nonsense. These indicators say the oxygen content is almost as high as on Neverend, no toxins in the air, plenty of plant life."

"Maybe. But throw a coin out there. See what happens."

"Just go on out there. We won't hurt you."

"Don't anybody move," Lan said forcefully to his friends. "Throw the coin. Then maybe we'll believe you."

Ellie shot an exasperated look at Wilby, who shifted his gun to the other hand and dug out a coin. Wilby motioned Carrie and Tessa to move farther away from one wall and proceeded to throw the coin. The coin shot straight and nearly level as far as the end of the corridor. About the time it hit the reddish sunlight, it dropped to the rocky surface as fast as if it had ricocheted off an invisible surface.

Wilby looked startled.

Lan said, "There are enough gees out there to keep us flat on the ground, maybe even kill us outright. Look at those stubby plants. And look at that stream; it looks nearly level, but instead of the water flowing slowly, it's racing. And a fast-running stream has ripples on the surface; this one is under such a high-gravity field that the surface is nearly flat."

"That's just great, Wilby," Ellie said. "You nearly killed them. Walking into a high-gee field might have broken their spines before they even fell down."

"You didn't say anything," he replied angrily. "Why is this my fault all of a sudden?"

"It's your fault because you and Rento pulled that stupid stunt. We wouldn't be having to deal with all these people if it weren't for that."

"How could I know they'd all—"

"Never mind that now. We've got to find another place for them."

Wilby shut up, looking irritated at *everyone* now. Together, he and Ellie herded everyone back into the airlock and went back into the topsy-turvy maze, Rento still trailing along, looking as if he was in a starship for the first time.

"Where to now?" Wilby asked Ellie.

Ellie thought for a minute, then looked almost every direction as she apparently tried to orient herself. "Up there." She pointed.

The group navigated another three chutes and stopped on command in front on another door. The tekker obediently stayed right with the group. On the door was the same handwriting, saying, "Forest."

From the other side of the airlock, Lan could see how apt the one word was. No more that five meters away was a mass of green and blue vegetation extending well over human head height. A green stalk supported a spiky blue mass of slender blades extending from the top of the stalk. Near it were several more similar but smaller plants. Filling in the rest of the space were other unfamiliar varieties. What little of the ground was not occupied by large bushes or tree-like growths with shiny black bark was covered with blue-green ground plants with fat, succulent-like leaves.

As the group stared at the vegetation, a small leaf or something shed from a plant higher up leisurely fell past their view.

"Satisfied with that gravity?" Wilby asked. The gun in his hand was steady.

Lan stared at Wilby. "Oh, yes, sir, that'll be just perfectly fine with all of us, I'm sure. There might be hungry carnivores just beyond what we can see here, or that bed of vegetation on the ground might be a thin layer of leaves covering quicksand, or there might be acid-dripping birds in the branches above, but the gravity looks likes it's just exactly what we were hoping for. Thank you so very much for showing us to our room, but I'm afraid I don't have enough money for the tip."

Wilby's face darkened. "You should be grateful. I could have just pushed you out where we were. Or put you out on an ice planet. Or just shot you immediately."

Lan said, "Well, I know that certainly makes me feel better. How about you folks?"

Parke said, "Maybe we shouldn't antagonize Rat Face."

Maybe Wilby was sensitive about his looks. Maybe he'd just had a long day. Whatever the cause, anger made his hand shake. "Keep it up, you two. Maybe I should kill you right now. Or maybe I should put the five of you out to separate planets."

Lan glanced down. "That's six of us."

"That's about enough—"

"You're right," Ellie cut in. "They're trying to make you angry, you idiot—"

"You, too, huh?" Lan said.

"—so don't let them. Just dump them here, and we'll let them out later."

Wilby calmed down. "You're right. Thanks." To the group, he said, "I'll do you a favor. I'll let you stay in here and decide to go out there when you get hungry. That square indicator high up on the right controls the barrier from this side. Don't waste your time trying to get back through this way though. It won't open."

Lan said, "We could still rush you. We still don't know that place is safe."

"Yeah, but it looks safe, and you'll probably be fine. You have to balance that against knowing that if you try anything some of you will definitely die."

Rento stood still as Wilby and Ellie backed into the open airlock. Wilby said, "We'll be back for you in a few days, so stay close."

Rento suddenly spoke. "Maybe he's right. You could be sending them out there to die."

Wilby looked at Rento as though for the first time. "That's *their* problem for now. If *she*—" Wilby gestured at Tessa. "—hadn't been so stubborn, none of this would be necessary."

"Yeah, but—" Rento started.

Wilby grabbed Rento's arm, twisted him around, and shoved him toward Lan. "If you're so concerned, *you* help them."

Ellie moved closer to Wilby but kept her eyes and her pistol aimed at the group. "Why did you have to do that? He only asked a question."

"I don't want to deal with it right now. He'll be fine. Think of it as a vacation." He reached toward the switch.

"But—"

"But nothing." Wilby pressed the control to close the airlock door.

As the door slid shut, Lan noticed motion at the bottom of his peripheral vision. Just before the door moved far enough to cut off the view of Wilby, the tekker raised one arm. With its small hairy hand and fingers it made a very expressive and surprisingly rude gesture at Wilby.

# 16

## THROWN OUT

THE GROUP OF six humans and the tekker stared silently at the closed airlock door for several seconds, everyone apparently sharing Lan's disbelief at the sudden changes in the last few minutes.

Finally, Rento surveyed the group, glanced back toward the strange scenery visible through the portal to wherever, then looked at Lan. "Look, I tried to help. Can we forget about the past?"

Lan ignored Parke's puzzled expression. "We're all in this together. Our survival may well depend on us functioning as a team. Act like a team member and there won't be any problems."

"Our survival?" Jarl said. "What are you talking about? They're certainly coming back for us if they left him here." He gestured at Rento. "As long as we have a little patience, this could just be a nice vacation. Right, Carrie?" He looked hopefully in her direction.

"A vacation?" she replied. "We don't even know yet if there's anything out there we can eat, or if there's water we can get to. Or if there's hostile animal life."

"She's right," Parke said. "Just because this place looks nice doesn't mean it's friendly. We've got to be very cautious if we go outside."

Jarl pulled his shoulders back. "We're going to *have* to go outside. The only question is when. How long can you go without relieving yourself?"

Parke said, "If I have the choice of relieving myself here and staying alive or doing it out there and dying, I'd have to pick here."

"I'm convinced," Lan said suddenly. "Anyone with that attitude has got to be a natural leader. I nominate Parke for the job."

"Fine by me," Carrie said.

"I'll go along with that," Tessa said.

"Wait a minute, wait a minute," Jarl said. "Things are moving too fast. Why him?"

"Why not?" Lan asked, turning toward Jarl. "Are you suggesting someone else?"

Jarl opened his mouth and shut it again. Finally he said, "Never mind."

Carrie knelt near the tekker, who had been looking first at the scenery and then at the group of humans. She started her speech by holding her left fist to her breast and moving her right hand up and down in a thumbs-up sign. "Dangerous out there. Possibly. No one does anything until we know if it is safe."

The tekker blinked its four blue eyes in succession, cocked its head and looked back through the portal for a moment, then shrugged its shoulders and nodded.

"And what is *that*?" Jarl asked.

"That is a tekker," Carrie said. "Don't worry; you're safe from it."

"But what's it doing here?"

Lan said, "Probably the same thing we are: wondering what's happening and how to get back home."

"And where the hell are we?" Jarl asked. "And what is this—this thing we went through?"

"We know what it *isn't*," Carrie said. "It isn't current technology. This is simply incredible. I really don't think it's new."

Jarl hit the wall with his fist. "Oh, sure. This has been around all the time. It's just that no one ever told us about it."

Lan looked out at the alien planet. "Keeping a secret is a lot tougher than you think. This is the kind of thing that everyone would know about if anyone knew about it a few years ago. Ellie and Wilby might have discovered this, but it's been around a long, long time."

"That's my bet, too," said Carrie. "These inscriptions aren't in any language I've seen. They have to be extremely old. Thousands, no, hundreds of thousands of years maybe. Could be even older."

Lan turned to Parke. "So, boss, until we know more about what this place is, what next?"

Parke looked through the portal. "Maybe we should try your gravity test here, just in case appearances are deceiving. Anyone have a coin to throw? And now that I think about it, we should do an inventory of what we've got. Those two say they'll be back in a couple of days, but we shouldn't count on it."

Lan picked a coin whose display said it was nearly empty and volunteered it. As the group watched, Parke threw it through the portal. The coin sailed smoothly across the clearing and smacked into a tree-like plant with shiny black bark.

"We'll, it looks like the gravity is—" Parke stopped. Instead of bouncing off the tree bark, the coin had stuck to it as though the black surface was thick tar. As the group looked on, the coin started to disappear into the bark.

Within a few moments, the coin had entirely disappeared, leaving behind no marks at all on the shiny black bark.

"Let me guess," Lan said into the silence. "Rule number one is don't touch the trees."

His gaze still locked on the tree, his voice hushed, Parke said, "Let's do that inventory now."

As everyone searched through pockets, Lan said, "Maybe high gravity wouldn't have been so bad."

"Four coins, a comb, a handkerchief," Tessa said.

Carrie said, "One computer, two coins, an audio cube, a watch, and a small mirror."

Rento said, "A video cube, six coins, a knife, and a watch."

Jarl said, "Four coins."

Lan said, "A pocket light, tool set, five coins, and a watch."

Parke reached into his pockets. "And I've got three coins and a small breath spray. How long's the light good for?"

"At a low setting, indefinitely. It's expensive."

"Meaning?" Parke lifted his eyebrows.

"Meaning it recharges from ambient light, heat, water vapor, pressure changes."

"Cute."

"I'm afraid of the dark."

"You might not have long to wait," Tessa said.

Lan glanced through the portal. "What do you mean?"

Tessa pointed. "That shadow line has moved just in the last minute or two."

She was right. As Lan watched it steadily for several seconds, the line crept away from them. He peered upward near the portal but the sun was out of view. "It must be late afternoon." Lan turned to Carrie. "While we can still see that tree, can you warn our undersized friend here about it?"

She nodded and proceeded. The tekker showed immediate signs of believing her. Evidently it had seen what happened to the coin.

As the night grew swiftly closer, a breeze began to jostle bristly turquoise branches harder and harder. The bristles seemed to shorten, as if they were pulling back for the night. The whole group watched as dusk turned abruptly to a dark night. Now that the planet beyond the portal was dark, the tunnel lighting seemed to brighten. Where intuition said there should be a pool of light spilling onto the vegetation just outside the portal, the ground was as dark as anywhere else.

"Wow," Parke said.

Carrie said, "Maybe I should get started with my computer. To see if I can figure out what this stuff on the wall says."

Without looking away from the dark planet's surface, Parke said, "Excellent idea. Do it."

Carrie began scanning the computer over some of the symbols on the wall.

Lan moved to the portal barrier, cupped his hands on both sides of his eyes, and let his vision slowly adjust to the darkness. When he could see clearly, he noticed stars rising in an unfamiliar pattern on the horizon. He heard one of the group join him.

He was about to voice a guess on the length of the day here when something in the darkness moved.

"Did you see that?" Tessa asked.

"Yeah. There's another," Lan said. "Birds?"

"Maybe."

Whatever it was had been moving fast, slicing through the air. As Lan struggled to hear sounds from outside, he was even more aware of the movements of his companions. Without turning his eyes toward the bright interior, he said, "Could everyone be still for just a minute or two? I'm curious about what we might hear from out there."

The sounds around Lan subsided and he moved his cupped hands from beside his eyes to behind his ears. The first noticeable sound was the breeze. From the distance came a soft rising and falling moaning as the wind surged then dropped off, as though the wind were whistling past resonant nooks and crannies. Almost submerged below the wails was a soft, deep sucking sound that made Lan imagine a starship slowing sinking into quicksand. Occasionally there came a short series of ticks like a heating system coming on and expanding with a succession of strain-relief pops. None of the sounds were those Lan associated with intelligent life. No distant mechanical throbbing or humming, no drums, no static squeals, no high-pitched whines, no sonic booms, no regular patterns. Just the intermingling of disturbing unknowns.

Lan became aware of motion near his leg. He looked down and saw the tekker staring into the darkness, too. The tekker trembled a little. Lan reached down to pat the tekker on the shoulder.

The tekker jumped and squealed. It whirled toward Lan, and crouched in defensive readiness. From above its small finger pads showed sharp claws.

Lan put his palms forward, fingers spread. Slowly he said, "Sorry. I didn't mean to startle you." Lan sat down beside the alien.

The tekker's blue eyes seemed even larger than normal, and its shoulders rose and fell quickly with obvious breathing. It visibly relaxed, retracted its claws, then nodded at Lan. The tekker spoke, in a voice pitched lower than Lan would have guessed. "Ont oo at," Lan thought it said. When Lan didn't respond, it made a short series of emphatic gestures.

"I don't understand," Lan said.

Carrie turned from her work long enough to say, "The tekker said, 'Don't *do* that.' "

"What is your name?" Lan said slowly. He turned to Carrie. "What's the sign for 'name'?"

Jarl said, "Oh, come on," and Lan ignored him.

Carrie placed two straightened fingers on one hand over the same straightened fingers on her other hand. "The fingers make an 'X,' like when an illiterate signs a document."

Lan asked his question again and made the sign for "name."

In a deep, scratchy voice, the tekker said, "Onta Antonk Oontah Usson." It hesitated, then repeated, "Onta."

Lan touched his thumb to his chest. "Lan."

"An."

*"Lan."*

"Lan," the tekker said, with an obvious struggle.

Lan looked back to Carrie. "When you finish there, maybe you should give us some signing lessons."

"Good idea," Parke said.

"I'm probably as far as I'm going to get for now," Carrie said.

Parke sat down and joined Lan and the tekker. "What did you find out?"

The rest of the group started to sit down. Jarl was last, as though to express his independence.

Carrie set the computer on the floor. "Whatever language it is, it does have some similarities with Agnerbreet. The computer doesn't recognize it as a catalogued language, but it did some comparisons using Agnerbreet and Xorn and has put together maybe a third of what's here into its best guess. Unfortunately, what we already guessed is what it's most comfortable with. Those control panels—" she pointed "—open and close the solid barrier. *Those* control the visual barrier. Blue in this context means 'functioning normally' or 'engaged.'

"The computer also indicates those symbols over there

probably represent atoms. The one word it could recognize near them is 'entry' or 'entrance.' The box of information near the—I don't know what it's called—the doorway—summarizes this planet. Some of the stuff makes sense. It gives the planet's diameter, its rotation rate—I could convert the units to ours, but I don't see anything else here measured in time units, so it wouldn't tell us much. It also gives what seem to be coordinates for the planet, but again, since we don't know their method for defining the origin, or the axis orientation or type, or their units, that doesn't mean much either.

"Some of the notations include words that apparently describe the conditions on the planet. I saw what seem to be words for 'water,' 'night,' 'air,' 'motion,' and 'temperature,' but the words in between I don't understand. The computer's got everything in memory now, and if it makes any significant progress it'll let me know. I saw one other word that's fairly likely to be correctly translated, but I don't know the qualifiers so I can't say if the message means 'no danger' or 'danger.' "

Parke said, "I think we'd better assume it means 'danger.' "

Carrie said, "I agree. Oh, one other thing—I did find out what one other control does. I think." She rose, and put her hand near a box that showed a symbol reminiscent of an explosion. "I think this turns the lights in here on and off. Want me to try it?"

Park said, "Sure. What can we lose?"

Carrie touched the panel and nothing happened. She rubbed the surface, and darkness enveloped the group. "Got it," she said, as Lan's eyes adjusted so he could see the stars outside become brighter. "Now I'll try to turn them back on."

The lights came back on and everyone squinted. Carrie sat back down. "Ready for that language lesson?"

"Sure. What should be in the basic vocabulary?"

"I suppose a list short enough to remember easily. How about 'food,' 'water,' our names, 'portal,' 'go,' 'stop,'—I don't know what else."

Tessa said, "How about 'night,' and 'day?' "

Lan said, "And we should probably include 'quiet,' 'danger,' 'safe,' 'dead,' 'avoid,' and 'hide.' "

Jarl said, "Why not add 'useless' and 'unnecessary?' "

Everyone looked at Jarl.

"Are you trying to tell us something?" Parke asked.

"Yes. I think you're overreacting. Sure we need to be careful here, but it's not like we're going to be here all that long. And most of us can talk to each other easily enough already."

Parke's mouth dropped open, so Lan responded to the comment. "One, I'm starting to get hungry already. It probably won't be that much longer before we start to get thirsty. If we wait until we have no energy left to try to at least find water, we might not be able to, so we'd better start planning now for survival. Onta here may have some skills we don't have, so it would be silly to exclude him or her from the plan. And depending on what hostilities we encounter out there, it may be to our benefit to be able to talk silently."

Parke looked at Jarl. "He's right." He looked around the circle. "Anyone else have problems?"

Rento had been silent, but now he opened his mouth and shut it again. Finally he said, "They're not going to leave us here long enough to starve. They just wouldn't."

Lan said, "Would you have guessed they'd throw you out here with us in the first place?"

Rento said nothing.

Parke nodded to Carrie. "All right. We're ready."

Jarl leaned against the wall and shut his eyes.

"There's going to be a test afterward," Parke said. "And anyone who fails goes out there first."

Jarl opened his eyes and looked at Carrie, avoiding Parke's gaze.

"All right," Carrie said. She looked at the tekker and said, "Onta?"

Onta looked at Carrie. Onta's front eyes blinked.

"Onta, we are going to have a language lesson," Carrie made signing gestures as she spoke. "We will all try to speak clearly and slowly enough for you to understand. We will try not to use contractions. We will try to use only words that are part of Standard. We will try to use signing for anything important."

Onta nodded.

"Are you male or female? Or does that question not apply to your species?"

Onta made a small fist with one digit extended. The fist moved along the tekker's jaw line, back and forth several times.

"Female."

Onta nodded.

Carrie said. "All right. Danger." She held her left fist next to her chest and moved her right fist, thumb pointing up, up and down a few times in front of her left fist. "Think of someone holding a shield with one hand and a weapon in the other. Next is quiet." She held a finger to her lips. "Let me see everyone do these."

The language lesson continued through the essential vocabulary. The lesson took no longer than fifteen minutes, but as they were finishing, Lan realized the sky outside had begun to lighten. Lan looked at the time.

Lan got up to stretch his legs. "Apparently, the sun is pretty close to the ecliptic. Day and night appear to be about the same length: seventy minutes." Everyone else followed his example and together they watched sunrise on the planet's surface.

The ruddy sun appeared almost directly opposite the portal opening, rising steadily through the turquoise tree branches. Bristles began to lose their pudgy appearance and straighten out to sharp points. The scenery brightened just as rapidly as it had darkened earlier, and the direct sunlight stung Lan's eyes.

The group watched in silence until the sun cleared the trees. Finally Lan said, "Is it just my memory playing tricks on me, or does anyone else notice something different?"

Awe filled Tessa's voice as she said. "I think you're right. That gap in the trees over there to the left. I don't remember that wide a gap, do you?"

Lan said, "No. Something's changed."

# 17

## DRAWING STRAWS

◆ "YOU'RE IMAGINING THINGS," Jarl said. "It looks exactly the same out there. A little strange, but just the same."

Lan turned. "If that's true, why do two of us think something's changed?"

"Because you've got an overactive imagination, and Tessa's suggestible."

"Maybe if you had a better imagination, you could think of another possibility. Like the possibility that something *has* changed out there. Maybe another opinion would help." Lan gestured at Carrie and Parke. "What do other people think?

Rento shrugged. Carrie explained the issue to Onta as Parke squinted in the direction Lan indicated.

"I don't know," Parke said. "You're talking about that gap between the trees there?" He pointed.

Lan nodded. "Doesn't the gap look wider than before to you?"

"Could be. But I couldn't say for sure. Anyway, what does it mean if you're right?"

"I don't know. That this place deserves even more caution than we expect so far. That something happened to one of those trees during the night."

"We can't be a whole lot more cautious than we are already. We haven't even stepped on the ground or smelled the air. And I'm getting hungry, too." Parke craned his head. "Hey, I see something shiny or a reflection in the distance. You suppose that might be water?"

"Where?" Lan said, as Tessa said, "You may be right."

Parke lifted Lan so Lan's head was slightly above Parke's.

"Yeah," Lan said. "Maybe you are. Good eyes." Parke put him back down.

"Now will you people stop being so paranoid?" Jarl asked. "If we've got water, we can last at least a few days. What's stopping us from going now?"

Parke looked blank. Lan said, "How fast can you walk?"

"What do you mean?" Jarl asked.

"How far away do you think that reflection is, assuming it is water?"

"I don't know. I bet I could get there in an hour. And what is it with all these questions? Haven't you done anything since graduation besides taking assertiveness training?"

Lan ignored the jab. "Perfect. Assuming you're not underestimating, that means you can't get there and back in a day. You'll be out there at night."

Jarl glanced at Carrie. "Not everyone's afraid of the dark, Lan. When are you going to grow up?"

Lan said, "All right. Assume you can get there and back. Are you going to be able to bring back enough water for everyone, or do we *all* have to go? And are we going to need water often enough that we spend most of our time walking back and forth between here and there? If we do, then the possible risk gets a lot larger, and we might not be here when our friends get back.''

"So, we go in shifts.''

Lan turned to Parke. "I suggest we give the computer a little more time to decode more of what's on the walls. We've wasted ten percent of the day already. I don't think there's any need for anyone to leave until right after the next sunrise.''

Jarl started talking to Parke as though Lan were not present. "I don't see any need to wait. We probably know as much now as we're ever going to know until someone actually gets some experience out there.''

Tessa shook her head at Jarl. "I think Lan's right. This planet doesn't seem safe. The more we know before we set foot on it, the better off we'll be.''

Carrie agreed. "They're right, Jarl. Let's not take any risks we don't need to take.''

Jarl angrily looked around the group. "I can't believe this. You're all cowards like Lan. All we need to do is open the portal—'' he rubbed the indicator Carrie had identified earlier "—and step outside.''

As Jarl walked toward the portal, Parke intercepted him.

"We're a group,'' Parke said. "We're conforming to a group consensus for our own safety.''

Jarl sighed dramatically. "I don't see the purpose, but if you—'' He suddenly ducked under Parke's arm and dashed out of reach, through the portal and onto the tendril-like matted vegetation. His skin took on a faint reddish hue from the sunlight.

He turned back toward the portal, obviously not able to see in. He spread his arms in the air and took a deep breath. "See?'' he said. "I'm fine. The air smells fine, the temperature is comfortable. I think I'm going to get a drink of water.''

Jarl turned toward the distant reflection and took two

steps. As he took his third step, a fast-moving blur hurtled out of the sky and struck him in the neck.

Onta squealed, making a sound that ended more like a scream.

Suddenly rigid, Jarl toppled slowly to the ground. As his body turned, Lan could see that what had hit him seemed to be a dark-blue bird with translucent feathers and a long, sharp beak. The beak had to be sharp for it to have penetrated so far. The beak was so long that it poked out through a jagged rip in Jarl's neck on the side opposite where it had hit.

Carrie sputtered an inarticulate word and started toward Jarl. Lan caught her before she could get to the portal opening. "It's too late," he said. "We can't do anything for him now, and it's dangerous out there."

Lan was right about Jarl. Jarl had probably died about the same time his body hit the ground. Blood quit spurting from the wound and started oozing into the mass of vegetation. Tessa turned her back on the scene. Rento just sat there, gaping dumbfoundedly before he finally grimaced and looked down at his feet.

"Oh, my God," Parke said softly. Carrie began to cry. Lan felt sick to his stomach, but he kept watching Jarl's body.

The bird was still alive. At first, Lan thought there was a chance the impact had been accidental, but he changed his mind. The bird pushed its tiny feet against Jarl's neck and slowly struggled to withdraw its beak. As the beak pulled out, Lan could see tiny suckers lining the surface. When the bird got its beak entirely free, it took three or four small steps as it steadied itself and balanced the long beak with the rest of its body, then flew away.

"How horrible," Tessa said finally.

Carrie no longer seemed likely to run outside, so Lan let her go.

"I agree," he said. "But I do see one small piece of

good news. Apparently there isn't a flock of those things."

"That's a big help," Parke said.

"I said it was small."

Just as Lan stopped speaking, there came another *whoosh* and a bird smacked into Jarl's back. The body shuddered with the impact. Carrie turned her back and began to cry again.

Parke glanced at Lan, as though to say, "Wrong again."

Lan said, "That's probably the same bird. And right now, it's vulnerable."

Tessa looked incredulous. "You're saying we should go out right now and try to kill it?"

"We might not have a better chance."

"Why risk it?" Parke asked. "There may be a hundred of those things circling."

"If that's so, why aren't they here now?"

Parke grimaced. "Are you volunteering?"

"I'm willing to give it a try."

Tessa took Lan by the arm. "You can't be serious. The same thing could happen to you."

"It's possible. But that bird *might* be the only one around for kilometers. We might not have a better chance."

Outside, the bird was struggling free again.

Lan said. "How about if we let it make the decision? If it comes back one more time, I'll give it a try. If it leaves, then it's safe."

"I don't like it," Tessa said.

"Me, neither," Parke said. "But he is making sense."

"Easy for you to say," Tessa said. "You're not the one going out there."

"I'm willing to go."

"No," Lan said. "It was my idea."

"That's not a very convincing argument," Parke said.

The bird flew away again. Lan moved closer to the portal. "Maybe not, but it's better than any argument you have. Would everybody back up to the airlock door, so I can run back in here safely when I'm finished?"

"Don't do it, Lan," Tessa said. Her eyes were large as she looked steadily at him.

Over Tessa's protest, the group backed up. Lan stationed himself near the door, ready to run. For a long moment, he thought the bird was not coming back after all, but then it plunged into Jarl's body again.

As Lan started to run, the back of his neck began to tingle. Four quick strides took him into the exposed outdoors next to Jarl's body, where the bird was extending its legs to help pull out its sucker beak. Without breaking stride, Lan delivered a kick as close as he could to the bird's neck, as though he were kicking a ball. His toe connected with a satisfying crunch of bursting flesh and cracking bones. The creature didn't even have time for a dying cry. Then Lan spun and was on his way back.

It took will power to run straight into the face of rock that rose before his eyes. Hoping he was going in exactly where he had come out, he shot back into the portal.

"Good job," Parke said. His voice was a little shaky, and held the suggestion of awe. Onta gave Lan a thumbs-up sign and Lan returned the gesture.

Lan looked back outside. To him, the bird looked dead. At least it wouldn't be able to harm anyone else. He looked back at Tessa. She still looked dazed. Rento didn't look as bored as he had earlier.

Lan said, "I obviously didn't spend any time sightseeing, but I didn't catch any glimpses of other birds. The portal door comes out the side of a small rock outcropping. The rock couldn't be any more than twice as tall as the portal door. The temperature is high—probably near body temperature. That's fine, though. The air must cool off some at night, and it wouldn't be too convenient if we were stranded on a planet where the nights got down near absolute zero.''

"Darned considerate of them, huh?" Parke said.

"Right," Tessa said, seeming to be recovering. "But we'd probably be better off making sure the nighttime temperatures *are* reasonable before anyone risks being caught out there at night.''

"Good idea," Lan said. "It won't be that much longer until we can check.''

As they spoke, Onta went over to where Carrie sat. She had stopped crying, and now sat silently, staring at the wall. Onta put a small hand on her arm. For a moment, she didn't respond. Then she glanced at Onta. Onta made a gesture, pulling her right hand away quickly from her chest.

Carrie made an answering gesture and said. "I will be all right. Thanks." She looked up at Lan and Parke and Tessa.

"Shouldn't we—I don't know—bury him? Or bring his body in here?" She started crying again.

Lan glanced at Parke. "Burying him is going to be a big risk. Just dragging his body away so it doesn't attract more trouble would be risky. Maybe it could wait a few hours until we know more about this place.''

Parke nodded. "I think we should at least wait until we're ready to hunt for water, then move the body.''

No one disagreed.

"So," Parke said. "What's the rest of the plan? Bright and early 'tomorrow' one of us tries to get water and bring it back here somehow?''

"Sounds reasonable to me," Lan said. "You want to flip a coin?''

"Flipping's easiest with two people," Tessa said. "I guess we'd better draw from a stack.''

Parke looked carefully at Tessa. "How many candidates do you think there are?"

"You used to know how to count, Parke. There are six of us here."

"Well, yes, I can see there are six of us here, but, but—"

"For one thing," Lan put in, "Onta's had a tough enough time already. That leaves us with five. If Rento gets killed, our pals back there might not let anybody back in. So we're down to four."

Rento unobtrusively expelled a large breath of air.

Parke said, "And I think Carrie's gone through enough recently. So we're down to—"

"Four," Carrie said determinedly.

"This is stupid," Parke said. "Those people should be back any time. If we just wait, we'll be fine. How long can it be?"

"A real long time," Rento said sullenly. He stared at the floor as he talked. "Half of what Wilby says is lies. They're never coming back."

"They'll be back," Lan said, wondering if they really would, but sure it wouldn't help the group's morale to dwell on the worst possibility. "Even if Wilby doesn't want to come back for us, your mother wouldn't leave you stranded here."

Tessa and Carrie both looked at Rento.

"Don't bet on it," Rento said, confirming the relationship. "She believes everything he says. He could tell her he came back to check and we were all gone and she'd believe him." He looked grim. "It might even bother her for a few minutes."

Lan said, "Maybe you're being too hard on her."

Parke blinked. "I can't believe this. You're telling him he's being too hard on her after all this?"

"I just meant—oh, never mind." Lan sat down. "I'm

tired of being on my feet. It looks like it's going to be night soon. Maybe a quick nap would help before we go out there."

Parke said, "Now you're talking sense."

Tessa said, "No, you're not. What's this 'we' stuff when you talk to Parke? I haven't seen any coin tossing or drawing."

Lan dug into his pocket and picked four coins. After a sleight-of-hand pretense of shuffling them, he took them and tossed three apparently at random to Parke, Carrie, and Tessa. "All right. How about this? The two highest amounts go together on the first trip, so each one can watch the other's back."

Tessa read hers. "Twenty-two."

Carrie said, "Eighteen."

Parke said, "Thirty-four."

Lan read the remaining-balance display on his coin. "Twenty-five. I guess it's you and me, Parke."

Tessa and Carrie both instantly looked suspicious. Carrie said, "Now wait a minute—"

Parke interrupted her. "We can't afford any dissent. You elected me leader, and I think Lan's suggestion is a good one. End of subject."

Tessa said, "At least let me see the displays."

Parke and Lan showed her the numbers.

Tessa still seemed suspicious, but she said nothing. Lan collected the coins.

Outside, shadows raced each other as they fled from the portal and night fell. Parke reached for the portal control. "Maybe we'd be safest if I close the door until daylight."

"Good plan," Lan said. He leaned against the wall for a few minutes. As he felt sleep coming on, he lay on the floor and tried to ignore the discomfort.

\* \* \*

When Lan awoke, it was still night beyond the portal. Everyone else seemed to be asleep, so Lan sat quietly. Minutes later, daybreak came. Lan looked at the view outside the portal, and he felt the skin on the back of his neck tingle.

Lan rose to his feet stiffly. Parke stirred and opened his eyes.

"Doesn't look great, does it?" Lan said softly.

"What do you mean?"

Lan cocked his head at the view.

Parke drew himself to a sitting position and looked the direction Lan had indicated. "I'll be damned."

"What?" Tessa asked, opening her eyes.

"Jarl's body is gone."

What Parke said was true. Not only was the body gone, but left behind was no indication that it had ever been there. The tendril-like ground cover looked as even and undamaged as it had when they first arrived. No sign of damage, and no sign of Jarl's spilled blood.

# 18

## GOSSIP

"I CAN'T SEE that reflection anymore, either," Parke said.

"Maybe the sun's not in the same place it was when you saw it before," Tessa suggested.

"No, it was just a few minutes after dawn. Just like now. What's going on here?" Parke looked at Lan.

Lan lifted one eyebrow. "You're asking *me?*"

Parke looked back out the portal and shook his head. "And bodies just don't disappear that cleanly. I don't like this place."

Even Rento got up and went to the portal to look. Carrie just stared blindly. Onta stood on tiptoe and moved her head from side to side, looking at the spot where Jarl had died. She looked quizzically at Carrie.

Tessa said, "Maybe we shouldn't go out there at all. Maybe we'd be best off trying to get through the door behind us, or just wait as long as we possibly can until they come back."

Lan moved over to Carrie and sat down next to her. Gently he said, "I know this is a bad time to ask, but we might not have any good times here. Has the computer made any more progress in decoding these inscriptions? Especially anything that might help unlock the door back to the—whatever you call it—the interconnecting area.''

Carrie sighed. She put the computer in her lap, traced a few lines on the screen with her finger, looked at the resulting display. ''Not a lot more. But it's still analyzing.'' She touched the screen a few more times and said, ''I don't see anything yet that might help with the door.''

Lan rose and moved over to Parke. ''I think it's time we were going.''

Parke nodded.

Tessa said, ''Do you really think it's necessary?''

Lan said, ''I'm afraid so.'' To Parke, he said, ''Any suggestions for a plan?''

''Watch each other's back. Keep an eye on the sky.''

Lan touched Tessa's arm. ''We'll be fine. And we'll be back soon. Can you keep watch for us so you can open the portal again when we get back, or wave to us from just outside if we can't find our way back to the opening?''

Tessa nodded.

Lan rubbed the panel that opened the portal wall. ''How about if we plan to go only as far as that tree over there—the large one—and re-evaluate there.''

Parke nodded.

They stepped out of the portal, Lan scanning to their left and above, Parke handling the right and also watching the sky. Lan saw nothing in the pink sky, not even clouds. He glanced back, trying to fix the image of the rock outcropping in his mind.

''It's quiet,'' Parke said as they walked.

Lan grinned and said in a stage whisper, ''*Too* quiet.''

''You know what I mean. It's eerie.''

The ground cover compressed under their feet and sprang back unhurt as they passed. Lan said, ''Of course it's eerie. It's someplace entirely new to us." He felt queasy as they walked across the spot where Jarl's body had lain.

Shrubs with spiky clusters dotted the ground so frequently that Lan and Parke had to thread their way among them. Occasional shoots of cobalt-blue wild grass gave Lan the feeling that he was looking at some hologram in which the hues were incorrectly rendered.

The sky remained clear. As they walked toward the large tree with shiny, black bark and blue, feathery leaves framing small clusters of spikes, Lan breathed in the aromatic air. It held a hint of peppermint and mildew. They seemed to be on the very gradual slope of some enormous hill. The land behind them rose ever so slowly in the distance. In front of them, the direction the portal faced, the land seemed to dip slightly as it stretched to a horizon that seemed an enormous distance away. The view in every direction showed similar plant life.

The reddish sun was already well into the sky. Lan could feel the heat sinking into his skin. They reached the shade of the tree and Lan felt more comfortable.

Lan said, "We're going to need water even sooner if we spend much time out here."

"Yeah. I'm starting to sweat already."

As they stood in the shade of the tree, under branches that spread over their heads, Lan said, "We'd better fix the image of the outcropping with the portal door in our heads. A person could get lost out here."

Theirs wasn't the only outcropping. From their current position, they could see several others, like giant round boulders sliced into hemispheres and stuck at random over the hillside.

"You're right," Parke said. He looked back at their outcropping for a long moment before swinging his gaze back toward the horizon. "I wonder what caused that reflection yesterday. Right now, I don't see anything that looks like water."

"I don't know, but walking downhill should be taking us in the right direction. That reminds me." Lan bent his knee and pulled one shoe up for inspection. "Looks like there's no damage to my soles. I wondered if somehow the ground cover disintegrates whatever touches it, but apparently we're safe. That's a little good news."

Lan squatted and ran a fingertip lightly and quickly across a tendril in the ground cover. "No pain. It just feels a little oily." Lan rose and waited a moment, looking at the finger tip to see if a slow reaction was going on.

"Yeah, but—what the?" Parke jumped sideways and rammed into Lan.

"What's going on?" Lan asked.

"Watch out! The branches overhead. They're folding down on us!"

Lan looked up. He saw no immediate danger, but the feathery blue branches were slowly drooping toward the two men. He and Parke crouched and scrambled away from the tree. As soon as they were no longer under the branches, the branches began to lift back up to their original position.

"Thanks," Lan said. "I didn't need *that.*"

"Me, neither. I wonder what that's all about."

"I don't know. Could be a reaction like a biwie swatting away pests with its tail, or something like a Venus's–fly-trap."

"Say, I see sun glinting off a surface over there." Parke pointed. "See?"

"Yeah, now that you mention it."

They resumed their walk, each trying to keep an eye on half the sky. They skirted a few more blue-feather trees before the texture of the ground changed suddenly from the tendril-like ground cover to a green surface that resembled an enormous lily pad. Ahead, near the center of what seemed to be a vaguely circular area of lily pad, were low-lying bushes with large red berries.

Branches in the bushes suddenly moved, and a fast-moving small form charged toward the two men. It made a sound like a snake hissing into an amplifier, shattering the stillness.

"Run!" Lan shouted.

They turned, Parke a little more slowly than Lan, and ran.

The creature waddled, but it waddled *fast*. Its coat was shiny green, and its back was a high arc, covered with ridges. It waddled faster than Parke ran. Almost at the same time they reached the edge of the lily pad, the creature reached Parke. Parke yelped and fell forward onto the tendril ground cover.

"It bit me!" Parke yelled, holding his ankle.

Lan turned to defend himself. Apparently, there was no need to. The creature stayed at the edge of the lily pad, pacing back and forth on six legs, snarling and hissing. Parke lay on his back, holding the hurt ankle, but the creature made no move toward him. Lan approached the lily pad and moved along the perimeter. The creature followed him, snarling and hissing, its black eyes squinting shut when it snarled the loudest, but it stayed on the lily pad.

"Territorial little bastard, isn't it?" Lan said. He came back to where Parke lay. The creature followed, apparently even more incensed by having both of the two invaders close to it. Lan searched the sky, then knelt next to Parke. "You going to be all right?"

"Probably," Parke said through clenched teeth. "Help me up."

With Parke's arm over Lan's shoulder, they rose. Parke took a couple of shaky steps, but the pain was obvious.

"We'd better get back to safety," Lan said. Parke didn't even argue.

As they walked and limped away from the lily pad, the creature's snarling grew more relaxed, as if it was satisfied that it had repelled the invaders. Lan kept halting to make brief searches of the sky.

By the time they got back to the rock outcropping that should have contained the portal, the sun was already on its final quarter of the sky. As Lan looked at the rock outcropping, trying to see if there were small bull's-eyes in the pattern, a pair of hands materialized, one apparently on each side of the doorway, guiding them in. Lan and Parke moved forward and walked through the wall image.

"Thanks, Tessa," Lan said when he saw who had been the helping hands.

"What happened?" Tessa asked. At the same time, Carrie asked, "Are you all right?"

Parke groaned and said "Probably."

Lan said, "Some nasty-tempered ground creature a quarter of Onta's size bit him."

"The size isn't important," Parke said. "It's the number of teeth. How many times do I have to tell you that?"

"I'm taking it to be a good sign that you're still alive, and still have something of your sense of humor, however tiny it is."

"Ha ha," Parke said, as Lan helped him to a sitting position. Rento and Onta joined the semicircle next to Parke.

Carrie pushed up Parke's pant leg to expose the bite. Six indentations showed. One of the teeth had hit right on top of the ankle bone, so that might have kept the others from penetrating farther.

Parke grimaced. "I can't believe it. Just a little whiny pest. And the stupid thing had to bite me."

Lan said, "You're probably just upset because this isn't very romantic. It could have been worse." He glanced out the portal toward the clear patch of tendril ground cover.

"Ouch!" Parke said. "What are you doing?"

Tessa had his ankle in her hands. "I'm forcing a little blood out of each of the tooth marks. There's not much we can do about possible infection, but that may force out some of whatever saliva that thing deposited."

"You think I'm going to be all right?"

Tessa said, "Too early to tell. At least you don't have such a severe allergic reaction that your foot swelled up to five times its normal size immediately."

"You're trying to comfort me, right?"

"Right," Tessa said. "Have you gotten any general immunizations lately?"

"Yeah. Just before I left home—for the trip to Neverend."

"Good. That should help. Some people get lazy."

"Well," Lan said, "Maybe this means we need a new leader. Do I hear any volunteers?"

"Why do we need a new leader?" Parke asked. "I'll be fine in an hour or two, and we can try again."

"Bad idea," Carrie said suddenly. "You go back out there limping and crawling and you'll just be committing suicide."

"All right," Lan said. "I nominate Carrie. Anyone else want to second the nomination."

"Sounds good to me," Tessa said.

Parke tried to sit up straighter. "No fair. My judgment is just as good as it was."

"Didn't sound like it to me," Carrie said. "All right, I accept."

"Accept?" Parke objected. "We haven't even voted or anything."

"I say Carrie," Lan said.

"Me, too," Tessa said.

"Me, too," Carrie said.

Lan looked at Rento.

Rento looked away, then back at Lan. "You mean I get a vote?"

Lan nodded.

Rento shrugged. "All right. I say Carrie."

"This is mutiny," Parke said.

"This is protection," Lan said. "You're in no position to go back there."

"This is stupid," Rento said. "They're not coming back. They're just going to leave us here." He looked at his watch. "By tonight, they're probably going to be so busy that they won't even remember who we are."

"What do you mean?" Lan asked.

"Just that I heard them talking. They're going somewhere tonight. They sounded really excited."

"But you don't know what they were talking about? What else did they say?"

"Not much. They didn't want me to know anything about it."

"Did they say anything else at all?"

"No. Well, they said something about a ceremony."

"What about it?"

"Nothing. Just some ceremony."

Lan looked at the date on his watch. After a moment, he said, "Did they say anything about Arangorta? Or maybe Helfing?"

Rento wrinkled his nose. "Maybe. Maybe they said something that sounded like 'Helfing.' Why?"

"Yeah, why?" Tessa echoed.

Lan sorted through what he'd heard at a recent security briefing and tried to recall what was classified and what was not. "I heard a news story on the way here, one about a new treaty about to be signed. Arangorta's way out in the fringe, and they're planning to join the Commonwealth. They're planning an elaborate ceremony because Arangorta will be the one hundred and fiftieth world to join the Commonwealth. I guess it's also important because Arangorta has been one of about a dozen holdouts, and some people think their joining the Commonwealth might mean some of the others will be more likely to do the same."

"I'm surprised there are that many hold-outs," Parke said. "Considering how much more nonmembers pay in tariffs and increased transportation costs."

"Me, too," Lan said. The Commonwealth, a rich and powerful core of ten worlds, allied with another hundred-plus human and non-human worlds, governed with economic persuasion. The closer a given world followed the party line on individual rights and a number of proscribed issues, the lower the fees they paid for everything from access to star gates to usage fees on Commonwealth-supplied equipment.

"But why would Ellie and Wilby be interested in the ceremony?"

"The news story said Arangorta's a very wealthy world. And they like showy rituals. They're expected to have on display a religious artifact of phenomenal value. If our friends have found a portal doorway that opens near or in the room where the ceremony is to take place, they could be planning to redistribute the wealth."

"So," Tessa said. "Even if they told us the truth about coming back for us, they probably won't do it until after they do whatever they plan on Arangorta. And for all we know, they could get killed while they're doing it."

# 19

## UNCHAPERONED

LAN TURNED TO Carrie. "Has your computer made any more progress?"

She sat back and took the computer from her pocket. A moment later she said, "Some, but I don't know that it's enough. It's decoded a phrase from that section up there—" she pointed "—near the symbols for atoms. It says 'combined'—or 'together'—and 'divided' or 'apart.' "

"That certainly helps," Tessa said.

Lan moved to the section Carrie had indicated. Just above the row of atom symbols was unintelligible text. "Maybe it does help. Think back to when our friends opened the door. What did they do?"

Onta suddenly hummed.

Lan spun toward Onta and squatted in front of her. "Exactly. Sorry I was a little slow."

Tessa said, "You're talking about that the tones that little gadget of theirs produced, right?"

Lan said, "Right. It sounded like four tones to me, but I guess it's possible they used three or five."

Carrie said, "And the drawing shows four atoms, a dividing line, and what may be a number."

Lan looked back up at the wall. "Maybe 'dividing line' is the key. If the people who left this installation behind wanted the gate to be open to people who had at least a minimum of knowledge, they could have left the atom symbols to represent numbers that only people with that kind of knowledge could convert to numbers."

"What kind of numbers?" Parke asked.

"I don't know. If it was just as simple as the number of protons or neutrons in the nucleus, then their picture could give that away."

"So," Tessa said, "if they meant a frequency associated with a particular atom—like an absorption frequency— that would be something we'd have to know about."

"Exactly."

Carrie frowned. "But if we need to convert that to some audible frequency, say by stripping zeros off the end, our units won't necessarily agree with theirs."

"They said 'divided.' Maybe we divide a frequency associated with each of those atoms on the left by whatever number that is on the right. Whatever time units they used wouldn't matter, because we'd take the frequency numbers in our own units, and after we do the division, they're still in our own units."

Tessa said suddenly, "And the 'combined' would mean the tones are played together, like Wilby did when he opened the door."

"Exactly. This may not be precisely the right method, but it fits what we see so far, and it fits what we saw them do. And we know they were able to figure it out."

Carrie said, "Unless that gizmo they had was left behind by the people who built this."

Lan shook his head. "It's possible, but I doubt it. The people who built this must have been pretty smart. And they left these clues for how to get in. It seems unlikely that

they would have forgotten and just left a key on the door-mat."

Tessa looked at the sealed airlock door. "So, all we have to do is have the computer generate the right four tones?"

Lan nodded. "Maybe. As soon as we have a guess as to the four numbers to pick. Wilby and Ellie could have had a computer working on it for weeks, but we don't have weeks."

Carrie began moving her fingers across the touch-screen. "I'll start on that. In the meantime, in case the tones don't have to be too precise, or last very long, I'll start the computer trying all the combinations that result from ten-Hertz increments."

Everyone watched her as she worked. Moments later, the computer produced its first sound, and one note rose quickly in pitch as the others held constant. The note fell to its original pitch, and the base chord changed subtly as the first note resumed its upward sweep.

"How long will this take?" Lan asked.

"A day or so. One of the days here, that is. An hour or two in our time."

"Then no one needs to worry about water," Tessa said. "We can afford to wait a while longer."

Lan glanced toward the portal door. Night had returned unnoticed to the planet's surface. "We can wait until daylight anyway. And if this thing opens the door before then, we don't have to risk it." He looked at Parke. "You feeling any worse?"

"No better, no worse."

Carrie left the computer where it was and came to stand near Lan and Parke. She said, "I questioned Onta while you two were out there. Apparently she was drugged somehow. She woke up in the chamber in the museum wall with Wilby. She pretended to still be asleep, and as soon as she saw an opportunity she ran."

Parke asked, "She have any idea why Wilby had her?"

Carrie shook her head.

Lan said, "Maybe Wilby was bringing back a specimen, something to use to convince someone else he really had access to other worlds."

No one had any countertheories.

Lan moved to the portal doorway. Whatever night sounds that might have been audible were masked by the computer as it continued to sound like a practice exercise on a badly out of tune instrument.

"You're not going out there alone, you know," Tessa said in a low voice from beside him.

Lan turned his head, glanced at her, and said nothing.

She went on. "I'm serious. The buddy system is the only thing that helped Parke get back here. I won't let you go out there by yourself."

"Carrie's the boss now."

"We'll see."

"Who then?"

Tessa glanced at the others. "Carrie's too valuable. If she doesn't unlock the door, we might never get out of here. Rento's just a kid. Onta—I don't know—Onta doesn't seem the right choice now."

"But that just leaves you."

"Maybe we won't have to go out. Maybe the computer will get the door open before dawn."

"But I don't—"

"I don't want to argue about it now. Let's shut our eyes for a little while so we'll be ready if we need to be."

Lan couldn't see any point in arguing against the immediate goal, so he nodded. He and Tessa sat down. He leaned against the wall, let his head fall forward, and tried to relax and ignore the ever-changing scale of discordant tones. His throat was dry and he felt thirsty. His eyes had been closed for less than a minute when Parke's voice intruded.

"Thanks for helping me back here, Lan."

Lan opened his eyes and looked back at Parke. "On a good day, you might have done the same thing for me."

"Ha ha ha. I don't need to remind you about the time you got that cramp while we were swimming in Lelanon Grotto."

"That bite must have affected your brain. I was joking."

Parke stared at him a moment. "I know. I guess I felt serious for a minute there. I mean, here we are, stuck in a closet light-years from home, an inhospitable planet on our doorstep, dependent on some conscience-dead people who may or may not let us out, if they're still alive. I guess it's kind of sobering."

Lan leaned his head against the wall. "Yeah, I guess it is. And yes, I remember swimming in Lelanon Grotto. I wouldn't be here remembering if it weren't for you. Thanks, friend."

Parke ducked his head. "And I remember that time Kellet and his two brothers planned to beat my insides out in front of everybody. I didn't want to look scared, and I didn't want to spend a month recuperating. Then I heard that voice from the crowd saying—what was it—'Three against one. That's probably the same odds they need to beat up their mother.' "

Lan nodded and grinned.

After a moment of silence, Tessa said, "That's *it?* That was enough to stop them?"

Parke said, "No. That was just the beginning. A bunch of the kids laughed at the comment. While Kellet was looking for a face in the crowd where the voice had come from, a different voice came from somewhere else and said something derogatory. I think it said something like, 'Did you know that weasels give birth to triplets?' Kids started laughing harder, and Kellet couldn't tell who made the joke. Then a third voice said something else and the whole crowd was laughing so hard Kellet and his brothers just went away. I don't know exactly why everyone laughed so hard. Probably it wasn't so much the actual comments, but that Kellet and his brothers looked so stupid, or the fact that by then almost everyone but me and the brothers was aware that all the voices were Lan's."

In the following silence, Rento frowned and said to Lan, "If you wanted to help him, why didn't you just join him?"

Parke snorted and started to say something, no doubt a comment about Lan's inability to do that, but Lan cut in. "Fighting isn't the only answer to a problem. It's the *last* answer."

"But—" Rento started.

"It's also an indefinite answer. Too much room for error."

Rento closed his mouth.

Onta changed positions. She lay flat on her back, her small furry legs bending forward and resting up against the wall. She blinked a few times in succession, then closed all of her eyes and gave a tired sigh that sounded human.

Lan let his eyes close, too. The only sound disrupting the calm was the computer playing its incessant discord.

"Lan, wake up," a voice said.

Lan opened his eyes. Tessa sat next to him. "It's almost dawn," she said. Near the door, the computer continued performing its prime directive, the tones generally higher than before. "It's about time we looked for water."

Lan swallowed, then swallowed again with an effort. "How about if we give the computer time enough to finish the scan? It may get the door open soon."

Tessa shook her head. "It's not going to get the door open. The tones are mostly higher than I remember from their key. We're going to need the exact frequencies to do

it, and we don't know how long that's going to take. You're just stalling because you don't want me out there."

"What makes you say that?"

"Because—you're doing it again."

"Doing what?"

"Stalling."

"No, I'm not. It's not even day out there yet."

"It's going to be in a minute or so. I see light on the horizon."

Lan looked out the portal and saw that she was right. As they watched together, the sun's arc suddenly lit a stretch of the horizon. In less than a minute, the full circle of fire had cleared the horizon. Lan looked over at Parke and saw his eyes open. "How's your foot?"

Parke stretched and rose to his feet, putting most of his weight on his good foot. He took a few steps and came back. Lan could see the pain flicker across Parke's face, but Parke said, "Fine. It's much better."

Lan didn't know what to say, but Tessa obviously did. "Oh, come on, Parke. That's very chivalrous of you, but you're wasting your breath. Lan and I are going out to look for water."

"Don't you think—" Lan started.

"We're losing time—" Tessa said. "I'm ready to go. Are you coming with me?"

"I still don't—"

"I'm leaving. Catch up if you decide to come." Tessa didn't wait for an answer, but instead rubbed the panel that opened the portal doorway and walked straight outside.

Lan scrambled to his feet, and said over his shoulder, "We'll be back. Don't wait up." He followed Tessa into the morning sunshine and made a quick scan of the sky.

"I see a reflection down that way," Tessa said, pointing. She spoke matter-of-factly, as though she had already forgotten the conversation moments earlier.

"All right. Let's go for it. You watch the sky to our left, ahead and behind?"

"Sure." This time her voice was a little shaky.

They walked as quietly as they could, the soft ground cover absorbing most of the sound except for Lan's pant legs brushing against each other. Finally Tessa said, "What do we do if we see one of those birds?"

"I don't know. Get under a tree, or lie flat and still on the ground." He cautioned her about the blue trees.

"I'm scared," Tessa said finally.

"Me, too."

They skirted the darker circle of ground cover surrounding another clump of bushes like the ones making a home for the creature that had bitten Parke.

The reflection had faded, but Lan thought he knew where it was. They walked under a pink, cloudless sky, passing between two large blue feather-trees with shiny black bark.

"You told Rento that violence was only a last resort," Tessa said, keeping her gaze on the sky rather than looking at Lan.

"Yes. Is that a question?"

"Why did you say that?"

"I don't understand the question. I said it because I meant it."

"If that's true, why were you so quick to use it the other night?"

"I didn't think I was all that quick to start."

"It seemed that way to me."

"I thought I did it only after I realized that nothing else was going to work."

Tessa was silent for a moment. "Maybe you thought about options faster than I did. That was a new situation

for me. I'm getting the feeling it wasn't a new one for you."

"You're trying to say maybe I was justified in what I did?"

"Maybe I am. I don't know."

"Maybe I did overreact. Maybe I should have seen an option I didn't. Maybe I got a little out of control because of having you threatened."

"So now you're trying to say maybe *I* was justified in feeling the way I did?" Tessa managed a weak smile.

They moved cautiously down an uneven slope, coming nearer to the place where they had seen the reflection. The morning heat was already considerable, and Lan felt the sudden fear that a sharp-beaked bird might have the instinct to attack by flying out of the sun. He glanced at the red orb, but it was too bright to stare at and left an afterimage that made it more difficult to scan the rest of the sky.

"Tessa, I'm still a decent person."

"So you say."

Lan couldn't tell if she was teasing him now, or if she was still half serious. "So I say."

"What else are you now?"

They walked across a clearing that exposed too much sky for Lan to feel comfortable. "I'm Lan. Your friend. Same as always."

"I mean what kind of job do you have now? Really."

"If I tell you, I'll have to kill you."

Tessa abandoned her scan of the sky and pierced him with a sharp, cold stare.

"I'm kidding. I'm kidding. And I'm sorry. But I can't tell you about my job. Except that it's honest, and it seems to fulfill some need for me."

"A need to beat up people?"

Lan looked at her, saw that she wasn't smiling, and resumed his scan of the sky without replying.

They moved between two irregular rows of feather trees and over a small rise. The years since Lan had left Neverend had been marred by sporadic periods of loneliness, but this seemed even worse. The sun beat down hotter than before.

"You're not going to say anything?" Tessa said after a dozen more steps.

"I don't know what to say. This is an emotional argument, not a logical one, so I don't know what there is to say." Lan didn't look at her. He pointed to a wide depression ahead. "Isn't this where we saw the reflection?"

Tessa had had her mouth open, apparently to say something. She looked where Lan had pointed. "Yes, I think so."

From where they were they could see nothing that might have generated a reflection. No shiny leaves, no water, nothing but more tendril-like ground cover.

Lan walked toward the lowest spot in the depression. There he knelt and felt the ground cover. "It's damp," he said, surprised despite having seen what could have been a water reflection not that long ago.

Tessa knelt beside him. "You're right. Condensation?"

"I'm not sure. The air doesn't seem very humid, and I didn't think it got very cold during the night."

"I don't know what else makes sense. We probably would have heard rain if it had rained during the night, don't you think?"

"Probably." Lan glanced back the way they had come, wondering which way rainwater run-off would flow. "That's certainly strange."

"What?"

"Those spots there, along the lip of that small rise we came over. They look so regular." Where Lan pointed was a row of five equally spaced discolorations in the ground cover.

"You're right."

Lan walked to the row of spots and knelt. Tessa was beside him. He made another quick scan of the apparently empty sky and reached toward the closest spot. A moment later, he felt goosebumps rise despite the heat, and he said, "Things are not at all what they seem, are they?"

Behind the ground cover he had pushed to one side lay a flat-black nozzle tip.

Tessa's eyes widened. "A—a sprinkler system?"

"That's my guess."

"So we're on what—a farm? A zoo?"

"I would lean toward 'zoo,' but this is a strange enough place that I don't have any strong idea which." As Lan spoke, he pulled up a short section of ground cover and exposed a long slit along the ground. He got a couple of fingernails in the crack and pulled. Apparently counterweighted, a panel pulled up and over, revealing a dark cavity below.

"What's down there?" Tessa whispered.

"I don't know. A way out of here? Storage for maintenance workers or robots?" Even as Lan spoke, there came a metallic rumbling noise. It grew louder, closer.

Wordlessly, Lan and Tessa stood, then slowly backed up together. The rumbling grew in intensity and was joined by an occasional high-pitched squeaking. By the time Lan and Tessa had moved ten meters away, staring at the dark opening, they could see motion inside.

Abruptly a servo whine began, and, like an automatic gun rising from a bunker, a dark shape began to ascend through the opening.

"Let's get out of here," Lan said softly. He took Tessa's hand and pulled her with him.

Tessa came with him. As she looked back over her shoulder, she asked, "What is it?"

"Could be a repair robot. I don't know."

The servo whine stopped, and a black, hemispherical blob pivoted until a couple of stubby protrusions pointed toward Lan and Tessa. They ran.

Tessa suddenly cried out, and Lan felt a flash of burning pain in the center of his back. Tessa stumbled.

"Keep going!" Lan cried. "We can't stop here."

They had wandered so far in the last ten minutes that the device now blocked their original path, so they raced up a short rise. Behind them, the device began to follow. Lan couldn't tell how it moved because its base stayed almost level with the ground cover, but it moved fast.

# 20

## CRUDE MUSIC

LAN AND TESSA scrambled over the small hill and momentarily escaped their pursuer's sight.

"Through there," Lan said, pointing as he ran. His back stung from the laser pulse.

The direct route back to the portal was blocked by the device following them. A gap between two large feather trees led to a large open area covered with more ground-cover tendrils. They reached the clearing as the black hemisphere topped the rise behind them. It seemed closer than before.

At the far edge of the clearing was a short bluff that the machine might not be able to handle. They ran for it. Lan sweated profusely in the midday heat, and he could hear Tessa's breathing.

Almost there, Lan felt another stinging bolt on his back. He sucked in his breath and heard Tessa do the same. They sped up the steep bluff, using reflexes tuned by years of cave climbing. The machine was definitely closing the gap.

They reached the lip of the bluff, sped over the top,

and put several strides between them and the black hemisphere. Lan was just starting to feel more optimistic when he felt pressure on his face and chest.

"What—" Tessa said.

Lan took another step and the pressure increased. He was forced to a stop, beside Tessa. Nothing he could see explained what was happening. Before him was more open land just like the area they had been in, but an invisible spongy presence forced him to back up another step. He put his hand forward and it met increasing resistance as he pushed it farther.

Tessa said, "Some kind of force field or something?"

"Must be. Let's go that way."

They resumed their run, at a right angle from their previous heading. Lan tried to scan the sky, but the way his head bounced from the running, small black dots would have been impossible to make out. As he ran, he wondered if the force field had been there all the time, the equivalent of a fence, or if their follower had somehow triggered it.

"We got rid of it," Tessa said between deep breaths.

Lan looked over his shoulder. "Not quite yet." The machine poked its hemispherical head over the lip of a small hill behind them and to their left. It rolled or crawled or oozed or levitated directly toward them, its turrets still pointing their way.

"We're almost there," Lan said. "Can you go any faster?"

In answer, Tessa sped ahead. Lan caught up, and they took a curved path past one of the lily pads and Lan deliberately cut across the side of the pad. Instantly, the nasty-tempered resident rushed from its concealment, snarling and hissing at Lan, but Lan was already back on the regular ground cover.

The black hemisphere swung into view, skirting the lily pad as it moved. The six-legged creature started snarling

at the hemisphere, and for the first time the hemisphere seemed to lose its single-mindedness. It slowed down, its turret first pointing at Lan and Tessa, then at the creature, and then back. By the time the hemisphere sped up again, the outcrop containing the portal doorway was in sight.

Tessa was breathing deeply as they raced the final few steps. Lan put a hand out so he wouldn't run directly into a closed portal door, but it was open. He and Tessa spilled into the portal enclosure.

"Close the portal," Lan said.

Carrie was already moving her hand against the panel. "All done," she said. In the background, the computer was trying more atonal variations.

As Lan watched the black hemisphere approach, he couldn't resist touching the portal barrier to verify that the entrance was sealed. He leaned against the wall and took a deep breath. Tessa leaned against the other wall, panting.

"What's going on?" Parke said. "What is that thing?"

Parke, Carrie, Onta, and Rento all went to the portal doorway to look at the device that had been following Lan and Tessa. The contraption approached within a few meters of the portal doorway and slowed to a stop. Slowly its turret swung through a full circle. Obviously it wasn't able to detect their presence. It just sat there, fixed in position, the edge of its shell so close to the ground there wouldn't have been room to slide a hand under, and its turret kept rotating. Each revolution seemed to take more time than the previous turn, as if the machinery inside was making a more and more thorough scan each time.

"I hope no one needs to go outside soon," Lan said.

"What is that thing?" Parke repeated.

Tessa said, "We don't know for sure, except that it's obviously some kind of robot."

"Yeah, but here?"

Lan said, "This whole place must be a zoo or something. There's a sprinkler system out there. We opened up a panel in the ground to see what it covered, and that thing came out to scare us away or to keep us from trying anything like that again, or something. Which reminds me. Check our backs, will you? We got a few jolts.'' Lan turned toward the wall.

A moment later, Carrie said, "It looks like you took some hits from a short-burst laser. You each have a few burned spots though the back of your clothing, along with small cauterized spots. I'm guessing the beam didn't go very deep."

Onta came to look, too. Rento stood up but stayed at the far end of the portal enclosure.

Tessa said, "I think you're right. They really stung, but I don't feel mortally wounded."

Lan said, "I agree. It must be set to scare the animals away, not kill them."

Carrie said, "If this is some strange zoo, and there might be people out walking around, wouldn't they be at risk?"

Lan said, "Could be they get clear instructions about not tampering, or they get some form of protection. Besides, this place is enough different from zoos I've seen that there could be a lot of rules and assumptions that aren't obvious to us."

The black hemisphere still sat there quietly, its turrets slowly scanning 360 degrees. As if for variety, it stopped its scan and started scanning in the opposite direction.

Parke said, "As long as you're both all right, this is good news then. This could be some Commonwealth world. If we can contact someone out there, we might be able to hop a flight back."

"True," said Lan. "But we can't afford to quit trying to open that door. It could be a long time before anyone shows up, if they do at all, and if they're not part of the

Commonwealth and don't have connections to the network, we're still back to having to open that door. We could be halfway across the galaxy for all we know." Lan turned. "Carrie, do you think you're any closer?"

"For a while I thought so, but now I'm not so sure."

Rento groaned.

Lan said, "Go on."

"I'm reasonably sure the elements those symbols represent are chlorine, iron, copper, and boron. I've had the computer crank out all the numbers it can associate with each one—atomic weight, density, wavelengths they absorb and emit—everything I can think of. Then I've tried taking each set of four numbers and dividing them by a number that gets them well down into the audible spectrum. Then the computer plays those four tones simultaneously and gradually ramps them higher, keeping the same ratios in case I picked the wrong divisor."

"What is it we're missing?" Tessa asked. "If Ellie and Wilby could figure it out, we should be able to, too."

Parke said. "It should be simple. Play four notes added together. Maybe you could have the computer go back to the dumb sweep but have it sweep in smaller steps but stay on each step a shorter time."

Rento cleared his throat loudly enough for the act to be a deliberate signal. Everyone but Onta looked his way. Rento looked down at the floor and studied his feet.

Lan said, "Was there something you wanted to say?"

Rento still hesitated. "It's just that I had an idea while you were talking."

"We're listening."

Rento looked up. By now, even Onta was looking at him. "Well, I just wondered if when they say to add the tones together they mean both ways."

Lan glanced at the others for signs of comprehension. "I don't understand. Can you elaborate?"

"I mean maybe if two of the tones are low tones, like bass notes, maybe you're supposed to add them together so you have a high tone."

Lan said slowly, "You're saying if one of the sets of numbers says we should try, say, 220, 330, 440, and 550 Hertz, instead of playing those four tones, maybe we should be playing 220, 550, 990, and so on, or some other combination where the numbers are added together?"

Rento nodded nervously.

"That sounds like an idea worth trying. Any other opinions?"

Carrie looked at her computer screen and then back at the inscriptions near the atomic symbols. "That could be a possibility. The meaning is certainly ambiguous enough to allow that." She started moving her fingers across the screen. "I'll start it out trying all the possible combinations for all the number possibilities."

"Thanks, Rento," Lan said. "That's a very good suggestion, and we appreciate it."

Rento nodded quickly and looked away. He actually looked embarrassed by the praise.

As the computer started a brand new tune, the sky outside the portal began to darken. Lan stared out the door at the robot. It seemed oblivious not only to the fact that night was approaching, but to everything. Its turret scanned just slowly enough to notice, and Lan could imagine it thinking angry or confused cybernetic thoughts. A moment later night arrived and the portal enclosure lighting took over.

"You've got a good sunburn started," Parke said.

Lan touched his forehead and nose, surprised to realize how tender they felt. "You know, I don't think I ever had a sunburn until I was almost twenty. I was on Kamerot for a week or so and I didn't even think about it, and I wound up with a really bad burn. Before that I never had to worry about it much. Growing up on Neverend was obvi-

ously a fairly low risk. Opendale had clouds so thick that the UV reaching the ground during the day was hardly more than the outdoor lights gave off at night." Lan thought a moment. "For some reason, I found that constant, thick cloud cover just as confining as Neverend."

"If you felt confined there, you should really feel great here. Locked in a closet and guarded by an idiot robot better armed than some peace offices. You think it will still be there in the morning?"

"I don't know. Jarl's body was probably disposed of by some automatic litter pick-up. But this thing isn't litter; it probably creates litter or disposes of it itself."

"Could be." Parke yawned. "I've been on my feet long enough. I'm going to rest."

Lan nodded, and Parke sat down beside Carrie. Lan turned his attention back to the night. A couple of minutes later, someone moved to stand near Lan. Lan looked away from the dark portal and found Rento next to him, also looking out into the night.

"Thanks for humoring me back then," Rento said under his breath.

Lan glanced back at the rest of the group to see how easily they might be able to hear, and replied softly, "I wasn't humoring you. You had a good idea. It's as simple as that." The computer's continuing music practice masked their voices.

"But—you really think so?" Surprise filled Rento's dark eyes. Lan had to look up slightly to make eye contact.

"Certainly. It may turn out that's not the right answer, but it could very well be, and we need all the options we can think of right now. Thanks for making the suggestion."

Rento was quiet for a moment. "Is there something you want from me?" He sounded puzzled, and Lan thought he could detect suspicion.

Lan frowned. "I don't understand. Obviously we need

your cooperation. We can't afford to be working against each other right now. Is that what you mean?''

"Not exactly. It's just that you're not like other adults."

"Yeah, I'm shorter."

"You know what I mean."

"No, I really don't."

"I mean you acted like you took me seriously back then. And yesterday you looked like you might have killed me."

"The way I act is a function of what's happening. If you were to threaten Tessa or any of my friends, you'd find me very difficult to get along with. Right now, we're dependent on each other and you're not acting in a threatening manner. You're making positive suggestions, just like everyone else. So right now you're like everyone else."

"So as soon as the door's open, it's just like before?"

"No. That's up to you. I don't get hostile for no reason. If you behave yourself on the other side of that door, I'll treat you with respect. If you start acting like someone who doesn't care what happens to anyone else, I'll respond accordingly."

"That's what I mean about you being different from other adults."

"We're all different. Don't try so hard to generalize. I'm no more representative of adults than your mother is. Everyone is an individual."

"But you *are* different. You could probably beat me into doing whatever you wanted, but I might not even know that if I hadn't—ah—run into you that night. And— wait a minute! When we were running from that store owner you acted like you look. And when we saw you alone you ran away. It was only when *she*—" Rento nodded toward Tessa "—was with you and she was in trouble that you—" Rento frowned. "I guess maybe I answered my own question, huh?"

"I think you did."

"So you really meant what you said—about fighting only when nothing else works?"

"What do you think?"

"I think you meant it." Rento looked back at the silent group, most of whom sat or lay down with their eyes closed. "But he doesn't pretend not to know how to fight."

"Parke and I aren't the same person. Like I said, everyone's different. But I'd rather you didn't talk about this with Parke. He likes to think of himself as my protector, and I don't want to spoil his fun."

A puzzled frown flitted across Rento's face, but he said, "All right. But I still don't think I understand you."

"What's new? I've known Tessa half my life and I don't completely understand her."

"What are you two talking about, anyway?" Parke asked, his voice raised to overcome the computer's efforts.

Lan turned toward him. "How such a big guy like you could let such a little, waddling, idiot beast bite you like that."

"I'm sorry I asked." Parke's tone said he wasn't sorry and he didn't believe Lan.

Lan grinned and looked back into the darkness. Beside him Rento did the same. After a while, light showed on the horizon.

Moments later, Rento said, "It's still there."

Disappointed, Lan nodded. The others gathered around the portal opening. Before them, the dawn light clearly showed the hemispherical robot, still swinging its turret in slow circles.

"That's just great," Carrie said. "Now how do we get out?"

"We can get out," Lan said. "Getting back in may be the problem."

"Right," Parke said. "And—"

As a group, the six turned toward the noise that had stopped Parke in midsentence. The door behind them slid slowly open.

# 21

## EXPLORING

IN TOTAL SILENCE, the portal airlock door swung open. Beyond it lay an empty airlock. "Great," Parke said. "I was afraid for a minute that our friends had come back."

"We did it," Carrie said, wonderingly. "We actually did it."

Onta stood up and bounced lightly on her legs.

Rento glanced at the others, his expression unreadable.

Nothing having informed the computer that its mission had been successful, it continued to produce its series of musical combinations.

"You'd better stop the computer," Lan said, "and try the last few combinations so we know which one opened the door. We may need to open other doors."

Tessa looked sharply at Lan. "You're suggesting we close the door again while we hope the computer can produce the right sequence and that this wasn't a lucky accident?"

"Yes, but with one of us on the other side so we can count on getting out if the computer can't do it again."

Tessa nodded. Parke moved forward and said, "I'll volunteer."

Lan said, "Fine. If you think your attention span is up to it, open the door if we don't get in within five minutes." He looked at Carrie and she nodded.

"I imagine I can do it." Parke stepped into the airlock, rubbed the panel to shut the door, and the door slid shut again, as if the ordeal was about to repeat itself.

Carrie was already at the computer. She stopped the progression. "I'll just have it go backward through the most recent tries," she said.

A moment later the door opened again to reveal Parke with his arms crossed. "Good job."

Lan, Tessa, Carrie, Rento, and Onta joined Parke in the airlock. Carrie was reaching for the panel that would close the door behind them when Lan said, "Wait just a minute. As long as this door is open, Wilby and Ellie probably can't open the inner door. This may be the only time we have to decide what to do next without the risk of being interrupted."

"What's to decide?" Tessa asked. "We get back to Neverend as fast as we can. We tell the authorities what's going on. And we let them deal with it."

"Sounds good to me," Parke said.

"I agree," Lan said. "But what happens if as soon as we get into the maze area we see those two again?"

No one said anything, so Lan continued. "We split up. Everyone try for a different direction. They can't get all of us. And, Carrie, tell us the frequencies the computer came up with so if some of us get out anywhere they have computers or audio generators they can get back in quicker than we did this time."

Carrie read the numbers from her display and Lan memorized them as the others did, too.

Tessa looked at Rento. "Are you for us or against us?"

Rento glanced at Lan, then back to Tessa. "I won't do anything against you."

Tessa caught Lan's gaze and he nodded, then rubbed the panel to close the airlock door. He said, "Everyone stays quiet when we get into the maze area."

Obviously everyone took the warning seriously because they all nodded rather than speaking their replies. Onta's tiny extended hand moving up and down said she understood.

Parke took a deep breath and rubbed the panel to open the inner door. The maze cubicle beyond was empty. The escapees closed the door behind them and moved to the center of what was currently the floor.

"Which way?" Carrie whispered.

They found no unanimity, but the majority of pointing fingers agreed. Parke took the lead and walked up the ramp to the wall pointed to by the most votes. The group followed him up the wall and over the next curved ramp. Again a direction vote ensued. This time the most popular vote was three pointing fingers.

The group went through two more six-floored rooms. In the next one, Lan saw a label he recognized as being in the room adjacent to the room with the door to Neverend. He caught Parke's attention and said softly, "Be ready to run if they're here."

Parke nodded. He went first, walking cautiously over the ramp leading "down" to the adjacent room. A moment later he turned back to the group and whispered, "There's no one here."

The rest of the group followed Parke into the next cubical room. Tessa said softly, "Maybe we shouldn't all go in together, in case they're in the museum."

Parke said, "Good idea. How about if—"

Lan interrupted, "I don't think it matters now. We're probably not going through this doorway anytime soon."

He ran his fingers up and down against the seam where the door met the wall. The surface was rough and uneven. "They must have sprayed this area with some sealer."

Parke rubbed the panel that should have opened the door. Nothing changed. "You're right, but why?"

"Because I'm always right." Lan gave him a meager grin.

"No, I mean why did they do it?"

Tessa said, "Maybe they were worried that people investigating in the museum might find their way in here. We *did* call the authorities before we disappeared."

Lan said, "That's possible. The implication is that they're still in here or on some other world, though."

The whispered conversation suddenly died as everyone looked around in all possible directions.

Parke asked, "Why didn't they seal *our* door?"

"Who knows? Maybe they ran out of time. Maybe they figured it would take us long enough to get out that they'd be finished with whatever they planned. Or that we'd never get out on our own. The reason doesn't matter now. What we've got to do is find out where they went."

Carrie stepped forward. "How? I don't see any footprints."

"We look for a doorway to Arangorta."

"Arangorta?" Parke said. "What—oh, the place you mentioned earlier."

"This is all going a little too fast," Carrie said.

Tessa pointed to the wall adjacent to the one they had come back over. "You see the 'A' next to the ramp? It looks as if they marked the path."

Lan looked where she pointed. Sure enough, a faint impression of an "A" on its side looked like partly erased graffiti next to the path leading up the wall, and the bottom of the "A" faced the path, as if the letter was written by someone kneeling on the path. "Let's see what's in the next chamber."

Parke shrugged and followed as Lan led the way up the wall.

"There's another," Tessa said, pointing to a new side wall. The scrawlings next to doorways here said, "Underwater," "green planet," and "small moon." At their feet was a faint "N."

They passed through two more cubicles with doorways marked "blocked," "Windchime," "Haversham," and "Hot" before they arrived at a doorway marked "Arangorta." Next to the ramp leading up the opposite wall was another "N."

"If 'N' leads back to the door to Neverend, I wonder where the 'S' leads to," Lan said, looking at a marking on another wall.

The five humans and Onta stood in a circle. Parke glanced at the door to Arangorta and asked, "What next?"

Lan surveyed five faces. "I think it's time we split up. Parke and I go through the doorway. We alert the authorities to the fact that they might have some uninvited visitors and let them handle the situation. The rest of you see if you can find a doorway to a friendly planet where you can get the authorities there to send net messages to Arangorta and Neverend."

"No, seriously, what do you propose?" Tessa asked. "The six of us all go through to Arangorta so we have the most chance of helping them catch the people who trapped us here?"

Lan was about to open his mouth when Carrie said, "That sounds best to me, too. Let's go." She reached for the panel to open the door.

Lan caught her wrist before she opened the door. "Wait. This isn't the kind of place you want to go."

"Oh, I don't know," Tessa said. "It might be very nice."

Lan said, "For all we know, there's a group of people

inside the airlock or the tunnel waiting in case there's trouble. We could all be back in their hands again.''

"All right," Carrie said. "We send in one or two people to check. The rest of us stay here ready to run. When we get the all clear then we all go in."

Lan glanced at the time. "Look, the ceremony starts in an hour or two if the news story I heard was right. We can't afford the time to argue about it."

"Fine. Then give in," Tessa said.

"Good memory," Carrie said.

Lan looked to Parke for support.

Parke grimaced and said, "I don't see much negotiation room. We'd better get going."

Lan shook his head in exasperation. "All right. You and me first. We'll call the others in afterward."

"How do they know we will?"

"Because we can't stop them from coming right after us if they want." Lan's gesture took in Tessa, Carrie, Rento, and Onta. "We'll come right back if no one's on the other side. I promise. But if we don't come right back, that means someone has us, and you'd better find another world."

"All right," Carrie said. She handed the computer to Parke. "You two will need this. It's all set so whenever you press this panel here it plays the combination."

"Thanks. Now how about if you folks spread out so you can get away fast if there's trouble."

Tessa and Carrie walked up one ramp; Rento and Onta took the one opposite. The all stopped when just their heads showed over the curve of the ramp, so Onta looked just as tall as Rento.

Parke glanced at Lan, then rubbed the panel. The door to Arangorta swung open to reveal an empty airlock. Parke said, "So far, so good," and they walked inside.

The short corridor beyond the airlock was empty of people, but several packs of supplies lay on the floor. The end of the corridor was opaque, so Lan rubbed the panel that turned it transparent.

"Nice place, huh?" Parke said into the silence.

Beyond the corridor lay a dark, brooding landscape, with patches of low-lying fog partly obscuring what seemed to be a large building in the distance. Between them and the building was uneven, rocky terrain punctuated by tips of large boulders punching up through the ground.

Parke had stood by the airlock door, keeping it open. "You want to make sure this door has the same combination?" he asked, offering the computer to Lan.

"Sure." After Parke had closed the airlock door from inside it, Lan waited a few seconds and then activated the combination. The computer dutifully regurgitated the tones and the door swung back open.

"Good," Parke said. "Should I get the others or should we go on and do this ourselves?"

"I think we'd better get them and just hope for the best."

Parke nodded and then said, "You know, you've been a lot more assertive lately. Maybe this whole experience will do you some good."

"Thanks, Dad," Lan said.

Parke shook his head, grinned, and closed the door again. Moments later, as Lan stood looking out at the view, the whole group was once again assembled.

Lan turned from the view and surveyed the group. "I want you to listen to me very closely for a few minutes before we go out there. I've done some reading on Arangorta and it's important that we all understand some basics."

Lan got acknowledgements from everyone. Even Rento looked attentive and serious. "All right. We're probably going to have to follow whatever trail Wilby and Ellie might have left. Arangorta's population lives in what's essentially one enormous, irregular building. People don't go outside. They have doors for the spaceport and for a seaport. Otherwise it's completely enclosed. Our friends must have gotten access to a map and cut their way through a wall somewhere. That's got to be how we'll get inside, too."

Carrie simplified some of the information for Onta as Lan continued.

"The way I understand it, the residents belong to two main races, united in some cross-cultural exchange centuries ago. One race looks enough like humans that we could pass for them if we wore the right styles and no one tried to operate on us. The other race is humanoid, but that's about as far as the resemblance goes. Apparently the two races each have their own religion, but a meteorite that crashed through the roof a couple of centuries ago has turned into a religious symbol for both groups. I don't know what it's made of, but visitors think it's worth an enormous amount. That rock, whatever it looks like, will be on public display as part of the ceremonies. I assume it's what our friends are after.

"Apparently the insides of their city-state are the haphazard product of ages of random building. If they wanted a new room next to an existing room, they just pushed the wall a little farther out at that point and built it. Finding our way around may be as tough there as in the lattice behind us. If we're lucky, our friends marked a path there, too.

"Finally, it's going to be cold outside, so make sure you keep track of which way we go. If we get separated, you'll want to be able to find your way back here. Any questions?"

Everyone else looked at Lan, then at each other. Parke said, "Yeah. Why don't we make you leader for now? You seem to know a lot about this place."

"All right," Lan said, without waiting for concurrence. "While we're out there, anything I say goes. And immedi-

ately. Anyone who doesn't want to abide by that rule stays here."

Everyone was silent. Parke offered the computer to Lan, and he hooked it on a belt loop.

"All right," Lan said. He knelt next to the packs. "Let's see what they left behind here."

"Food!" Carrie said. "They've got hiking rations in this one."

"Pass them around," Lan said.

Lan peeled a wrapper off a chewy ration bar and savored the taste as he examined the pack in front of him. Inside were a spray can of sealer, partly used, two coils of thin high-stress cord, powered suction-grippers for climbing, cutters, and extra needles for a weapon not present. In the packs opened by Tessa and Rento were light clothing, more food, a couple of lamps, and a few light tools including a drill. Onta picked up the drill, aimed it out the portal as if it were a weapon, pulled the trigger, and the bit spun soundlessly. She put it back down.

Tessa shook out the pack and a mapstack fell onto the floor. "This may give us some help," she said as she turned it on and angled the display so everyone could see it.

The group formed a semicircle around the image. Obviously the contents were homemade because the map that showed on the wall was unlabeled, an excerpt from some reference library. It showed a long, irregular building wall dividing a featureless outside area from the inside room layout. The map of the rooms looked more like a map of many separate, small countries than an architectural drawing. Each "country" had a label like "storeroom," "archive," and "maintenance." Superimposed on the map was a hand-drawn line from a point well away from the wall to one of the rooms.

Tessa pushed one of the mapstack buttons and a red overlay of other rooms apparently one floor below the first was superimposed on the original. Another button push made the top floor display disappear and the new floor was alone in the display. More button pushes took the display all the way down to the ground floor. Additional hand-drawn line segments showed a path from the top-floor room to a small room directly over a large room labeled "Grand Hall of Abersorn."

Lan stepped over to the portal doorway and looked out at the shadowy scene. "We've delayed too much. We'd better get going."

# 22

## BAD TASTE

"It's cold out here," Carrie said.

The group stood on rocky ground in the gray mist, a dark boulder containing the invisible portal door looming next to them.

Lan looked over Parke's shoulder as Parke rotated the mapstack display until it matched their surroundings. "There," Lan said and pointed.

The rest of the group followed his pointed finger and looked back at the map. "Looks right to me," Parke said.

Rento, who had been last in line, came back around the boulder from his emergency bathroom break and rejoined the group. Lan said to Parke, "You know, this portal system is going to revolutionize travel. Until now, most people have gone to other planets for vacations or business. Now we can use the portal just to find a planet for a bathroom break."

Parke seemed to laugh, but cold made the sound come out more like a loud shudder.

They began to walk over the rocky, barren surface. The slate-gray cloud cover was so thick it seemed to be a perpetual feature of Arangorta. Their surroundings were utterly quiet. A sporadic breeze occasionally tugged at Lan's hair and added to the chill. Lan put his hands in his pockets to try to stay a little warmer. Footsteps crunched and expelled air made tiny clouds in front of people's faces. The group turned slightly to the right and followed Parke's directions past another large, partly exposed boulder. As they were leaving the boulder behind them, Lan took the packs he and Rento had been carrying, carried them around the side of the boulder, and left them on the ground. He caught up and said, "They'll be there if we need them, but at least no one else will be able to find them without wasting a little time."

They continued walking. Lan occasionally looked back the way they had come, not because he feared they might be followed, but to fix the return path into his memory. Ahead of them, the side of the building stretched into invisibility in both directions, as if it somehow bisected the entire planet.

"What a zipoid place," Rento said.

Lan took his gaze off the irregular building wall ahead. "It's really a lot like Neverend in its own way. Apparently they're as locked into their large building as we are locked into the caverns. Neither of us sees the sun. Neither of us feels the weather."

Rento crossed his arms and shivered. "Well, I can see why. Who would want to be out here?"

"Someone dressed for it who wants a little variety."

Parke stopped, inspected the mapstack again, then pointed at the new course.

The map took the group toward an even gloomier area. As they walked, the windowless building loomed still larger, finally seeming tall enough to contain the eight levels shown on the mapstack. A section near the ground seemed obscured by a thick patch of fog, but when they drew closer it became obvious that two facing surfaces of

the building were joined above ground by a tall walkway. The facing surfaces angled in to a point beyond the overhead walkway.

They walked under the overhead structure, now close enough to see textures on the walls. The patchwork surfaces looked to have been constructed from a variety of materials, some flat black, some with the brushed gleam of aluminum, others with the marbled appearance of congealed aquasteel. Some junctions were lined with rivet heads, others looked seamless but for the texture change, and a few seemed fused as if a giant torch had heated up one panel of aluminum and one panel of dark glass and let the materials somehow swirl together into a wide boundary layer. Here and there on the surface, individual cubes stuck out, as though the builders had wanted one room to be slightly larger than its neighbors.

Onta didn't lag behind the group of humans. She didn't seem cold, but she had to scamper to keep up.

"It shouldn't be much farther ahead," Parke said.

The breeze had changed from a steady current to sporadic swirls and gusts. The tapering alley seemed even gloomier than their path had been.

"You see what I see?" Parke said, gesturing ahead.

Carrie asked, "You mean the cord?"

"Yeah."

At the spot indicated by the mapstack, the group stopped before the dark wall. Hanging from some point far above and out of sight was a thin, white cord, long enough to coil at the base of the wall. Near the cord, the ground was smooth with footprints.

"This must be our ticket inside," Parke said.

Tessa said, "Will they ever be surprised to see us."

Parke grabbed the cord and tugged on it. "Seems secure to me. Want me to go first?"

"No," Lan said. "Second. I'll go first. After you, Tessa, Rento, Onta, then Carrie."

"All right, boss."

Lan surveyed the group. "From now on, no noise. If you stub your toe, tell us with hand signs. If you have to sneeze, muffle it. When you're on the way up, don't drag your feet on the walls or clunk your feet against the walls. We could be a meter away from a room containing our friends from Neverend or from people even less friendly. Is that understood?"

All the others nodded.

Lan took the cord in one hand and tugged on it to satisfy himself that Parke's assessment was accurate. "I'll see you upstairs. Everyone after Parke, we can probably pull up." He looped the cord under one arm, around his back, then under one foot. He pulled himself upward, then tightened the cord so his leg now supported his weight. He pulled himself upward again, and repeated the process until his feet cleared Parke's head.

Once when he looked down he saw nothing but four pale faces and Onta staring up at him. Onta's blue eyes seemed almost black in the faint light. He kept going, keeping his motions smooth and making sure he didn't bump the wall too hard. The exercise helped take the chill away.

The rope's path led him past the side of a large, square protrusion formed apparently by another room that the builders wanted slightly nonstandard. He reached the top of the bulge and found a level space to rest. He must have been next to the top floor, because the roof wasn't far enough above him to squeeze in another level. At chest height, near where the line was tied to an eyelet anchored in the wall, was an outlined square of light where someone had apparently cut out a section of wall material and then fitted it back into place. To the left, adhering to four patches of solidified goo, were two large hinges. In the center of the square was a small dot of light. When Lan put

his eye near it, he could see a fish-eye view of a closed room inside.

The light inside was little stronger than a night-light, but the room was still brighter than outside. Directly opposite Lan was a closed door with a lever handle. The door contrasted strongly with the bleak exterior of the building they were about to enter, because it was a vivid swirl of hot, fluorescent reds and greens and blues and yellows, with sparklies embedded in overlapping arcs.

In further contrast, the nearby walls made the vibrant door seem drab. Crisscrossing the walls were reflective strips that seemed to vibrate, giving the feeling that the surface was in motion. Between the reflective strips were more hot colors, a few with matte surfaces, but most with glossy, metallic finishes. A little light would go a long way here.

On one of the walls Lan could see was some sort of potted plant with spiky red leaves and what looked like blue icicles or stalactites growing down from some of the branches. Draped over the plant were some streamers of turquoise and cobalt blue. Also in Lan's field of view was a table with fuzzy, orange strips of material hanging from the front edge.

From what Lan could see of the room, it was apparently unoccupied. Who could blame the residents? He looked down and saw Parke pulling himself up the cord. When Parke was close enough, Lan gave him a hand up.

They stood together on the building outcrop. Lan didn't remember the sign for "wait," so he brought down one fist with thumb and little finger extended to say "stay" to those below. He watched Parke for a second as Parke made a quick scan of their surroundings, and then he said softly, "I want to go through there before we call the rest of them up. That way, if anyone's inside, they'll get only us."

Parke nodded. He put his mouth near Lan's ear and said, "You're adapting to this very fast."

Lan made no reply at first, but then said just as quietly, "Probably some racial memory just waiting for the right time. Look, I'm going through. If I don't give you an all clear, get away as fast as you can."

Parke nodded.

Lan pulled open the cutout wall panel. Warm air smelling slightly of machine oil and dust filled his lungs and felt good. No sound came from within. He cautiously poked his head inside and still saw no one. The bottom surface of the cutout square had been taped and padded, so he leaned forward into a controlled roll and used his grip on the padded section to ease his motion until his whole body was through the opening, then slowly lowered his legs to the floor. Still no sounds of alarm.

Lan got to his feet. The room was empty. He crept to the door and put his ear against it. All he felt was a faint background vibration that was probably the result of having every room in the world connected to each other. He almost missed seeing another pinhole viewer cut into the gaudy door. Through the viewer he could see another empty room, also lit, also garishly appointed.

Lan turned back toward where Parke's face showed in the wall cutout and signaled an all clear. Parke pulled enough cord through the window for Lan to get a grip. With Parke outside and Lan inside they had enough strength and leverage to hoist Tessa up so she could join them. Minutes later Carrie completed the procession, looking totally out of place in her dinner dress, and the six stood inside the soundless room.

Carrie frowned and she paused to take a good look around the room with its flashy colors and gaudy patterns, then whispered, "Where did we wind up? On The Planet of Bad Taste?"

Lan said softly, "I think we're in part of their church.

That's probably why our friends picked this place to enter. With only one ceremony every couple of months, this place must stand idle most of the time."

Tessa frowned. "That must have been a really long report you saw on this place."

"I'm a fast reader." Lan turned to Parke. "Which way does the line on the map point?"

Parke turned on the mapstack display and aimed it at the floor for all to see. The display was hard to read because the floor was covered with bright paisley patterns, so Parke went back to using the viewfinder. Finally Parke said, "Straight ahead through that door, through another, then we make a right turn."

"Let's go then. Everyone quiet."

Lan took a final glance through the pinhole viewer, then twisted the door lever and pulled open the door. The room beyond was also empty, but aside from that seemed to share few features with the first room. In one corner of the room was a fountain of sorts. Blue-tinted water or some other liquid spewed from a dozen small jets up to a small, black, circular dish at the top of the fountain. Liquid spilled from the top level into a silver, triangular dish just below, and from there into a gold, square dish below that.

This room had five walls. One corner of the square room was cut off by what seemed to be an afterthought wall that turned the room into an irregular pentagon. About three-quarters of the ceiling sunk slightly lower than the rest of the ceiling. A door-sized opening in one of the full walls led to what looked to be a bathroom. Standing in the corner was a fountain similar to the one in the main part of the room, except that its jets were supplied with a clear liquid, presumably water. Next to the fountain was what had to be a sink, a large pink bucket underneath a large spigot connected to a long lever. Transparent tubing ran from the drain over to the fountain. The walls were covered with alternating strips of vivid blue and red. The room smelled like cheap perfume. Lan backed out, trying not to inhale.

Moving quickly and silently, Lan moved to check the viewer in the door beyond to make sure they were still far from other people. So far, so good. They moved into the next room.

The next room made Lan feel they had stepped into a gravity anomaly. Green and red *nearly* vertical strips were close enough to vertical to make it seem that they should actually be vertical. The door opposite their entrance bore the now-familiar pinhole viewer, and through this one Lan could see a long empty hallway meandering into the distance. The corridor walls were broken at intervals by doors and stairways, and the walls made occasional small curves. Along the seam of the door leading that direction had been sprayed more sealer.

"The map says we go this way," Parke said, pointing to a narrow pair of sliding doors set into the adjacent wall. Parke slid one of the doors aside and as it came almost all the way open, Parke rocked back then recovered. "A mirror. I guess I'm a little jumpy."

Lan poked his head into the closet. A mirror occupied the center third of the wall. A couple of boxes lay stacked against one end of the closet.

"This can't be right," Parke said. "The map says we go through here."

Lan pressed his fingers lightly on the back wall, opposite the end with the stack of boxes. He pressed several more places on the wall until when he pressed the wall next to the mirror about waist high the surface gave. He looked closely and he could see a narrow seam running all the way from floor to ceiling. Two more seams traveled along the wall near floor and ceiling. A pinhole near the center of the panel was dark. "Let's see your map again."

The group gathered around the map display. Appar-

ently the room next door had a closet facing this side. Lan moved back to the closet. "Let's see what's behind here."

He carefully pressed the panel along the seam, slowly widening the dark gap. Finally the panel that had been pressed back into place pivoted, held in place only by pressure at the top and bottom corners. Lan edged into the dim area beyond.

His eyes adjusted to the darker space and another pinhole showed up in front of his eyes. He had to stand on tiptoe to see through it, but beyond was yet another unoccupied room. His fingers found the edges of another set of sliding doors and he pushed one door silently aside.

The group followed him and assembled in an irregularly shaped room that could have been a bedroom. Next to one crooked wall was a bed-sized platform covered with a soft pad and suspended from the ceiling with four chains. Unlike most of the garish furnishings so far, the chains were actually a single, solid, non-metallic color. The ceiling was covered with a mottled fabric with the texture of thick carpet. Large, fabric-covered cabinets framed the bed.

"Looks like we go through there and down," Parke said. He pointed to sliding doors on the opposite side of the room.

Inside the other closet, a section of the floor had been sliced on three sides and pushed down at a steep angle. A flexible ladder anchored to the wall showed the route leading down into a dark closet on the level below. Lan yanked on the ladder to make sure it was secure, then started down to the next level where he reached a much larger closet, with cabinets on both sides. Sliding doors formed another barrier to the room beyond and, true to form, another pinhole viewer provided a view of an unoccupied room beyond. Lan signaled for the others to follow.

When all six of them had reached the level below

safely, Lan slid open the closet door and moved to a door on the adjacent wall. This view showed a narrow corridor, also unoccupied. "This must be a seldom-used section also, or everybody must be at the ceremony," he said. "I still don't see anyone." Lan moved to another door opposite but it was sealed shut and bore no pinhole viewer.

The group filed into the room. This one faintly resembled a waiting room, with low-slung chairs around the perimeter, and a window-like wall cutout to the small area beyond. Lan couldn't see how to get into the small area other than by climbing through the cutout.

"What's this?" Rento asked, pointing at a pair of small square panels, one on each side of the sealed door. He touched one and nothing happened.

"Probably something best left alone," Lan said. "They may be light switches or something."

Before he finished speaking, Rento touched the one on the other side of the door and the room turned into a blazing white place where no shadows could possibly survive. Even through Lan's closed eyelids, the light level in the room seemed much higher than before. "Turn it off!" he snapped.

Despite the confused cries from everyone else, Rento must have heard Lan because he said, "I'm trying. I'm trying."

"Try the other panel."

Lan started in the direction his memory told him was correct. He got perhaps halfway to Rento when suddenly the illumination level snapped back to where it had been.

"Got it," Rento exclaimed.

"Whew," Parke said. "What was all that?"

"I think we've been wandering around in the dark," Lan said. "Or at least using only whatever the residents use for night lights. The article said the people here like much more light than we do, but I didn't realize how much more."

"Sorry," Rento said. "I was just curious. And when I pushed the one panel that turned on the lights, pushing it again wouldn't turn them off."

"Which is *on* and which is *off*?"

Rento pointed to the panel to the left of the door and said, "That one's *on*."

"All right," Lan said. "No more experimenting. We need to hurry. The ceremony's probably started by now."

As Lan turned toward the door to the short corridor beyond, the door burst open and Onta squealed. In rushed two familiar people.

Wilby and Ellie looked even more startled than the six of them did.

# 23

## ARRESTED

WILBY WAS THE first to speak. "How in the name of Beezle did all of you get here?" In his hand was a laser pistol aimed steadily at Lan and his companions. Over his shoulder was slung a bag. Ellie held a gun similar to Wilby's. They both wore glittery and colorful pants and shirts that would have made good camouflage outfits at a circus. Their faces looked a little comical, too, because they both wore goggles.

Lan gestured toward the restructured closet. "We came down the ladder."

Ellie spoke impatiently. "We don't have time for stupid questions. Obviously they got out and followed us here."

Wilby said, "Well, I can see—"

"We need to *move*. But these meddlers can come in handy. They should slow down the pursuit."

Lan edged very slowly toward a light switch behind him. The goggles Wilby and Ellie wore could very well be flash protectors that let them see in brightly lit rooms or "dark" ones, but he didn't see many options. Trying to gain an advantage and failing was preferable to doing nothing.

"Stop right there," Ellie said.

Lan made a pretense of looking at his companions to see who she was talking to. They all looked around, too.

"Everybody over to that wall," Ellie said. She gestured toward the wall with the receptionist's cutout. "Fast!"

The group moved.

"Get inside there." Ellie pointed through the opening.

Parke lifted Onta up to the lip of the opening and over. He climbed in and Tessa followed him.

"What about me?" Rento asked.

Wilby said, "Get in there with them. They'll let you all go as soon as they figure out you don't have this." He touched the bag slung over his shoulder.

Ellie said, "Now wait a minute. That might take a while."

Wilby scowled. "That's too bad. But we can't take him along where we're going. Too much has gone wrong already."

Ellie hesitated.

"He'll be fine," Wilby said. "They'll run everyone through a lie detector, verify they're innocent, and he'll be out in two hours."

Ellie gave in. "All right. Everybody in there." She gestured again. To Rento she said, "I'll make it up to you later." Rento scowled.

Carrie and Lan climbed into the small receptionist's area. A concealed doorway cut into the side wall was also sprayed with sealer. At Wilby's insistence, Rento climbed over and made the group complete.

Ellie gestured with her pistol for emphasis. "You people stay there. Try to follow us and we'll shoot." She looked directly at Rento. "No matter who's in front."

She and Wilby backed toward the closet containing the ladder up to the next level. She slid the doors to a position where she could watch the group while Wilby climbed up.

Holstering her pistol at the last minute, she scrambled up after him.

Lan waited five seconds, then scrambled back into the main room and cautiously approached the closet, listening for sounds from above. He heard nothing but sounds behind him of his companions coming back into the room. He crouched so he could see up the path Ellie and Wilby had taken, and he heard a *thud* from the floor above. An instant later the opening above suddenly darkened. Lan jerked back as a large cabinet fell heavily into the opening leading up, jamming it.

Lan waited a few seconds for Wilby and Ellie to continue along their escape route, then said to Parke, "Help me get this thing out of the way, will you?"

"Whatever you say." Parke took the spot with the most leverage, and Lan applied pressure as close to that point as he could. The large, rectangular cabinet was too large to twist out of the way. It had to go back up into the room above.

"Oof!" Parke said, "This thing is heavy."

"Push," Lan said. "Tessa, grab the mapstack. In case we can't get this out, tell us the best route back up to the room above us."

"Right," she said.

Lan and Parke continued to struggle with the bulky mass. Parke said, through clenched teeth, "It's moving, I think."

The cabinet did move. It rose half a meter then stopped. Parke grunted.

Tessa said, "It looks as if we could go into the hallway here, down a ways, and take some stairs to the right."

Carrie said, "But that takes us toward whoever's following them."

Lan said, "Push harder!"

A moment later, Parke said, "It's no use. I can't do it. We've got to shift it or something."

"All right," Lan said. "If we can push the other corner up, maybe—"

The door Ellie and Wilby had come through burst open once again. In rushed a group of three very tall humanoids with weapons drawn. Their faces were gray, with patterns of lines like sun-baked mud cracks, and they showed expressions of an emotion that seldom needed interspecies translation: anger. Tight lips, clenched jaws, creases around the narrowed eyes.

"Halt!" the one in front shouted in Standard. One of the others reached for the light switch, and the room flooded with light strong enough to throw shadows of people's skeletons.

Lan's eyes squinted shut, and he let the cabinet slowly back down, then raised his hands. "We're not the people you're after," he said, still unable to see. "We just got here to try to stop them. They went up to the next level through that closet and they're getting away."

"Enough lies," one of the new arrivals said. "Where is the Kalamati?"

Lan heard sounds of someone walking quickly around the room, obviously looking for the Kalamati. Lan said, "We don't have it. The people robbing you took it with them. Let me show you my identification, and I can prove we're not the ones you're after."

"What are you talking about?" asked Parke.

A lower-pitched voice said, "We are wasting time." The sound of a pouch snapping open was followed by the same voice saying, "Top level above the entry-gateway. We have six in custody one floor below, but there may be more."

Lan's eyes had adjusted enough that by squinting through nearly closed eyelids he could almost tell where he was in relation to the room and the newcomers.

The third newcomer said, "How foolish of you to try to escape. The door to the spaceport is guarded. Come along."

According to what Lan recalled about this society, detention might be the room in which they spent the rest of their lives. He stumbled forward toward the door, letting his hands fall enough that he still looked subservient but trying to look as if he was feeling his way in the too-bright room. The three natives began herding the group toward the door to the hallway. Parke made a sudden lunge toward the weapon held by the closest guard. The weapon holder reacted too quickly and used Parke's momentum to shove him into the wall.

Near the door, Lan slapped his hand against the *off* panel. Even as the room plunged into what would be darkness for the guards, Lan was moving backward and to one side. The one weapon pointed toward the group arced into the corner of the room, driven by Lan's kick. Ignoring the owner of the first weapon, Lan moved toward the second guard, relieved that no one had fired at random. A strong blow to the gun-holding arm and an elbow to the face took care of the second guard.

Lan made it to the third guard almost in time. The guard must have sensed the motion or heard the cries from the other two, because he fired in Lan's direction and a white-hot needle of nerve disruption burned through Lan's upper arm. Lan kicked the gun upward, but the guard managed to hold onto it. Fortunately that left the guard's midsection exposed and Lan crashed a fist into the guard's chest, then kicked, spinning him into the wall. The guard who had been disarmed first was still blinking quickly, obviously trying to see what was going on. Lan punched him a couple of times and he folded over, temporarily not a threat.

"Run!" Lan shouted. He whipped the door open and had to squint in the bright hallway lights. No one was responding, probably because of the sudden shock. "Down the hall and up the stairs on the right! Let's go!"

Tessa was just to one side of the door. Lan grabbed her

hand and pulled her with him. Behind him he heard steps of the others finally reacting. Parke's voice sounded above the confusion. "Lan, what the. . . ."

"Faster," Lan said, still pulling Tessa. The corridor was deserted when they entered it, but before they reached the stairs leading up, more guards appeared at the far end. They were starting to draw their weapons when Lan and Tessa whipped into the opening leading to the stairs. Only there weren't any stairs. Instead, a ramp led upward.

"What about the others?" Tessa cried as soon as she reached the same conclusion that Lan had: that the others were no longer following because their escape had been cut off by the new group of guards.

"We'll have to come back for them later," Lan snapped as they pounded up the ramp to the next floor. "If they get all of us, we'll never get a chance to go home. Regardless of what Wilby said, their court system isn't like ours, and no one will know to try to get us out."

"But we didn't *do* anything."

They reached the top of the ramp and found another hallway. Lan spent an instant integrating the route they had taken from the room below and decided which room they needed to get into.

"If we can't give them back the Kalamati nothing is going to matter." He tried the door. It wouldn't open, and he remembered the sealer. He could hear footsteps in the distance as he forced his shoulder against the door. The door held.

Lan stepped back a few steps, then ran toward the door and kicked hard about waist level. A splintering sound reached his ears as the door flew open. Tessa ran inside and Lan followed. The relative darkness let him open his eyes completely again. Lan slammed the door shut behind them. As fast as he could, he levered another cabinet into position and let it fall so it blocked the door from opening. "Come on," Lan said, moving quickly toward the closet connection to the adjacent room. Tessa ran with him. By now, Wilby and Ellie had to have a large lead, so Lan didn't pause to listen before he scrambled through the cut wall.

The room was unoccupied, as was the next. They sped through the series of empty rooms, oblivious to the noise they were creating, stopping only when they arrived in front of the wall cutout leading outside. Lan pushed on the cutout. It swung away from the wall and fell back to rest in the closed position. He pushed it out and held it while he listened for noises outside. He heard nothing but the faint internal building rumbling, so finally he pushed the cutout side open and looked out.

He saw no sign of Wilby and Ellie and heard nothing of their flight, so he scrambled over the lip of the cutout. Standing on the outside ledge, he could still detect no sign of the pair. "Come on," he whispered to Tessa, and he helped her over the lip.

Lan pulled the cord up to Tessa's hand. "You've got to hurry. Let yourself down hand over hand."

Tessa glanced back the way they had come, then toward the gloomy cloud cover in the direction of the portal, and she sighed. She gripped the cord and tentatively let herself over the edge. As soon as she was a body length down, Lan grabbed the taut cord and followed.

Tessa was waiting for him when he dropped the last couple of meters. She wrung her hands and shivered. "Follow them, right?" she said.

"Exactly." Lan began to run lightly, retracing their path. Tessa matched his pace. As soon as they were a safe distance from the building, he slowed. "Not too fast now. Since they're armed, we need to follow, rather than catch up."

"Lan, just how is it you know so much about the customs here? And why would your ID prove anything to them?"

"I just read a lot. And I thought the bit about the ID might give us a little time for a diversion."

"There's something you're not telling me, and I—"

"Quiet!"

Noise from back in the distance told him their followers had found the cutout in their wall. They would take some time to adjust to the new situation, and now they had a choice of possible paths to worry about. The sounds of Lan's and Tessa's feet crunching softly against the ground and their audible breathing were almost enough to completely cover the distant muffled noises. The chill had already begun to overcome the warmth generated by the recent exercise. Lan wondered how long he and Tessa would be able to stay free if somehow Wilby and Ellie were able to lock them out of the portal, or if they decided to wait just inside, using their weapons to bar the way.

"What if they're waiting for us just inside the portal?" Tessa asked, her thoughts obviously moving parallel to Lan's.

"Then we're out of luck. But I'm hoping they won't do that. They can't know for certain that we weren't able to convince the natives that we were innocent bystanders. They have to operate on the assumption that whoever's following them is armed and irritated. That means they'll continue their flight to wherever they had planned to go."

"You hope."

"I hope."

"What about Carrie and Parke and the others?"

"If we can send a message to the Commonwealth explaining what happened, I'm sure they'll send out investigators and legal experts to make sure they're set free as soon as possible. Without that outside pressure, I think these people would keep them forever."

Tessa looked back over her shoulder and shivered.

"That looks like our boulder ahead," Lan said. "Wait here just in case."

"Just in case what?" Tessa asked, and continued walking.

"Just in case something happens to me."

"If something happens to you and I'm trapped out here, I'm not sure I'd be any better off than if I just went with you."

"I *am* sure about one thing."

"And what's that?"

"That you're just as stubborn as you always were."

"And you're not?"

"Maybe I am. But this time you have a point."

"*This* time?"

"Don't start."

They walked the remaining meters to the portal wall. Lan reached out to touch the wall, and felt the solid rock-like surface indicating Wilby and Ellie had shut the door behind them. Lan knelt beside the boulder and tried to make out small bull's-eyes in the weak light. He touched the two spots that looked probable, and the surface turned as insubstantial as the mist around them.

"Go in together?" Lan asked. "If they're still inside looking at us, we're not going to surprise them."

"Fine by me."

Together they stepped through the portal doorway and found themselves inside the deserted portal chamber. The comfortable air temperature helped take away the chill.

"That's a relief," Tessa said. "At least one thing in a row has gone right. What now?"

"Simple. We follow Ellie and Wilby, get the Kalamati back, and use it to get the others loose."

"Oh, good. For a minute there I was afraid it would be complicated."

Lan moved to the airlock and reached for the computer to open the door.

Tessa said, "Hey, I didn't sign up for all of this."

"Me, neither. But what choice do we have?" Lan pressed the switch, and the computer spewed out the tune. "It's playing our song."

The airlock door swung open to reveal an empty chamber. Lan swung one arm low in an inviting gesture, and Tessa preceded him inside.

"How are we going to follow them?" Tessa asked. She leaned against the wall, as well as she could with a wall that slanted toward the middle of the chamber.

"We're going to hope their 'S' marks lead us to them. 'S' could stand for Sarratonga or Sengoful. Sarratonga wouldn't be a bad choice if they want to convert the Kalamati into spendable assets."

"And if they went someplace else?"

"Then we go there."

"But they could go through *any* door."

"I know. Let's worry about that later. If we have to."

Tessa took a deep breath and nodded. She faced the inner door as Lan reached for the panel to open it. "Wait a minute. What was that about showing them your identification back there?"

"Nothing. Just a ploy to gain time to think."

Tessa looked unconvinced, but the door was starting to open, so the conversation stopped.

The matrix room on the other side of the door was silent and empty. Lan stepped softly through the doorway and listened. Nothing. He located a faint "S" on one wall and turned to gesture to Tessa. At the same moment, she put a hand on his shoulder. She looked serious and puzzled. She put her mouth near his ear and said very softly, "You and I are going to have a frank talk as soon as there's time. I think there's a lot you haven't been honest with me about."

Lan met her gaze and swallowed. "As soon as there's time."

They walked up and over the first ramp, and again Lan

was disconcerted by the feeling that as he walked on a level path the entire matrix shifted in position around him.

Several more faint "S"s showed them the way. They saw no sign of Ellie and Wilby, the two fugitives having apparently been worried about armed followers, and no doubt unable to find the stashed container of sealer to help delay any pursuers.

Unmolested, Lan and Tessa arrived at a doorway with the legend "Sarratonga" scrawled next to it.

"Very good guess," Tessa said.

"Sarratonga has a reputation for being a place where the locals don't have a history of being petty about details like enforcing the laws. It attracts a fair number of people with money to spend—and a fair number of people with plans for encouraging spending."

The door opened promptly on command. Lan and Tessa moved through the airlock and reached the chamber beyond. Tessa drew in a sharp breath, and Lan's ears popped with the pressure change.

The view was spectacular. The portal faced a distant, steep hillside covered with dense habitation clinging to the slope. The level, multicolored striations could almost have been an aerial view of a flat planet's surface, but for the people that were visible. Far across the chasm, almost three kilometers away, were the tiny shapes of people walking along sidewalks, stopping to talk or examine the outside of a shop before going inside. Two isolated, fluffy clouds moved slowly through the gap wide enough to turn the distant environment a faint blue.

# 24

## CURSING

"So THIS IS Sarratonga?" Tessa asked. She stared out the portal gateway at the expanse of city carved into the steep slope across the chasm. Sunlight lit narrow horizontal strips that divided the patchwork metropolis into mottled stripes. At several points cable cars stretched over the depths. Two colorful large balloons with suspended passenger carriers drifted slowly with the air currents in the chasm. Several individual helium balls suspended fancycle riders as they pedaled this way and that.

"This is it," Lan replied. "I was here a couple of years ago. That trip took much longer than this one." He nodded toward the portal airlock.

"You travel a lot?"

Lan nodded.

"You like the travel?"

"Mostly. I guess I have this need for frequent change."

Tessa kept staring. "It's so *big.*"

"That's, I think, North Face, only half the city. This slope is mostly covered, too."

They moved closer to the portal gateway. To both sides

and above, nearby rock outcroppings were all they could see from inside. Near the bottom of the gateway, requiring a step up, was a black-and-red walkway extending at least ten meters out, ending at a guardrail. The walkway surface closest to the gateway was black, and the outermost third of the walkway was red. Lan reached out and his fingertips confirmed that the portal gateway was closed. "They locked the door behind them here, too. We'd better get out of here in case they come back after they put the Kalamati somewhere safe."

"Suppose they've made plans to sell it immediately?"

"If they sell it before the news that it's been stolen reaches here, they might have to explain how they got here so fast. If they're smart, they'll keep the portal a secret."

"All right. But I still don't know what we're going to do."

"Me, neither. But we'll figure something out." Lan reached for the panel that would open the gateway.

"Wait!"

"What?" Lan asked. He held his hand poised over the panel.

Tessa pointed, at an angle off to the right. Lan moved so he could see what she was looking at, and saw two young men sauntering along the walkway, walking as far out as they could on the black portion. They came closer, seeming to be paying no attention to the portal. They passed by, directly in front of the portal, then continued on. Lan pressed the panel to open the portal. He put a finger to his lips to indicate silence.

Together they listened to the two men talk as they strolled out of sight. The conversation was inconsequential, focusing on where they should eat dinner. By the time their footfalls became inaudible, Lan was convinced it was as safe as it was going to get. He poked his head through

the portal and looked quickly in both directions. No one was coming.

"Let's go," he whispered. He and Tessa stepped up onto the walkway, and Lan quickly found the bull's-eyes to lock the doorway closed. He stood up beside Tessa, grateful that no one had happened along while they were emerging from an apparently solid rock wall. He fixed the image in his memory before making an arbitrary decision and leading Tessa the same direction the strolling pair had taken.

The air outside was slightly cooler, but comfortable. Now they were outside the portal, the bottom half of their bodies fell into sunlight reflected by enormous mirrors at the top of the far chasm wall. As they walked, Lan started to talk, just loud enough for Tessa to hear. "I'm going to have to ask you to trust me for a little while. We've got to do several things as fast as we can. When things slow down, I'll answer all of your questions."

Already they were approaching a cluster of people. Tessa said quietly, "All right. What's first?"

"We need to change our appearance and send a message. In that order, unless we see something convenient first."

Lan kept a close watch for Wilby and Ellie, but saw no sign of them so far. The walkway followed the contour of the side of the chasm and ahead on their left was a bar called Alonzella's cut into the side of the rock wall. Stone steps led upward to the establishment. Aside from the sun and the open air, the construction techniques reminded him of Neverend. Fortunately the doorway was the only opening to the bar, so they had little risk of being seen by Wilby or Ellie through a window that would let them see but not be seen. To minimize any chance view through the door, Lan put his arm around Tessa and leaned his head toward hers. A friendly, leisurely couple wouldn't be what

they would be on the watch for. Tessa stiffened at first, then relaxed.

Past the door, Lan let go. "I see a utility plate ahead. Good timing."

Mounted on the rock wall was a large touch screen. Lan put his hand on it, and it came to life, displaying choices that led quickly to a map of the chasm wall they were on. A "you are here" highlight came up in red, identifying their location as South Face, with a level number and longitude. Moments later Lan had highlighted communications terminals, clothes stores, elevators and clip shops. He pointed at the display. "Clothes and clips two levels up, and there's a comm nearby. Remember this location."

They walked a little farther in the same direction and came to a plaque showing a vertical double-headed arrow. Next to the plaque, a wide tunnel led into the rock wall.

At the end of the tunnel, a couple of people waited on a down elevator. An "up" elevator arrived first, and Lan and Tessa got in with four others, none of whom spoke.

Two levels up, the construction style was identical. The clothes shop was nearest the elevator. Lan said, "Get one change of clothes, including shoes—something functional and moderately drab. Keep your old stuff if you want, but wear the new outfit. We don't want to stand out. I'll meet you here in a few minutes."

They each moved off in appropriate directions. When they met a few minutes later, Lan wore brown pants and brown shoes and a jade-green pullover. Tessa had picked pants, too, a subdued blue. Her blouse was a dark gray.

"Good choices," Lan said, approving. He looked at his reflection in a nearby window and saw the tanning cream had almost completed its job on his face.

At the clip shop, Lan said, "Have your hair cut to half its length, and choose any other color."

Tessa frowned and paused just a moment, but then went silently away.

When they met in lobby, Tessa was a blonde with short, straight bangs. "I see you didn't cut yours," she said.

"If I cut mine, I'd stand out as unusual. The color change and style are going to have to be enough."

"Doesn't seem quite fair."

"True. But there's no help for it. Now, about your walk."

"What about my walk?"

"If they see you from a distance, they might recognize the smooth way you seem to glide. Make it more jerky, as if you had on uncomfortable shoes."

She tried a few steps.

"We can *make* your shoes uncomfortable if that will help."

She walked a few more steps.

"Terrific. You learn fast. But I already knew that. Now the comm booth."

Twenty meters along the walkway was the booth the map had indicated. It was idle.

"I won't be long," Lan said.

Tessa said nothing.

Lan stepped into the booth and shut the door. The booth was instantly quiet as the noise cancelers activated. From his pocket he took a small cylinder with a flattened end and inserted the cylinder into the corresponding hole on the comm unit panel. A number flashed on the screen. Lan added twenty to it and entered the sum. A second number came up. Lan subtracted twelve and entered the difference. Two more combination numbers completed the sequence. From the panel, a voice said, "Everything is in order, Mr. Dillion. You have no messages waiting." A list of menu choices filled the screen.

Lan selected the *send distant message* option and identified the recipient. The panel voice said, "You may begin recording."

Lan faced the blinking light. "I need assistance. I may not have time for you to send backup here, but at the very least I need help in altering a soon-to-break news story. The Kalamati has been stolen from Arangorta by two people: Wilby Hackert and Ellie Troughteral, both recent residents of Neverend. I and several civilians tried to intervene and four of the group were caught by the Arangortan authorities who believe *they* are responsible for the theft.

"The assistance I need is: One, start immediate diplomatic sessions to free the four captives. Two, if possible, alter any news stories about the theft to indicate that *six* captives are in custody. Do not add anything about the actual thieves. Three, prohibit any commercial travel for the two people I identified. Four, have anyone leaving Sarratonga by commercial means searched for the Kalamati. Five, start some backup headed here—as soon as possible.

"I have no time to spare now to elaborate. I'll send more when I can."

Lan touched the *message complete* selector, and the panel reported that delay along the chain of transmissions could be as much as twenty hours. A touch on the *transactions complete* was met with a confirmation voice.

"Who'd the message go to?" Tessa asked when Lan opened the door.

"My employer. I said I'd tell you more, and I will, but we're not done with the things we need to do immediately."

"Such as?"

"Such as verifying that Wilby and Ellie are really here, and somehow preventing them from going back through the gateway that brought us here."

"We could spray paint over that whole area so they couldn't find the bull's-eyes to unlock it."

"Good idea, but I'd rather they didn't know we were here."

"Something from the inside, maybe a clear thin panel that covered the airlock controls?"

"Maybe. Yeah, something from the inside. Have you seen bubblehard—those inflatable maintenance bubbles that expand into a cavity and harden to support it temporarily? I bet they're available here. Cutting into rock they way they do here is enough like Neverend that they probably have some of the same tools."

"I see a utility panel down over that way," Tessa said, pointing.

They hurried toward the panel, moving much faster than the average pedestrians. "Why the red and black?" Tessa asked, indicating the division of colors on the walkway.

Lan pointed up. "The black is under the lip of the next level up. The red is open to the sky, so if someone above drops something, or a rock falls, your risk is higher out there. Not that it's all that high."

The utility panel product search indicated a source for bubblehards, so Lan and Tessa took an elevator up two more levels, a speedwalk over about a kilometer, and an elevator down twenty levels. Less than an hour later, they strolled casually on the same level as the portal. They hung back to let a lone woman ahead pull away and when they reached the portal Lan quickly unlocked the gateway. He peered in to make sure the chamber was unoccupied, then armed the bubblehard with a pull-twist-push motion, tossed it inside, and quickly relocked the door. In Tessa's bag was a small spray can of solvent, in case they needed to reverse their action.

Lan started walking back the way they had come. "I'd like to keep the location in sight for at least ten minutes, so we know for sure that stuff has set."

Tessa nodded. "So if they unlock the door now, they'll just feel the bubblehard and think they didn't unlock it after all?"

"Right. I hope."

At a prudent distance, they stopped. Lan walked across the red section of the walkway and leaned on the guard-rail, taking in the view he had been largely ignoring.

Tessa joined him, then immediately backed up. She took a couple of deep breaths. "It's almost like a cliff, it's so steep. How can you stand it?"

Lan glanced down. From here he could see nothing but a series of red walkways extending into the depths, the ones farthest below so distant that they seemed to be a continuous ramp. In three places, probably where construction was going on, room-sized balloons bulged out from the side of the chasm. The bottom of the chasm, four or five kilometers below, was a white thread. "Just lucky, I guess. The drop doesn't bother me much." He looked up and saw a series of guardrails.

"Well, I'm staying back here," she said. As Lan looked at Tessa, her mouth opened and she gasped, "Oh no! Someone's falling from that cable car."

Lan turned and saw what Tessa did. Almost in the center of the chasm, a lone figure was falling through the air. A second later, a second figure leapt from the same cable car, and the first person moved into the spread-eagle jumper's posture, slowing the fall. Lan said, "They're going to be all right. It looks like sport jumping. They must have parachutes."

A few more seconds passed, and by the time the second jumper caught up with the first, a third person left the cable car. This one had a hang glider unfold over his shoulders. Finally a fourth jumper appeared, also with hang glider wings snapping into position. The two hang gliders spiraled slowly, maintaining their distance. Tessa moved closer to the guardrail, holding Lan's arm, as the

two chutists fell below their level, neither having opened a chute. Finally, when it seemed they must have waited too long, two colorful chutes shot up like fountains and unfurled at almost the same time.

"Those people must be crazy," Tessa said, backing away from the guardrail.

"Maybe," Lan said.

"The bubblehard must be solid by now. I've been starving for so long my stomach has stopped sending signals. How about if we get some food?"

"Good idea. I noticed a place not far from here."

They ate slowly, in case their stomachs protested the sudden change in activity. Heldekurt's restaurant, like most other places of business, was cut into the side of the cliff. Small cubbyholes the farthest inside gave the place a feel similar to Neverend, except that the rock wasn't volcanic. The walls were flecked with tiny exposed surfaces that reflected the light, and Lan couldn't decide if it was the natural appearance or if the management had sprayed the walls with some mixture.

With her plate still over half full, Tessa leaned back and said, "Isn't it about time you told me whatever it is you need to tell me?"

"Not here. I'll do it soon, but not in a public place."

Tessa blinked then frowned. "I'm not going anywhere with you until I know what's going on. I've accepted the situation until now, I guess because I didn't seem to have much choice. Now I have a choice. That's it."

Lan suddenly felt very tired. He glanced out the open doorway to the narrow hallway cut through the rock. "I'd really rather wait just another hour."

"No."

Lan met her gaze, then glanced away. Making up his mind, he took out his wallet. "Do you promise me you will keep this to yourself? I mean absolutely to yourself."

Tessa nodded.

Lan pressed both fingertips against the card. As it turned blue, he pushed it toward Tessa.

She stared at it a moment. "You mean—"

"Keep your voice down," Lan whispered.

" 'Commonwealth Covert Corps. Undercover Operations'?"

"Some peace officers are selected partly for their body type. It helps, if you're in uniform and on patrol, if you look tough and competent. Sometimes, that's enough by itself to keep trouble from starting in the first place. Other people, a few people, are selected because they *don't* have that image. Someone who looks as unthreatening as I do can get into a wider variety of situations unsuspected. And if that someone is trained thoroughly in the regular peace officer skills, as well as being trained to retain the unthreatening image, then that person is a different kind of tool to be used."

"This obviously isn't what you told me your job was. So you lied even to me?"

"I lie to everyone," Lan said. "It's *not* something I like about the job, but you can see that if I tell people my job, that has a tendency to defeat the whole purpose."

"So almost everything you've told me has been a lie?"

"A lot of it. I'm sorry, but like I said, I can't do my job if everyone knows what it is. I felt guilty every time I withheld some of the truth."

"Oh, you felt guilty. Now I feel so much better."

Lan felt his chest tighten. "I lied because I was afraid."

"Of what?"

"Afraid that you'd hate me. I've turned into the kind of man you have a lot of reasons to hate. I solve some problems with violence. That's my last resort, but it's part of me now. I don't want you to hate me." Lan sighed. It shouldn't be possible for Tessa to hate him if he loved her, should it?

Tessa looked away. "So, what happens next? You find Wilby and Ellie and arrest them?"

"It's not that easy. Sarratonga is a free zone. They have their own laws, their own enforcement, their own penal system. More to the point, they don't choose to enforce much, unless a citizen gets into the practice of killing lots of people in public places. I'm essentially a private citizen here. And I'm sure Wilby and Ellie picked this place mainly so they could turn the Kalamati into money with the least possible interference." Lan didn't add that to protect his friends he'd be willing to break a few laws and dangle Wilby over a ledge until he was ready to give up. He could think of little that would push Tessa farther away.

"So following them was for nothing?"

"No. Nothing in the law says I can't apply my own pressure."

"What do you plan to do?"

"I don't have the wildest idea yet. I'm hoping that something will come to me. The only sure things are that I need to find them and start watching their moves. If they're dumb enough to leave it hidden wherever they're staying, I can just steal it back."

"That's not against the law here, either?"

"No. Not much is. You ready for a cable car ride over to North Face?"

Tessa looked down at the remainder of her meal. "Sure, why not?"

When they left the restaurant, darkness had fallen and the temperature had dropped a few degrees. Lights sparkled from the opposite side of the chasm. The regular rows of levels with random lights on each could have been a field planted with phosphorescent sprouts. Unfamiliar stars pricked the dark band of sky overhead.

"It's beautiful," Tessa said.

Lan agreed.

As they stepped into the cable car, Lan could feel the floor bounce slowly, almost imperceptibly. A molded observation window curved completely around the circumference of the cable car, except for a gap for the door. Inside the car, two pillars kept the bottom from separating from the top. Centered on the floor of the car was a hinged round hatch currently secured closed. Above the hatch was a low-gee pole that could be lowered through the open hatch when a skydiver departed. About a dozen more passengers entered and took seats around the perimeter before the door closed, and the cable car accelerated into space over the abyss.

Lan glanced at Tessa. At first she looked down at the view behind her seat, but then adopted the safer technique of looking over the shoulders of the passengers opposite them.

"How deep is this chasm anyway?" she asked finally. "It looks like a *long* way down."

"The bottom is maybe three kilometers below us. The top is up probably a kilometer, maybe a kilometer and a half. Near the top, the air pressure is low enough to make you be really careful when you exercise. Yallerts and Gronkos like it up there more, because it's closer to what they're used to."

"Lucky for us we came in at this level."

"Yeah," Lan said. "Yeah." His eyes focused on the distant chasm wall, but he was thinking about Arangorta.

"What?" Tessa said. "You're off somewhere."

"Sorry." Lan snapped his gaze back to Tessa's concerned expression. "You just said something that triggered an idea. Luck."

"We really don't seem that lucky so far."

Lan lowered his voice. "I was thinking about Wilby and Ellie's luck. Some of the briefings I read about Arangorta and the ceremony mentioned the fact they are superstitious. Supposedly the Kalamati is protected by the gods.

Anyone who tampers with it is supposed to receive bad luck."

"Sounds like an ancient curse or something."

"Yeah, it does. You heard Ellie mentioning Wilby's lucky jacket? Maybe that's where we need to start."

"Start?"

"I'm not sure exactly how yet, but I think Wilby and Ellie are going to start having accidents."

Tessa took a moment to absorb the idea, but then she began to smile.

# 25

## FAST TALKING

"There," Lan said as he came out of the comm booth. "When the news of the theft arrives, the 'curse' should get prominent coverage."

"Your employer can change the news?" Tessa asked.

"They have limits, but emphasizing an element that's already part of the news isn't too demanding."

"What next, then? Find a place to stay and get some sleep?"

"Soon."

"Don't you think you've bought enough?" Tessa asked.

Lan glanced at Tessa, then at the pile of gear on the counter down the aisle, then back at the shelf. "I keep thinking I'm forgetting something."

"Get it later, all right? I'm so sleepy I won't make it much farther."

"All right. Sorry I took so long."

At the counter, Lan paid an exorbitant amount for the stack of video and computer equipment, and they left the store. On the walkway outside, the air temperature had

dropped another degree or two. Across the chasm, lights of South Face shone in their agricultural constellations.

Nearby on the same level, they found an illuminated sign saying, "Cozy Caverns. Vacancy." Lan walked right on by.

"What's the matter with this one?" Tessa asked.

"We need one with a view."

Up one level they found Outlook Overnights. A wall screen indicated two adjoining units facing the chasm were available, so Lan paid for three nights in each. He entered fake names for both rooms, and the wall slot disgorged two coded keys.

At 224, Lan waited until Tessa had her door open.

She looked at him bleary-eyed. "Don't wake me up before you have to, all right?"

"All right."

In 226, Lan unpolarized the window to make sure the view was adequate. Then he polarized it again for privacy and unpacked and connected his purchases. He set it up next to the window and took his old shirt and draped it over the equipment so it covered everything except the lens directed at South Face, and the controls. With the lights off, he unpolarized the window again and started defining the sequences and limits for the equipment.

Light against Lan's eyelids woke Lan before he expected it. Daylight streamed in through the window. He got out of bed, still fully clothed, looked at the viewer long enough to make sure the camera was compensating correctly for the increased light levels, then went back to bed and pulled a pillow over his head. Before the mattress had finished conforming to his changed position, he was asleep again.

A rapping noise woke him sometime later. He pulled the pillow away from his head and heard knocking on the door to the adjoining room. He rubbed his eyes and got out of bed.

Lan opened the interconnecting door. He was so tired that for an instant he didn't recognize Tessa with her blonde hair.

"You look terrible," Tessa said.

Lan shut the door.

After a pause, Tessa rapped on the door again.

Lan opened the door.

Tessa said, "You look great in the morning."

"Thank you. Would you like to come in?"

Tessa scooted quickly through the open door, as though it might close again. "Nice tan."

Lan sat on the bed and rubbed his eyes some more.

"How's all this doing?" Tessa asked.

Lan opened his eyes and saw she was referring to the array of video and computer equipment on the table next to the window. "With any luck, it's found Wilby and Ellie." He stood up, still feeling a little groggy. On the control panel viewer flashed an array of still images, changing too fast for persistence of vision to do anything but turn them into a vague blur. Lan gave the unit commands to keep busy at its primary task but to show him sorted scenes from its memory. A still image came up on the viewer. It showed four people, all strangers to Lan, on a walkway at night. In the lower right corner were the time the view was taken, along with azimuth and altitude. Lan gave a few more commands.

He turned to Tessa. "I've had it capturing anything that moves in a square that goes a couple of dozen levels above and below the level the portal is on, and almost a half-kilometer on each side. Its sorted all those images by original coordinates and then by time." The four people started moving on the screen, looking a little like an ancient archive film because, while most of their motions were tracked smoothly, occasionally the image would jump noticeably.

"Why is the image jerky sometimes?"

"Apparently at those times the camera had enough other motion in its field of view that it couldn't keep up." Lan pushed a control and the camera skipped the rest of the recording for the foursome. The next segment showed a woman apparently in a restaurant bay window lifting a glass to her lips. "Normally, all the windows on that side are polarized vertically when they're open, and the ones on this side are polarized horizontally, so you can't just use a telescope from here to see inside. This little attachment between the lens and the window sets up a field to neutralize the window."

Tessa scrutinized him. "Seems pretty easy for someone who wants to get around it."

"It is. Just the same way a lot of laws can be skirted. Laws have a history of having loopholes that benefit people who'd like to break other laws. Like allowing receivers for peace officer frequencies. At least this time the good guys benefit."

Next on the screen was a segment showing a Delpok triple making their way from an elevator stop, along a walkway, and into an odor bar. A cable car moved slowly across the chasm. In what seemed to be a private apartment with an open window, a naked couple displayed their ignorance about the magnification possible with surveillance lenses.

Lan skipped past several more sequences as Tessa said, "So, is this the model a junior voyeur buys, or is this only available to the serious buyer?"

Lan glanced up at her, startled. He was trying to decide how to respond when Tessa said, "I'm sorry. Maybe I'm teasing too hard because after all this time it seems I know so little about you."

"You know a lot about me. I haven't changed what I am or who I am just because I work out of a peace office."

"The Lan I knew in school wouldn't use force on someone, or lie to a close friend."

"Force is a last resort. I wish you could understand that."

Tessa sighed. "I know. I'm sorry. I'm trying to adjust to this, but it's difficult."

"I know. Look, I have no intention of finding Wilby and Ellie and beating the Kalamati's location out of them." At least not as long as there was any way Tessa could find out about it.

"Its location? Why wouldn't they have it with them?"

"They've gone to too much trouble to take a chance that it might get stolen if they're carrying it around, or get stolen if they left it in a hotel room someplace. My money says they had it in a lockbox ten minutes after they got here."

"You're saying you *wouldn't* try to beat the location out of them, under any circumstances?"

Lan hesitated, then told her the truth. "No. Four innocent people stand to spend the balance of their lives in confinement, and two of those people are close friends. If that's what it took to get them out, that's what I would do. I'm not saying I'd like doing it, just that if I had to I would. But it's not my preference. I think that's a distinction you're ignoring." Lan continued to scan through the sequences of images as he talked.

"You're right," Tessa said. She stared at the distant wall of the city. "I guess I understand it intellectually. The emotions take a little longer to deal with."

Lan put the image on hold and turned to her. "I think I understand. I wish you didn't have to go through the things you did."

Tessa nodded, and Lan turned back to the images. The next sequence showed a restaurant employee

loading a tray of glasses and dishes onto the input tray of a cleaner. The employee left the room and the image jumped forward in time to show the sorted and cleaned utensils rise back out of the machine. Next, a man standing at a railing flicked a wadded up wrapper into space.

"You really—" Tessa started.

"Jackpot," Lan said.

Clearly visible on the screen was Wilby Hackert. Lan glanced at the time display. Next to the standard time recorded at the lower corner of the display was the Sarratonga time, 28:32:17, near local midnight. Lan tagged the video sequence with an index mark.

Wilby was alone as he exited the Rigel Bar. He wore casual clothes, including a lime-green windbreaker. He looked both ways on the walkway, seeming to be verifying his directions rather than looking for someone following him. He turned left, moving out to the red section of the walkway. He took a deep breath. He looked happy, and his walk had more of a saunter to it than Lan had seen before. The frame tracked with him as he walked.

"Looks cocky to me," Tessa said. Her voice was quiet, as if Wilby could somehow overhear.

"With some luck we can change that. He probably assumes we're all stuck on Arangorta, surrounded by disbelievers."

Wilby continued his stroll, passing businesses mostly shut down for the night and an occasional open restaurant or bar. He occasionally passed other people, and the video unit indicated it had tracked the others, too, and those independent segments were also available for recall. Lan kept the focus on Wilby as he turned into a tunnel leading toward an elevator. The dark walls to his side lightened as the camera boosted the gain. The segment ended with Wilby turning a corner. Next on the screen was a view of two Kadergans leaving a stimulant store. One shook his head at the other, and his large ears flapped.

"Now what?" Tessa asked.

"Now we look for where he came out." Lan backed up to the Wilby segment and issued a few commands to the video unit. The view pulled back until the walkway Wilby was on extended for the equivalent of several blocks and about ten levels of walkways showed on the screen. The rest of the image was in lower resolution than the square showing Wilby frozen in mid stride. Lan positioned a narrow vertical rectangle on the screen, bracketing the elevator shaft Wilby had picked. Then the screen split into sixteen smaller views, each one showing activity somewhere in the selected area during the five minutes following the end of the segment.

"There he is." Tessa saw him first, pointing to a square in which a figure in a green windbreaker was shown coming out of an elevator tunnel.

"Good." Lan indexed the new segment, and blew it up to occupy full screen again.

Wilby walked back the direction he had come from and stopped outside a large double door bearing the legend "Hillside Haven." He pushed his way through the door and the view changed to another look at someone else.

Again, Lan backed up the video, and selected the surrounding area to include the front of the hotel. Split-screen multiple views now showed several windows, most of which were opaqued enough that the motion showing was indistinct. Lan kept the same area selected and sped ahead until morning light began to make the colors more vivid and make the views through partially opaqued windows impossible. The video continued to speed forward jerkily until almost at the same time three windows turned transparent. Framed in two of them were strangers, but in the third were Wilby Hackert and Ellie Troughteral.

With the image filling the screen, they could see that Ellie had been the one to clear the window. Wilby sat on the edge of the bed looking tired and squinting in the sudden light. Ellie looked wide awake and was already dressed for the new day, in a shiny tan pants and a magenta jacket with epaulets.

"Thank you, Ellie," Lan said. He issued commands to the video unit, froze the current image and expanded it, and moved a cross-haired circle over to cover a section of the material on her jacket. At the top of the screen, a duplicate of the colored circle appeared next to the number one. Lan returned to the scene and played it twice real time until Wilby had dressed and they left the room.

"All right," Lan said. "Now we can save some time because we can search for scenes that show that same color." On the screen came a wide view of the side of the chasm, not blown up much at all from what they could see through the window. Narrow blue borders indicated the physical locations of the scenes Lan had indexed, a horizontal line on one level, another shorter line several levels up, and a couple of small squares at Hillside Haven. Eight blinking magenta circles showed where the camera was currently scanning significant occurrences of the same shade as Ellie's jacket. Of the eight frames brought up by Lan's commands, one was closest to the other marked areas. That frame contained Ellie and Wilby, seated outside at a walkway restaurant, eating breakfast. When that frame filled the screen, the word "live" came up at the top of the display and the image of the pair was now in high resolution. To get a feel for how much resolution was available with these optics and their current range, Lan slowly zoomed in on Wilby.

When Wilby's face filled the screen, anti-jitter filtering kicked in, and Lan continued the zoom until a Rorschach freckle on Wilby's cheek occupied nearly the entire screen. Lan pulled back until Wilby and Ellie were once more framed against a darker background.

Wilby and Ellie were finishing breakfast. A waiter

removed a few plates from their table, and they began to talk.

"You read lips?" Lan asked Tessa.

"No. Do you?"

"No. They have programs that can do a mediocre job, but I don't have one with me."

Wilby and Ellie seemed content, which was pretty good evidence that they didn't yet know the portal was sealed.

"Their meal looked good," Tessa said. "What about us?"

"You can go out for something if you want, or we can order from room service. I've got to set up the first accident before the news of the theft reaches. I want them already worried."

"I'm beginning to think I wouldn't want to have you on the opposite side."

"That actually sounds enough like a compliment that I'll take it that way." Before she could say anything, Lan added, "I need to go buy a few more things. Can you wait an hour until I'm back, or order stuff for here?"

"I'll order something for here. You want anything for when you get back?"

"Maybe just something to drink and a sandwich. Thanks."

"What do I do while you're gone?"

"Keep recording whatever you can see of them. Here, I've got it set." The view pulled back so Wilby and Ellie occupied about the center ten percent of the screen. A dotted box surrounded them. "Whatever's in the box gets recorded. You can shrink it or expand it this way. It's set to motion track that shade of Ellie's jacket, but you can override it."

"What are you going to buy?"

"I don't know the whole list yet. I may just surprise myself."

"Somehow I doubt that."

* * *

"You must have a liberal expense account," Tessa said.

Lan looked up from the array of equipment he had spread over the bed. "Yeah. And I haven't even spent any bribe money yet." He took another bite of his roll.

"What *is* all this stuff?"

"I'll show you all about it when we get more time. But first I need to run another couple of errands. Here, take this."

Tessa accepted the small, molded earpiece. Lan put an identical unit in one ear and gestured for her to do likewise.

"You hear me?" Lan asked.

Tessa shook her head. "You mean through this thing, not—oh, I just heard you."

Lan waited another couple of seconds, then Tessa's voice sounded in his ear, speaking rapidly. He nodded and said, "Good. They seem to be working fine. These are chirpers. They wait for a silent second, or until they've recorded about ten seconds, then they transmit the audio in an encrypted microsecond burst so it's difficult to detect or triangulate. The receiver plays it back triple-speed with pitch correction. Much safer than using simple two-way gear." Lan looked back at the video screen as he stuffed a couple of items into his pockets. "I'll be back as soon as I can. Can you stay here to let me know where our friends are?"

"So you can stay where they're not?"

"Exactly."

"Are they still in the store?" Lan asked softly. He stood alone at a South Face walkway railing, looking across the expanse, thinking he could identify the hotel Tessa was in, but far enough away that he was dubious.

A moment later her accelerated voice answered, "Yes."

"Warn me the instant they leave."

"Right."

With Wilby and Ellie safely four levels below, Lan moved away from the guardrail and toward the couple's hotel room. As he walked along the front of the Hillside Haven, he reconfirmed the distance from the pair's window to the front door. Especially careful with his cultivated bumbling image, he tripped on an almost nonexistent ridge across the doorway, then recovered and moved inside to the reservation screen. Matching the map against his recollection placed Wilby and Ellie in room 118. Across the hall, room 119 was available, so Lan registered and paid. The key maker ejected two copies of the little punched-hole ticket.

Inside room 119, a room with no view except a hologram of some seaside scene, Lan pocketed one copy of the key and proceeded to use a pen to transform the printed label on his 119 key to the number 118. When he was satisfied, he tried unsuccessfully to tear the key. Only by wedging it partway into a drawer and pulling hard enough to make his fingers ache was he able to produce a short rip through the new "8" and into the uppermost coded hole. Satisfied, he left the room.

The hallway was vacant, so he inserted the damaged key into 118's lock, then banged heavily on the door a couple of times. He had gone through the motions of inserting the key, trying the doorknob, cursing, and trying again more than a dozen times before his peripheral vision picked up someone approaching. To himself, but loud enough to be overheard, he said, "Oh, come on. Don't do this to me."

"May I help you, sir?" Suddenly at Lan's side was a rotund Tarnsdweller, his eyestalks twitching, blue teeth gleaming.

Lan pounded on the door once more. "I'm beginning to think no one but someone on the hotel staff can help.

I'm locked out of my own damn room and my wife won't be back for hours."

"I *am* hotel staff, sir," the Tarnsdweller said with the formal bow to a stranger.

"Oh, good. You can let me back in." Lan promptly stood aside.

"I am sorry, but hotel rules forbid me from letting just anyone into a room."

"Even when the anyone has a proper key? Never mind. It'll open eventually, I'm sure of it." Lan inserted his key again and resumed his pounding.

"Sir, sir! Please stop."

Lan glanced at the staffer.

"Please let me see your key."

Lan pulled it out of the slot and held it up, hoping it was just beyond the optimum range for the Tarnsdweller's vision.

The Tarnsdweller's eyestalks arched forward. "Very well. I see the date is current, so I will retrieve a replacement. I will return speedily."

"Thanks. I appreciate it." Lan put the key back in the slot again, as though he would continue to try until the Tarnsdweller returned, and the Tarnsdweller hurried off, his serious demeanor and businesslike image diminished by a slight waddle.

"Here we are, sir," the Tarnsdweller said on returning moments later. "I'm most sorry for the inconvenience."

Lan accepted the "replacement" graciously. As the hotel staffer moved off, Lan let himself into the room.

As the door closed, he said, "I'm inside. You still there?"

"Still here," came Tessa's voice. "I hadn't realized quite how obnoxious you could be."

"Be careful. That's two compliments in one day." Lan hesitated. "I *think*."

# 26

## NOSY SNOOPS

LAN WANTED TO set the door indicator to *do not disturb,* but if he kept the room from being cleaned while Wilby and Ellie were out, and they complained, they couldn't help being alerted. And, unfortunately, the place definitely needed cleaning. A stack of trash too big for the disposal sat in a bag nearby. The bathroom was a mess.

He completed a quick survey of the room before starting a thorough search. One of the few lucky things about the whole mess was that Wilby and Ellie had stolen a physical object rather than just information. That put an obvious limit on hiding places.

Having seen no likely hiding places other than the wall safe, he moved back to the bathroom. He said, "As long as everything is safe, would you just confirm that fact every five minutes until I'm out? If anything disrupts communication, I don't want my first indication to be that Wilby finds me here and shoots me."

"All right," Tessa's voice chirped in his ear a moment later.

Under the assumption that nothing hidden in the

room would help him as much as being able to monitor what went on in the future, his top priority was getting snoops in place. Standing on a chair, he pulled up one pant leg and exposed a small kit of items he had bought earlier in the day. He took out a sticky, pinhead snoop and pushed it into the corner where two walls met the ceiling. He repeated the procedure with three more snoops and placed one at the head of the bed, then began on clothes hanging in the closet. Into tiny crevasses formed by hems and pleats, he stuck several more snoops. They would run for about a week before they died and began to decompose, but until then they offered a capability similar to the chirpers, except they were only one way, and their range was much lower.

With all the snoops in place, Lan began his search, being as thorough as he could be without leaving obvious signs of his presence. The wall safe, potentially the longest job, turned out to be unlocked and empty. The much larger baggage-protection wall unit employed a simpler lock, one which gave way to Lan's efforts in a couple of minutes. Lan flipped through the clothes in two cases and affixed another couple of snoops. An examination of toiletries turned up nothing more exotic than hair-tint pills and toothshield, but behind the back panel of a mapstack was a rectangular flimsy bearing a number and the legend "Safestore." A lockbox key.

Lan's shoulders twitched as a voice in his ear said, "Everything is still all right."

"Thanks, Tessa."

The lockbox key wouldn't do Lan any immediate good, because the box would also be coded to Wilby's or Ellie's prints, but he withdrew it, placed the paper-thin key on a flat plate, and made an impression of the hole pattern, just in case.

At the bottom of one bag was a pistol outlawed on a long list of worlds. Here on Sarratonga, it could have been brought in through what was laughingly called customs, even if Wilby and Ellie hadn't had a shorter route. Or it could have been bought in a number of stores here. Lan deposited a drop of strong adhesive where the back edge of the trigger entered the body of the gun.

With a tiny power-driver, he unfastened panels in the bathroom and the bedroom, finding nothing concealed behind any of them. Behind one of the panels that didn't fit as tightly as the others, he stuck a tall capillary tube filled with a thin column of an amber fluid that would slowly evaporate. He heard two more "all clears" from Tessa before he completed his search.

In the bathroom, he took another vial from his kit and let three drops of a clear liquid fall to the floor of the shower. In the bedroom, he applied two different powders to the pillows and the bedding, using them sparingly because he didn't want Wilby and Ellie to change rooms, especially now that he could monitor the place and had his own key.

He still had time, so he went back to the clothes bags and deposited a tiny drop of clear liquid on each of several seams. As he snapped the compartment cover closed, a knock sounded on the door.

Lan whirled, thinking fast. The knock would be visitors or staff. Visitors would probably come back later; staff would be interested in cleaning. He moved quickly to the closet. He was inside it, hiding behind one side of the sliding door, leaving the door open just enough to present a convincing view of an empty closet, before the main door opened. "Cleanup," said a hesitant male voice.

At the same moment, Tessa's voice chirped in Lan's ear. "They're leaving."

The housekeeper came into the room, trailing a long flexible tube.

"Did you hear me?" Tessa asked. "They're leaving."

After the housekeeper had moved into the bathroom

and turned on the suction hose, Lan said softly. "I hear you. I can't leave yet. Keep me up on where they are, especially if they come back here."

Tessa acknowledged, and the worry in her voice came all the way through the compression process.

In the bathroom, the housekeeper cursed, presumably at the mess. No one was happy with Wilby and Ellie. He came back into the main room, and Lan could hear the sound of the vacuum pump move to a higher pitch as the housekeeper began to run the hose over the carpet. From where Lan stood, he could see the carpet fibers stand on end in response to the floor being heavily charged. The skin on his ankles tingled.

"They're taking the elevator," came Tessa's voice.

Through a small crack at the edge of the door, Lan watched the housekeeper stop vacuuming, make the bed, and resume. The housekeeper was a teenage human male who shook his head from side to side with the beat of music Lan couldn't hear, presumably coming from an implant. His mushroom-style hair must have been caked with fixer; not one strand was dislodged by his dancing. Thanks to his gyrations, the wide, positively charged suction tool on the end of the hose covered some sections of the floor thoroughly and some not at all. Lan began to feel more comfortable.

The housekeeper continued his solo performance for an unappreciative audience, moving nearer to the closet. Lan began to feel less comfortable.

"They're off the elevator," Tessa said. "On *your* level."

Lan gave up on being able to get out of the hotel before they returned. He retrieved his key to the room across the hall and held it ready while he considered alternatives.

The housekeeper worked his way sporadically toward the closet. Miraculously he stopped short of opening the door. From there he moved into the bathroom.

"They're going into the hotel." Tessa's voice was anything but that of a dispassionate associate.

Lan stepped out of the closet, facing into the room, prepared to start walking toward the housekeeper the instant he was noticed, but fortunately the housekeeper currently faced the shower. Lan walked quickly backward. He reached the open hallway door without being noticed, feigned nonchalance, and turned to open the door across the hall.

His peripheral vision caught no activity in the hallway in the direction of the entrance as he entered the room. He closed the door behind him and let out a long sigh. No more than fifteen seconds after he started watching through the door viewer, Wilby and Ellie returned.

"I'm all right," Lan said quietly, even though the door should have been good enough sound insulation that he could use his normal voice.

Tessa's "Whew!" was made to sound almost comical by the compression circuits, but it still managed to sound heartfelt.

"I'll give you an update in a few minutes," Lan said, turning away from the door viewer. From his kit he retrieved a repeater cylinder no bigger than a writing stylus and with a half-twist turned it on. By lying on his back next to the bed, he was able to stick it under the very center of the bed.

Still lying down, Lan said, "I've just turned on a transmitter that should be strong enough to get voice over to you. Do you hear anything from the computer?"

After a pause, Tessa said, "Yes. It sounds like Wilby's voice. He's asking how soon their room will be ready. And the speech is normal, not like these chirper things."

"The snoops I just put in are chirpers, too, but the computer delays all the audio for several seconds so it can splice the pieces together." Lan got up and peered through the door viewer. Across the hall the door was still open.

A couple of minutes passed and the housekeeper came out and the door shut. If he had been embarrassed at being seen performing, he gave no indication.

Lan said, "Tell me as soon as you're sure they won't be opening the door for a minute or two."

"Now. Wilby's in the bathroom and Ellie is talking to him through the door."

Lan ducked his head, pulled open the door, and strolled down the deserted hall. The dancing room-cleaner would just have to make his next performance to an empty house.

"There," Lan said. "Now the video is delayed, too, so it should be in sync with the audio. Don't you enjoy home videos?"

"About how many laws do you suppose you've broken today?" Tessa asked. She sat on the bed, watching the screen.

"Percentage-wise? Or numerical count?"

Tessa didn't look amused.

"None, actually. Sarratonga is fairly loose about things like that."

"Even breaking into people's hotel rooms?"

"Actually, I didn't break in. And I didn't steal any-thing. I think they do have a law against theft, but I would have broken it if the Kalamati had been in the room. Still, that would have been more a matter of retrieving stolen property than stealing. Sarratonga doesn't have any laws about searching and retrieving."

Ellie's voice suddenly sounded over the speaker, and on the screen she rose from her chair. "Let's turn the news on. The story's got to reach here soon."

Wilby said, "You're wasting your time. Tonight's about

the fastest it can make it. Let's go out and have a good time and forget about everything until we can do something about it."

"Forget about it? Maybe I could if things had gone according to plan, but—"

"They went closely enough. No one on Arangorta is going to believe those idiots aren't guilty. And the courts there move so slowly that by the time they start to have doubts, we'll be different people, with enough money that a good lawyer can get Rento out of there in no time. If anyone got loose and followed us, we would have seen them by now. And even if they did follow us, there's no way they can get to our lockbox."

Ellie's voice carried more emotion than she'd ever displayed. "Well, I don't like it. You got that? He's my son."

"I know you're worried. But Rento is going to be fine. Think of how rich we're going to be, and think about how happy the kid will be living in luxury for the rest of his life. He'll forgive you. Trust me."

Ellie ignored his assurances and turned on the wall-screen. Conversation stopped, and Ellie sat back down.

Lan settled back into his own chair for the wait. After fifteen minutes, he let his eyes close but he kept listening.

"This is pretty exciting work," Tessa said. "Aren't you kind of afraid you'll burn yourself out?" She was smiling.

Lan opened his eyes. Tessa still sat cross-legged on the bed.

"Would you actually rather it was exciting all the time? Usually, excitement is proportional to risk."

Tessa drew in a breath without replying.

The silence grew longer until Lan said softly, "My profession is the only thing I've ever lied about."

Tessa looked up. "I don't doubt that. I understand now that you can't just tell people what you are."

"I'm sorry, too, that I handled things the way I did. I never meant to hurt you."

Tessa nodded. "I know that, too. And thanks."

On the screen, Wilby and Ellie looked at their own screen.

Tessa said, "How did you get into the business, anyway?"

"I was recruited. In my final year at school, we all took the standard series of tests. About a month later, I was invited to interview for a company that seemed to be fairly diversified because they had lots of different positions open. They also had a reputation for being picky, because no one knew anyone who had ever gotten an offer from them. While I was there, the interviewer put me through several more tests without me realizing exactly what they were testing for.

"Later on I found I tested high in loyalty and responsibility. And I tested low in looking like a conventional peace officer and in having active attachments."

"You mean like having a wife and a family?"

"Right. Please don't hate me for what I am. I couldn't stand that."

"I'm trying to understand. I really am. I know I react more strongly to violence than some people do."

"For what it's worth, I take no pride in that aspect of my job. I do like the knowledge that I can defend myself in most situations, but I don't encourage fights, and I feel like I've failed when I have to resort to that way out of a problem."

"I'm sure that's true, but why is force ever necessary? If no one were violent, the universe could be heaven."

"I feel the same way, but the basic problem is that if one person is violent, all people have to be violent. If whoever starts using violence takes whatever he wants and no one stands up to him, no one is really free except the violent person. What's worse? Living life as a tolerant victim, knowing what's within your grasp, but unable to reach for it, or becoming violent when it's necessary to defend your freedom?''

"I used to think I knew. I guess I'll have to think some more.'' Tessa was silent for a long moment before she jogged closer to the first subject. "In college, did you date much?''

"Some. I guess I just never found anyone I couldn't live without.'' Lan came close to adding, "None of them was enough like you.''

Before Tessa could respond, Lan noticed motion on the video display. Ellie rose from her chair and conceded Wilby's point that the news of the theft hadn't arrived yet. Wilby announced his intention of taking a shower before they went out to dinner.

"Good,'' Lan said.

"Why is that good?''

"I hate to spoil the surprise. I hope you'll see the answer in a couple of minutes.''

Wilby left their screen. Moments later the sound of running water joined the newscast audio. Lan adjusted the volume from the snoop in the bathroom, and the water sounds were mixed with bumping noises as the newscast grew fainter. The next sound was that of a shower door sliding open until it gently hit the stops. The sound of the shower water hitting the floor shifted and Lan could imagine Wilby putting his hands under the water flow to satisfy himself that the temperature matched the readout.

An instant later came a loud, resounding crash and a cry of pain. About the same time Wilby's moans were audible, Ellie said from the other room, "What happened? Are you all right?''

Wilby moaned again as Ellie knocked on the bathroom door.

Lan turned to Tessa. "The shower floor was unexpectedly *very* slippery.'' Tessa looked puzzled.

Ellie opened the bathroom door. Wilby moaned again,

and Ellie said, "Oh, my God. Are you all right?" She vanished from view of the camera.

Obviously in pain, Wilby said, "You ask the stupidest questions." He groaned. "Of course I'm not all right. Help me up, will you? And turn the water off."

"What happened? You're bleeding."

"I slipped, all right? It happens. I hit my head on that thing. Ooh."

Water in the shower stopped, then a different sound of water started, no doubt from the sink.

"Ouch! What are you doing?" Wilby cried.

"Don't be such a big baby. You're bleeding and we need to get it to stop. I'll spray some superclot on it, but I need to get it clean first."

Wilby's noises of irritation and pain continued until Ellie said, "There. Hold that tight against the back of your neck for a minute."

Lan decided the next noise was that of Ellie snapping open the emergency kit on the wall.

"All right. Take that off." A *whoosh* from a mist sprayer blocked the background noise. "Where did you slip anyway, on the shower floor?"

"Yeah."

A moment later. "Well, it seems all right. You should be more careful."

"Thank you very much," Wilby said, plainly irritated.

Tessa turned to Lan. "What did you do?"

"I applied a little mixture of ingredients to the shower floor. It doesn't feel slippery to the touch, but under pressure microscopic balls break open and release a superslip compound. By now, the water should have washed the whole mess down the drain and whatever was left on his feet should have evaporated."

Ellie asked, "What happened to your hand?"

"Oh, I guess I banged it on the door, trying to grab something to keep from falling."

"That really helped, huh?" Now that Wilby was obviously recovering, Ellie's concern seemed to be changing to match Wilby's irritation. "I guess we'd better get you to a clinic just in case."

Wilby grumbled.

"Oh, come on. It won't hurt. In fact, you'll probably feel better."

Finally Wilby gave in. As Ellie waited in the main room and Wilby got dressed again, Tessa said, "They seem a little more like business partners than lovers."

Lan turned from the screen. "Yes, they do. And with luck that may go on for a while. I stuck some phellotankum where its fumes will stay in the air there."

"And what does that do?"

"It has a tendency to make people cranky."

# 27

## PLAYING PRANKS

TESSA LOOKED INCREDULOUSLY at Lan. "You put some drug in their room that will make Wilby and Ellie irritable?"

"Yes. Actually, though, I'm not sure it was necessary. They probably haven't had enough exposure for it to be affecting them yet. They may just be naturals."

On the screen, Wilby and Ellie left the hotel room. Lan widened the viewing angle to include the entrance, and moments later Wilby and Ellie came out to the walkway and turned left. Wilby looked a little unsteady.

"You sure this is really necessary?" Wilby asked, his voice muffled.

"Good," Lan said. "He's changed to clothes with a snoop stuck inside."

Ellie's voice was fainter but understandable. "It's your head. You want to be wealthier than you ever dreamed of and be sick the whole time? Besides, you shouldn't be the one complaining. Rento's the one who's going to be held up for a while, and this is your fault after all."

"My fault? How can it be my fault the floor was slick?"

"Wet floors are *always* slick. It's your fault for not being more careful."

"Hey, I'm the victim here. You don't need to keep piling it on. This could just as easily have happened to you."

"No, it couldn't. I'm always more careful than you."

Lan turned very slowly to Tessa and gave her an extraordinarily large grin. "Sounds like a dare to me."

Tessa shook her head and rolled her eyes. But she grinned, too.

"It's not my fault," Wilby said. "Besides, not everything bad that happens is because of me. When that Farlon woman and her friends showed up on Arangorta that wasn't my fault."

"All right, all right. You've just had some bad luck."

"What do you mean 'me?' Them showing up there was bad luck for both of us."

"You're right. *We've* had a little bad luck. But you're all right. Everything's going to be fine."

"It had better be. If anything goes wrong with Ferelto I'm going—"

"Quiet," Ellie whispered urgently, and Lan pressed a panel to index the name.

On the screen moments later, Wilby and Ellie passed a trio of Knooters shuffling the other direction, their hands almost dragging on the walkway.

"We're outside," Ellie said after they had passed. "Try to use a little restraint."

Wilby looked around. "What are the odds that someone is listening to us? They'd have to be on the other side of the gorge, and at that range they'd probably need a dish the size of a planet. Besides, no one who knows anything about us realizes we're here. There's no way we can even *be* here."

Ellie said, "It's unlikely. But a few months ago you probably would have said all this would seem unlikely."

"All right. I just want to hear the news, wait a few hours, arrange a transaction, get paid, and get out of here. Is that vague enough for you? Who's going to know, even if they could hear us?"

"Only someone who would bother to spy. You can talk in code, but if people know enough to be listening, they probably know enough to break the code."

"But no one—" Wilby started.

"Here's the turn."

They rounded the corner toward the elevator.

Tessa turned to Lan. "He must have been talking about a telemike or something. He must not know about the things you bought—the snoops."

"He may know about them, but also knows they're expensive enough that few people use them casually. I'm going to have some expense account explaining to do."

The ambient background noise picked up by the snoop gradually faded to nothing. Tessa glanced at Lan. "Why can't we hear anything?"

"The snoops aren't strong enough to go through much more than one wall. While they're in the hotel room, we have a booster nearby, but when they leave the room, we'll have to make do with just hearing while they're outside. Unless I go over and try to get close enough to hear. And that's got its own risks. If they frequent some place we want to hear them from, I can install another booster."

Lan adjusted the camera to sequence through views aligned on the elevator column. So far he saw no indication that Wilby and Ellie had exited. "If they're in a room with a large window, we might be able to hear what they're saying, but farther inside we don't have much choice."

"Who's this Ferelto?"

"No idea yet. I'll have to start on that pretty soon, though. Seems likely to be the potential buyer, so if we can make whoever it is nervous, maybe we can slow things down until more help gets here." Lan watched the screen for signs of the pair.

"There they are," Tessa said finally. "Near the top of the screen."

Voices began coming through again. The level the pair was on now was much more crowded than the hotel level. Wilby and Ellie were not talking, but as Wilby passed people, the speaker produced meaningless snippets of conversations. Lan reestablished Wilby and Ellie as the motion to track, and the camera resumed its automatic pan.

They neared the Hillside Clinic where a short line had formed, visible through the half-open doorway. Leaning against the counter inside was a man with his back to the camera. Three people behind him formed an irregular waiting line. Wilby stepped into line behind a woman with her back to the camera and who was dressed in a very tight-fitting malachite-green outfit. Ellie fell in behind Wilby, leaving the woman in green partly visible. She looked back at the newcomers, revealing a pretty face and an unimpressed expression, and turned back.

"I've got an idea," Lan said suddenly. "Let's see how well this laser works." He flipped the video display into real time, and turned on the UV-spotting laser-sighting crosshairs. He set the primary laser for a single, short, low-power pulse, and centered the cross-hairs on the wall above Wilby's head. He fired the laser. The display confirmed that the laser had fired, but no visible damage showed on the wall.

"Oh no," Tessa said, as Lan proceeded to line up the cross hairs on the one malachite-green buttock visible on the screen. The image rippled over the contours and came to rest. "Don't tell me—"

"All right," Lan said. "I won't tell you."

Lan pressed the trigger. Instantly, the woman's hand showed in the display and began to massage the area that had been under the cross-hairs. She turned toward Wilby. The sound lagged because the chirpers didn't keep up with the live video, and a moment later, the sound of a woman clearing her throat came over the speaker.

So far Wilby was oblivious. The line moved forward at that moment, and people shifted into positions that still managed to leave some green buttock exposed. Wilby faced sideways, one hand falling near the greenery. Lan lined up the cross hairs and pressed the trigger again.

The reaction was much more satisfying this time. The woman whirled angrily to face the unaware Wilby and slapped him hard. Wilby, obviously surprised and unapologetic, turned to face her. His expression was lost, but there was a good chance it was irritated, because an instant later a malachite-green knee smashed upward into Wilby's groin. The sound of the slap arrived just as Wilby bent double, and a moment later came his gasp of pain. The woman stomped away, apparently deciding whatever medical problem had brought her there could be dealt with later or elsewhere.

Lan turned to Tessa and innocently said, "It's a dirty job—"

Tessa kept her eyes on the screen, not entirely successfully suppressing a smile. "But someone's got to do it. And you love your work."

On the screen, Wilby was on his knees, moaning. Ellie was asking what he had done to prompt the action from the woman who was already off the screen.

Tessa said, "The woman. You might have—" She choked back a laugh and regained her composure. "You might have hurt her."

"This power level is set really low. If Wilby had pinched her hard she would have been hurt more. And besides, we need to get Wilby and Ellie thinking the world is out to get them. Unfocused paranoia. If they start to think one person is behind this all, then we lose."

"What's going on?" Ellie asked. She sounded more irritated than sympathetic. Apparently she suspected the obvious explanation for what might have happened.

Wilby moaned again.

"Did you touch her?"

Wilby looked dazed, unsure whether to clutch at his most recent injury, hold his hurt neck, or respond to Ellie. Most of the people in the line ahead had turned to see what all the excitement was about.

"I *said*, did you touch that woman?" Obviously Ellie had her own opinion already.

"I don't think so," Wilby finally said. He should have been more definite.

"You don't think so? What kind of an answer is that?" Ellie was oblivious to the nearby audience.

Wilby struggled to his feet. He glanced toward the people in the line ahead, then looked back at Ellie. He massaged the back of his neck. "I said I don't think so. If I did, it was an accident, all right?"

Ellie crossed her arms against her chest and stared him down. The people in the line ahead gradually turned around to face the front again.

Wilby gave her a little-boy look. "I'm innocent, all right?"

In response, Ellie feinted a knee kick.

Wilby gasped. Reflexes doubled him over, and he clutched his latest injury. "Don't *do* that. If I touched her, it was an accident." His voice was still a little squeaky.

Ellie turned away from him and said nothing.

The line moved forward again. A moment later, another woman stepped into line behind Ellie. She was a short redhead, wearing a brown business coat and brown pants. Wilby glanced back at the woman, and Ellie glanced at Wilby. She must have glared a don't-even-think-about-it message, because Wilby spread both palms and instantly looked away.

Wilby and Ellie exchanged no more words before they reached the front of the line. A male voice attached to a body off screen asked for a short description of Wilby's ailment, and shortly Wilby went one direction while Ellie presumably sat down in a waiting room somewhere. Both audio and visual contact were temporarily lost.

Tessa shook her head. "I don't know. I'm still having trouble with all of this. You think you'll really be able to convince them they're having a streak of bad luck?"

"It's genuine. They really do have bad luck."

"No, they don't. You caused both of the things that have happened to Wilby."

"They said it themselves. They had the bad luck to have us find out about their plans. They had the bad luck to have someone escape and follow them. If Parke and Carrie had been the two to escape, they would have done their best to do what we're trying to do for them. It's Wilby and Ellie's bad luck that it was you and me who escaped, because I'm probably better equipped to deal with this. Unless Parke lied to me about *his* job, too. So Wilby and Ellie have the bad luck to have me on their trail."

"I certainly agree with that much. They chose the wrong person to pick on. What kind of work do you actually do? Normally that is."

"A little bit of everything. I've done anti-terrorist work. I can pretty easily pass for a reporter or an assistant, so I look unthreatening. Sometimes I work as a decoy or a target in a high-crime area. I've been a bodyguard for some people who didn't want it obvious—again I make a good assistant."

"Do you normally enjoy your work as much as you seem to now?"

Lan thought a moment. "No. I get a strong sense of accomplishment, satisfaction. But I have to admit I'm getting more pleasure from this case than most."

"Because these two took advantage of you personally and it's revenge time?"

"No. Because I'm with you."

Tessa actually blushed. "I'm glad I'm here, too."

Lan really hated to get back to work, but they couldn't afford to lose their advantage. "We've got a few minutes. Let's see what we can find out about Ferelto." Lan had no intention of letting Wilby and Ellie pass the Kalamati to anyone, but the more he knew, the better.

"From here?"

"Right." Lan left the clinic entrance showing while he connected the computer to the central facility on Sarratonga. He entered a password. On the computer screen, a message said, "Hello."

"I need to ask you to look the other way for a minute," Lan said.

Tessa obliged.

Without being prompted, Lan entered a different password. From there, three questions came up. After answering each one, another short message came up on the screen: "Level one is ready."

Lan told Tessa she could look again. "We're connected to a local database that should have information on known criminals."

"If they're known, why are they at large?"

" 'Known' can be in the 'statement of fact' category rather than the 'provable in court' category. Or they can be back on the street after having served time." Lan entered the name "Ferelto."

A woman's picture came up on the screen underneath the legend "Jasmine Ferelto." Ferelto had wide-set, lava-black eyes that a holo-star would envy. Smooth, ageless cheeks showed small dimples. Only the mouth seemed at odds with the rest of the picture. Lips slightly pressed together seemed to show a trace of impatience. Her hair was deep red, well past copper and nearly ruby. Narrow eyebrows looked more blonde than red.

Next to the picture was a column of text, with a few cross-indexed words highlighted. The summary at the top said, "Self-proclaimed 'trader.' Deals publicly in rare art, especially early Menzoan frozen paintings. Firmly believed to also handle illegal transactions. Two alleged criminals, on separate occasions, have permanently dropped from sight during suspected dealings with her."

A larger block of text below the picture expanded on her background, past home worlds, associates, and included several hyperlinks to additional material. When Lan had finished the summary page and saw that Tessa had also, he flipped to the section on associates. Two smaller faces filled the area where Ferelto's picture had been. The pairing was a disturbing testimony to interspecies rapport. Despite the fact that one face was human and one face was Wark, both were male, both were smiling in a way that didn't really suggest humor, and both managed to generate the feeling that between them they had heard as many last words as an emergency medic did.

The screen window displaying the clinic doorway showed more people in line, and a few leaving, but still no sign of Wilby or Ellie.

Silently Lan flipped through the rest of the available information about Jasmine Ferelto.

"What do the 'two' symbols indicate?" Tessa asked.

"Another layer of protection. You can get to the information under them only if you've got two agents simultaneously using the terminal, or if your rank is higher than mine. For now, we'll just have to make do with what we've got. But it's obvious from what we've seen here that we've got to keep Wilby and Ellie from connecting with her. The Kalamati could vanish in a black hole along with the two of them. As soon as they get the Kalamati out of storage, I'll be there to retrieve it." Lan stared at the screen for a moment, lost in thought.

They heard Wilby and Ellie before they saw them reappear in the video. Lan enlarged the primary camera view to cover most of the screen.

". . . did she say?" Ellie asked.

"I just . . . to be careful and take it easy."

"More careful than you were while we were waiting in line?"

"Don't start on that again." Wilby walked out the clinic door with Ellie at his side. "I told you that wasn't my fault."

"It just happened, huh?"

They turned along the walkway and walked in the direction of the elevator. They traveled a moment in silence, then Wilby said suddenly, "You don't think—nah, it's stupid."

"Think what?"

"It's nothing."

"Think what? Come on, you made me curious."

"I just thought about that superstition, the one, you know, where we were last. The superstition about bad luck coming to anyone who, ah, takes something that's not his. Something important."

Ellie glanced at him sideways while they walked. "You know," she said slowly, "when you're right, you're right. That really *is* stupid."

# 28

## EAT AND RUN

"THEY'RE MAKING ME hungry," Tessa said, watching the display screen. She paced back and forth on one side of the bed.

"Me, too," Lan said.

Wilby and Ellie had decided to eat dinner at an open-air walkway restaurant. Although they had ordered ordinary dinners, the choices sounded extraordinarily delicious. An array of round tables with red and white awnings spread across the walkway and required that passers-by walk right next to the guard rail or against the restaurant wall on the inside of the path. A restaurant employee holding high a very overloaded tray walked quickly past Wilby and Ellie's table.

"How can you stand all this waiting and watching?" Tessa asked.

"It's tolerable. And it's one way of getting to know the suspects better."

"I think I know those two as well as I ever care to. I need to eat or do something."

On the screen, Wilby and Ellie bickered about how

long it would be before the news of the theft reached Sarratonga. Another busser came by with a huge load of dishes and glasses.

Lan said, "You could go out and eat dinner and come—"

"Wait! Wait!" Tessa said. "That busser. Did you notice him?"

"Sure."

"You saw the tray he was carrying, and the way he carried it?"

"Yes."

"You're looking for another accident, right? One for Ellie this time?"

"Yes."

"How good a shot are you with a moving target?"

Lan's lips curved up. "You're suggesting we poke the busser and make him drop a tray?"

"If you can do it. You might be able to get him in the ticklish part of the underarm."

"You know what? I like it."

Tessa dimpled at the praise, obviously uncomfortable with it. Lan wondered if even Tessa had her breaking point, a point at which she finally wouldn't take any more and would resort to doing whatever was required to keep from being a victim.

On the screen, a waiter brought Wilby and Ellie their dinners. Lan pulled the view wide enough to see that several tables were still in need of cleaning. Apparently a large group had just recently finished their meal.

Lan made sure the laser was set for no more power than he had used earlier. He aimed and in a second the spotting cross-hairs showed up on the awning over Ellie's head. With the screen split into two views, one close enough to aim with, and one wide enough to see who was going to enter the field of view, Lan lowered his aim until it was at the level he guessed would be about right. Fortunately, that left the cross-hairs on another reflective table awning.

"The first time will be a dry run," Lan said. "I want to make sure I can see the cross-hairs against that green uniform, and make sure the height is about right."

Tessa stopped her pacing and stood close to the screen. Moments later the busser, a lanky man with hair dyed to match the uniform, made his way past Ellie's chair again. The cross-hairs were almost even with the man's blue-and-white checkered neckerchief. Lan lowered the laser just a hair.

"This is great," Tessa said, her voice more energetic than it had been all day. "He turns to go through that aisle right when he passes near Ellie. If you get him right then, the timing couldn't be better."

Lan turned to face her, and he smiled. Tessa smiled back and for an instant she seemed to be the Tessa of ten years ago.

"You know," Lan said. "We used to have some pretty good times together."

Tessa's smile diminished a tiny bit as her expression became more serious. "Yes, we did. God, I missed you."

Lan nodded, unable to speak. He reached out and touched her hand. Tessa turned her hand and clasped his silently. Moments later, he had to consciously break the spell and turn back to the screen. They waited silently, as Wilby and Ellie talked about how good the food was, and the waiter came back for another load.

"Here he comes," Tessa said.

Lan nodded, his gaze locked on the close-up view, the waiter moving through the field of his peripheral vision. Closer, closer, closer, *there!* Lan fired.

As soon as he was sure he had hit his target, Lan flipped the video into delayed mode so it would match with the audio.

The busser's image froze on the screen for a few seconds, then he lurched. The height of the tray dropped suddenly, but he managed to hang onto it. It was no longer exactly level, though. Liquid sloshed onto the waiter's arm, and he tried to steady the platter. He tipped it forward and plates began to slide away from him. He tried to correct in the opposite direction, but it was too late. The center of gravity of the jumble of plates, glasses, and utensils had already shifted too far forward. The whole mess slid down the tilted tray and cascaded over Ellie's head.

A large, partly full pitcher of water hit Ellie on the back of the head. The water sloshed out and drenched the entire back of her outfit. Remains of meals left on plates slid just past her head and splattered onto the table, mixing in with the meals they had just received, knocking over glasses, and showering both Wilby and Ellie with a mess of water and leftover food. Ellie screamed. Wilby yelled.

Ellie backed her chair away from the table to get out from under the water still sloshing over the edge. She started to get to her feet, and she slipped. She caught the chair with her elbow, and must have hit her funny bone just about the time she landed on her bottom in a mess of water and noodles. She screamed even louder and clutched her elbow. Wilby got up and rushed around the table to help her, slipped but caught himself at the expense of plunging one hand into the mess of utensils on the table. He yelped in pain. The waiter stood petrified.

Wilby reached Ellie and tried to help her up. As he did, he grabbed the elbow she had fallen on and she shrieked again.

In the next few seconds, more hotel staff started toward the disturbance, and Wilby satisfied himself that Ellie would survive. Wilby turned toward the busser who was apparently just then reaching the point where he could speak.

"I'm *terribly* sorry, sir. I don't know—"

Wilby didn't let him finish. "You moron! *Look* what you did."

"Sir, I'm—"

Wilby stepped forward and hit the busser in the face. He followed the blow with a punch to the man's midsection. The busser crumpled to the floor, and Wilby started to move closer when a huge hand came in from out of the frame and clamped onto Wilby's shoulder.

Lan expanded the view as Wilby swung to meet the new arrival, who also wore the uniform of a busser, and who wore a blue-and-white checked neckerchief that matched the one on the downed busser. The main difference was that the new arrival might have weighed twice what his friend weighed.

"This idiot—" Wilby started, but he was interrupted, too.

Still holding Wilby's shoulder with one hand, the busser smashed a massive fist into Wilby's stomach. The breath went out of Wilby instantly, and he was still looking like a fish opening his mouth and not breathing, the busser hit him again. And again. Lan cringed in empathy.

The busser released Wilby's shoulder and pushed him toward Ellie. Wilby crumpled limply to the food-strewn floor next to Ellie, looking as if he didn't have a rigid bone in his body. She sat there dazed, just staring blankly at him.

The muscular busser picked up his friend, slung one of his friend's arms over his shoulder, and put a hand around the man's waist. Together they walked slowly away from the disaster area. The view would have made a good scene in a war chronicle, and lacked only a few sporadic fires to be complete.

For another long moment the other bussers and bystanders looked on in silent surprise, then a couple of bussers started to move, helping Wilby and Ellie to clean chairs, and beginning to clear away the enormous mess. Wilby and Ellie sat down and stayed put. Ellie closed her eyes and rocked back and forth on the chair in a tiny arc. Wilby clutched his ribcage and just stared.

Lan caught Tessa's gaze. "You do good work."

Tessa looked almost as shocked as Wilby. "I had no idea so much would happen."

"Wilby may be one of those people who contribute to their own bad luck."

"I guess with you, me, and Ellie contributing, he'll probably have enough to last him until retirement. However soon that might be."

As Wilby and Ellie sat motionless, the restaurant manager approached them and offered Wilby a chit good for a free dinner. Wilby took it into his hands, looked up at the proprietor, and tore the chit into tiny pieces.

"More bad luck," Lan said.

Wilby got up, took Ellie's hand, and walked her away from the people still cleaning up the damage. He said, "I think we'd better go back to the clinic."

Ellie took a deep breath and felt the back of her head. "I think I'm all right."

Wilby inspected his hand. "That's good. But I meant for me. I've got a bunch of cuts. And I might have a busted rib."

Ellie said nothing as they walked another twenty meters. Occasionally the snoop picked up the sound of a squishing shoe.

"Now what do you think about a curse?" Wilby asked finally.

Ellie snapped her head around and shot him a piercing glance before she winced from the pain. A couple of noodles shook loose from her hair. "I don't want to even hear about it."

Just as Wilby and Ellie reached the door to the clinic, the same woman in green they had encountered there earlier started out the door. Wilby backed away as fast as he could, holding his hands up, palms forward. He backed up so fast, he ran his head into the door frame.

As Wilby moaned and held his head, Ellie said, "You idiot."

The woman whisked by him without touching him. She didn't look any happier with him than Ellie did. She raised one eyebrow at Ellie's appearance, then she was gone.

The gesture was apparently enough to remind Ellie what she looked like. She listlessly picked at stuff in her hair, and another glob of pasta fell to the ground. "I can't stay here looking like this," she said to Wilby.

"It won't take long." He coughed, then grimaced.

"No."

"Come on. You need to be looked at, too." Wilby gripped her arm to tug her inside, and he grabbed the injured arm again.

"Ow! You're hurting—"

"Sorry. Sorry." Wilby got his arm around her and pushed her through the doorway.

The last thing that came over the speaker before Wilby and Ellie vanished inside the clinic was, "You idiot."

After a few moments of silence, Lan looked at Tessa, finally able to say what he'd wanted to earlier. "I really missed you, too."

Tessa looked up. "I'm glad you're here. I was angry with you, with myself, when you left. But I never stopped missing you."

"We're a couple of stubborn people, aren't we?" Lan almost told her about how lonely it could be sometimes, always playing roles, never letting anyone get close enough to catch sight of the truth.

"I think that would be fair to say."

Lan sat still, feeling better than he had in too long a time. Even better than when the woman in green had kneed Wilby.

                           *    *    *

"Wilby and Ellie are coming out," Tessa said.

Lan nodded and looked at the screen.

As Wilby came out of the clinic, he looked like a child's pretend patient. He still had a patch on the back of his head. In addition, he had a patch on one hand, and he wore a stiff, form-fitting, sleeveless flak jacket, the kind designed to prevent further damage to patients with rib injuries. He now limped noticeably. Ellie looked much like she had before, except that she had cleaned out the worst of the mess in her hair. Instead of looking like they were sitting on top of a fortune, they could have been the "after" pictures in a malpractice story.

"I'm still hungry," Wilby said.

"So am I, but I've had enough excitement for today. I'm going back to the hotel."

Wilby just shook his head and acquiesced.

"So, do we get to sleep while they do?" Tessa asked.

Wilby and Ellie had gone directly back to their hotel and were getting ready for bed. They had set the window into the privacy state, so the audio from the snoops accompanied a screen view of an uninteresting flat gray rectangle.

"You can," Lan said, "but I've got to do some work. I'm guessing the news will arrive sometime tonight. I want to do what I can to make things more difficult just in case Wilby and Ellie try to make a deal with Jasmine Ferelto. If we can keep the accident pressure going, and keep Ferelto from making a deal, maybe we can get Wilby and Ellie to turn over the Kalamati to the authorities, such as they are, without me even having to intervene. I'm hoping Wilby and Ellie decide that having the portal system available will mean they can easily find another way to get rich."

"What can I do?"

"You can set the receiver to record the news if anything comes on about the Kalamati or Arangorta, and you can get some rest. I'll call you if I need help."

Tessa didn't look pleased. "And you know how to look for her from the information in the file?"

"Right?"

"And you'll be all right?"

"Nothing is guaranteed. But I'm careful and I'm good." Lan grinned. "I'll be fine."

"You make sure of it."

Lan stepped into the S&S Sailing Club Bar. He threaded his way through the crowd, avoiding direct eye contact with everyone, observing all he could as he moved. He saw nothing of Jasmine Ferelto, but in a corner booth he saw one of the faces from the file information.

Lan continued to move toward the bar, ostensibly paying the most attention to the tablecloths made from nautical windsails and squares of impossibly thin, glossy polymers hanging from the ceiling, fluttering with every word anyone in the room spoke. Hanging in one corner was a hologram of a sea-sailboat. Hanging in another corner was the spiderweb holo of a solarsailer.

Light in the room came from an overhead hologram, backed up with some carefully constructed indirect lights and optics, giving the illusion of a sky containing a half dozen bright stars close enough to be called suns, and an expanse of more distant stars filling in the blackness between. Every wall held a flat, moving display of an ocean surface with waves energetic enough to have whitecaps. The floor displayed a sandy beach marred by scuff marks and litter.

No one seemed to be paying Lan undue attention, so he approached the bar and took an empty seat next to a pair of older men engaged in their own private conversation. When the bartender looked at him, Lan ordered a "Beached Sailor" on her recommendation. When it arrived, Lan gave her a tip large enough to make it obvious he wasn't cheap and small enough to avoid arousing too much interest. Moments later, he dropped a coin on the floor, then retrieved it as his other hand stuck a repeater under the lip of the bar.

Lan sipped his drink slowly, then swiveled enough to keep watch on the Wark face familiar from the file.

The Wark male, sitting with two men and a Wark female, had recolored his ears since the picture Lan had seen was taken. In the picture they had been a translucent amber, and now they were opaque and light blue. The eyes were the same as before, the lids forming a rectangle around each one. A swirl marked the craggy, gray flesh above his right eye.

Lan was on his second drink, cautious about moving too fast, when one of the two men at the Wark's table got up and moved to a game area to one side of the room. The holoboxing game was already in use by a Feldner whose reflexes were very quick. The game was set for a speed so high that an unaugmented human would wear out in a minute. Lan had to watch carefully to even see the feints, they were performed so quickly. During the crescendos of motion, the Feldner seemed to have four arms.

The man from the Wark's table activated the knife-throw game. He picked up a knife from the dispenser, and a moment later the target screen showed a display of several dangerous looking opponents. The man's knife found the armed opponent almost instantly. Had the target screen been composed of a hard surface like dense wood, the hilt probably would have twanged for an instant. In the everflow putty, the blade just sank halfway to the hilt.

As Lan watched, undecided what the best approach would be, someone turned up the volume on the news screen behind the bar. On the screen was a picture of what looked vaguely like a shoe, except that most shoes didn't look like they'd been dipped in a sticky fluid filled with impossibly large gemstones. Between the largest of the stones adhering to the surface was a barnacle growth of smaller stones. Below the picture was a text insert saying, "Kalamati stolen." The Kalamati's ugliness fit right in with their decor.

Lan got up from the bar and did his best drunken lurch toward the man at the knife-throw game. He had his plan.

# 29

## BAR TRICKS

LAN LURCHED THROUGH the crowd in the S&S Sailing Club Bar. He held onto his second drink, barely managing to keep its contents from slopping over the rim as he moved toward the man at the knife-throw game.

He passed the man as he threw another knife and stopped at the game adjacent, darts. He fumbled with a coin and inserted it. As he threw the first dart, missing the board entirely, he heard the newscast voice say how valuable the stolen artifact was. He wobbled a little as he readied his next shot. Beside him, the man had stopped throwing knives and was paying attention to the news.

Lan glanced back at the screen, let a lopsided grin come across his lips, and he laughed. He turned back to the dart board. The display said, "000."

His next dart caught the edge of the board and he grinned broadly. The newscaster started talking about how unlikely a crime this was, and Lan turned back toward the screen and laughed again. Softly he mumbled, "Not *that* old trick? Bunch of vacuum-heads."

Lan's peripheral vision told him he had caught his neighbor's attention. Lan proceeded to throw another dart, and laugh, softer this time. The dart caught the very edge of the target.

"What say?" the man next to him asked, matching the slang.

Lan tilted his head toward the man, then looked around the room, as if he had just heard a voice from nowhere. He turned back to the dart board and grinned his idiot grin.

"Hey, you," the guy asked again. "What say?"

This time Lan looked directly at the man. "Didn't say nothin'." His next dart missed the board completely.

"You say 'that old trick.' What mean?"

Lan frowned at the man, looked back at the screen, and turned back to the dart board. "They're so stupid. No new tricks."

"What that mean?" The man moved closer, took Lan by the shoulders, and looked down into his eyes.

Lan blinked hard several times. "I know you?"

"Yeah. I'm friend. What you mean about a trick?"

Lan blinked some more, and twisted his lips into a grimace. "They pulled that same scammy on—on Rasmussen I think. Or Ramdelk. One of them two. They wanted to trapper—to trapper someone. They did."

"What they do?"

"Buy me a drink, huh?" Lan blinked again, and scratched his nose.

"Sure, sure." The man punched in an order at a nearby panel. "Coming. So, what they do?"

"Big news. The Kalamati stolen—as if anyone could ever entrance there. Some forcers tricked a guy into buying it. But he never received it. He went to forcer retirement." Lan laughed. "What a stupid. Some undercoforcers had it. So said. They went to deal. Undercoforcer had this hospital shirt on—like injured. Was wired. The stupid delivered the good stuff. And got nabbed up."

Lan glanced back at the screen. The announcer was talking about how the natives believed in a curse that accompanied the Kalamati, and how the curse would never leave the thieves until the Kalamati was back in the hands of its true owners. "Curse!" Lan laughed. "Curse. Curse for stupid who bought. Probably still in arrest home."

"When this happen?"

"While back. Where's drink?"

The drink arrived on the tray of a man from behind the bar.

Lan gulped it down.

"When this happen?" the man asked again.

Lan rocked on his feet and rubbed his forehead. "While back. Just said." He frowned.

"Wait minute. I want to get a friend."

Lan squinted. "I know you?"

"Yeah, we through that."

"I think not friend. I think don't talk more. Goodbye." Lan took a gamble and spun around. He lurched off through the crowd. The man follow him for a few steps, but Lan stopped suddenly and stared hard at him, then turned back toward the door. Lan zigzagged for the front door and reached it without being stopped.

In a doorway nook close by, he whipped off the checkered shirt he had on, reversed it so the solid brown surface showed, and put it back on. He matted his hair back down from the stand-up style, and moved off along the walkway, steady on his feet and moving briskly.

"That was terrific," Tessa's voice chirped in his ear. "I've got you in sight and no one seems to be following you. Wilby and Ellie are still in their room."

Lan gave a noncommittal grunt.

In a nearby hotel room, Lan discarded the clothes he'd been wearing, showered to get rid of any snoops that might have been stuck in his hair, and put on clothes that should be snoop-free. The white powder that had temporarily transformed the appearance of his hair rinsed away, too. Rather than put the old clothes down the disposal, he left them in the room with an entertainment channel turned on, for the benefit of any snoops stuck to the clothes.

Back out on the walkway, Lan scratched his nose to conceal the motion of his lips, and he said softly, "Thanks for the backup. I'm coming home." The lights of North Face shone more brightly than before.

"You didn't want to talk earlier in case they had put a snoop on you?"

"You got it."

"They're still sleeping," Tessa said when Lan got back.

"Good. We should probably do the same. We may not get another convenient chance soon." Lan felt more tired than he had in months.

"Fine by me. You know, you seem very good at your job." Tessa got up from the chair in front of the screen, and she stretched.

"When you do only one thing, you do tend to get better at it." Lan took in a deep breath as Tessa stretched. The fabric across her breasts tightened, and Lan was suddenly aware of her sexuality, as if he'd deliberately forced himself to ignore it as long as he could. She looked sleepy, and Lan wondered how it would feel to wake up beside her.

"You don't do only one thing. Acting drunk is a whole lot different from breaking into a hotel room, for instance."

"True. I just mean my job is all I do. It's my life."

Tessa nodded and gave him a long pensive look before she said, "Wake me up if anything starts happening, all right?"

"Sure." Lan changed some settings on the computer. "This thing should wake me up if they start talking again."

As Tessa moved past Lan toward the door to her room, Lan put his hand against her waist and stopped her. She turned to him and suddenly they were almost nose to nose. Lan leaned forward and kissed her gently on the lips.

Tessa's hand reached the back of Lan's neck and pulled his lips tighter against hers.

Lan was breathless when they finally pulled apart. Tessa's eyes gazed directly into his. "I missed you so much," he said.

"Not as much as I missed you."

Lan brushed his fingertips along her cheek, and she reached up and pressed his hand harder against her flesh.

She smiled. "I'm glad we're together again, even if we're spying and causing accidents." She pulled Lan's hand from her cheek and kissed it. "But I've got to get some sleep before I die of fatigue."

Lan nodded, knowing it was true for him, too.

Tessa turned and walked tiredly into her room and shut the door.

"What's happened so far?" Tessa asked. She rubbed her eyes and blinked at the screen.

"Nothing really," Lan said. "But they're up, so it shouldn't be long. They know the news reached here, and they're about to play it back."

As Lan spoke, the flat gray of Wilby and Ellie's polarized window cleared, and the camera could see into the room again. Ellie moved away from the edge of the window. She was still moving tentatively after her dinner mishap the night before.

"All right," came Wilby's voice. "Here it is."

The same newscast Lan had heard the night before began, but this time he could devote more of his attention to it.

Wilby and Ellie sat in chairs visible from the window, their entertainment screen out of view. When the newscaster talked about how difficult and unexpected the theft had been, they both laughed. When the subject turned to the "curse," they quit laughing.

"What did I tell you?" Wilby asked.

"Just shut up," Ellie said.

"No doubt many scoffers will have a difficult time taking this seriously," the newscaster continued, "but the Kalamati has quite a history of bad luck for people who tried to keep it away from its normal resting place on the Altar of Henkalt. About four hundred years ago, Peneg Farhorn, the then leader of Arangorta, put the Kalamati in his personal residence. Within days, his health began to fail. No more than a week later, he was so ill he had to have his subordinates return the Kalamati to its proper place. His health improved for another week or two, but he never regained enough strength to return to power, and his daughter came into power.

"As recently as eighty-five years ago, a group of five influential members of the house of Gammenket plotted to hold the Kalamati for ransom. They succeeded in buying the assistance of two guards. Within two weeks, three of the seven were dead. One fell down a stairway and hit his head on a step. Another slipped while bathing and drowned. The third committed suicide in apparent remorse."

"They did a terrific job with the newscast," Lan said.

"The Arangorta council has strongly urged the captives to tell where the Kalamati has been taken. So far, they have refused, claiming they do not know. None of them have suffered any tragedies clearly attributed to the curse, but Arangorta council members have expressed the opinion that if they don't divulge any information soon, that bad luck will be forced on them.''

Wilby got up and cut the sound as the recorded segment finished. He moved very stiffly. He glared as he turned toward Ellie, his whole body moving like a solid object with feet, but he didn't say anything.

"What?" she snapped.

"I didn't say a word," Wilby said innocently.

"Well, why are you looking at me like that?"

"How would you like me to look at you?"

"From a greater distance."

"What's *that* supposed to mean?" Wilby demanded.

"I'm sorry. I'm getting a little testy, I guess. I just don't buy all this curse stuff. We had a bad day; that's all. Don't try to make anything more of it."

"So you think our luck has changed?"

"I don't think luck had anything to do with it. It's just a statistical thing. You have so many accidents in your life. Some of them get spread out; some come in bunches."

"So today should be back to normal?" Wilby asked.

"Sure. In fact today should be a lot better than normal. We contact Ferelto. And by tomorrow, things should be terrific."

"If you say so."

"I say so. We'll have so much money that we could pay a thousand legal people to get Rento out of there. They can't hold him when there's no evidence."

Lan stood up as Wilby shuffled out of sight of the camera. "This is great. Wilby's so suggestible that if an unassisted accident happens today, he'll blame it on the curse. He might even be nervous and suggestible enough that he'll help cause his own accidents."

"But Ellie doesn't believe in the curse."

"That's all right. The tension between Wilby and Ellie because of that is just as good."

The sound of a crash from the bathroom interrupted the conversation. When Wilby finally spoke, his voice held the flat, overly calm tone that suppressed anger generates, and he asked one of the most universally useless questions: "Why did you leave all this stuff on the sink?"

"I think you'd better let me do the talking," Ellie said. "We can't afford to have anything go wrong."

Wilby and Ellie were on the walkway, moving from the elevator toward the S&S Sailing Club Bar. Ellie wore a tight skirt and looked less businesslike than she had at dinner. Wilby turned stiffly toward Ellie, and his irritated look intensified, but he said nothing.

"You heard me?" Ellie asked.

"You said you were going to do all the talking," Wilby said.

"Good," Lan said, watching the image. "Having Wilby so angry that he's acting childishly has got to help." Both Wilby and Ellie seemed to be wearing clothes with snoops, because both voices were clear.

Tessa looked up from where she sat on the floor with her legs crossed. "I'm getting the feeling that this Jasmine Ferelto may outclass these two."

"No doubt about it. We just need to make sure that Ferelto stays out of it. With some luck, she'll send Wilby and Ellie away without even listening to them. That might be enough to push them over the edge. After all, they don't know the portal is sealed, so they probably think they can use it again for getting money some other way."

The pair on the screen reached the entrance to the bar.

"You ready for this?" Ellie asked.

Wilby turned stiffly toward her. "Is being poor boring?"

They went inside. Sound from their snoops died, and Lan switched to the repeater inside the bar. Instantly a multitude of voices and noises erupted from the speaker. Lan touched a panel that cut out everything but voice frequencies and switched on a signal processing module that would separate voices by their characteristic voice patterns as well as reproducing them all at the same volume. Finally he told it to boost the gain on any voices that matched Wilby's or Ellie's.

Wilby and Ellie must have had a picture of Jasmine Ferelto, because they didn't need to ask directions of anyone. While the motionless door to the bar filled most of the screen, Lan and Tessa heard Ellie say, "You're Jasmine Ferelto, right? We'd like to talk to you a minute if we could."

What must have been Jasmine's voice responded after a long pause. "All right. Have a seat." Lan managed to tag her voice pattern and have it boosted, too.

Tessa asked, "What if Ferelto thinks they're trying to set her up and kills them?"

"Then I suppose after some delay we could get the right people to find their lockbox and open it up. I'd rather have it sooner than later, though."

Ellie's voice said, "We understand you do some trading in artwork."

Ferelto said, "Occasionally. If I find something that appeals to me quite a lot."

"Could we talk alone?"

"This is as alone as I get, darling. I'm a people person. I like having my friends around. Do you not want to talk after all?"

Ellie hesitated. "All right. We have a piece of what some people might call art, but we're not really art connoisseurs, so we're looking for someone to take it off our hands."

"And just what kind of art would that be?" Ferelto asked, too innocently.

"It was mentioned in the news yesterday."

"Why don't you just tell me? I don't pay much attention to current events."

Wilby spoke up. "Oh, just tell her."

Ellie said, as though she didn't want to speak the name out loud, "It's kind of a sculpture, with quite a few gemstones." She lowered her voice. "It's the Kalamati."

"The Kalamati? Now how about that," Ferelto exclaimed. "You know you're the third person today to offer me that?"

"I don't understand," Ellie said.

"I mean after that news last night, probably every con man on this planet is offering the Kalamati to anyone stupid enough to believe."

"But we really do have it."

Ferelto must have looked closely at them, because Wilby protested. "Not *with* us. Not right now. But we really do have it."

Ferelto said, "This is all very interesting, but even if you actually had it, I wouldn't be interested."

"Not interested?" Ellie said. "We're willing to take less than ten percent of its actual worth."

"But if I paid you for a stolen object that would make me a criminal, too," Ferelto said, as if explaining to a school child.

"But you—" Wilby started.

"I need to confer with my colleague for a moment," Ellie said. "Would you excuse us?"

As Ferelto responded and Ellie and Wilby moved away, Tessa said, "It just occurred to me. Wilby and Ellie might be naive enough not to know about snoops, or to think there's no way anyone could be interested in the two of them right now, but what about Ferelto? Wouldn't she know about snoops? And wouldn't she have a detector?"

Lan shook his head. "She almost certainly knows about snoops. But they transmit such a short blast, they're really difficult to detect unless you know the exact frequency.

What she can do is jam them. Since we're hearing all this, the implication is that she doesn't think the conversation is threatening.''

Ellie's voice was breathier than before. "She doesn't think we have it. That's the problem."

"Well, that's just great. We're sure not going to bring it here," Wilby said. "This is just more bad luck. I think we should get that thing out of the lockbox and hand it over to the authorities—tell them we found it. And then get out of here and come up with a new plan. Too much is going wrong. And if that curse is genuine, we'll be regretting this as long as we manage to live."

"You idiot. There is no curse. Can't you understand that? Come on."

A moment later came the sound of Ellie saying, "Sorry about the delay. We just wanted to discuss a few details." She hesitated. "Look. I know the problem here is that you don't believe us. You don't believe we really have it. But we do, and we can prove it. Give me something, anything you pick. Within six hours we'll be back with a hologram of the Kalamati and whatever you give us. Together."

"Computers can do a lot of things," Ferelto said.

"Then we won't just give you a still frame. We'll give you one minute's worth, and we'll be in it. If you figure a computer can do that as realistically as what we bring you, we'll go away."

# 30

## TELLING STORIES

◆ "I STILL THINK we should just give it up," Wilby said. He and Ellie walked along the walkway after having stopped in an electronics store. They both carried packages of new purchases. "Too much has gone wrong. And I wouldn't trust that woman as far as I could carry her on Heavyhaven."

"Listen to him, Ellie," Lan implored.

Ellie listened, but she didn't give Wilby the answer he wanted. "We've come too far with this one to just give up and start on something else. I agree we need to watch ourselves with her, but we can do this if we're careful. She stands to gain enough that what she pays us will seem small to her, so she should be satisfied to deal straight. And what she pays us should set us up for years." Wind whipped her hair back as she spoke.

"Oh, no," Tessa said. "If the Kalamati gets out of their hands, we may never get it back."

"True," Lan said. "We just need to make sure it doesn't. If they make plans to meet Ferelto, we should find out when they plan to take the Kalamati from the lockbox, and I can intercept them."

"Shouldn't your backup person be here by now?"

"Could be any time."

On the screen, Wilby and Ellie were approaching a sign saying, "Mountainside Vaults and Storage." Two men came out the door that stood propped open.

"Oh, just a minute," Lan said. He hurriedly enlarged the display of the door and found the thin cord at the top holding it open. He centered the cross-hairs and increased the laser output. Satisfied that the aim was accurate and stable, he flipped back to the frame with Wilby and Ellie fast approaching. Closer, closer. At the instant his instinct told him, he punched on the laser.

In the display, Wilby had politely offered Ellie the chance to enter first. As she turned her head toward him to acknowledge the gesture, the cord holding the door open snapped, and as it started to swing slowly close, Ellie walked right into the edge of the door. Choreography could not have improved the timing. One hand swung to the right side of the door, the other hand on the opposite side, and Ellie collided soundly, connecting at nose and forehead.

As this happened, a passing woman diverted Wilby's attention just long enough for him to miss what was happening directly in front of him. Wilby's packages rammed into Ellie's back and knocked her into the door a second time.

Seconds later, the snoop transmitted the sound of Ellie's scream, and Lan switched the video back to delayed mode to match the audio.

Ellie dropped her packages. Her nose was bleeding already, blood dripping down her chin and onto her blouse. "What the hell happened?" she cried.

By now Wilby, who was unhurt, realized part of what happened. "The wind blew the door shut. Are you all right?"

"What a *stupid* question!"

"Who are you calling stupid? I told you this wouldn't stop. But no. You wouldn't believe. You—"

With both of her hands clutched to her nose, Ellie twisted toward Wilby, ignored or forgot about her tight skirt, and kneed Wilby where he'd already had more than enough pain the day before. Saddled with packages, stiff in his hospital coat, he dodged too slowly to avoid the blow. He cried out and dropped his packages, then crumpled to the ground, moaning.

Under other circumstances, Ellie's knee might not have reached him, or she might have lost her balance when her leg reached the limit the skirt put on her motion, but one of the seams Lan had treated gave way instantly and Ellie's skirt had opened at the side, all the way from hem to waist.

"What a destructive relationship," Lan said.

At first Ellie didn't seem to notice that, besides her bleeding nose and bruised forehead, her skirt was no longer doing its job. The skirt flapped wide as she squatted, sorting through her dropped possessions, presumably searching for something to stanch the blood.

"You're a mean man, Lan Dillion," Tessa said softly.

At almost the same time that Ellie realized a small crowd was gathering, she noticed her bare legs. Her double-take from the crowd and back to her exposed thighs made her surprise and irritation unmistakable. She quit holding the tissue to her nose and tried to wrap her skirt back into place. Blood dripped onto the skirt.

Wilby's moans had quieted by now, but he was still no help to Ellie because he seemed only half-conscious, and his hands were occupied.

"That sure is one persistent woman," Tessa said.

On the screen, Wilby and Ellie were again approaching Mountainside Vaults and Storage. Wilby still carried a snoop somewhere on him, but Ellie had changed clothes and no longer carried one. For the moment, that was no problem. Not only were neither Ellie nor Wilby saying much; what was said was usually said so angrily that the voice carried well to Wilby's snoop.

"Do me a favor and don't distract me while I'm going through the door this time, all right?" Ellie said.

"That's right," Wilby snapped. "Blame your own clumsiness on me."

"I'm *not* clumsy."

"Maybe not normally, but right now, because the curse—"

Ellie couldn't have stopped more suddenly if she had run into a wall. "Don't say one more idiotic word about that. You hear me? That's insane."

"You know I'm getting a little tired of you calling me an idiot."

Lan said, "Good, Wilby. Stick up for your rights."

Ellie started walking again, leaving Wilby behind. "Well, then stop acting like an idiot."

Tessa said, "I'm beginning to think that if they do manage to get away with this, one of them is going to kill the other one before very long."

The two on the screen didn't say one more word during their walk. At Mountainside Vaults and Storage, Ellie made a production of carefully opening the door and walking calmly through. The door looked undamaged.

"What's the plan?" Tessa asked, when the sound from the snoop on Wilby had faded to nothing.

"If we're lucky, Ferelto won't believe their hologram isn't rigged. That might be the final blow that will convince them to give up the Kalamati. If we're less lucky, Ferelto will arrange to meet them somewhere. Then I wait near the lockbox place and take the Kalamati away from Wilby and Ellie when they get it out. More risk than I like, but still better than trying to get it away from Ferelto."

"And if we're not lucky at all?"

"Then we improvise."

The motionless, closed door to the bar filled the central screen window. Sounds of the conversation came over the speaker. This time, Jasmine Ferelto was harder to hear, but Wilby and Ellie's voices were reasonably plain.

"Very interesting," Ferelto said. "It would appear that you really do have the object you spoke about earlier. I have to confess that from your appearance I would not have guessed that you would be actually able to secure such a find. I hate to think my judgment is so unreliable. Is there some explanation that accounts for how you managed such a feat?"

"I don't think I like—" Wilby started.

Ellie cut in. "We don't like to reveal our methods. Our current concern is to find a new home for this piece of property."

Ferelto said, "I understand. The news reports say this object carries with it a curse. From the looks of you two, the curse seems to be working."

Ellie said, "There is no such thing. We've just had a little bad luck in the last couple of days."

"I'm sure you must be right. But the stories I've heard certainly make me uncomfortable."

"Stories?" Wilby asked.

"Oh, you would not be interested in them. I'm sure they're just exaggerations."

Tessa raised her eyebrows and looked questioningly at Lan. "Ferelto seems to be helping us. Is everybody on our side?

"I doubt it," Lan said. "But she heard the news, too, and she can see that Wilby and Ellie have had a rough time lately. If she can strengthen the worry about a curse, then they'll be that much more agreeable about letting go of the Kalamati, and the price may drop."

Ferelto continued. "In any case, I certainly understand why you would want to be rid of the object. In your position, I would, too. I, however, am only interested in seeing such an item up close. I certainly wouldn't be a potential buyer if that's what you're looking for."

"But that's not what we understood," Ellie said.

Tessa glanced at Lan again.

Lan said, "Ferelto must be saying that for benefit of any snoops. I would guess that any second now she'll start jamming the snoops so she can speak freely."

Lan was right. Ten seconds passed, then another ten, all in silence. "Ferelto will be making arrangements for the purchase now. The odds are such that she figures, rightly, no one would risk such an expensive method to entrap someone at her level. Still, I'm a little surprised she believed the hologram so quickly, without having anyone run some tests on it to see if they can find any evidence of tampering or computer generation."

"Maybe she doesn't actually intend to follow through with anything they talk about so it doesn't matter."

"Certainly possible. But I'd feel better if I knew for sure." Lan rose and stretched. "At least it looks like things are starting to move." From a shelf in the closet, he pulled down one of his purchases and opened the box.

"What's that?" Tessa asked.

"Insurance." He withdrew a pressure pack and looped it over his belt. Around one wrist he snapped a firm band. He uncoiled a spool of thin hose, screwed it into the pressure pack, and threaded it up the back of his shirt and through a sleeve. As he connected the free end of the tubing to a small needle-gun and then snapped the gun into the band mount, he said, "I don't think I'll have much trouble with Wilby and Ellie, but it can't hurt to be sure." The gun pressure and load indicators both read full.

"Why hasn't any help arrived?"

"It should be just a question of time now. With luck,

it'll arrive before Wilby and Ellie go back to the lockbox."
Lan fitted the small sites into narrow grooves in the side of
the needler. He took off the safety, extended a pointed
finger toward the base of the wall, and squeezed the body
of the gun. An almost imperceptible sigh from the gun
and a faint click from the wall said the unit was functioning. Lan shoved a few magazines of needles into one
pocket and turned the safety back on.

Tessa was watching him silently. Her eyes were large.

"If it makes you feel any better, these are just tranquilizers."


"They sure have been quiet lately," Tessa said as she
watched the screen.

She stood behind Lan, near enough that if he leaned
back slightly, his head would touch her breasts. The temp-
tation to do just that was almost overwhelming, but he
tried to keep his mind on the task. As long as their friends
were depending on them, he couldn't let up.

Wilby and Ellie had left the bar, stopped at a different
storage company twenty levels down and six elevators east,
and now appeared to be going back to their hotel room.
Wilby carried a box slightly larger than Lan guessed the
Kalamati would be. Besides a couple of brief exchanges,
one of which implied that they planned to get the
Kalamati and meet Ferelto in about six hours, they had
spoken less than two introverts on an arranged date.

"Sure is a pleasant change, huh?" Lan said. "It's hard
to see why they've stayed together so long."

"Well, they haven't had you to play—what's the reverse
of matchmaker?"

"You're telling me I can be a strain on a relationship?"

Tessa just looked at him. Idly she picked up the writing
stylus from the table next to her.

As Lan looked back at the screen, he heard the stylus
snap in two.

\* \* \*

"I don't like this," Lan said. "I still can't figure out what that stop at the other storage company was for. They obviously had something saved from a previous trip, or they made two stops right after they got here this time."

"They're bound to say something about it eventually," Tessa said.

Wilby and Ellie were back in their hotel room, saying nothing. Occasional random sounds came over the speaker.

"I'm sure you're right, but it still makes me nervous not to know things. I'm getting impatient. I'd like to go ever there right now and wait near the lockbox, but that runs the risk of making people suspicious."

Tessa looked at the time. "Just about three more hours."

A phone chirp sounded. Lan looked instantly at the instrument on the nearby table; its light was off. The chirp came again, and he realized the sound was coming from the room they were monitoring.

"Hello," Ellie said.

The voice on the other end was buried in the noise.

"Yes," she said, tentatively, and then asked, "Right now? But you said—" She listened for a moment.

Lan rose to his feet and moved quickly to the door.

"But we're—" Ellie started. Seconds later she said, "All right, all right. We'll be there as soon as we can."

Tessa said, "What's happening?" She looked from the screen to Lan.

"Ferelto must have accelerated the schedule. I don't know why. But I've got to run. You've seen the console operations. Can you track them, and keep me up on where they are?"

Tessa nodded. She looked worried, but she didn't say anything.

Lan fingered the chirper in his ear, pulled open the

door, and left. He ran down the hall, hoping no one would suddenly step into his path. He bounded down the stairs, feeling the pressure pack bounce lightly on his waist. "Can you hear me?" he asked as he reached the landing and followed the turn.

He was halfway through the lobby, slowed to a jog, when Tessa's voice in his ear said, "Yes. Clearly."

Lan pushed rapidly onto the walkway outside, the cool air helping to dissipate the sudden heat he felt. He started running to the left, toward the nearest elevators. As he moved through a empty section of walkway, he said softly, "Start a running commentary on anything they say and do. If I clear my throat a couple of times, that means to hold off until I say OK."

Lan attracted more interest than he wanted as he ran along the walkway, but it couldn't be helped. If the Kalamati got into Ferelto's hands, the odds of getting it back would suddenly have too many zeros in front of the other numbers. She must have accelerated the plan so she could keep Wilby and Ellie off balance. Lan wished even more that he knew the meeting location. If he knew that, he could move to intercept rather than merely to catch up.

Several levels above, a cable car was slowly approaching the face of the cliff. Lan picked up speed.

In his ear, Tessa said, "They're leaving the hotel room now."

A man stepped out of a door ahead, his back to Lan. He held the door open for someone with him, and he backed onto the walkway, continuing a conversation. The man must have reacted to the look on his companion's face, because just as Lan neared him the man whirled to see what was behind him, and Lan had to dodge past his outstretched arms.

Lan reached the elevator corridor and took the turn fast as Tessa said, "They're leaving the hotel. They still have the box."

Ahead at the elevator bank were six people. As Lan got close enough to see that both the up request and the down request were lit, he wondered if he'd have to lie to get space on the next one going up, or if he'd have to resort to throwing someone off. Within moments the decision was past. An up elevator and a down elevator arrived almost simultaneously. Five of the group were going down, so Lan had to compete with only one woman for a space going up. The people already in the car squeezed back toward the rear as much as they could, but that wasn't far. Lan had to squeeze in right next to the woman.

The woman was about Lan's age and wearing a frilly, full dress that would have taken up the space another person would have if Lan hadn't had to press so close. Her black hair smelled faintly of perfume or soap. A small, blue genetic earring grew on the earlobe closest to Lan, and her eyelashes bore tracery shadow so regular that it was probably grown, too.

She avoided his gaze, but she could hardly avoid him since he was so close. After a couple of floors had passed, mercifully without any stops, she said, "Where I come from, people have to be engaged to get this close." From the back of the car came a snicker.

Lan watched the elevation counter approach the level the cable car docked at. The indicator reached the right level, and the gravity lessened as the car pulled to a stop. Just before Lan got off, he said, "So, was it good for you, too?"

He didn't wait for her reaction, but instead ran for the walkway. He nearly knocked over a pair of Warrows wearing plaid capes as he spun around the corner and spotted the motionless cable car. In his ear, Tessa said, "Sounds like you just love them and leave them. By the way, Wilby and Ellie just reached an elevator."

Lan reached the cable car and moved quickly through the open door. He reached a seat with a good view of the far side, and sat down, breathing hard.

If his timing had been perfect, the car would have departed at that instant. Instead, it sat there as Lan grew more and more impatient. He looked across the chasm, but he couldn't decide which elevator bank Wilby and Ellie had just reached.

A voice from over his shoulder, not Tessa's voice, said, "Kind of in a hit-and-zip mood today?" The woman from the elevator took a seat across from Lan.

Lan couldn't decide if she was irritated, or was teasing. "You know how it is. So many elevators, so little time."

The woman smiled and nodded.

In Lan's ear, Tessa said, "They're off the elevator, on the lockbox level. You remember them, right? I hope I'm not intruding."

Two more passengers entered the cable car and took seats.

"Seriously," the woman said. "Is there anything wrong?"

Lan hesitated. "No, not really. Well, yes there is. A couple of friends of mine have gotten themselves in trouble. So I'm trying to help."

"What kind of trouble?"

"I hate to admit this, but they were shoplifting. Ellent's basically a compulsive, and Willer's not as watchful as he should be. They're at a stim shop somewhere down by that place that sells floaters. I can't think of the name."

"Hi Sky?"

"Yeah. Near there. Anyway, I'm trying to get over there before the badges show up to escort them someplace they don't want to be. Maybe I can explain it away again, and pay for the stuff Ellent tried to lift."

"That's terrible," the woman said.

Yes, Lan thought, I should have been able to do better than that.

# 31

## AMUSEMENT PARK

"GOOD LUCK WITH your friends," the woman with the eyelid tracery said. "I hope you get to them before any more damage is done."

"Thanks. Me, too," Lan said. Even though the cable car was approaching North Face, it seemed to be going even slower than it had while they were suspended over the middle of the chasm. Lights flicked on here and there on the canyon wall as dusk began to fall. Tessa's reports had indicated that Wilby and Ellie were almost at the lockbox establishment several levels below. If the levels weren't so tall, Lan might have considered jumping from one down to the next rather than using the elevator.

In Lan's ear, Tessa said, "They're getting near the lockbox place."

Finally the cable car slowed to a stop at the dock. Lan rose and stood by the door. As the faint whine from on top of the car died, Lan glanced at the woman again, and she gave him a thumbs-up sign. The doors spread open, and Lan was moving fast toward the nearest elevator bank.

"They're inside the lockbox place," Tessa said.

The first downward-traveling elevator was empty. Lan selected the level of the lockbox business, pressed the close-door button, and pretended not to see the man running for the door as it shut. To Tessa, he said, "I'm on my way down." In the privacy of the elevator, he double-checked his needle gun.

"They're still inside," came Tessa's reply.

The elevator pulled to a stop, and the doors opened, but it wasn't Lan's destination. A man wearing a blue shirt and red pants looked up and casually started toward the door as Lan pressed the close-door button again. The man's carefree expression passed through surprise on its way to irritation. The closed door cut off the view of any further transformation. As the elevator continued its interrupted descent, Lan heard the pounding on the door slowly grow fainter. The pounding had seemed awfully loud from someone who looked so leisurely. Lan's ears popped.

Just as the elevator door finally opened on the right level, Tessa's voice said, "They're leaving! They must have it with them! They're heading east, away from you."

A man in a hurry to get in stepped in front of Lan. Lan stepped aside and the man stepped aside at the same time. Lan reached out, grabbed the man's arms, and swung him aside. He ran.

From behind Lan came a voice calling him a rude name.

Lan skidded around the corner and onto the walkway. He just missed colliding with a woman carrying a large parcel. He ran along the outside edge of the walkway, near enough that his peripheral vision showed the tapering slivers of walkways below, but he couldn't see far enough ahead to see Wilby and Ellie. The walkway curved out and then back in with the contour of the chasm wall, and the pair must have been on the far side of the curve or obscured by the few people ahead on the path.

"I can see you now on the wide view," Tessa said. "You're gaining on them fast, but I don't know how long they plan to be on this level."

Lan found a small reserve of energy he hadn't been tapping and pumped his legs a little faster. He was doing well at avoiding occasional pedestrians, but a group of six forced him to slow down enough to navigate, and then he was running fast again.

"You're gaining. You're gaining. Oh, no! They went into an elevator entry."

Lan had come close enough that he had just caught a glimpse of a distant pair that seemed to be Wilby and Ellie, and they had just turned off the walkway. He was in good shape, but despite that, his breath was coming in ragged gasps now as he forced himself to keep up the pace. Two more surprised expressions flashed past. He managed to force out the words, "Tell me up or down as soon as you know."

"Will do."

Lan still had hopes of catching up to the pair as they waited for the next elevator, but the hopes faded with each step, as the elevator corridor seemed barely closer. He kept telling himself he could rest inside an elevator, and he kept going as daggers of pain slid between his ribs.

Lan flashed past Mountain Vaults and Storage and moments later reached the elevator corridor. He slowed to a fast walk, trying to breathe quietly through his mouth. He readied his gun and rounded the corner.

Twenty steps brought him to where he could see that Wilby and Ellie were no longer there. He pressed both the up and down requests. "Up or down, and what level?" he said.

"I don't know yet. I can't see them."

The elevator doors opened for an empty elevator going up. Lan stuck his foot in the door and looked at the time. The seconds turned into the kind of seconds he experienced when someone was dying.

Before Tessa could tell him which way to go, a man and a woman arrived. The man, a head taller than Lan, said, "Oh, thanks. I was afrai—" He stopped as he realized Lan wasn't exactly holding the door for them. "What's the problem?"

"A small emergency," Lan said. "A couple of doctors are on their way with a patient. They should be here any second."

The woman nodded politely, and so did the man, but then she whispered something to the man. The man's gaze moved from Lan and apparently settled on the pair of lit indicators.

Abruptly his face darkened and he frowned. "Say, buddy. What's going—"

At the same moment, Tessa's voice in Lan's ear said, "Down! They're way down! I'll get the level in a minute."

Even as Tessa's words reached Lan, the down chime rang.

"—on here?" The man asked. He released his grip on the woman's hand.

The down elevator doors began to open as Lan said, "All right. You can have this one." He took his foot out of the door to the up elevator and moved to board the down elevator. As he moved, the man got even angrier, because the up elevator door slid shut before he could reach it. For an instant, he stood transfixed, incredulous. Lan joined the other four people in the down elevator and pushed the close-door button.

Just before the doors came together, the man's hands grabbed them and began to pull them back apart. "Listen, buddy. You and I are going to have a talk."

Lan looked through the widening gap at the fury on the man's face, and he snapped his needler into his palm.

He squeezed off one needle into the man's chest. Time froze. The man slowly looked down at where he must have felt the pinprick. He looked back up at Lan, and squinted. He released his grip on the elevator doors. As the doors closed again, the man fell over backward.

Lan glanced at his elevator-mates, four young women with tourist t-shirts and hats. In unison, the women backed up against the rear wall and sent each other darting glances of worry.

"No cause for alarm," Lan said. "He'll be fine when he wakes up. He's been seeing my wife while we're here on vacation. He didn't like it when I sent a picture of them together to *his* wife."

The only reply was four slow, solemn nods. No one was going to disagree.

"They're almost at the bottom of the chasm," Tessa said. "Level four. And they're heading west."

As the elevator slowed for the next stop, Lan pushed the *four* indicator. The women edged closer to the corner opposite him. When the doors opened, a lone man stood right directly in front of the elevator. He would have entered immediately except the four women nearly knocked him down in their haste to get out. Lan had the feeling it wasn't even their stop.

The man peered around the corner, as though to see if anyone else was getting off, then he entered and pressed a floor indicator below Lan's. As the door closed, he glanced at Lan and shook his head.

Lan said, "I thought I heard one of them say something about being late for a time-management class."

The man glanced at Lan again, gave him an uncertain grin, then stared at the decreasing digits.

After a minute of silence, Tessa's voice said, "They're going into something called 'Fun Fun Fun.' It looks like it could be an arcade or amusement park. They're inside now. I've lost visual contact."

Lan watched the digits drop, and he swallowed to clear his ears again. Wilby and Ellie couldn't be stopping there to play or pass the time. As he reached that conclusion, Tessa said, "I can't hear them anymore. The only thing I heard was just after they entered. I think Ellie said, 'There. To the right.' "

When the elevator deposited Lan at the correct level, he moved quickly along the corridor out to the walkway. He couldn't afford to attract attention this close to what had to be the meeting point. If he could only get close enough to Wilby and Ellie, he could pick up the snoop's transmissions directly.

From the walkway, the overhead slice of darkening sky seemed much narrower than it had been from higher levels, more like a cobalt-blue river than sky. The other side of the chasm was so close that Lan could easily see faces on the people opposite, and a few bridges spanned the gap. Along the bottom of the chasm, the surface was covered with plazas and patios with frequent areas marked off for parachutists and hang gliders to land.

Strategically positioned, skyward-pointing, orange sensors formed a detection grid to warn pedestrians if an incoming flyer was on a course for a populated area. Lan had wondered if reactions would be fast enough to handle the case of an unopened chute, but few people who came to Sarratonga expected it to be risk free.

Lan approached the door to Fun Fun Fun. The entrance was a huge clown's face, the walkway an enormous tongue. Lan stepped onto the tongue, momentarily disconcerted by the spongy texture of the ramp, and walked up and into the mouth. "Here we go," he said under his breath.

He didn't have to stoop at all to get past the teeth. The tongue started to slope downward about the time that grinding noises sounded from all around Lan. As he walked partway into the throat, the sound of someone swallowing echoed loudly. A door opened in the back of the throat. Lan avoided thinking about what the exit might look like.

Beyond the door, Lan paid his admission and wandered into the busiest, largest, and noisiest room he'd been in on Sarratonga. People of several species filled the large, semicircular hall. Holos pointed the way to concessions and amusements. Six large archways led off the main chamber. Holos over them showed choices from "Games of Skill" to "Water Sports" and "Rare Wonders." On the far right, the holo said, "Fast Action and Rides." The arch next to it led to "Sexual and Sensuous."

Lan moved carefully through the crowd as the noise level rose to the point where people near each other almost had to shout to be heard. It struck him that they could all talk comfortably if they used a normal tone of voice, but as soon as one person raised a voice, others nearby had to do the same, and soon so many people had raised voices that only one alternative was left if you wanted to talk. Lucky thing that voices can only be so loud.

Lan kept his eyes open for Ferelto and her associates as he walked. All he saw was a group of boisterous, loud people with apparently nothing more than entertainment on their minds. He threaded through the mob, listening intently for audio from Wilby and Ellie. They must have been on the other side of too many walls.

The crowd was so loud now the noise was more like vibration than sound. People had to use body language to make their communications clear. A woman bumped into Lan, giggled, and moved back to her cluster of companions. For an instant, an awareness of loneliness displaced part of Lan's thoughts about Ferelto, and then he pushed the feeling aside.

The archway labeled "Fast Action" was less crowded than the main floor since it had moving slideways on both sides of the wide corridor and people would have to make an effort to stand in one place and block traffic. The surface led gently upward, not so fast that a slightly inebriated game-player would have trouble balancing. At intervals on both walls were doors surrounded with colorful motion holos showing what a great time you could have in each game. The returning slideway bore people glistening with sweat, breathing hard, leaning against one another. Wilby and Ellie were not among them.

The ramp slid past the door to something called "Death Raid," and a couple of people got off.

Lan scratched his nose to conceal the motion of his lips as he spoke. "I'm in the Fast Action corridor, still looking for them. Make sure you let me know if you see them or Ferelto leaving."

The slideway took Lan past the entrance to "Roller King" as Tessa's voice said, "Will do."

On the opposite side of the corridor was a large holo with misshapen stalactites and stalagmites forming the letters in "Cavern of Fear." Next to the entrance itself was a thin banner saying, "Closed for Repairs."

As Lan slid past the door, he heard Wilby's voice say, "Of course she's here somewhere." The voice had come through Lan's earpiece. Lan looked around slowly, and saw no sign of anyone familiar. The slideway carried him farther, and he heard nothing more.

"They must be in the Cavern of Fear game," he said softly. "It's closed down, and I heard Wilby's voice."

Lan stepped onto the path between the slideways, and then onto the slideway talking him back toward the closed entrance.

Tessa said, "Understood."

A short entrance corridor led to a closed door that didn't slide open as Lan approached. He looked for a handle and found nothing but a card slot on the wall. He pushed on the door, and pushed sideways with his fingertips, but the door was not going to open accidentally. Lan retreated, crossed to the far slideway, and continued up the corridor. Two games later, he found what he was looking for: a door marked "Employees Only."

He crossed to the door and found that it was locked solidly. The nearest game to it was "Pinnacle." Lan entered the short corridor, went through the open door, and stopped in front of an overweight man with a bulbous nose, a full red beard, and a pass card showing in his front pocket. Fortunately, Lan was the only person wanting in at that moment. Lan held a few coins in his hands, preparing to pay, and then he looked down the hall leading into the game and did a double-take. As the ticket-seller glanced where Lan was looking, Lan shifted position slightly and shot him.

As the rapid-acting tranquilizers started their work, the man had time for a slightly puzzled expression to come over his face before he slumped to one side. Lan steadied the man so he leaned into the corner, balanced on his stool. As Lan drew his hands back, one contained the pass card.

The slideway took Lan back to the employees-only door. He wasted half a minute changing directions on slideways until only a few people were in sight. With studied nonchalance, he slid the pass card through the grooves, pulled the door open when he heard the *click*, and walked through.

The lighting inside was harsh compared to the indirect lighting in the public area. Overhead naked lum panels gave Lan a shadow again. Narrow corridors led in three directions: straight ahead, left, and right. Lan took the left, taking him back toward Cavern of Fear. The walls still had their factory barcodes meant for the construction phase. A dull throbbing seemed to come from every direction. A distant, excited cry sounded, and occasional thuds came through the floor and walls.

After twenty steps, Lan followed a narrow stairway leading upward, edged with handrails. He slowed as his eyes came level with a higher floor, but he could see no one for the length of the next corridor section. Once on the new level, he walked quickly and quietly. He passed a closed door with the legend "Pinnacle, Flightpath maintenance. Danger." Below the bold letters was a you're-here map. Lan wondered how many new employees had been lost in the twisty maze of access passages before the signs had gone up.

Occasional side corridors at odd angles fed into the corridor Lan followed. He saw other signs indicating maintenance entries for Pinnacle, then Speedship, and finally reached one saying, "Cavern of Fear, Lagoon maintenance. Danger."

Almost at the same time, he heard Ellie's voice through his earpiece. "They *can't* have changed their minds." She sounded angry.

Lan examined the you're-here map. Ahead in the same corridor should be a branch corridor that led into the heart of the game area. He moved forward silently.

Wilby's voice said, "Would *you* be late for something this important?"

Lan said very softly, "No more transmissions unless it's vital. I can hear them now."

He reached the branch corridor and moved into it. After twenty meters it dead-ended at a wall-mounted ladder going up. At the top of the ladder, the corridor walls were no longer featureless. Access panels with numbered designators turned the walls into a patchwork grid. Lan had to stoop to get under a lowered section of the ceiling, and the corridor gradually curved to the right. A clear panel covered a body-sized, humming piece of equipment that could have been anything from a large holo projector to a target positioner. Winking green lights on the back of it indicated it was doing its assigned job successfully, whatever that was. The corridor continued to twist up and

down and through the maze of access panels and auto-
mated devices.

Lan was starting to worry that he had taken the wrong
path when Ellie's voice sounded, louder than before. She
said, "Time to key it in again."

"I know. I heard." Wilby sounded irritable.

In the silence after Wilby's words, still through the earpiece, Lan could hear what sounded like water crashing
into a pool. The high frequencies were absent, as though
the source of the noise was at a distance.

Ahead of him was another corridor junction, one way
with stairs leading upward and to the right, the other
down and to the left. The you're-here map needed four
layers to show all the surrounding features. Lan found a
waterfall in roughly the direction he was headed and a
large fountain back along the way he had come. He moved
down the stairs on the left, keeping in his mind a basic
map to the waterfall.

"All right," Wilby said. "We've got ten more minutes."

"Ten more minutes for what?" said a new voice.
Ferelto's voice.

# 32

## SURPRISE

◆ LAN MOVED QUIETLY along the corridor, looking for another you're-here map. Softly he said, "I'm patching in what I can hear from the snoop on Ellie." He spoke a couple of key phrases, and his earpiece softly beeped to acknowledge the commands.

As he followed a series of steps upward, he wondered why Ferelto hadn't started jamming transmissions if she was in voice range? Did she have some reason for trusting that Wilby and Ellie weren't entrapment personnel? If so, turning on a jammer to block supposedly nonexistent transmissions could just call attention to her.

As Lan thought the situation through, Wilby answered Ferelto's question. "Ten minutes for our protection."

Ellie cut in. "It's just a little insurance. We didn't want you thinking you and your friend could just take the Kalamati without giving us our cut."

"Is that right?" Ferelto asked. Her voice was softer than either Wilby's or Ellie's, and the waterfall noise was louder. From her companion mentioned by Ellie, Lan could hear nothing.

Lan reached a map at the point where the access corridor split once again. The corridor walls rattled, apparently due to a high volume of water flowing somewhere nearby.

"Yes," Ellie said. "The Kalamati is locked in this container. The container is armed, ready to explode. Unless my friend sends it commands from his transmitter every ten minutes, it will explode, taking the Kalamati with it. And it will take you longer than ten minutes to figure out how to open it. So if you try to get it without paying, you'll get nothing."

Ferelto said, "It sounds as if you've given this some thought."

Ellie said, "We have. Your assistant and I will take the container to a safe distance. While you and my friend watch, I will enter the combination, take out the Kalamati, and put your trade items back inside. If anything goes wrong, my friend immediately detonates the explosives in the container, and you lose the Kalamati, your assets, and your assistant. Obviously, my friend loses me and the Kalamati, but we think you wouldn't be here unless you wanted a successful transaction. When the trade has been made, we slowly separate. If you decide to try anything after the trade, you'll still lose the assets, because they'll be destroyed no more than ten minutes after something happens to us."

Lan took the passageway to his left, hoping he was correctly interpreting the map. The vibrations intensified, then started to diminish. He stopped in front of an access panel and unsnapped it. On the other side was a dimly lit cavern. Below him, running along the bottom of the cavern, was a pair of levitational tracks gleaming like strands of an enormous spider web. From the distance came the sound of crashing water. Lan replaced the cover and moved farther along the corridor as Ferelto said, "That sounds fair to me. May I suggest the bench over there as a comfortable place to work?"

Lan opened another access panel, just a hair. Below was another cavern, with a track running through it, also. He opened the door farther. In the darkness below, he could see rungs leading toward the floor. He snapped the panel latch into a position where it would stay unlocked, moved onto the ladder, and closed the access panel quietly behind him. Fortunately, most of the light that had escaped while the panel was open reached no farther than the nearby rock wall.

"All right," Ellie said.

Lan froze.

Ellie's voice had reached Lan's ears without benefit of the snoop, which a moment later echoed her words.

A trick of acoustics had bounced her voice to Lan, because the cavern he climbed down into showed no sign of her. He continued quietly downward, one rung at a time, wondering for a moment why the cavern felt strange. Then he realized the cavern shape was wrong somehow, an artificial construct patterned after limestone caves, cut and enlarged by underground rivers, rather than the volcanic, bubbly way Neverend had been formed.

A glance over his shoulder showed stalactites that felt more like cancerous growths than natural parts of an underground setting. The rungs set into the wall became more like small steps as the wall curved to meet the floor. Finally Lan was on the relatively level ground next to the tracks. He moved in the direction the sound had come from, in the direction he could hear the waterfall pounding. He quietly snapped his gun out into his palm and started walking lightly, as though the floor was a thin layer of mica rather than bedrock.

The levitational tracks sat atop antique railroad ties and cinders. Lan walked along the tracks, hoping no cars were currently running, glancing back occasionally so a silent car wouldn't overtake him while he listened to the conversation. The cavern was faintly lit by silvery streaks on the walls, probably meant to look like ore deposits. Lan wasn't sure if limestone and ore deposits went together. The top of the cavern was totally dark, probably flat black so it could be undecorated. The distant sound of moving water covered Lan's footfalls. Ahead the tracks banked and curved.

A group of a half-dozen stalactites ahead each had a matching stalagmite below it, and water dripped regularly from each stalactite tip. At least it looked like water. Lan's path took him close enough to that he was aware of hearing no sound accompanying the drips. A hand passed through the path found a hologram instead of water. The stalactites and stalagmites were physical models, but perfectly dry.

Lan crept around the curve to the point where the cavern opened onto an enormous chamber. To his left was the waterfall shown on the map. To the right of it was a medium-sized lake, fed by the waterfall, whose waters looked calm near the far shore. Masses of blue-green water plants floated in several spots. To the right of the lake were Wilby, Ellie, Ferelto, and one of Ferelto's helpers, a big guy with hands the size of boxing gloves. None of them seemed to be enjoying the beauty of the place.

Lan searched for a way he could get close enough for needle fire without being seen, and saw only one. A cavern mouth just past the group was, according to Lan's memory of the map, joined to the cavern just to his right by a twisting series of small artificial caves. The tracks should lead the way. He convinced himself it was just as well that he'd have to take the long way, since Ellie and Wilby's explosive meant he couldn't just grab the Kalamati right then. He'd have to knock everyone out after the exchange started. He ducked low behind a rock shelf and moved for the next cavern.

Just before he reached it, he took one more look at the group. Wilby and Ellie were sitting on a bench, facing the lake. Between them sat a large canister. Lan decided where he would have more backup people if he were Ferelto.

The first cave received a fair amount of light from the brighter chamber, but the next was dim. Lan moved quickly, cautiously. His eyes adjusted to the darker cave beyond, but he almost ran into a boulder. After that, he stuck closer to the tracks as they wound through the twisty path.

"No. Stay there," Ferelto said suddenly.

"That's not the plan," Wilby said. "I'm going over there. Your associate brings your trade items here. My partner will perform the trade with your man. Then my partner comes away with me and your partner goes away with you. Simple."

"Yes, simple. Too simple. Please stay where you are."

"No, that's not—" Wilby's voice filled with pain and surprise. "Hey! Tell him to put the weapon down. If you hurt us, you'll never get the Kalamati."

"That was merely a warning shot. I must ask that you stay exactly where you are. You will be paid for your efforts. I just believe you are asking too much."

"You agreed to the price already," Ellie said. "And we've explained the arrangements. You don't get the Kalamati unless we get our price."

"Sit down." Ferelto's voice lost all its social charm.

Apparently Wilby and Ellie complied.

"Now we wait," Ferelto said.

"For what?" Wilby asked.

"For you to open the canister, place the Kalamati on the bench, and walk away with the canister."

Lan suspected Wilby and Ellie were just now seeing the loophole in their plan. He kept up his pace, still moving quietly.

"We're going to do no such thing," Ellie said indignantly.

"We're going to wait here until you do exactly that. And my associate will shoot you if you try to leave."

"But if you shoot us, the Kalamati will be destroyed before you can get it out."

"True. But I'm not risking my trade, and I'm not risking my associate. I really have nothing to lose. You two, however, stand to lose your lives and the Kalamati. Wouldn't you rather just lose the Kalamati? I will pay you a quarter of what we discussed earlier."

"Of what we *agreed to* earlier," Ellie said icily.

"You're making a common mistake," Ferelto said. "Deals are conducted in the present, not the past."

"We're not interested," Ellie said.

"Let's talk about this." Wilby's voice was almost lost in the noise. Obviously he was directing his words just to Ellie. "This has been a disaster from the beginning. Let's just cut our losses and get out of here."

By Lan's estimate, he was nearly to his destination. He slowed down and started moving carefully from one shadow to the next. The cavern sounded unnatural to him. Instead of the sharper echoes he knew so well from Neverend, the fake-cave walls gave dull, building-like echoes.

Finally, Ellie said, "What reason do we have to trust you now? You haven't been too trustworthy so far."

"I don't expect you to trust me. I expect you to take the only option open to you that offers any hope of success."

Suddenly Ellie said, "That isn't the only option, though. We worried that you might be a little aggressive, so we planned for that. A heavily armed backup team will be on its way here in—" she must have looked at her watch "—five minutes. So we do this the way we agreed, or you—"

Ferelto laughed. "You two are so transparent. Do I look that incompetent to you? I've been in business for twenty years. That locket I gave you to photograph with the Kalamati has a transmitter in it, so I know every word you've said since then. And so I know you're alone. Very alone."

"You're lying. If that were true, you'd know we were telling the truth right now."

"I'm lying, am I? Go ahead, prove me wrong. Conceal it in your hand and tap it a few times. You pick the number."

Lan moved closer to the light coming from the lake area.

"Five," Ferelto said with satisfaction. "Now who's lying?"

"I'm telling you the truth," Ellie stubbornly insisted.

"And I disagree. I thought at first this was some inept scammy. But you two convinced me it was legitimate, if I may use that word. The only thing I'm surprised about is that a couple of people with your obvious lack of talent could steal something so valuable."

"Maybe you'd be—" Wilby started.

"Shut up," Ellie snapped.

In the silence, Lan heard the waterfall sound louder than before.

Ferelto said, "Before we go any farther, get rid of the weapon."

"What weapon?" Wilby asked.

"Oh, please. The pistol you have concealed at the small of your back."

Lan heard nothing for a moment, and then a short clatter sounded, apparently Wilby's pistol being discarded.

"It's time to open the canister," Ferelto said.

"Go fly," Ellie said.

"I really must insist."

"Now." Ferelto seemed to be speaking to her associate rather than to Ellie and Wilby.

"What was that?" Wilby said suddenly.

"A slow-acting tranquilizer. You have a few minutes of lucid thought left before you go to sleep for a while. Start unlocking the canister now, or you'll be too sleepy to do it. If you fall asleep before it's open, my associate will shoot your partner. Then she will have a few minutes. If she falls asleep before it's open, we will just walk away from here and leave you to your own device. As soon as you open it, I'll give you the trade."

"You can't be serious," Ellie said.

"What part do you doubt?"

"Let's just open the damn thing," Wilby said. "Let's get it over and let's get out of here."

"But we stand to get nothing."

"We stand to get worse than that. I'm starting to get woozy. She's not kidding around. I believe her."

"But we've come so far—"

"Give it to her! If she has it, at least she has no reason to kill us."

Lan crept closer, moving behind an artificial boulder. He was close enough to hear their voices directly, so he touched his earpiece and turned off the reception. From the darkness behind him came ultra-faint echoes from other nearby games.

Ellie finally reached a decision. "All right. All right. I'm opening the canister. I hope you're happy now."

"*I'm* happy," Ferelto said.

Lan finally got to a shadow from where he could see Ellie and Wilby. Ellie was fumbling with the top of the canister.

"Can't you hurry it up?" Wilby's speech was slightly slurred. He pushed at her arm.

She gave him a withering glance and kept at her job. A moment later the lid popped open. "All right," she said.

"Take it out. I want to see it." Ferelto's voice came from the right, out of Lan's view.

Slowly, gingerly, Ellie pulled the Kalamati out. It still

looked vaguely like a really flashy shoe, but the way Ellie's hands moved suggested that it was heavier than most shoes Lan had ever worn. Beside Ellie, Wilby slumped onto the bench and then fell to the ground.

"Bring it to me," Ferelto said.

Ellie looked undecided for a moment, but she rose and walked toward Ferelto.

"Stop there," Ferelto said. "Put it down."

Ellie stopped, just at the edge of the space Lan could see, and put it on the ground.

"Now back up to where your friend is."

Ellie obeyed. She looked beaten.

A moment later, Ferelto said, "Again," and Ellie suddenly clutched one arm.

"What did you do that for?" Ellie asked.

"I would just feel more comfortable with you going to sleep with your partner. When you wake up, you'll have your payment, and I will no longer be near."

"Sure," Ellie said.

"Believe what you want, but just stay there."

Before long, Ellie began to droop. And then she was out, too.

"This was almost too smooth," Ferelto said. Her voice had a slight vibration to it, as though she were walking as she spoke. "I like sure things, but this was almost too easy." She hesitated. "Kill them and conceal their bodies. You can call the rest of your team in."

Lan went cold. There could be someone behind him in this tunnel for all he knew. And if that someone got a summons to join Ferelto, the squeeze would be on. He had no time to figure out a better plan, so he made sure the needler was in his hand, and he bolted from his hiding place. As soon as he saw Ferelto and her associate, he began rapid-firing needles toward them.

As he ran, he heard the clatter of pellets spewing against the tunnel wall behind him. He had moved just in time. Ferelto and her associate wasted little time on surprise as they ducked for cover. Continuing to fire steadily in their direction, Lan passed the motionless forms of Wilby and Ellie. He zigged and zagged until he was close enough to snag the Kalamati, which thankfully was a manageable weight.

No other options. He ran ten more steps, firing the whole time, and launched himself into the lake. It seemed to Lan that he floated through the air for ten seconds before he splashed into the cool water. Underwater, the pounding sound of the nearby waterfall sounded more like a symphony of bass drums coming from all directions. The Kalamati helped pull him toward the bottom of the lake. He set it on the smooth bottom and pushed off toward the surface as fast as he could.

He was just in time. He broke through the surface, shook the water from his eyes, and pulled himself up just far enough to see over the edge of the retaining wall. Ferelto and her associate had come out from concealment and covered half the distance to the edge of the lake. A lanky guy with a black shirt was about even with them, coming from the direction of the cave Lan had vacated. Lan's needler was virtually silent, so he made a point of having his hand show as he fired several times. He heard startled cries and bodies suddenly reversing directions. He ducked behind the lake wall and dog-paddled sideways far enough that they would have to take a new aim. He waited several long seconds, and repeated his procedure.

Good. The three he knew about had all stayed behind protective cover. He ducked and moved again, this time waiting slightly longer. He kicked off his shoes as he took a series of deep breaths and rechecked his bearings. Off to his right was a circular growth of surface plants that could provide some cover. To his left, farther away, was the waterfall. He rose up to deliver another barrage of needles toward the trio, then took a last breath and silently slipped under the water's surface.

He kicked himself away from the wall, moving deep, toward the Kalamati. At first he saw no sign of it, but then its glittery surface reflected enough light to spot. He reached it and held it between his knees to weigh him down as he pulled his belt from his waist, looped it around the Kalamati, and then back through a belt loop, and then knotted it through another belt loop. He pushed off to his left, toward the waterfall. If the maps were current, the waterfall held a chance of escape.

He stayed deep, near the bottom, hoping the water was dark enough and he was now far enough out from the shore that no one could see him.

The pounding of the waterfall grew steadily louder. Lan's lungs grew steadily tighter. He expelled his air little by little as his head started to pound along with the water. He was aware of nothing but the pounding and the shimmering light created by the waterfall. He let it guide him.

The Kalamati dragged from his waist, slowing him. His head felt larger than before. His chest felt hot, and sparkles formed before his eyes. He wondered which would explode first, his head or his lungs.

He was under the waterfall, in water so turbulent that suddenly he didn't know which way he was headed. It pounded at him, tossing him from side to side and twisting him like a small plane in a hurricane.

He turned in the water, suddenly unsure of his directions.

His lungs were on fire. He had to surface. But the Kalamati dragged him down, and the pounding water from the waterfall made him feel like a fly going down a drain.

# 33

## ROLLER COASTER

LAN'S LUNGS WOULDN'T last another second. He had
to get fresh air. He imagined what it would feel like to
make that gasp and feel water jerked inside instead and
wasn't sure he cared anymore.

The light around his head seemed to brighten then,
and just when he knew he couldn't last any more, his head
broke the surface of the water and he gasped in a lungful
of precious air. It took him another instant before he
began to worry about such mundane things as which side
of the waterfall he was on.

The stars in his vision began to fade, and the waterfall
noise grew louder than his heartbeat. He realized he was
having to paddle hard to stay afloat. The Kalamati wanted
to be on the bottom. And he realized he was behind the
waterfall, cut off from view. He spent no time reveling in
his good fortune. If the map was accurate, behind the
waterfall should be a ladder and a couple of access panels.
Lan shook the water from his eyes and looked up.

The ladder was exactly where it should be. It rose from
the water to a height of about thirty meters, just below the

top of the waterfall. An enormous flow of water spewed from the pipe at the top, through a mesh of nozzles apparently designed to prevent the output from looking like water spewing from a hose, cascading over Lan and the shallow enclosed area behind.

Lan grabbed the bottom run and began to pull himself up. Mixed with the incredibly loud sound of the waterfall came a sharp *crack* and a dull *whump*. Lan looked over his shoulder as he climbed four more rungs. The Kalamati bumped into the ladder too hard, and he shifted position. The rungs bit into the arches of his bare feet. As he climbed, he realized he no longer wore his chirper.

There came the sound of another *crack* and another *whump*. Through one of the thinnest spaces in the cascading water, Lan could see the circle of watery surface plants. Water was raining down on a huge hole in the center of the circle. As he watched another blast from somewhere ripped another huge hole out of the circle of plants. Someone was really irritated.

He said thanks for not having picked that concealment as he rose three more rungs and reached the lowest access panel. He wasn't sure if his needler would still operate after all the water, but he readied it as he swung open the panel. On the other side was a dry access corridor. He would have stayed on the ladder to let more water drip from his clothes, but the longer he stayed next to the loud waterfall, the longer he'd be vulnerable to someone approaching.

He lifted the Kalamati so it wouldn't bump into anything, and he swung into the corridor. With the door shut behind him, the sound of the waterfall was much softer, more a deep rumbling than a broad-spectrum noise. He could hear the water dripping onto the floor.

Quickly he unfastened the Kalamati and set it down. With circled hands, he tried to squeeze as much water as he could from his shirt sleeves and pants legs to avoid leaving a trail of water spots. After a short glance at the you're-here map next to the access door, he walked to the right, frequently looking over his shoulder. As soon as his footprints had been invisible for a meter or two, he reversed his path, careful to keep to the other side of the corridor. If they had brought infrared sensing gear, the ploy wouldn't help at all, but he had to go with the odds.

As he ran lightly along the corridor, past access panels and occasional signs, he debated whether to hide the Kalamati someplace safe. While it was out of Ferelto's hands, Lan's life was valuable to her. And its obvious presence might keep someone from firing an explosive bullet at him. He kept running.

Ahead was a split in the corridor and another you're-here map. One fork led downward and almost directly toward the outside. They would expect him to take it if they suspected where he was. The other fork led up and to the right, toward a virtual maze of corridors, a couple of which eventually led outward. He went up.

His clothes had stopped dripping, and the cool dampness felt good. His head reached the level of the next floor. Far in the distance he saw sudden motion. He ducked.

He turned and took the stairs back down and turned into the other corridor below. It took a quarter turn and straightened out. Ahead was a straight corridor perhaps thirty meters long and at the end was a turn. If someone waiting at the turn let Lan get halfway to him, then Lan would be totally out of luck.

An access panel nearby seemed to be the only answer. Lan imprinted the you're-here map into his brain for as many seconds as he felt he could afford. Once back in the caves, he knew how easy it could be to get turned around.

Lan stepped through the access-way. Beyond the panel was a pseudorock floor that felt rough on his feet. He snapped the panel closed and let his eyes adjust to the dimness of the cave. The waterfall sound was softer than before.

He had to know if his needler was still operational, or if the water had gotten to it. He pointed it at the far wall and squeezed off five needles, greatly relieved that the manufacturer's claims had not been exaggerated.

Lan stood there, reviewing the you're-here map in his head and deciding which way to go. He stayed there just long enough for a lucky break to arrive. As he was making up his mind to leave his concealment, he heard a whooshing sound, like wind gradually picking up. He looked to his left, through the cave and through the adjacent one, and saw a levitational car approaching, silently guided by the rails. He got only a glimpse before its path took it momentarily out of sight again, but that was enough. He ducked.

Riding the car were Ferelto and a very big guy, both wearing goggles. The goggles were the worst part of the news. They were undoubtedly searching infrared, looking for hot spots or footprints. For now, Lan's damp shirt and pants helped reduce his visibility, but that would change. As he kept his head low, the car *whooshed* through the cave he was in, not more than a few meters away from him.

The sound subsided. Lan moved. If he could stay in the wake of the search car, his footprints would have the most time to fade before the car returned, and this direction took him toward an access corridor far enough from the waterfall that it should be safe.

Lan jogged quietly, his bare feet helping to keep his steps from giving away his presence. When the noise from car ahead had completely vanished, he slowed down. The Kalamati seemed to grow progressively heavier in his left hand, but he kept his right hand free and his needler ready. He passed through several small adjoining caves, more and more worried about the possibility of being spotted. As he moved, he passed occasional holo projectors, all currently inactive. He supposed that during normal operation they would generate scenes of mine workers, or scary apparitions to thrill the paying public.

He went through another cavern, then another, until he came to a dead end. The tracks led straight into a wall. Lan stopped abruptly, puzzled. Then he saw the seams. The wall was apparently meant to scare the customers, and would spring open at just the right moment. Lan moved closer and pressed on one of the surfaces. It gave so easily that it had to be servo assisted, and several other wall sections folded back in unison. He pressed his way through the opening.

On the other side was another empty cave, which held a sudden grade, slanted downward steeply enough to guarantee weightlessness for a moment. Lan was about to continue down the slope when an idea occurred to him. He looked back at the mass of hinges and servo controllers designed to flip the wall sections rapidly out of the way, then glanced around the cave. Maybe it would work.

He hurried over to an equipment box near the fake wall. He snapped open a small access door, and inside was a lighted touch panel. After staring at the display for a moment, he pressed the "maintenance mode" selection, and then the "disconnect power" selection. The panel indicated that it had followed his commands. He pulled on the back of one of the wall sections. It moved as he did, but it was much heavier now, no longer power assisted. Perfect.

Lan scrambled around some fake boulders, along a ledge. He put the Kalamati down beside him and settled into place. Fake rocks in front of him formed a comfortable arm rest. He forced his breathing to slow, and he tried to relax. He wondered how long it would take them to make one circuit. If he could knock them both out and take over the car, then he could try propping up their bodies for cover as he used the car's speed to advantage.

The wait was much shorter than he thought it would

be. He heard a muffled *whoosh* just before a car crashed into the fake wall. The wall segments flew out of the way under the impact, but not as quickly as they would have if power had been applied. The top segments bashed into the heads of two goggle-eyed guys, and as they floundered, trying to right themselves, they hit the drop-off. A second later, Lan released two quick volleys of needles.

The car sped down the slope. Lan listened for it to slow down at the base of the slope, but apparently it was running a preset course. Lan was sure his aim had been accurate. With no one awake to override it, Lan guessed the car would probably just keep following the course. That was fine with him, now that he knew Ferelto wasn't on that car, and that at least two cars were circling through the maze.

With luck, the car would attract no attention, and Lan could still wait for Ferelto's car to return. At the worst, someone would see the two drugged bodies in the car and guess what had happened. But for all they would know, Lan had left the scene immediately and was far away from the tracks. And they wouldn't know which section of track had allowed the assault.

He stayed where he was. Running through caverns that could hide other searchers had its own problems.

He listened. Now there was no sound of an approaching car, but he could make out a faint throbbing beat that must have been coming from some other game, loud enough to travel through lots of insulation.

He knelt in position, ready for the car to return, listening to every creak and echo, having second and third thoughts, wishing he could talk to Tessa.

Suddenly, the sound of whooshing air came from beyond the closed door flaps. Lan shifted position and hoped this was Ferelto's car.

The car collided with the door flaps, and history repeated itself. The riders *were* Ferelto and the large man. They, too, were caught unaware by the sections that smacked them across the face and chest. One pistol went flying as Lan aimed and fired at each of the pair. An instant later, the car was plunging down the slope, leaving Lan fairly confident that he had hit both targets.

He scrambled off the shelf he had used and hurried down the steep slope, trying to keep his balance with the Kalamati. Halfway down the slope, lodged against a large rock, was the dropped weapon. Lan folded his needler back against his wrist and picked up the dull-black pistol. Its status display said it had over a dozen pellets left and they were the explosive variety that had been used in the lake.

Lan reached the bottom of the slope, worried about the next car broadsiding him before he had space to get clear of the tracks. Facing across the tracks, he could see through several caverns to a point where the tracks curved back on themselves. He moved off the tracks, into a protective niche. He took careful aim and waited. Only a moment later, Ferelto's car sped past the gap. Lan waited less than a second for the car to pull out of view, and then squeezed the trigger.

The wall opposite the far tracks burst into an incandescent display of bright colors, and a big hole appeared, exposing further caverns beyond. Even as debris was still raining on the nearby area, the car following Ferelto's burst through the wall at the top of the slope again. It flashed by Lan, carrying two men slumped over the railing in front of them, their bodies swaying as the car headed into a turn.

Lan ran in the car's path, hoping the explosion would attract the remainder of Ferelto's crew. Thirty meters ahead, he dodged left and found rungs leading up to another access panel. At the top, he quietly pulled open the panel, wishing he could look both directions simultaneously, and settling for listening closely for a long moment before daring to stick his head into the corridor.

No one that direction. And no one in the other. He pulled himself into the corridor, tugged the panel gently closed, and moved off toward the exit.

After ten minutes he was convinced he had escaped the net. He followed the access corridors past several more games, and finally found a hiding place behind some seldom-used maintenance equipment and left the Kalamati and the pellet gun there.

He moved past several more games until he was finally ready to go back to the public walkways. He took off his shirt, reversed it, and pulled the wrinkles out. When he stepped into the corridor, his heart rate was back to normal and, except for missing his shoes, he looked like any other game player.

At the first communication booth he passed, he made an anonymous call to the authorities, saying a group of people were busily vandalizing the Cavern of Fear game. He hoped the car with Ferelto on it would continue to move fast enough that her people wouldn't be able to get her off it until they had visitors. As angry at Wilby and Ellie as he had been, he hoped that Ferelto's people had ignored the orders they got just before things had started getting more interesting. And now, there would be little point in carrying them out.

Lan's second call was to Tessa.

"Everything's all right," he said as soon as he saw her face in the screen.

"Oh, thank God. I've been trying to decide what to do. I just about went crazy when you lost contact."

"I was a little worried myself," Lan said.

Tessa took a deep breath. "You had me worried."

At that moment, Lan saw motion in the screen. Someone was behind Tessa. He opened his mouth to warn her just as a second face joined Tessa's on the screen. A woman with green eyes and short black hair.

Tessa shifted position, making room for the other

woman and said, "Oh, I should have known it would work out like this. The help you sent for arrived."

Lan vaguely recognized the woman behind Tessa, who said with a grin, "I got here as fast as I could. Can't you get into trouble a little closer to home?"

Lan said, "Actually, I'm probably closer than you think."

# EPILOGUE

◆ THE AIR IN Neverend had rarely smelled as sweet. Lan
drew a deep breath and leaned back, totally relaxed.

Distant motion in the adjacent cavern caught his attention. A couple strolled along the walkway. The boy, a head
taller than the girl, seemed oblivious to everything but the
girl. As she talked, she gestured excitedly. A man approaching the couple from ahead had to swerve out of the
boy's way because the pair didn't seem to realize anyone
else existed.

"Lan? Lan? Are you still with us?"

The sound of Tessa's voice snapped Lan's attention
back to the table. "Sorry. I guess I'm still a little tired. My
mind was wandering. What were you saying?"

Carrie and Tessa exchanged an indecipherable glance.
Tessa said, "I said Parke must have found out something.
He's coming back."

Lan looked in the direction Tessa had cocked her
head. A woman wearing a green peace-officer uniform was
leaving, and Parke was approaching, wending his way up
the slope, through the maze of restaurant tables at Mer-

caldo's. The party sat not far from the table Lan and Tessa had used when they first tried to confront Wilby. Lan watched Parke's springy steps as he came closer.

Parke looked satisfied as he reached the table and sat down with the trio. "It's official. We got a public apology from Arangorta. They have the Kalamati back on display and everyone's happy. The people here heard from our short friend with the blue fur. Onta's safely home. And we all have free lifetime passes to use the portal system whenever we want, once they open up public access. The experts say the system is hundreds of thousands of years old, and that apparently the race that left it behind is long dead."

"That's terrific, Parke," Lan said. "Great negotiating. I know—a toast." Lan raised his glass. As the others raised their glasses, he said, "To Parke. To the guy who complained so loudly that Arangorta eventually *had* to believe him—a world-class whiner."

Parke squinted, no doubt deciding if the toast was complimentary or not, then looked suitably proud. The others joined in, and Tessa gave Lan a look that lasted just a little too long. Lan bumped his glass against Parke's glass hard enough to spill a little. "Oops."

"There you go again," Parke said. "Back to normal. I'm still astonished at how resourceful you seemed while we were in the portal."

"It must have been an adrenaline rush. It lets us all exceed our normal capabilities. But I've had enough of being scared stiff." Lan glanced at Tessa and received a return glance that said she would keep his secret.

Carrie raised her glass again. "I have another toast." As glasses rose, she said, "To Neverend. It seems like a better place than ever—because Parke is going to stay around."

Lan and Tessa both raised their eyebrows as they toasted. Tessa said, "Tell us more."

Carrie looked to Parke, who said, "Well, yeah. I'm going to be staying."

The silence lasted a moment before Lan said, "And?"

Parke ducked his head and tried to suppress a stupid grin. "Well, I'm staying. So—ah—so I can be with Carrie."

Lan shook his head. "Settling down? Why I remember one time you told me—"

"Hey, I know what I said. Things change, that's all."

Tessa said, "Well, I'm really happy for you both."

Lan said, "Me, too. That way I'll get to see all of you more often."

Parke leaped on the opportunity to avoid the focus of attention. "And what does *that* mean?"

Lan glanced at Tessa and then back at Parke. "Just that I'll be visiting a lot more often now. The portal system puts a new perspective on a lot of things. If I get a little claustrophobic, I can always go for a stroll on Widemeadow. And you ever notice that sometimes just knowing you can do something reduces the need to actually do it?"

Parke and Carrie nodded.

"And," Tessa said, "I didn't do as badly as I thought I would when I didn't have rock walls overhead. Maybe I can join him on some of those walks."

Lan and Tessa left a lot unsaid. In long talks that lasted far into the night, they had each finally admitted they didn't want to live life without the other. They still had some sorting out of schedules to do, but they'd found that each time one of them bent a little for the other, it was that much easier to reciprocate.

As Lan took a drink, Tessa tapped his arm and pointed. On the walkway below, someone waved. Lan glanced that direction and waved back. "We've got to go," he said. Tessa rose with him.

"What's happening?" Parke asked.

"We promised Rento we'd take him up on the beanstalk. He's never seen Neverend from the outside."

"I haven't either," Tessa admitted. "It's about time. It's funny—I've been to planets hundreds of light-years from here, but I haven't seen the surface of Neverend."

"I hope you enjoy it," Carrie said, smiling. "Come back and visit, won't you, Lan?" Carrie stood up and Lan gave her a hug.

Lan offered his hand to Parke. "See you around."

Parke grinned as he shook Lan's hand. "I'm glad to hear it."

On the way down to meet Rento, Lan said. "Oh, I forgot to tell you. I got a message back from a friend involved in getting Wilby and Ellie into custody. Neither of them got a good view of the man they saw steal the Kalamati back. All they know is that someone did." They were also convicted of Kentin's murder, but this didn't seem a good time to remind people.

"What happens to them now?" Tessa asked.

"They get a vacation from all this. They'll be spending some time on Freezemelt, probably cursing the seasons." Lan tried unsuccessfully to suppress a sudden smile.

"What?" Tessa said. "What is it? Tell me."

"Oh, I don't know. Sometimes I just hate myself. A friend of a friend is a guard on Freezemelt. I get the feeling this guy's sense of humor is a little like mine. He's already mentioned some possibilities for nurturing Wilby's and Ellie's run of bad luck."

"You mean he's going to arrange some more 'accidents' for them?"

"Apparently so. He doesn't think the curse is ready to die just yet."